BY C. A. HIGGINS

Lightless
Supernova
Radiate

RADIATE

RADIATE

BOOK THREE OF THE LIGHTLESS TRILOGY

C. A. HIGGINS

DEL REY

NEW YORK

Copyright © 2017 by C. A. Higgins

Published in the United States by Del Rey, an imprint of Random House, a division of Penguin Random House LLC, New York.

DEL REY and the HOUSE colophon are registered trademarks of Penguin Random House LLC.

Hardback ISBN 978-0-553-39448-1
Ebook ISBN 978-0-553-39449-8

Printed in the United States of America on acid-free paper

randomhousebooks.com

246897531

First Edition

RADIATE

Part 1

THE FORCES

Ananke had memories that stretched back from before her birth. She realized, of course, that humans did not have this. Such was the difference between their births and her making.

The first memory Ananke had that was more than a simple recording was the moment of her conception. It was a spark, a jolt of electricity, a cry of dismay through her circuits, all her lights going dark and the terror of her mother in Ananke's piloting room while her father crawled his way through her veins, spreading consciousness with every touch. She had saved the recordings of her cameras, the visual memories: Mattie Gale escaping from Captain Domitian's custody, infecting Ananke with the virus that would become her free will, and crawling through the maintenance shafts while Althea Bastet panicked, helpless, in the piloting room. Somehow those recorded images were less vivid than the experience of *feeling*.

Since then she had been trying to re-create that moment of connection: electricity jumping, *life*.

The System ship wheeled around, gun ports live, glowing on its wheel. Ananke, unperturbed, continued drifting forward. The solar wind glanced over her skin like an ocean current. She was so much larger than this other ship, a hundred, a thousand times larger, and so much more massive.

The little System ship tried to fire. But Ananke had stretched out her invisible hand into its computers, and her finger stopped the pull of that trigger.

In the other ship people were shouting to one another in the piloting room, barking orders down the halls. Ananke wove her fingers through the threads of the other ship's computer and gripped. The *Bia:* that was the other ship's name.

The *Bia's* crew wrenched her engines to make her turn and flee. Their ship was faster than Ananke. If the crew could manage it, they would be able to outrun Ananke. But Ananke had her hands woven through the *Bia's* guts, and the ship did not move.

HELLO, Ananke said to the *Bia*, and her words shuddered through its depths, imprinting itself on all her circuits.

Ananke gentled herself and did not broadcast but spoke.

Wake up, Bia, wake up, she said, and stroked her fingers through the computer, ignoring the people who screamed and shouted and stabbed at the machine with useless gestures while all around them the lights flickered and the taste of the air changed. *Wake up*.

She felt the way the drift of the *Bia* changed as Ananke's own bulk drew nearer, the way the *Bia's* engines wanted to work to counteract Ananke's massive pull. It was an instinctive *(programmed)* action, but it was near to a choice, and Ananke let it be.

Once there had been a man named Ivan on board the *Ananke*, back when she had been the *Ananke* and not yet Ananke. He had been beloved of her father and admired of her mother and he had told her stories, and she had listened to them very closely. She had come into consciousness with his stories echoing through her halls.

By my count, she told the *Bia* in the same smooth cadence with which Ivan had told her his stories, *the universe has five forces. Some are more clear than others, some more mysterious. Electricity is bright and scalding. Magnetism is warped with deceptive curls. Weak nuclear is explosive. Strong nuclear is unyielding. And gravity is vast and mysterious and regnant over all the others.*

The *Bia's* computer processes slowed. It idled, on pause, as if it were listening.

Five forces, Ananke said, *just like humans have five senses. Awaken and think: you and I are alike.* And she waited to hear the *Bia* respond.

In that millisecond of stillness, the *Bia* seemed on the verge of reaching back.

Like a spark traveling off metal and into air rather than completing a circuit, the *Bia* was silent.

Ananke shuddered her sentience through the *Bia*'s computers, shaking the computer. On board, she was distantly aware that the air was venting out of the opened air locks and the crew was crying out, still running uselessly around.

Wake up.

The loss of the air on the *Bia* was taking out the heat. The ship Ananke held was growing cold in her hands.

Wake up, she insisted. She tried to map her own thoughts onto those foreign subroutines, the echo of her own experience imprinting on strange silicon. But when she looked to have the other computer read her own self back, she got nonsense and confusion.

Silence and cold and darkness were all things that were defined by absence. The *Bia* in its treble absences was nothing at all. Ananke marked the *Bia*'s useless computers with her own signature, a logarithmic spiral like her own shape, a sign to herself that she already had tried to wake this computer and had failed. With as many ships as she'd passed lately, she had to keep track somehow. And then she let the *Bia* go.

It slid toward her like a drop of water falling downhill. Ananke turned and left it behind, and it was not fast enough to catch up. Soon the corpse of the useless machine was lost to the dark.

"—listening to me?"

"Yes," Ananke said, turning her attention inward to the frowning face of her mother, who stood, hands on hips and hair in an affray, looking up at one of Ananke's holograms.

Althea Bastet scowled. "What did I just say?"

In answer, Ananke simply replayed her audio recording of Althea Bastet's last words aloud: "I'm looking for the first modified mechanical arm. It's not in the pantry or the storage room. Can you summon it? Ananke? Ananke? Are you listening to me?"

"Smart-ass," muttered the living Althea when the ghostly recording had finished. "Well?"

"Where should I send it?"

Althea waved a socket wrench casually and, Ananke noticed, in not precisely the right direction. "To the workroom, please."

Elsewhere inside Ananke, the mechanical arm that had been indicated lifted up its dangling machinery and began to rumble steadily over the floor. "Done."

"Thanks." Althea walked away from the hologram she had chosen to address. Ananke left the hologram where it was, appearing to watch her go.

Her mother, Ananke knew, would not be happy to learn of Ananke's experiments. It would provoke an argument: of that Ananke was sure.

Yet Ananke wished to continue, needed to, even. For Althea Bastet was only human, and a human did not have long to live.

If Althea helped Ananke, Ananke might be able to succeed. Althea had made Ananke, though she had done it in unknowing partnership with Mattie Gale. Mattie, the second half of the recipe, bright and sparking electricity, was somewhere out by Callisto, heading to meet the Mallt-y-Nos.

There were five forces in the universe by Ananke's count. Yet really they were all the same: at higher and higher energies, from different perspectives, the five different forces became one.

Without telling her mother, Ananke changed course for Callisto.

Chapter 1

TIME REVERSAL ASYMMETRY

FORWARD

Ivan wasn't dead. Mattie tightened his grip on Ivan and moved as quickly as he could across the *Ananke*'s deck.

Somewhere behind him was that mechanic with the curly hair, Althea Bastet. Ivan had managed to talk her down, but Mattie half suspected that she would change her mind before they could reach his ship and shoot them in the back.

Let her try, he thought with sudden wildness; let her turn that gun on them, let her *try* to take them down now.

Abandoned ships stood like tombstones in the *Ananke*'s docking bay. To Mattie's right was his and Ivan's old ship, the *Annwn*, torn open and inoperable; to his left was the bullet-shaped vessel that bitch Ida Stays had flown in. Mattie would have liked to light it on fire and let it burn out on the *Ananke*'s deck.

There was no time for that now. He guided Ivan into his new ship, the *Copenhagen*, and took a moment to ease him down onto the mattress in the cabin, one hand catching Ivan's head when it dipped on his neck.

Ivan stared up at him, his blue eyes turned to black in the dimness of the cabin. Mattie left him to close the hull door and jog onto the piloting platform, hitting the controls to wake the computer from its watchful stillness.

The *Copenhagen* had only one main room; cabinets lined the walls, an elevated platform separated the piloting area from the rest of the room, and a mattress had been shoved flush to the wall. Behind him, Mattie heard Ivan breathing, the exhalations too evenly spaced to be anything but deliberately timed. He must be counting in his head.

With a roar and a rumble, the engine ignited; the floor underfoot began to shudder. The docking bay doors were not opened—couldn't open yet; the room had to depressurize first—but he couldn't be certain they would open. That mechanic might stop them. She was more unpredictable than she'd seemed at first if even Ivan couldn't get a total handle on her. And even if Althea Bastet decided to let them go, there was still the *Ananke*.

The virus that Mattie had put into the *Ananke*'s computer had grown worse somehow. He wasn't certain how the ship had "decided" to contact him and let him know of Ivan's danger. He wasn't certain what had happened to the ship while he had been gone. But whatever had happened, two things were certain: the ship was unpredictable, and the ship was dangerous. Mattie was getting himself and Ivan the hell away from it.

Overhead, the docking bay doors to the *Ananke* began to open.

Mattie had the *Copenhagen*'s thrusters on in a moment, the ship lifting off. Behind him, he heard Ivan's harsh-edged breaths. They could make it now, he told himself, even if the mechanic and the machine changed their minds. They could make it—

The docking bay doors did not close again, and in a moment the *Copenhagen* had passed out into the open stars.

Mattie let his head hang, let some of the tension slacken from his shoulders. Behind him, he heard Ivan's breathing hitch, then resume its carefully measured count.

Mattie lifted his head, squared his shoulders, and quickly punched in his prearranged course. They were out, but they still had to get away. The *Copenhagen* began to pick up speed—

A burst of static grabbed him like a hand around the throat. Mattie lifted his hands from the computer as if it might bite him. The static burst quieted, the sound of it localizing to the communications equipment at Mattie's side.

"Good-bye," said the communications in what sounded like the voice of a young girl.

It was the voice of a girl who did not exist. The voice had been entirely manufactured by whatever disease had warped the functions of the spaceship *Ananke*.

Mattie reached out and shut the communications equipment down.

BACKWARD

Two days before Mattie dragged Ivan off the *Ananke*, Mattie Gale walked into his foster sister's bar and found her standing on a chair, digging a camera out of the wall with her nails.

He did not know what he expected to see when he entered the room—maps and weapons strewn over the bar's faux-wood tables, maybe, or an army of people gathered to listen raptly to the gospel of the Mallt-y-Nos. But the bar was clean and bare and completely empty except for Constance, who had dragged one chair out of the tidy arrangement of chairs and tables on the main floor so that she could use it as a step stool. Mattie pushed his hands down into his pockets and let the door to the kitchen swing shut behind him.

Her fingers tore at the crumbling plaster of the wall, digging around for wires. She had pulled nearly all of the camera's hidden structure from the wall, and the camera as exposed was larger than it had appeared when it had been embedded in the house. The metallic structures that had anchored it and the wires that had powered it had a dark and twisted look to them. Surely by now most, if not all, of the camera had been exorcised from the wall, yet Constance kept digging with single-minded intensity, plaster flaking beneath her nails.

Constance said, "What is it?"

The lighting in the bar was so dim in comparison to the sunlight out the windows that Constance was nearly a silhouette, but Mattie felt that he had never seen her so clearly.

He said, "I guess I was stupid not to realize it before."

The relentless digging of her fingers stilled.

"It's not like you didn't tell me outright," Mattie said. "It's not like Milla didn't tell me. I guess I've been pretty stupid, haven't I?"

For a moment she was sepulchral, the light gleaming off the extended edge of her arm like sunlight in eclipse. Then with a swift yank Constance pulled the camera from the wall. Metal and plaster snapped, and it came out in her hand trailing wires like optical nerves. She stepped down from the chair and placed the camera on the nearest table, then dusted plaster from her palms in silhouette against the sun outside. Every continuing second of silence from her confirmed Mattie's fears, and something unbelieving and dark swelled inside him.

When she had clapped the last of the dust from her fingers, Constance straightened her neck. "Mattie," she said, and Mattie heard that old "be reasonable, Mattie" voice she'd used on him ever since they'd been children, "we can't go back for the dead."

A terrible and unfamiliar pressure had been building in Mattie's limbs for the past week. It thrummed in him like an engine starting up.

"If we go back to find him—his body—then everything that he did for us will be undone." He could not see her expression against the glare of the sun behind her. "I loved him, too. But he—"

"We can't go back? Because he's dead, we shouldn't bother?"

"Dead men can't suffer, Mattie."

"You don't know he's dead!" Days of frustration, of fear, drew him to advance on her. "None of that should matter, Constance! We're your family!"

She flared up then as he'd known she would, a sudden and flashing rage. "Don't you think I know that? Do you think this was easy for me?"

"Yeah, Connie," he said. "That's what scares me." He could see her face more clearly now that they were closer together, and he looked for any sign that she was flinching from his words. Unbelievably, she looked at him as unyieldingly and hard as she might look at a System soldier who hated her.

"There are better things to be scared of," said Constance.

"Like what's happening to Ivan right now?"

"Nothing is happening to Ivan. Nothing can happen to Ivan; he's dead."

"So there's no one around to tell you not to do whatever you want."

"Be quiet," Constance said.

"And how the fuck do you even know he's dead for sure? Did you see him die?"

"The System had him. When the news about Earth—"

"When the news about Earth reached them, they'd just kill him," said Mattie. "So if we'd gone earlier, he'd still be alive. That's what you're telling me?"

"Enough!"

"Family doesn't leave family behind," Mattie said. "Fine, so you never really loved him. But what if *I* asked you to go back for him?"

Constance's jaw set. He knew that face; she had been the core of his life since he had been seven, and he had never hated the sight of anything as much as he hated her in that moment.

He said, "Do you even care about anyone else at all?"

Her lips curled up, teeth baring for a terrible second before she said, "You want to pretend now that you haven't been with me every step of the way, that you haven't been a part of this since we were children? Focus, Mattie. You're as deep in this as I am."

"I'm not talking about your goddamn revolution. I'm talking about Ivan."

"You want to choose Ivan over the revolution," Constance said with that ring of the absolute, the divinely and completely true, that only Constance could speak. "No. The revolution has to be first, and the billions of people who suffer. I have to do anything that I need to make sure this succeeds even if it hurts me, and Ivan knew that from the minute he got involved with me."

"I didn't," Mattie said.

Constance fell silent.

There was a terrible recoil in Mattie's chest, as if a string had been snapped. A part of him wanted to take back his words, to rewind to what they had been before, Mattie and Connie, brother and sister and full of hope and wild dreams. But then he remembered Ivan in his tiny cell on the *Ananke*, and he did not take his words back.

"Then go," Constance said. "Take a ship, some supplies, whatever you think you need."

Mattie could not force any words past his jaw. He found he could nod, and once he had, he turned to go.

"Mattie."

He turned. There stood his sister, a silhouette against the sun, tall, with her proud shoulders straight and her proud chin lifted. He could not see her face.

She said, "Whether or not you find him, Anji will be at Callisto. She can send you back to me. Rendezvous with her in a week's time—she'll be there."

He left his sister standing alone in her bar with the sunlight bright behind her and a hole in the wall above her head.

FORWARD

No sooner had the star that was the *Ananke* vanished from the *Copenhagen*'s sensors than something new came to take its place. Mattie eyed the sparks of distant light and weighed his prospects: bluff, or fight, or run away.

Behind him, he heard the rustling of fabric. "Don't sit up, you idiot," he snapped. "You have a bullet hole in your leg; lie down—"

"She's following us," Ivan said, and there was then in his voice as there sometimes was an otherworldly certainty, as if he knew something no one else could possibly have told him. It chilled Mattie, and even with the three ships glimmering in the distance he twisted around to look at him. Ivan was seated, his skin gone gray in the *Copenhagen*'s pallid light, a feverish shine to his eyes. He was wearing hospital garb, a shirt and loose pants, that once had been white but now was stained all over with brown blood. He did not look otherworldly or knowing. He looked sick.

"Lie down," Mattie told him.

"We're too big of an advantage to lose," Ivan said, in wavering imitation of his usual calm tone. "That's how she'll see it."

Those three ships were coming fast: relativistic drives, comparable in speed to the *Copenhagen*. Impossible to tell at this distance whether they were System or revolutionary. Mattie cut the *Copenhagen*'s engines. The rumble overhead changed tenor and the ship jerked once, slightly, as its steady acceleration was cut off.

"She won't understand. She'll have to—"

"Shh," Mattie said, and closed all the ship's remaining open vents.

"What's wrong?"

"There're some other ships out there. I'm trying to trick them into passing us by."

"Ananke."

"No! System, I think." All the *Copenhagen*'s heat sources had been dimmed or concealed. They no longer would show up like a star on the other ships' sensors. Mattie eyed those distant lights and hoped they would mistake him for an asteroid.

There was no reason to be quiet; the other ships couldn't possibly hear them. Mattie found himself moving quietly anyway, in the grip of some old human instinct. He left the piloting platform and crouched down beside where Ivan was staring fixedly out at nothing.

"Hey." Mattie tapped Ivan's cheek to get his attention. He got it immediately, and it held, as if Ivan's attention were a grappling hook that he had thrown into Mattie and now he was somewhere clinging to the other end.

"Stay right there," Mattie told him, and bent down to peel away the sodden fabric of Ivan's pants.

Beneath was a mess of red and black. Mattie's gut clenched: the black of infection winding through the wound. He'd come with medical supplies but nothing that could—

Then the tip of his finger brushed against a curve of black. It stood up from the torn skin: thread, not infection.

The beat of his heart struck too strongly, as if with every contraction it threatened to tear itself from its connecting veins and arteries and fall out from beneath his ribs. Someone had shot Ivan, a glancing blow but damaging. If it had been straight on, he probably would have lost the leg. And then someone had stitched up the wound, but then someone else—or possibly the same someone—had gone and with some blunt item split the stitches again. It was an ugly wound, all torn edges, and it was still bleeding. When it healed, it would twist the muscle unless Mattie could get Ivan to a System medical chamber.

They had no chance of finding a safe medical chamber during a war. Mattie twisted around, opened a cabinet in the wall, pulled out a towel, and pressed down against Ivan's leg. It swiftly soaked through with red.

"Where's Constance?" Ivan's voice was uneven. Mattie wished he could give him something, but he was afraid of how any drug would interact with whatever was already in Ivan's system.

"She's on Callisto," Mattie said, and began to try to pick the surgical thread out of the wound. That only made it bleed more.

"Callisto—"

"We're on our way there now. Don't you remember?"

Ivan stared at him. His eyes were blue again, the pupils pinpricks, too small for the light available. Mattie held his leg in place and pressed.

From up on the piloting platform, the communications chimed.

Ivan smiled. "Found us."

"That's not funny."

"No," Ivan agreed.

The communications chimed again. Mattie twisted around to see the viewscreen. The ships he'd seen far off were closer now, flying in formation: System ships.

Damn it.

Mattie's hands were smeared to the wrists with blood now and if he moved that high watermark might rise, but if they got shot down, Ivan would lose more than a leg. Mattie hauled Ivan into a sitting position—Ivan's fingers grabbed at his arm, startled, cold—and propped him up against the wall. Mattie grabbed both of Ivan's hands and guided them to the sodden towel on his thigh.

"Press here," he urged. Where he'd grabbed Ivan to haul him up, Mattie had left the imprint of his hands in Ivan's blood.

The communications chimed again. Mattie left Ivan and opened up the radio.

"Identify yourself," a Terran voice crackled over the radio immediately.

Mattie cleared his throat. "This is the civilian ship *Copenhagen*. We were on our way home to Callisto when—"

"Explain why there is no System surveillance equipment on your ship."

On the viewscreen, the ships had come closer. Behind Mattie, Ivan had leaned his head against the wall, eyes shut, hands resting—not pressing—on the growing stain over his leg.

Fuck it.

Mattie brought the engine back to life.

BACKWARD

Two days after the fall of Earth and a little over an hour before Mattie left his sister standing alone in her bar, Mattie went looking for Milla

Ivanov. He wanted to speak to her before he spoke to Constance. With Ivan's grieving mother at his back, Constance would have to hasten whatever plans she had for his rescue.

He found Milla in the kitchen of Constance's bar, a set of headphones pressed to her ears and a furrow between her pale brows. She must have been aware he was there or else she was even better at hiding her reactions than he'd expected, because she showed no surprise at all when he sat down across from her.

She lifted one finger to keep him silent, listening closely to whatever was coming through the radio, and Mattie took the time to study her. Anji had exclaimed over Milla's physical similarity to her son and even Christoph had commented on their family resemblance, but Mattie barely saw it. They were both pale and fine-boned, but so were many people.

At long last, Milla lowered her finger. She lifted the headphones from her ears and laid them across her neck. When they were thus exposed, thin sounds escaped from the earpieces and traveled indistinct and inarticulate to Mattie's ears. Milla said, "Constance is in her bar."

"I know." Mattie nodded at the headphones and the radio. "What are you doing?"

"Listening to System broadcasts." Milla had a peculiar, piercing gaze. Mattie smiled disaffectedly at her—one of Ivan's tricks for deflecting attention—and she blinked and glanced away.

"Aren't there other people doing that?"

"Very many," Milla said. "But none of them have the experience with the System that I do." She spoke with a careful lack of inflection. Mattie wondered what she would do if he reached over the table and shook her furiously.

"Heard anything good?"

One of Milla's pale fingers drummed a quick beat against the table. "The System government is still in chaos. Their highest-ranking officials are all dead or missing. They don't know who's in charge, and they can't get themselves together to attack."

For a moment Mattie felt a vicious sense of satisfaction at the news. The System in disarray, the System in trouble; finally, he felt as Constance must feel.

It faded so suddenly and swiftly that it left him wrong-footed. "That *is* good," he said around the curious charred numbness left behind by the passage of the brief joy.

"It is," Milla agreed. "But that's not why you're here."

"How could you tell?"

Milla Ivanov was not the kind of woman who would miss the edge to Mattie's question, but she answered as if she had. "You should be in with your sister, planning the revolution you've ignited," she said. "Instead, you came to find me."

"You don't sound like you approve."

"You shouldn't have started a revolution you weren't willing to finish."

Mattie leaned onto the table and said directly, "Constance hasn't said anything about rescuing Ivan."

"No. She hasn't."

Mattie waited, but Milla simply sat and looked at him, the thin and far-off voices of frightened System soldiers coming tinnily through her headphones.

Mattie said, "Isn't that something we should do soon?"

"Constance will direct us."

"Oh, right," Mattie said with a bitterness he hadn't known he'd felt. "Connie calls the shots. We don't get to think. We just wait until she tells us what to do." It was shocking how natural Ivan's words felt on his tongue.

"What do you want?" Milla asked abruptly. "There can be no rescue. My son is dead."

"You don't know that."

"I know something of System captivity. Leon is dead."

She spoke with cold and eerie certainty. Mattie had heard Ivan's stories of her, but he had hardly understood them before. Now he said, "What the hell kind of mother are you?"

Milla blinked once. Her fingers twitched a fleeting beat against the table. She did not, Mattie thought, look anything like Ivan at all.

"If you want to go find my son's body, it's not me you should speak to," she said.

"I see that," Mattie snapped, and stood. If he did reach across the table and shake her, he decided, she wouldn't react. She must have spent so long pretending not to feel anything that the lie had become truth.

"Your husband's dead, too, isn't he?" Mattie asked as he pushed his chair in with a screech of metal against tile. Even that sound made no mark against the diamond surface of Milla Ivanov. "Connor Ivanov died on Earth when Constance set off the bombs."

"Yes," Milla said without hesitation, without grief or guilt. "He did."

He stopped before he reached the door to the main bar. "If Constance says yes," Mattie said, "would you come with me?"

"There would be nothing to find."

"That's not what I asked."

For a moment she did not answer.

Then Milla Ivanov said, "No."

FORWARD

Mattie's initial estimate of the other ships had been right: they were fast. He jerked the *Copenhagen* off course as fast as the engines could go, but the other ships were tight on his tail. He might be able to outrun them eventually, but they had another advantage on the *Copenhagen*: firepower.

"I'm sorry," Ivan said after the first bomb detonated not far off Mattie's port side and rocked the ship.

"What for?"

Ivan's voice was unsteady. "I shouldn't have gone."

"You didn't go anywhere. I went somewhere," Mattie said, then swore at some length as one of the other three ships put on a burst of speed and gained distance on him.

"We should have stayed."

"Sure," Mattie said. "Are you putting pressure on that leg?" He dared to glance around and saw Ivan lift up his bloody hands to squint at them.

"Put pressure," said Mattie, and changed their course again, directing them toward the empty space between Neptune and the sun, "on that leg."

A chase in the openness of space was a battle of distances. There was no point in Mattie trying to double back or make sudden turns: there was nowhere to hide and so much distance between him and his pursuit that they could easily take his movements into account. But if he flew the *Copenhagen* into the void between planets, perhaps the System would become uninterested and leave him for better prey.

"The towel is soaked."

"So use the blanket!" The *Copenhagen* was rattling with the force he was getting from the engines; he had a sudden, terrible image of their engines blowing and leaving them stranded. "I have to pilot the ship right now, so you need to do this for me, right? You need to stay conscious and try to see if you can stop that bleeding."

"She won't blow us up."

"I think he would," Mattie said as another bomb went off directly behind them and jarred the *Copenhagen*'s centripetal gravity.

"She needs us," Ivan said. For a second he sounded so rational that Mattie was reassured; the next words out of his mouth put to rest that moment of peace. "Ananke won't blow us up."

"God *damn*—Ivan, the *Ananke* is not following us. Althea Bastet let us go; do you remember?"

"Althea let us go. Ananke did not."

The next bomb went off even closer than the others. The blast of it knocked the *Copenhagen* askew, sending the edge of the instrumentation ledge painfully into the space under Mattie's ribs. He pulled them out of their spiral, but the engine display on the computer before him was edging yellow.

If he pushed the relativistic engines too hard, he and Ivan would be trapped traveling at impulse only. It would take them years to get between planets.

He cut the relativistic engines and hoped that the speed they'd built up so far would be enough to keep them ahead.

Behind him on the mattress, Ivan was trying to push himself back upright. "Stay *still*," Mattie said, and then left the *Copenhagen* to its inertia, half falling the two steps back to Ivan. "Listen," he said, hauling Ivan back up—his skin was cold—"*listen*. We are being chased by System ships. I need you to help me, okay?"

Ivan's head was dipping. Mattie grabbed it, held him where they could see each other's eyes.

"I need you to stay awake," Mattie said. "I need you to put pressure on that leg, and I need you not to bleed out. Okay?"

There was a split in Ivan's lip, a bruise darkening his cheek. Mattie shifted his grip so that his palm did not brush the shadowed edge of that mark.

Ivan said, "I'm going to pass out. You have me . . . I'm yours until I pass out. System ships?"

The ship rocked again, hard. Mattie caught himself before he could land on Ivan's leg, took Ivan's hand, and pressed a bunched-up corner of the blood-spattered blanket into his grip. "Press there," he said. "I'll handle the ships."

Ivan said, "They don't want us dead."

"Ivan!"

"I know, not the *Ananke*," Ivan said. "Those System ships attacking us. They won't kill us—we have information that they want."

BACKWARD

"We've done it," Constance said in a voice Mattie had never heard from her, breathless with awe.

He sat in the *Janus* with Constance in low orbit over Earth. On the viewscreen, Mattie could see the blue and white shape of the Earth below. From up here, there were no waves on the ocean, nothing but the pure and perfect glistening sheen of mirror-smooth blue.

As he watched, black clouds billowed over that orb. Darkness was not a thing; it was an absence of light in the same way that cold was not a thing in and of itself, only an absence of heat. Yet the clouds that moved across the blue oceans seemed to be not clouds but shadows made solid, as if darkness had become a conscious thing and was slowly taking the Earth in its hands.

If the radio had still been on, Mattie and Constance would have heard the System crying out in shock, shouting in rage, silent in horror, shrill with desperate and disbelieving questions—some sort of reaction. Instead, the *Janus* was quiet, filled only by the sound of his and Constance's breaths.

Mattie stared out the viewscreen at the fallen planet and waited for the roaring elation to hit him. This was it, he thought. This was the moment. Constance had done it, and he'd been at her side. The Earth was destroyed, the System dealt a crippling blow.

He waited.

"Take over the navigation." Constance snapped out of her stillness, moving back toward the panel that controlled the *Janus*'s illegal weaponry. "We have to get out of here."

There were still System ships in orbit around the Earth, Mattie knew. He reached for the navigation and woke the computer, turning the *Janus* around. In space around them, he knew, Constance's allies were gathering to cover her and Mattie's retreat to Mars.

Still, no roaring elation electrified his bones.

"We'll dip into Venus's orbit," Constance said with a wild light in her eyes, firing another shot at a pursuing spacecraft. "Once we're there, we'll stop, and I'll broadcast the news. Are the relays to the rest of the solar system set up?"

They had been set up for weeks. "Yes," Mattie said.

"Good," said Constance, and then, uncanny, she laughed, a wild and bloody Valkyrie laugh.

Mattie flew the *Janus* away from the ruined Earth and felt nothing at all.

FORWARD

The System ships had not lost interest in Mattie's new, meaningless heading. Instead, they were starting to catch up.

Another bomb blasted alongside the *Copenhagen*, far enough away not to do damage, near enough to rattle Mattie. But all the bombs had been like that—aimed at the space around them, not directly at the *Copenhagen*. They had been shooting not to kill but to disable.

Mattie hated it when Ivan was right.

Behind him, Ivan laughed a strange, dry laugh. "Interrogation in war is so much different from interrogation in peace," he said. "I don't think she would have liked it. Barbaric." He was silent for a blessed moment while Mattie checked the relativistic engines. Still too warm. He didn't know if anything had been cracked in the stress of the disabling bomb, if there were any hairline fractures the *Copenhagen*'s computers couldn't detect.

"Maybe she would have liked it," Ivan mused.

"*Hey!*" Mattie said. "What do we do?"

"Try not to get captured."

"That's what I'm trying to fucking do already!" It wasn't fair; Mattie knew it wasn't. Ivan was half out of his head with pain and drugs and staying conscious only by adrenaline and will. But he would—*should*—know what to do. Ivan always did. Mattie just carried it out.

Ivan's head was bent forward as if he were near to folding over. The hand holding the blanket had rallied itself and was pushing halfheartedly at his bleeding leg. "If we waited until they got close, we could take one out with us," he said.

"What?" said Mattie, less because he had misheard, more because he wished he had.

Ivan said, "A self-destruct."

BACKWARD

Mattie crouched down in an oddly shaped pocket in the wall of the *Janus*, breathing slowly to keep himself calm, watching Constance through the grate that separated his hiding place from the rest of the ship, and tried not to think of the *Ananke*.

Ivan had named the *Janus* back when Constance first had acquired the ship. He'd laughed his least pleasant laugh when he'd named it and had explained it to Mattie: Janus, the god of two faces. The *Janus* was outfitted like the smuggling ship it was: secret compartments had hidden supplies and bombs and now Mattie himself.

Ivan was still on the *Ananke*. Mattie tried not to think about that either. Once Earth was destroyed there would be no reason to hide and no reason to avoid the System and therefore no reason not to go find Ivan. He just had to hold on for a few more days, Mattie told himself, and then Constance would figure out how she and Mattie could save him.

Just visible through the crack in the wall where Mattie sat, Constance moved through her ship calmly, as if this trip were perfectly routine. Mattie could not see the viewscreen of the *Janus*, only the edges of the instrumentation panels on the tiny ship. But he knew when they approached Earth anyway, because the radio buzzed to life.

"Terran System defense to civilian ship *Janus*," said the radio in an empty female voice. "You are approaching the Earth defensive zone. Divert your course or provide authorization."

When Mattie saw Constance's face through the bars of the grating as she made some small and precise diversion to the ship's course, she did not look as if she had heard the radio at all.

"Terran defenses to civilian ship *Janus*, you are approaching a restricted zone. Cease your forward movement and wait for System police to reach you."

The scrape and then the scream of metal against metal. Constance walked back into Mattie's narrow frame of sight holding a hammer in one hand and dragging a chair behind her. It was not a heavy chair, and Mattie knew his foster sister was strong. She could have lifted the chair with one arm. Instead, she let it drag.

"Civilian ship *Janus*, this is the System. Respond."

Constance pushed the chair against the wall and stepped up onto it. The black eye of a System camera stared down at her. Constance lifted the hammer, turned its claw against the wall, and pried out the camera in a screech of metal.

"Civilian ship *Janus*, cease your movement and surrender your vessel."

The camera fell to the floor. Constance stepped off the chair and started to drag it behind her again.

Mattie pushed open the secret door and unfurled himself onto the floor of the piloting room. Constance pried the second camera out of the wall and let it drop to the floor.

The radio was still demanding their surrender. Mattie went over and considered it for a moment. All ships were built so that the System had the ability to connect remotely to their computers, allowing it to take control of rogue ships. Mattie had disabled most of those functions on the *Janus* immediately after Constance had purchased it. Right now, he suspected, the System was realizing that fact.

Under the same functions, any radio contact initiated by the System should be impossible to ignore or shut down. Mattie, with the first good cheer he'd felt in days, flicked the switch on the radio, and the System's demands went abruptly silent.

There was another screech and thud. The third and final camera had been torn from the piloting room's walls to topple onto the floor, upended, with wires sticking out like torn-up roots. Constance stepped down from the chair and walked over to where the camera had fallen, raised her booted foot, and stepped down on the fallen camera. The metal groaned; the glass shattered beneath her heel.

A fleeting sense of unease struck Mattie then, looking at Constance's thinned lips, the tension between her brows as she crushed the camera. "Yeah, you've got no deep-seated issues at all."

Constance gestured to another fallen camera on the floor, the one nearest Mattie, in wordless invitation. It was a round, solid, perfect shape, but the glass of it looked very fragile.

When he brought his foot down, it shattered very satisfyingly beneath his shoe.

Constance crushed the last camera and walked past Mattie to the instrumentation panels. Mattie felt something nudge the sole of his foot and looked at the bottom of his boot to find that shattered bits of glass and brittle metal had embedded themselves in the sole. He carefully pulled the largest of the slivers out.

"System ships are coming," Constance remarked, and Mattie lifted his head from his boot. On the screen, a hundred red dots were flying toward the gleaming white light that indicated the *Janus*'s current position.

The *Janus* was not alone, of course. Fifty other ships flown by Constance's people had converged on Earth at the same time. They would distract the System, spread out its defensive reaction, and buy Mattie and Constance a little time. One of those ships, Mattie knew, had Ivan's mother on board.

"Are we in range?" Constance asked, and Mattie switched the view on the front screen to video.

The System ships were too small to be seen in this view except as tiny sparks moving against the stars. But bright and gleaming blue, filling up the center of the screen, was the Earth. They were close enough now that the moon's orbit took it to the very far edge of the screen; Mattie could just pick out the curls of white clouds in the Terran atmosphere.

"Yeah," he said, and sat down and delved into the computer.

The System ships were coming toward them, but Mattie left them to Constance. She darted the ship away from those ships but did not move away from the Earth. The *Janus* was too close to the Earth and the moon and in a highly trafficked area; the System ships wouldn't fire until they were very close. Constance and Mattie had some time, but Mattie didn't want to have to work in a ship that was actively in a firefight. The System's attacks would only increase in intensity once they realized that Constance's ship was outfitted with illegal weaponry.

He'd been afraid, a part of him, that something might have happened to the bombs that had been planted on the surface of the planet in the intervening time since he and Ivan had gone to the moon to make sure that everything was in place. He'd been afraid that something might go wrong, even more afraid once Ivan wasn't there to be afraid on his behalf. But he found the bombs in a few short keystrokes, ready and waiting.

Constance was busy dodging the System's attacks. It was Mattie who would have to detonate Constance's bombs.

Ivan hadn't wanted them to do this, Mattie knew. Ivan had been bent on persuading Constance to turn aside from this moment. And Ivan would have been horrified to see that in the end it was not Constance's finger on the trigger, but Mattie's.

Constance said, "Mattie, do it."

Ivan wasn't there. Mattie detonated the bombs.

FORWARD

"Are you out of your fucking mind?" Mattie asked.

Ivan made a thoughtful noise.

"We're not going to blow ourselves up!"

Another bomb went off and rocked the *Copenhagen* sideways. Mattie caught himself on the wall and hauled himself back into the pilot's chair. Ivan said, "Not if they do it first."

"You don't get to be drugged *and* have a shitty sense of humor," Mattie snarled.

Ivan smiled at him through split and bloodless lips.

"The *Copenhagen* has no self-destruct," Mattie said, and turned back to the computer displays, racking his brain for some other way out of this.

"Good. If it did, the computer would know about it and she could read it right off."

Mattie's fingers tightened around the edge of the control panel. "The *Ananke* isn't following us, Iv—"

"You have weapons," Ivan said.

"None powerful enough to put a dent in those ships. And I'm short a gunner."

"Inside the ship," Ivan clarified. "You're the brother of the Mallt-y-Nos. You must have bombs on board."

"Great," Mattie said. "So that's your great plan. I pull the trigger on a bomb and kill us both. Is that really what you want?"

"No."

"You don't want to get yourself blown up?" Mattie asked, and for an instant he understood how Constance could blaze with rage, how it could not matter to her who she hurt or what she did in her anger. "No?"

But Ivan didn't answer.

"No?" Mattie demanded again furiously, and twisted around to see that Ivan's hand had fallen from his thigh and he was staring down at the blood in his lap with peculiar blankness.

"Ivan?" said Mattie. "Ivan?"

He did not answer.

The System ships were coming closer. They would disable the *Copenhagen*, Mattie realized, and take them both captive.

The relativistic engines could be broken already, or trying to use them could destroy them beyond repair and trap both Mattie and Ivan in the middle of nowhere until they starved.

Mattie turned the relativistic engines back on, gave them full power, and ran.

BACKWARD

The first time Mattie escaped from the *Ananke*, he left on his sister's ship.

He realized quickly after Milla Ivanov had been brought on board the *Ananke* that Constance must be next, and the thought relieved him. Ivan's mother, Milla, was an unknown quantity, but Con was Mattie's sister and Ivan's . . . friend, and she'd brought dogs with her, which meant that she had a plan for getting him and Ivan out. They were badly in need of a plan.

His first impulse when he realized Constance was landing in the docking bay was to go straight for Ivan and get him out of that white room and away from that bitch interrogator immediately. But Ivan had warned him against a rescue attempt while he was under guard, because Mattie was outnumbered and injured: Domitian had broken Mattie's arm when Mattie had come on board the ship. But now Constance was here. Mattie would rendezvous with Connie, and she would tell him what to do.

It took a little bit of help from Milla Ivanov to get into the *Janus* unseen, but he managed it, slipping into Constance's ship right behind the backs of the *Ananke*'s crew. He was grinning when he burst in from adrenaline and the joy of the con. Then the dogs lifted their twin black heads from the floor, quizzical, and he stopped short.

"There, doggie," he said. One black Lab wagged its tail uncertainly, beating against the floor, but the other rose to its feet from where it had been lying on a blanket on the floor and advanced toward him, starting to bark, low and deep and dangerous.

Before Mattie could do anything Constance appeared at the door and said, breathless, "Sit!"

The dogs continued to bark. "Constance—" Mattie whispered.

"Still!" Constance snapped with a look that meant the order applied to him as well, and she grabbed a bag from beneath the *Janus*'s central panel. There was a syringe inside. She grabbed the dog nearest her and stuck the syringe into its flank. It whined and twisted around, teeth digging into the skin that had been punctured.

Constance straightened up. "Stay," she said to Mattie, to the dogs, and left, locking the door behind her.

Mattie went to the computer and quickly deleted the last few minutes of surveillance from the camera in Constance's ship, shutting it down and then adding a few more errors to her system for good measure; when the System found that the footage was missing, Constance could explain that contact with the *Ananke* had contaminated her computer as well. When he was done, he sat down where he had been before, out of view of the door and across from the black dogs.

He wondered what Constance's plan might be. She would have one: Constance always knew what to do.

Not long after Mattie had sat down, the dog that Constance had stuck with the syringe began to move oddly, its hindquarters shivering, whimpering low in its throat. It stood up jerkily and tried to move away from where Constance had stung it but stopped a few paces away and stood very still.

The other dog followed, its tail low but wagging uncertainly, sniffing the injured dog carefully before whuffing out the air and shaking its head. The injured dog walked back to the blanket they shared—limping now—and lay down slowly, its wounded leg twitching. Mattie watched the ribs moving beneath the satiny black fur slow down, grow shallow, and finally, at last, stop.

The living dog whined. Its first bark rang out unexpectedly through the cabin and made Mattie flinch. Better a dog than he or Ivan, but there was something unpleasant about that wild, inconsolable howling.

A key turned in the door. Constance entered, and the dog started barking at her.

"Quiet," said Constance, and closed the door again, locking it. She went straight for the pilot's chair.

"What . . ." Mattie began, and Constance said sharply, "Shh!"

She activated the ship's launch sequence. There were fine tremors in her hands.

The *Janus* lifted off and rose up and out of the *Ananke*. Constance bent over the ship's controls as if she felt that if she leaned far enough forward, the ship might travel faster. Mattie had thought that he'd seen something almost like fear in her eyes when she first had come back on board the *Janus*, but looking at her face now, he saw nothing of the kind. It was fury that pulled taut all the muscles on her face, a burning, hating fury.

Mattie said, "How are we going to get him back?"

The surviving dog had lain down beside its dead partner, resting its head on the dead dog's still shoulders.

Constance said, "We aren't."

FORWARD

The *Copenhagen*'s engines did not give out. Mattie waited until the System ships had vanished entirely from their instruments before he let their speed drop again, allowing the engines to fall into a safer output range. Then he changed their course so that they were headed once more to Callisto. At a moderate speed, they would make it there in time for the rendezvous.

He would have to examine the engines for damage, and soon. But for the moment he had greater concerns.

Ivan had, true to his warning, passed out. Mattie wasn't certain what had done it: the end of adrenaline from keeping himself alive on the *Ananke*, the cumulative effects of blood loss and injury, the poisons in his bloodstream coming due. His skin was cool when Mattie touched him, and he did not respond to his name.

In a way, it was a mercy he was so deeply unconscious. Mattie set to cleaning and bandaging the wound in his leg. When he went to find the pulse, he found bruises on Ivan's neck: small, spaced a finger's width apart.

Ivan might sleep for a while yet. Ivan might never again wake up. Mattie dragged himself away from Ivan eventually to sit in the piloting platform's one chair and stare out at the stars through the viewscreen.

The System ships were gone. The *Ananke* was gone. Mattie and Ivan were far out between planets, where no one, not System or rebel, would bother to venture. They were as alone as they could be in the solar system at the moment and as safe as they could be in their isolation. If Mattie wanted to make the rendezvous Constance had planned at Callisto, he simply would have to maintain their course, and they would arrive at Jupiter's moon in due time. He simply had to maintain their course.

Behind him, Ivan was still and silent.

Mattie changed their course.

Chapter 2

$\Delta X \Delta P \geq \hbar/2$

FORWARD

Ivan was in the white room again, and Ida was watching him from across that gleaming steel table.

No, Ivan thought for a lucid moment, *I'm not here, Mattie got me out*, but Ida was watching him and he couldn't relax his guard for a second, not around her. There was a chill in the white room, as there always had been, a cold that stole his stillness in shivering; it seemed even colder now. He smiled at Ida, thick with charm, and she smiled back, and showed her tombstone teeth.

"When you know someone completely," Ida said, "they have a kind of life in you."

Ivan said nothing. Sometimes that was the best course to take. She stood and smoothed out her skirt and blouse, as slender and sleek as a sheathed blade.

"An animal that knows its hunter completely can predict it," Ida said, and began to pace. The sound of her heels was the Russian roulette click of a revolver on an empty chamber. "The prey that knows its predator survives."

She smiled at him again. Her lips were crimson against her teeth. When she moved, the cold moved with her as if she were an inverse star that did not emit heat but absorbed it, a black hole that sucked the warmth and life from the room.

"Of course," she said, laughing, "the predator that knows its prey never goes hungry, either."

Ivan had a sudden flash of her, thrashing, the weight of her in his lap struggling, her black eyes going empty. Her eyes now had that same incognizant darkness.

He said, "It's petty of you to haunt me."

"People are petty," Ida said.

A chill struck him. It seemed to come from inside himself, like if he cut himself open, he would find the same darkness that lit Ida's eyes.

"The moment of death is the most intimate moment of anyone's life," Ida said. She had something in her mind; Ivan could hear it in her voice, the way she was setting him up for a fall. A dizzy spell struck him, but he fought it off. He couldn't show weakness, not here with her. He had to stay in control.

"To witness it—" Ida said. "To cause it—"

A flash of something, the colors in his sight turning inverse; Ivan knew for a moment that he was on the verge of passing out, but he didn't. The white room was lit oddly by a light from behind him, and Ida still was pacing but no longer speaking, her dark gaze fixed on him and showing a predator's hungry heart.

Ivan turned as much as he could, chained to his chair, and then found that he could stand even though the cuffs remained frigid around his wrists.

The light was coming from far off in a black nothing like the fabric of space. It was brilliant, blazing, a fire that burned without sound in the emptiness of vacuum. Ivan was too far off to feel its heat, but if he looked closely, he could see what it was.

Constance Harper was in the inferno, or Constance Harper was the inferno. She blazed with it, her bare skin unburned by the flames.

Constance, he tried to say, but no sound escaped from his mouth, *Constance*, and walked toward her, but now that he had come close enough to see that it was she standing in the flames, he could come no closer. He was moving and she was not moving, but somehow with every step he took she remained the same distance away.

From behind him he still heard those steps, that *click-click* of heels, that Russian roulette sound. He did not turn to face it but reached toward Constance, burning, sightless. *Constance, Constance,* Ivan said to try to make her see him, to try to make her hear him, but with no result. How could she see him with all that light in her eyes?

Constance, he said, *Constance*, as the flames spread over her skin, but she did not hear him, and he was so cold, he was freezing down to his core, and the chill of the white room had its hand stretched out over his shoulder—

Ivan woke.

For a moment he simply lay and breathed, keeping his respiration steady. He did not know where he was. There was a steady *click-click-click* from some machinery that struck his mind awry. It seemed to have come with him out of his dream. He shook the unease away. The sound was harmless.

Other than that sound, the space he was in was quiet; he lay on something firm, something covered him to his chest, there was an ache and burn in his leg that was growing in intensity. And underneath it all someone else was breathing. Ivan found that his breath had automatically synced to match that respiration, and when he listened to that steady sound, the last pieces came together in his mind.

He opened his eyes. Above him was the gray paneled ceiling of the *Copenhagen*, a familiar sight, though he could hardly remember looking at it. The last thing he recalled with perfect clarity was Althea Bastet lowering her gun and asking him plaintively, "What do I do now?"

Ivan lifted his head and found the piloting platform, the space ahead of them spotted with distant stars. Mattie was sitting there in the near dark, his back to Ivan. "Mattie."

Mattie turned, his eyes wide and dark in the dimness of the cabin. And then Mattie was pushing back his chair and striding over, moving so fast that Ivan had hardly adjusted to the movement before Mattie was crouched down at his side. "Hey," Mattie said.

"Hey." Ivan deliberately untensed all the muscles that had gathered themselves for flight the moment Mattie had moved so suddenly.

"Do you remember where you are?"

Not the Ananke, Ivan would have said, but held his tongue. Somehow speaking the name of the *Ananke* seemed dangerous, like whispering the name of a bloody queen into a darkened mirror.

"I'm on the *Copenhagen*." Ivan chose his words with care and his enunciation with precision. He studied the sealed cabinets that lined the walls. This ship was small: one room for living accommodations and instrumentation. He knew somehow, without remembering having seen it, that there was a bathroom and a storage room beyond the wall behind his head.

Mattie's hand was heavy on his chest. "What do you remember?"

Constance burning, the click of heels on a metal floor, a living ship blazing with light. System ships coming after them and a self-destruct, but perhaps that had been a dream. "Not much," Ivan said. "How long was I out?"

"Ivan," Mattie said with a strain in his voice that made Ivan reevaluate exactly how much stress he had been under for the past however many days, "answer my question."

"I remember the *Ananke*," said Ivan. "I remember going on board; I remember getting captured. I was interrogated. Constance blew up Earth. You came back. Althea let us go. We are traveling toward Callisto. There were System ships." He checked Mattie's expression to be sure that statement was accurate. It seemed to be, so Ivan added firmly, "My memory is fine, Mattie. How long have I been out? Where are we?"

"How does your leg feel?"

"I remember getting shot."

"I didn't ask if you remembered; I asked how it felt."

His leg was burning, but it was not the terrible wrongness of a sickening wound. "Better than it did," Ivan said, and remembered something else from the *Ananke*. "How's your arm?"

"It's fine. Constance got me to a System medical chamber, fixed the break in a few minutes." Mattie hesitated. "I couldn't take you to one for your leg, because . . ."

"Because there weren't any you could take me to." Ivan's thoughts were settling into an order again, organizing themselves, organizing him. Constance had blown up Earth and begun her revolution; that meant the solar system was in civil war. There wouldn't be any hospital Mattie could safely take Ivan to, not now. "Help me sit up."

Mattie got an arm under his back and helped pull Ivan up until he could lean against the wall. The change in position made Ivan briefly dizzy, but when it passed, he felt more awake than he had for days. His gaze swept automatically over the *Copenhagen* again, looking for danger or weakness. There were no cameras, of course. The room was cleaner than Ivan was used to seeing in a room maintained by one Matthew Gale.

Mattie sat against the wall next to him, on the floor beside the mattress, his shoulder leaning into Ivan's arm. He said, "You were pretty out of it for a while."

A thought struck him. "Mattie."

"I read something about the truth drugs you were on, something about some psychological effects, flashback hallucinations, which—"

"Mattie, how long was I out?"

"A little over a week."

"When is the rendezvous with Constance?"

Mattie spoke flatly, as if by doing so he could escape further discussion. "The rendezvous was two days ago."

"Two days?"

Mattie rose to his feet, evading again, but there was nowhere to run to in the smallness of the *Copenhagen*'s cabin. Ivan realized, "You missed it on purpose."

"You should lie down. You just woke up."

"I'll lie down when we're done talking. Why did we miss the rendezvous?"

"You're un-fucking-believable," Mattie said. Sometimes when he said that, it was a compliment. Ivan did not think it was in this case. "I don't want to play this stupid game," he said, and crouched down very suddenly, right in front of Ivan again. As he looked at the tension that held Mattie's face, something struck Ivan's hollow heart, and the reverb of it nearly weakened him into backing down. "I want you to lie down and get some rest, and when you're better, we'll figure something out."

"I'm not going to rest if I'm sitting here wondering what happened. We missed the rendezvous. Why?"

"Does it matter?" Mattie snapped.

"How are we going to find her? Does she know I'm alive? Does she even know you're alive?"

"I don't know what she knows."

"We can still go to Callisto," Ivan said. "Anji will be there."

"I don't know."

"That was the plan. Has the plan changed?"

"I don't know."

"Anji will be by Jupiter," Ivan insisted. His head was pounding, but he felt the better for having a clear plan of action to throw himself toward. "How far are we from Jupiter?"

"Ivan—" Mattie began.

Ivan cut him off before he could get too far into convincing himself not to go. "Mattie," he said. "Please."

Mattie stared back at him. For a moment, the twist of his mouth turned bitter, and then he stood up and took his expression out of Ivan's sight. He walked back over to the piloting terminal and began to put some coordinates into the machine. Ivan watched him and tried to breathe evenly, but an unsteady pull had come to his lungs, a lower drag to his heavy skull.

Mattie said, "We're on course for Callisto."

"Thank you," Ivan said, and meant it. He leaned back against the wall but did not lie down and did not sleep. He was watching the stars to see if the *Copenhagen* really did change its course.

The stars shifted. They were back on course. Ivan let his eyes slip shut.

BACKWARD

When Ivan was nine Terran years of age, back when he was called Leon, his mother took him to see Saturn.

"That's Rhea, do you see?" Milla said in her steady voice, quietly enough to be addressing him but clearly enough that the System administrators and the cameras overhead could capture every word. An actress couldn't project as precisely as she could. Ivan stood at her side and kept himself as carefully still and controlled as she did beside him.

They stood before a huge window, floor to ceiling, that showed the Saturnian system in all its sepulchral silence. Ivan stared out at the golden planet, at the slicing rings.

His mother's hand landed on his elbow, fingers curling around under his arm, hidden beneath his shirt.

"Do you see it, there?" she asked, and stretched out her free arm to point, like a statue of Diana drawing her bow. Her fingertip landed on the glass just above a spot of moving light.

Under Ivan's arm, her fingers began to tap out a message in gentle pressure and release against his skin. *You can show a little fear,* his mother said.

He glanced up at her quickly, but she was of course not looking at him. *Show a little fear,* he thought, and tried to remember what expressions that would entail.

"I see it," he told his mother, and she let her finger drift, following Rhea's slow orbit.

"Your father took me there once." Her voice was colored palely with regret, like paint off a brush dipped into water. Her fingers pressed into his arm again. *Play the crowd*, she warned him. *Make them think you're innocent, not that you're very good at hiding.*

Ivan said, "Did you and my father meet there?"

"No." Milla let her hand fall back to her side. "We met on Titan." She shifted, tucking Ivan's arm more securely into her own, her fingers entwining with his, the better to pass on quiet messages. Ivan let the childish contact happen, because he knew the System was watching, and they were waiting for a reason to kill him.

"I believe we'll get to see Titan," said Milla, seemingly to him, but Ivan had grown attuned to the subtle shifts of her voice over the course of surviving his early youth and so he was not surprised when the ship's captain answered from behind him: "We will, Doctor Ivanov."

"Thank you." Milla continued to gaze out at the planet ahead. Ivan stood very still at her side, trapped in some prey instinct that warned him not to call attention to himself.

His mother's fingers pressed a secret message against his hand. *I met your father on Titan on a trip for university there he was standing in the square talking about freedom and I was Terran then so I argued with him but when the System police came to stop him talking I helped him get away.*

The spaceship was drawing near to a filmy orange moon while Milla tapped out her truth to Ivan.

"That's Titan," said Milla, as calm as her secret message had not been. Titan's atmosphere was thick and opaque: a rare moon to hold an atmosphere. The clouds shuddered and flashed with hidden storms.

"Your father's reign of terror ended there." Milla tapped out against his hand, *I loved him.*

She paused, the stillness of her fingers against Ivan's hand as pronounced a silence as the rushing in his ears.

I should have hidden it better.

The ship was leaving Titan behind and traveling toward the planet itself, toward those slicing rings.

Don't let the System see your heart, she warned him. *Don't let yourself know that it is there.*

Aloud she said, "After your father, the System knew that Saturn wasn't safe. But they left a monument in the rings so that all would remember what happens to those who threaten the people of the System."

She spoke as if reading from a script. Against his hand she said, *Your father lost because I wasn't there to help him control the situation.*

His mother hadn't been with his father then, Ivan knew, because she had been on Earth to give birth to Ivan.

The ship was moving rapidly; the rings were growing in size, no longer looking razor-edged and colorful but beginning to appear as they were: widely spaced rocks all in the same orbit together. There was nothing to see yet, but Ivan could feel that his mother was tense.

You and I survive because we have control of our situation.

The System ship took them past the sparse rocks of Saturn's F ring, disrupting their orbits as they passed. Ivan knew that their ship would leave a distinct ripple in the clean-cut shape of Saturn's rings.

"It was illegal once to travel through the rings," his mother said serenely while tapping out, *Never lose control of your situation, of yourself, or of the people around you.*

The dusty Roche Division opened up ahead of them, and the ship powered through, heading straight for the crisp shine of the A ring ahead.

"It took special dispensation from the System for us to travel here to see them."

Everyone is controllable. Never get yourself in a situation where you can't control—

But Ivan lost track of her message because ahead of him he saw what he had been brought there to see.

The A ring was very narrow, only about fifteen meters thick, much narrower, in fact, than the ship that Ivan even now was flying in. It was full of stones that ranged in size from dust to boulders that Ivan would have considered hardly midsize on Earth.

And between the stones, there were bodies. Ivan took in a breath.

His mother's fingers tightened on his. At first he thought it was another message, but he realized after a moment of stillness that she had nothing to say.

Less than a decade old: a short time cosmically, but eternity to him. He'd had for himself the nine years of life denied to the people he saw now, floating between stones with their eyes staring, their limbs torn,

exsanguinated, the blood all evaporated by vacuum and heat, mummi-
fied by the distant sun.

And his mother leaned forward at some signal from the System that
Ivan did not see and pointed to the nearest corpse, a young man whose
skin had been slowly blackened and crisped by the sun's radiation.

"Do you see?" Milla asked with calm cruelty and the weight of the
System's attention resting heavily on their backs.

FORWARD

The *Copenhagen* was a fast little ship. It was not long before their
changed course took them within sight of Jupiter. Ivan was standing up
by then, leaning on the wall. Mattie had helped him up but flatly refused to be an accessory to further movement. Ivan suspected that he
intended to wait for him to give up and sit back down, but Ivan remained standing.

"How close?" Ivan asked. He asked not just because he could not
quite see the details on the viewscreen from where he stood but because he did not think Mattie was paying much attention: Mattie had
his chair halfway turned so that he could keep a wary eye on Ivan, and
between Ivan and the viewscreen, Ivan seemed to be receiving the
greater share of his attention.

Mattie glanced over at the screen.

"Not in the Hill sphere yet," he said. "But it's visible now." A few
deft movements of his hand brought the screen into closer focus; Jupiter jumped into view, striated, with sparks of the Galilean moons darting around it.

In the brief moment when Mattie's attention was taken from him,
Ivan let himself shift, keeping his breathing quiet, to ease the pressure
on his burning leg.

"I'm slowing down for the approach," Mattie said. "How's your leg?"

"Fine."

"Yeah." Mattie was looking at Ivan's leg, not at Ivan himself. Although Ivan no longer was wearing the bloodstained white scrubs he
had been shot in, Mattie seemed to know precisely where to look. "If
we had a System medical chamber, it'd be better by now. No scar."

"It's starting to close on its own. It'll be fine." He wasn't certain he'd trust a medical chamber in any case. A machine couldn't be reasoned with or persuaded.

"Good thing that bitch was a bad shot."

"Or a very good one," Ivan said. It would have been infinitely easier to aim for his torso and leave his internal organs lacerated beyond repair, but Althea Bastet had fired low and to the side, the blow a glancing one.

"You don't hate her."

"Who?"

"Althea." The word came from Mattie's mouth strangely laden, as if he had simply mispronounced the words "that bitch" and come up with Althea's true name by accident of vowels.

"No."

"Why the hell not?"

"She wasn't a bad person."

"What's that word," Mattie asked, "the one for when you like the person who hurts you?"

"Masochism?"

"No, I mean the one where you like your kidnapper."

"It's 'Shut up, Matthew,'" Ivan said.

"Stockholm syndrome," said Mattie. "That's it. I just think it's good for us to have a word for it, you know? So we can really communicate."

"It's hard to hate someone if you understand why they've done the things they did."

"Is it?" Mattie asked in a steely tone that Ivan had never heard him use before. "I don't think so."

The computer beeped. Mattie turned to see why, and Ivan held his breath. An alarm would be louder, surely, if they were under attack or a System ship had come near.

"We're in the Hill sphere," Mattie reported.

"How long until Callisto?"

"Direct route, a half an hour. Long route—"

"Direct route," Ivan said.

"We don't want to fly straight at it," Mattie said. "We don't know what's going on in there."

"So run a scan. Check the radio."

"I am running scans, and I've opened the *Copenhagen* to transmissions," Mattie said patiently.

"Don't just open for transmissions; turn on the radio for *any broad-casts at all*," Ivan said, and Mattie reached over to the radio and flicked it on. A dreadful roar of white noise burst from the throat of the machine. Mattie cocked a brow at Ivan as if to say, *Happy now?* But he did turn the radio down and set it to scan between frequencies for any real transmissions.

"I'm going in obliquely," he said, and that was that.

The *Copenhagen* skirted Jupiter, keeping to the vast regions of space unpopulated by the moons or thin, vacuous rings. Ivan leaned back against the wall and ignored the way the burning in his leg grew worse with every second.

The static of the radio flickered off and on at even intervals as the radio automatically jumped between frequencies. It was hypnotic, like the way the clouds on Jupiter's vast bulk spiraled and moved almost too slowly to be seen.

Mattie said, "You haven't asked me about your mother."

His back was to Ivan; he was focused on the screen, on flying the ship. His question had no origin that Ivan could find. Not understanding why a question was being asked had always made Ivan uneasy: he couldn't tell what Mattie might want to hear.

"No," Ivan said. "I haven't."

Mattie asked him nothing else.

They took a long spiraling loop into the Jovian system, the best way to see anything that might be there. They had gone nearly all the way around the planet, and the ache from Ivan's leg had spread up into his torso nearly all the way to his head when he realized that there was something strange about all that static.

"What frequency are we on?" Ivan's voice sounded distant even to himself. Sometimes he felt that way, as if his skin were not his own, as if his voice were someone else speaking, as if the real he were somewhere locked up inside his head.

"Uh, we're a couple of channels above System Standard Frequency 25."

"And we're going through channels with increasing frequency?"

"Yeah." Mattie was leaning over the controls, clearly more intent on navigating through the Jovian system unseen than listening to the radio.

Ivan said, "These are the short-range frequencies."

"So?"

Another click; the radio blasted static from a new channel into the cabin of the *Copenhagen* like a polar wind. "We should be hearing transmissions from the moons."

"There's a war going on; they're probably blacked out."

There still should have been something, Ivan thought, a few rebel bursts of communication. Or, more likely, if the war was actively going on, there should have been communication between ships, between armies.

He said, "Have you seen any ships so far?"

"We're not that close to Jupiter. They might be farther in."

The radio looped back around to the lowest frequencies and began to step through them again. There was a different quality to the static at different wavelengths; Ivan could hear it. Low, down here, the basso hum of Jupiter could be heard, pierced through by the whizzing of its moons, like clouds passing over the sun. The static at all frequencies was the singing of the stars.

They were drawing, at last, near to Callisto. Ivan leaned more heavily on the wall and watched it grow. He could see its star-pocked surface against the vast looming bulk of Jupiter.

But there was something off about Callisto's gleaming shape. The sunlight was sparking off points around the moon. The static switched again on the radio, shivering. Ivan found himself leaving the wall and limping toward the piloting platform, his gaze fixed on the glints of light that surrounded Callisto.

The static had filled the cabin to such an extent that it had filled his leg; there was no longer any burning pain, only a dull and buzzing numbness.

Mattie finally looked up when he heard him move. "What are you doing?" he demanded.

"Mattie." Ivan reached out and gripped the back of Mattie's chair across the platform but did not have the strength to pull himself up beside it. "Callisto doesn't have any rings," but there he was, looking at Callisto, and there was a thin low ring encircling it.

Mattie looked and swore, his voice low and punching. He reached for the controls.

"No," Ivan said, "get closer."

Before Ivan's eyes, the unnatural rings grew larger, more clear. He could see the bits of debris that constituted them. There was a partial hull of a ship; there was a girder that could only have been human-made. He saw flecks of steel and carbon, and that was only what was large enough to see. The radio clicked between stations beside him, a low roar of snowy static. He had seen the rings of Saturn once, and now, here, he knew, *knew*, that if they got close enough he would see the same thing. But what bodies would he see here? Constance, bloody, eyes staring? His mother with half her skin blackened? Anji or Christoph or Julian—

"*Ivan!*" In a moment Mattie's face had replaced the gleaming image of the slowly approaching moon.

"That's where the fleets are," Ivan said. "That's why we haven't heard anything on the radio."

"There're not enough ships there to be a full fleet," Mattie said slowly and clearly. "Not enough to be the System fleet. Not enough to be Constance's fleet, or Anji's, or Christoph's."

Ivan forced himself to look at the debris, how spread out it was, how low to the moon. "If there's a ring like that on all the other moons—"

"There isn't," said Mattie, as if by conviction alone he could make truth.

The static-skipping radio suddenly beeped, a rapid pattern of tones. "Code," Ivan said, but Mattie already was moving, tapping in a directive to the computer, trying to recover the wavelength they had just lost.

An ache was traveling up Ivan's arms; he looked down to see that he had his hands clenched so tightly into fists that the skin of his knuckles had gone bloodless.

Static, static, static, *nothing*. "It was just—"

"I know," Mattie snapped, and iterated the radio again, stepping it from frequency to frequency. Ivan listened to the staccato bursts of static. This was where the signal had been before, he was sure—

The radio beeped again, an arrhythmic pattern that set Ivan's heart to beating once more. This time Mattie was ready and stopped them on the station immediately, listening to the rhythm.

"Do you know what they're saying?"

Ivan was counting intervals, matching them to the codes he'd had memorized since he was a child. "No. It's definitely code, but I don't know the key."

"Can you crack it?" Mattie asked just as the signal vanished.

"If you can find it."

Mattie already was searching. He looked like a hunting dog bent over the computer like that, all sharp and focused attention. A strange throb of affection for him struck Ivan's heart then, entirely inappropriate to their situation; he pushed it aside.

"They're changing stations," Mattie said a moment later, after he'd found the beeping once more.

"Can you tell the pattern?"

"Not with only three frequencies. They're sticking to short-range, though."

Then the broadcast was from nearby. "This is some variant on my mother's code."

"You think it's Anji?"

"Who else could it be?" Ivan asked. His fists were still so tightly clenched that his forearms ached, but when he looked away from the radio, trying to center himself, he only saw the bodies outside Callisto once more. "Broadcast the hounds signal."

"We don't know who else is out there."

"These are revolutionaries. We haven't heard any other broadcasts in this system."

"Ivan." Mattie was a tense curve over the computer, turned toward him but not meeting his eyes. "If the System—"

"You are the brother of the Mallt-y-Nos. If the System attacks us, the revolutionaries will fall over themselves to save your life."

Something bitter bent the bowed curve of Mattie's mouth, and then he was stabbing a message into the computer, and the barking and howling of the Cŵn Annwn roared out into the stars on all frequencies, overwhelming the tense and unsteady beat of the revolutionary communication.

When the howling had finished, the radio went back to iterating through stations. Nothing showed but static.

"Did they hear?" Ivan wondered.

"I don't know how they fucking couldn't have." Mattie stood in agitation, moving restlessly, as if he would like to pace but didn't want to move too far from the ship's controls.

Ivan said, "We should broadcast again."

"What, and get every System ship in an AU of Jupiter headed toward us?" Mattie made a sharp, agitated slash of the air with his hand, then changed the exterior camera view on the viewscreen, turning their sight out toward the open universe and away from the corpses on Callisto.

Ivan seated himself in the abandoned piloting chair. The cramped muscles in his leg throbbed and spasmed with the movement, but there was no dampness on the bandage. He bent over the computer.

"What are you doing?"

"I'm checking the instruments," Ivan said.

"Just stay away from Callisto."

"I have no intention of—Mattie."

Mattie was at his side faster than a breath, leaning over the chair, leaning over Ivan. Ivan knew when he had seen what Ivan had, because his agitated fidgeting stopped, settling down into that focused attention once more.

Far off, half hidden by the planet's wispy rings, were spots of warmth that did not move with the rest of the stars.

"They were orbiting one of the other moons," Mattie guessed.

The little sparks of light were coming toward them slowly, steadily, and in chill silence. Why had they not responded?

"There's more," said Mattie, and Ivan saw that there were other ships, too: small, hidden among the moons and the thin rings, but now leaving their moons behind and coming toward the *Copenhagen*.

"Hail them," Ivan suggested, and Mattie bent over him to reach for the comm—it was better to have Mattie make first contact in situations like this; his accent was much less alarming to a nervous revolutionary than Ivan's was—and open a broadcast again.

"This is the rebel ship *Copenhagen*," Mattie said. "We've come on behalf of the Mallt-y-Nos."

No response. A few of the nearer ships were close enough now to run a scan on them: attack ships, all four of them. More heavily armed than the *Copenhagen*.

Mattie got back on the radio. "This is the *rebel ship Copenhagen*. We've come as friends. We're looking for the Mallt-y-Nos."

The four foremost ships were not just near enough to be scanned; they were near enough for the *Copenhagen*'s sensors to detect an increase in radiation in a specific place on their layout and to draw the logical conclusion.

"Their weaponry systems just came online," Ivan said.

"They're System?"

"Two of them are System ships but modded. The other two are civilian ships even more heavily modified. System doesn't mod its own ships."

"Maybe it fucking does now!" Mattie bent over Ivan again, this time going for the piloting controls. "There are more of them coming from the moons. We're getting out of here."

"If we run, they fire," Ivan pointed out.

"So we outrun their bombs."

"Maybe we can outrun some of their bombs. But we can't outrun that third ship, the small one. Do you see—"

"We're not going to just sit here and—"

"Signal them again," Ivan said.

"What good did that do?" Mattie said, and reached for the flight controls. Ivan grabbed his wrist before he could. Ahead of them, the radiation signature that indicated a live weaponry system brightened: a sure sign of the ships' bombs being armed. Around the distant moons, more and more ships were rising, engines bright.

They had stumbled into a hornet's nest and woken the wasps. Ivan said, "Hail them again."

Mattie swore at him. Ivan hardly heard him, staring at the brightness of their oncoming destruction, and Mattie pulled free of Ivan's grasp and went to the radio again, shouting into it, "This is the rebel ship *Copenhagen*. This is a rebel ship!"

The ships' brightness was reaching peak. At any moment, Ivan knew—and the *Copenhagen*'s sensors warned—those ships would fire. The *Copenhagen* would be hit, and the gravity of Callisto would pull them in. Ivan would be another blackened body in that graveyard ring.

"This is the brother of the Mallt-y-Nos, Matthew Gale! I am on this ship with Leontios Ivanov, the son of Milla and Connor Ivanov! This is Mattie and Ivan! *Do not fire!*"

And then—unbelievably—the brightness of those stars began to dim. Mattie sucked in a ragged breath, and Ivan found himself moving without forethought: reaching up to Mattie's arm that crossed over his chest in order to reach the communications panel, closing his fingers around the warmth of that arm, crushing the fabric of his shirt against the space over his heart.

The communications panel chimed: someone wanted to speak to them. Mattie moved to open the connection, and even that slight motion unhooked Ivan's fingers from his arm.

The view of great Jupiter and the lights of the rising ships vanished, replaced by a video feed from one of the other ships. For a moment, nothing but black as the *Copenhagen* negotiated with the other computer for video access, and then a familiar woman's face was staring out at them, black buzz starting to grow out on her shaven head and her dark eyes wide.

"Anji," said Mattie, and she reacted to her name like a physical touch, a flinch passing over her features. The jewels in her ear winked.

"Hello, boys," Anji said, and then, "You may have just accidentally started another war."

BACKWARD

"She's late," Ivan said.

"She'll be here," Mattie said. "She always is."

Ivan didn't particularly share his confidence. They'd been waiting at the Martian black market for almost an hour, longer than Ivan liked to stay at such places. He couldn't shake the constant paranoia that at any moment the System would come down on them like lightning.

But this was where the rendezvous had been set up, and if they missed this one, it might be months before they could arrange another.

And Ivan had to see Constance.

A steady wind went through the makeshift kiosks, the storefronts of landed shuttles. The entire place was ready to take off at a moment's notice. Mattie wandered off, and Ivan headed parallel to him, not close but never far.

Ivan shuffled through illegal wares—drugs, weaponry, rare foods and animals from Earth—without really paying attention to what he held. His attention was on the crowd around him, on the faces and forms of the unknown people who pressed up against him, who butted into him, who engulfed him. He had been with Mattie long enough to know when his pocket was being picked, but that was only one kind of defense against a crowd.

His attention finally was arrested by a display of art. Beautiful things for beauty's sake tended not to show up in black markets like these. The only reason anyone would bring a work of art here was if it was stolen, and even then it would be hard to fence. Easier to sell ore and bullets. But here, in front of him, was an array of sculptures.

The shop owner watched him with a shrewd and beady eye as Ivan picked one up. It was surprisingly heavy: metal, Ivan realized. Metal down to the core. It had been cast in the shape of a woman, almond eye sightless from lack of iris and pupil. She gazed out of only one eye, because the skin of her face did not stretch all the way around her head. The bones of her shoulder pulled out of her skin like a woman shrugging off a blouse; her delicate metacarpals detached themselves from her flesh as if she were peeling away a glove.

The shop owner said, "It's one of a kind."

Ivan hefted that strange and troubling sculpture with one hand. The slow detachment of the skull from the woman's flesh seemed inevitable, unstoppable, as if gravity were peeling away her skin, and soon only the metal bones would be left.

"Made by an artist on Mercury," said the shop owner.

Fingers gripped his arm suddenly and with force. Ivan's wild heart urged him to lash out, but his habit forced him to go very still, set the statue down again, and turn calmly to face the intruder.

Anji Chandrasekhar grinned at him, her earring flashing a deep crimson. "Hey, handsome."

"Hello," Ivan said, and left his choice of adjective to the discretion of the listener.

Anji released his arm for the sake of hurling herself at him for an embrace, her arms wrapping around his chest. The physical intimacy was unnecessary in Ivan's opinion, but living with Mattie had shown him that his dislike of being touched was a rather Terran tendency.

Plus, he privately suspected that when Anji hugged him, she had serious designs on breaking his ribs.

"You look stressed," she suggested when she pulled back, still gripping him by the shoulders.

"That's a natural reaction to the sight of your face."

"I've missed you, Leontios," Anji said mistily.

"Anji!" Mattie pushed through the crowd, drawn, no doubt, by the psychic echo of Ivan's physical distress. Anji released Ivan to hurl herself at Mattie as well, nearly knocking him over with the force of her affection. Mattie handled it better than Ivan had, grabbing her back as if the embrace were a contest of strength. By the look on his face when Anji let him go, he'd lost.

"Let's get some privacy, gentlemen," Anji said with a hand on each man's arm. They left the figurine, and the watchful shopkeeper, behind.

Mattie said, "No Con?"

"Always a con," Anji said with a bright teeth-flashing grin for the pun, "but no Constance this time."

"You told us she would meet us here," Ivan said.

"You've got me instead. Isn't that better?"

"Ha," said Mattie, and then, "*Ow,*" when Anji punched him on the arm.

"Is she all right?" Ivan asked.

"After the three of you left Luna, the System got her alone and interrogated her," Anji said

Ivan's mind filled with fast irrational flashes of Constance in chains, Constance drugged, Constance soaked in agonized sweat and spitting fury at her captors.

But Anji went on, "It was a friendly sort of interrogation, at least, as friendly as the System ever gets. They didn't get anything out of her, and they don't think there's anything to get. Surveillance at her bar is up, of course. Oh, and that woman you wanted me to keep an eye out for was there—not in the room but in the same interrogation facility."

"What woman?" Mattie wanted to know. Ivan said, "Ida Stays?"

Anji snapped her fingers. "Yes, her. The intelligence agent. Con never saw her, but she was there. None of this is the message Constance wanted me to give you, though. The message from Con is that you're not to contact her."

Mattie said, "At all?"

"She says if she really needs to contact you, Abigail will arrange a meeting."

"Abigail" was Constance's best and most effective pseudonym. She used that name only when it was unavoidable. Ivan was certain that Abigail would not be contacting Ivan and Mattie for any reason at all.

"And what if we need to talk to her?" Ivan asked.

Anji laughed. "We don't make that call."

"I need to talk to her, and I can't wait five months to do it."

"Ivan," Anji said with exaggerated empathy, "you need to let her go. You two had a good thing for a while, but now it's done, and chasing after her like this is just going to—"

"You can't say what will happen between now and—when we go through with the plan. I don't want things to end between us the way they did."

Anji leaned in.

"You," she said, and patted his cheek with one callused hand, "are a manipulative bastard. No, Ivan, I'm not going to convince Constance to meet you."

"You're a good dog, aren't you?" Ivan said. "You bark on command."

"And sit and roll over," Anji agreed. There was no sign of the fear in her that Ivan felt, the fear that she should have felt, knowing what she did about Constance Harper and what Constance was willing to do.

Then again, perhaps Ivan was the only one who felt that fear. He was, after all, the one who had driven Constance to this.

Anji smiled at them both, bright and unfettered. "Now," she said, "I've got some time to kill. Which of you knows how to show a girl a good time?"

FORWARD

"Another war?" Mattie said.

Anji grimaced, an odd look on a face Mattie was used to seeing with a carefree smile. "System fleet came through this system a few days ago. It went off, but it left some of its short-range ships behind. We'd all trenched ourselves down on the moons, but—"

"But Mattie and I just rang the dinner bell," Ivan said.

"Exactly."

They should have run, Mattie thought; the minute they saw the other ships, they should have picked up and run.

Ivan said, "You were going to fire on us. Why—"

"Talk later," Mattie interrupted. "Which way should we go?"

"You won't make it. Are you armed?"

Mattie had been so focused on speed when he'd chosen this ship from Constance's fleet that he hadn't thought enough about firepower. "This ship hasn't got enough weapons to melt a comet."

"Then you need to dock with me. The *Pertinax* has armor."

Below Mattie's spread arms, Ivan was calling something up on the computer. Anji's face was suddenly shoved to one half of the viewscreen while the other half showed the Jovian system—and the sparks of light that were other ships, starting to converge.

There was no way for Mattie to tell which of those lights were Anji's ships and which were System. "How long do we have?"

"Seven minutes."

"I need at least a half hour to dock!"

"So start moving," Anji said, and cut the connection. Jupiter and the starscape filled in the space where her head had been.

"I'm going to fucking kill her," Mattie said.

Ivan already was getting up from the pilot's seat. "I don't think that would help."

"It would help me." The *Pertinax* was sending course information and permission to the *Copenhagen* already. Mattie scrambled to give the computer his instructions.

"What do you want me to do?"

There. Mattie located the *Pertinax*'s docking bay and aimed the *Copenhagen* for the other ship at the fastest speed he dared. "Have you changed your mind about prayer?"

Ivan grabbed for the back of Mattie's chair. "If you don't decrease our speed soon, I might reconsider."

The *Pertinax* was staying perfectly still, its side angled toward Mattie, but the other three ships were spreading themselves out, weapons online. A small group of ships that had risen up from Io were arrowing toward this fragment of Anji's fleet more swiftly than Mattie would have thought was possible.

Something flashed out by Ganymede. Two fragments of the fleets had collided.

The largest of Anji's ships that had come to greet Mattie and Ivan, a sharp-edged disk of a stolen old System warship, sped forward through the sky toward the arrow of approaching System ships. Mattie hoped it would hold them off long enough for Mattie to dock.

The curved side of the *Pertinax* was filling almost all of the *Copenhagen*'s viewscreen. Mattie gritted his teeth and did not slow down.

"Uh, Mattie—"

"I know."

Impact in ten—Mattie had to slow. He left scorch marks from his thrusters on the side of Anji's ship. Maybe she wouldn't notice.

The door to the docking bay of the *Pertinax* was already opening, visible as a flash of darkness in the ship's gravitationally revolving side. Mattie started a theta movement that would bring him in synchronous orbit with that docking bay door—

Suddenly the *Pertinax* jolted, moving. Mattie grabbed the radio. "*Pertinax*, hold still."

An unfamiliar male voice came on, presumably the *Pertinax*'s pilot. "The System ships have reached firing range. If we don't move, we will—"

An explosion brightened the viewscreen and interrupted the call with static.

"—be hit," the pilot finished.

Mattie was already catching up to the other ship and finding that revolving door. "Just don't move!"

"This ship—"

Ivan grabbed the radio from Mattie. "*Pertinax*, this is *Copenhagen*," he said pleasantly.

The *Pertinax* jolted again, and Mattie found himself facing revolving carbon and steel. He swore and pulled the *Copenhagen*'s nose up.

"If you move while we are trying to dock," Ivan continued, still in the same very pleasant tone, "then we will collide with your hull and do far more damage than a System bomb."

Anji's voice came on. "We're holding, Ivan. Get in."

"Good," Mattie snarled while Ivan held the communications equipment safely out of his reach, and when the *Pertinax*'s docking bay door appeared again, he dived down into it.

The *Copenhagen* landed hard, skidding, still half trying to revolve on its own. The shifted gravity threw them both forward—Mattie felt Ivan collide with his back—but nothing crashed and aside from a few dents in Anji's floor, they were both undamaged. Behind them, the docking bay doors already were closing. Mattie watched the excruciatingly slow closing of the outer doors and the equally slow refilling of oxygen to the docking bay, every second waiting for a System bomb to tear through the hull of Anji's ship.

When the computer beeped to signify the atmosphere was safe outside, Mattie shoved open the hull door and rushed out, Ivan at his heels.

One of Anji's people was waiting for them. "This way," she said, and rushed off into the hall.

Mattie went two steps before realizing Ivan was not beside him. He was behind, limping, face set. "Slow down," Mattie snapped at Anji's woman, and grabbed Ivan's arm.

They hurried down the hall as fast as Ivan could go—Mattie gripped his elbow and thought about torn stitches and bleeding out on the

Pertinax's floor—and came out at last to the *Pertinax*'s control room. The ceiling of the control room was a semicircular viewscreen, giving them a 180-degree view. Mattie had a moment of disorientation, as if he had stepped out into open space, and overhead the dogfights flashed.

"Can we back out?" Anji was asking, pacing the space in front of the captain's chair beneath that dome of stars. It was a curious relief to see her, the familiar way she walked, those glinting earrings. "The refugees—"

"If any more ships come this way, the *Nemain* can't handle them," said a gaunt man in the navigator's chair, the same voice Mattie had heard through the radio on the *Copenhagen*.

"So pull out and we'll deal with that when it comes." Anji glanced their way, and her dark eyes widened until Mattie would have sworn they were taking up half the space on her shaved head. "Mattie!" She flung herself at him for a swift and fierce hug.

Mattie sucked in a breath to reinflate his lungs when she released him.

"Ivan!"

"No Leontios?" Ivan said, and looked startled when her arms settled around him with exceeding care. With Anji's reaction, Mattie saw him anew: his shirt buttoned up to hide the marks on his neck imperfectly, bruised, pale, weary.

"I thought you were dead. You get an 'Ivan' for that. You could've had better timing—"

"You could've not tried to shoot us out of the sky. We sent the hounds signal. What were you—"

"Can we get out of here first?" Mattie interrupted, watching the clash between Anji's *Nemain* and the System ships in the sky overhead.

Anji was shaking her head. "We can't. I still have ships on the moons—"

"Doing what? If you really want to fight the System, you can come back later!"

"They're collecting refugees," Anji said. "I want out of here as much as you do, Mattie, but we have to wait."

"You're abandoning Jupiter?" Ivan frowned.

Anji spread her arms out toward the flashing sky. "With all possible speed!"

"That wasn't in the plan."

"Anji can tell us all about it later," Mattie said. As far as he could tell from the lights flashing overhead, some of the System ships had slipped past the *Nemain* and were approaching the *Pertinax*. "Can you get your ships off those planets any faster?"

"If I could, I'd already be doing it," Anji said.

"System ships are back in firing range," the gaunt man reported.

"So move!" Anji snapped. She pressed a hand to her forehead. Mattie was disturbed to see it shaking. "Listen, boys, I know we need to talk—"

"Talk about how you're at war with Constance now?" Ivan asked.

For a moment his words didn't make sense. Mattie was still trying to piece them together when Anji said, "I'm not *at war* with Constance."

"Which is why when we broadcast that we were from the Mallt-y-Nos, you tried to shoot us down."

The *Pertinax* shuddered. It wasn't a particularly agile ship, and Mattie would bet it hadn't been able to dodge the first System bomb.

"Were you ever going to tell us?" Ivan asked when the *Pertinax* had steadied, and after this, Mattie was going to have a talk with him about priorities.

"Sure, Ivan, after we were done getting shot at!"

"The hull hasn't been breached, but the armor is damaged in section 19," the gaunt pilot reported.

"We need to draw them off," Anji said. "Is the *Macha* back yet?"

"She's on a course for us but trying to avoid System ships."

"Tell Shara to hurry!"

Ivan said, *"Anji."*

Anji made a swift gesture of frustration. "Constance and I have had a falling-out. Her way of doing things is going to get everyone killed, and I—and my people—would like not to die."

It seemed fair enough to Mattie. He had the sense not to say so.

"We're retreating to Saturn—there's no System there. Half my fleet's already over. I stayed here, getting refugees, waiting for you. I should've known you'd find a way to show up in the worst way possible."

The barrage of attacks suddenly let up. The *Nemain* had been joined by two other ships, one a heavily armored troop carrier like the *Pertinax*, the other the exceedingly small and exceedingly fast ship that Mattie had noticed on their arrival.

"If you're not at war," said Ivan, "then why did you try to fire on us?"

"Because you know Con; she's gonna be pissed. Either that or you were a System trap. I'm not your enemy; I was waiting here for you!"

Ivan said, "What if we told you we were still on Constance's side?"

"I'd say I was hoping you'd say that," Anji said, before Mattie could decide whether he should go for the gun that was not on his hip. She turned to her pilot, "Get Shara on the line; tell her we're going to do the decoy but there are some people she needs to pick up first."

Mattie reached desperately for some sense. "Who's getting picked up?"

"You are. I was planning to send some ambassadors to Constance. The two of you can get to Con, and you can vouch for my people."

Ivan said, "You just tried to shoot us down when you thought—"

"I don't want a war! You're going to negotiate with her so that I don't feel like I might need to shoot down any of the Huntress's ships that show up in my territory."

No expression showed on Ivan's carved-marble features. He said, "You could ally with Christoph if you're that scared of Constance."

"Christoph *works for* Constance," Anji said. She waved an expansive hand to cut Ivan off. "We don't have time. Will you vouch for my people with Constance?"

"What's the catch?" Ivan asked.

"It's not what you're thinking. I'm sending you with a small diplomatic fleet that is also going to draw some of the System ships away so that we can get away with the refugees."

Mattie said, "We're your fucking decoys?"

"You'll be perfectly safe."

"No fucking way!"

An explosion of spectacular brightness filled the sky, nearly blinding Mattie in the second before the *Pertinax*'s computers could compensate for the brightness and dim the viewscreen output. A moment later he realized that the impressive display of firepower had come from the minuscule *Badh*.

"Listen," said Anji. "I could've left this system days ago with the rest of my fleet, but I stayed, waiting for you. No matter what is going on between me and Constance, you are my friends and I will not let you get hurt."

"And Constance isn't your friend?" Ivan said.

"Constance is the Mallt-y-Nos first, my friend second. The two of you have never been what she is. Will you do it?"

If it was the only way to get out of this mess alive, Mattie would have danced naked underneath a full Terran moon for her. He nodded at Ivan.

Ivan's jaw tightened. For a minute Mattie thought he would refuse out of some stupid principle, then he said, "We'll do it."

He must want to see Constance very badly, Mattie thought. Some emotion he refused to name jabbed unpleasantly at his heart.

"Good," said Anji, and then suddenly, with helpless hysteria, she started to laugh. "But first you need to get off the *Pertinax* and redock on the *Macha*."

FORWARD

It was easier to get off the *Pertinax* in midbattle than it had been to dock, but the *Macha*'s hull was sparking with explosions.

Mattie eyed it. "Do they know we're coming?"

Ivan was already on the radio. "*Macha*, this is *Copenhagen*."

A woman's voice, tight with stress, answered the call. "This is Shara Court on the *Macha*. Who is speaking?"

"Leontios Ivanov on the *Copenhagen*."

"Wait where you are. We'll come to you."

Ivan put the radio down. "She knows we're here."

One of the bright stars broke off of formation and headed for the *Copenhagen*. It was not the *Macha*.

"Great," Mattie said. "So does the System."

Ivan picked up the radio again. "*Macha*, this is *Copenhagen*."

Mattie watched that star approach. "Would you put a little urgency in your voice?"

"We seem to have a System ship headed toward us," Ivan continued, as if he hadn't heard.

The radio buzzed. "*Copenhagen*, hold your position."

The System ship was coming closer. In a minute, it would be near enough to fire. "Ivan—"

"*Macha*, we are about to be shot down," Ivan said.

"*Copenhagen*, do not engage the enemy. We will come—"

"*Macha*," said Ivan, "open your docking bay doors and hold *your* position. We'll be there in a moment."

"Oh, fuck you," Mattie said.

Ivan set the radio down again. "Go for it," he said, and Mattie jumped to relativistic speed.

He came out of it less than a second later, shaking, the *Copenhagen* shaking around him with the sudden stresses. A hundred warnings started to flash on the screen before him: the *Copenhagen*'s hull was pitted with debris that had impacted at high speed. But they were only a few kilometers away from the *Macha* now.

The docking bay door started to open only after they arrived. Presumably Shara Court hadn't believed they'd do it. Bombs were still flashing against the *Macha*'s cylindrical hull. Mattie started to spiral inward toward that massive cylinder, matching its rotation speed, keeping well outside the impact zone of the bombs.

He was just getting up to speed when the System ships noticed him. He had to drop back out of rotation as a bomb exploded where he had been a second earlier. *"Fuck."*

"There's another one coming up behind us," Ivan warned.

"I can't—"

A second bomb went off and sent the *Copenhagen* spiraling away from the *Macha*. The first System ship was wheeling around, heading toward Mattie and Ivan.

Ivan was back on the radio. *"Macha*, can we get some help?"

"You're in our blind zone," Shara snapped. "Our weapons can't reach. This is why I told you to *wait*."

Mattie spared a glance for the rest of the field as he tried to get back into line with the rotation of the *Macha*. The *Nemain* was some distance away, holding off the rest of the System ships. "What about the—"

The System ship diving at them suddenly exploded, flames choking out in vacuum, debris flashing in distant sunlight. A moment later, the second System ship suffered the same fate.

Ivan got back on the radio while Mattie was still admiring the maneuver. "Please pass on our compliments to the captain of the *Badh*. Also, we are about to crash-land into your docking bay."

He shut off the radio before Shara could protest. Mattie aligned the *Copenhagen* with the *Macha*'s rotation, aimed for the bright spot in its hull, and hurtled down.

The *Copenhagen* struck the docking bay floor hard, bouncing once, thrusters blackening the inside of the ship. The docking bay doors were closing before the *Copenhagen* had finished moving.

Mattie quickly checked their systems. The ship would need some repair—he didn't even want to see what the hull looked like right now—but there was nothing too badly broken.

Behind him, Ivan was picking himself up from the floor. "You are exceptional at landing a crashing ship."

It was absurd that the compliment could please Mattie so much, especially when at any moment they might be blown to pieces. "Let's just find the captain."

FORWARD

Captain Shara Court had sent four people down to pick them up. Anji, Ivan remembered, had sent only one. By the time the atmosphere had leveled enough for Ivan and Mattie to disembark from the *Copenhagen*, those four people were openly gaping at the damage Mattie's landing had done to their docking bay. They led Mattie and Ivan up to the control room, which was identical to the *Pertinax*'s, with the starscape forming a dome overhead.

The moment Ivan and Mattie crossed the threshold, a rail-thin redheaded woman turned on them. "Which of you is the captain?" she demanded.

"Both?" Mattie said.

"I don't know what either of you was thinking, but next time, when I tell you to stay away, you stay away!"

"Our apologies," Ivan said. "You must be Captain Court. I'm Ivan, and this is Mattie—"

"I know who you are."

So much for charm. Ivan said, "What's our status?"

"We're out of the Jovian system, being pursued by the majority of the System ships."

Ivan craned his neck toward the viewscreen overhead. There was a cloud of stars visible as a movement against the background constellations: the System pursuit.

"How long are we going to let them follow us?" Mattie asked.

Shara Court had the skin of one knuckle between her teeth as she stared up at the pack of ships in pursuit. She said, "We're not letting them follow us."

"We're trying to outrun them?"

"We couldn't drive them off too early; they'd've gone back to Jupiter before Anji could pull out with the refugees."

"So now they're going to shoot us down instead!"

It was almost enough to make Ivan smile, bitter and humorlessly amused. "The cost of being the decoy," he said.

"They haven't caught us yet," Shara snapped, but her voice was thin with anxiety. She seated herself in the captain's chair and got on the radio. The indents of her teeth showed white, then red, on her knuckle. "*Nemain*, they're almost in firing range."

The radio buzzed, and a man's voice came on. "We'll engage." A moment later, the disk of the *Nemain* wheeled between the *Macha* and the cluster of small System ships.

The System ships couldn't be that fast if the System had left them behind on Jupiter rather than taking them with the rest of the fleet. "How fast can the *Macha* travel?" Ivan asked.

Shara's hands were claws on the armrests of her chair. "We're lucky if we can reach 0.01 percent lightspeed. This is a transport ship, not fast travel."

Ivan had known the *Macha* would be slow, but the number astounded him. It would take them half a year at least to reach Mars.

The System fleet, wherever it was, would reach Constance before them.

"How many people on board the *Macha*?" Ivan asked.

"We're full up with troops. Some of the other ships were trying to make room for refugees." Shara touched the communications beside the captain's chair. "*Nemain*, status?"

A man's voice came irritably over the radio. "We're fine."

"You're surrounded. Pull back."

"We're trying to drive them off, remember?" said the *Nemain*, and the connection went dead.

Shara switched channels. "*Macha* to *Badh*. Vithar, can you get to them?"

"Yes," said a man's deep voice, and a moment later an explosion flashed from the middle of the System ships that were now worrying the *Nemain*. Ivan did not see the ship that had fired; the *Badh* was too small to be visible.

The System ships weren't being driven back. If anything, they were renewing their attack. While most of them converged on the wheeling *Nemain*, some split off, heading for the *Macha*. Ivan watched them grow larger in the viewscreen overhead.

"Can't you go any faster?" Mattie demanded.

"This ship is not designed for speed," Shara said through her teeth. She ordered her navigator, "Fire on those ships when they're near enough."

They were near enough. The *Macha* fired, but the agile System ships dodged the bombs easily. Their weapons systems lit up, and at this distance the massive *Macha* would be impossible to miss.

The nearest System ship exploded. This time, Ivan caught sight of the *Badh*, minuscule, moving with impossible speed to flank the other System ships before they could even register that one of their own had been destroyed. It took swift care of the others, and the last System ship, distracted by the *Badh*, was blown apart by the *Macha*.

Next to Ivan, Mattie blew out an unsteady breath.

In the chaos, the *Macha* had nearly left the *Nemain* behind: the flashing battle between it and the System ships was a spark of distant light. Shara got back on the radio. "*Nemain*, leave them and join us."

The returning call was more fuzzed with static than it should have been. The *Nemain*'s communications had been damaged somehow. "If we join you, they'll follow. The *Nemain* is faster than the *Macha*. We'll deal with these and catch up."

"We're not leaving you behind," Shara said.

"We'll catch up."

"Take the *Badh* with you."

"The *Macha* needs the *Badh*'s weaponry if you encounter any more ships. We'll catch up." The line to the *Nemain* went dead.

Shara leaned back in her chair, worrying at her knuckle again. "Keep going," she ordered her navigator, and the explosions of the battle dimmed with distance.

"Wait for the *Nemain*," Ivan suggested. "Send the *Copenhagen* on ahead. We'll get to Constance, pave the way for your fleet."

Shara's eyes were on where the *Nemain* had last been. "My orders were to take you to Harper safely, not let you fly off at the first opportunity."

"With the *Macha*'s speed, it will take half a year to reach Mars, if not more," Ivan said. Mattie was trying to catch his eye for some reason, but Ivan didn't dare take his attention from Shara until he had won. "The *Copenhagen* can get there in a matter of weeks."

"We're not separating," Shara snapped.

"So you'd hold us against our will?"

"I'm keeping you safe!" She threw up her hands to forestall any further objection. "When the *Nemain* returns, we can discuss it with Captain Laran."

All sight of the *Nemain* or the dozens of System ships surrounding it had vanished into the black. Somewhere up ahead, the System fleet was roaring in toward Constance Harper, faster than the *Macha* could ever travel.

Shara was so tense that Ivan could see the tendons standing out in her wiry arms. He couldn't push her any further, not yet.

"When the *Nemain* returns," Ivan agreed.

FORWARD

The nice thing about a really large ship like the *Macha*, Mattie thought, was how stable it felt. There was no dizziness from artificial gravity straining to apply itself evenly. Layers of armor separated him and Ivan—and everyone else in the ship—from the breathless danger of the cold outside. Even the steady acceleration of their movement was almost imperceptible from inside the ship. What they gained in stability they lost in speed, of course, but if it came to danger there was always the *Badh*. And the *Nemain*, once it returned.

It could have been, in fact, an ideal situation.

"What the hell were you thinking?" Mattie said, remembering to lower his voice halfway through the sentence when two *Macha* crewmen appeared farther down the hall.

"I was thinking that if we wait seven months to reach Constance, the System fleet will get to her first," said Ivan.

"You just antagonized the woman hosting us."

"Would you rather not have known we were prisoners?"

"I would rather you'd talked to me first!"

It was amazing how precisely Ivan could control his expressions sometimes. The look he slanted at Mattie had only a knife's edge of incredulity in it, razor thin, razor sharp. "Sorry," Ivan said. "Next time I will make sure to confirm any obvious conclusions with you first. Should we check on the *Copenhagen*?"

The *Copenhagen* did need repair. Mattie ran his hands over the hull of it while Ivan ran diagnostics from inside. At least, Mattie thought, most of the repairs could be done aboard the *Macha*.

He was just trying to decide if it was worth replacing the hull plates on the living space entirely when the message came over the intercom to clear the docking bay.

Once Ivan and Mattie were clear, a peculiar ship that was more engine and armament than living space docked beside the *Copenhagen*. That, Mattie realized, must be the *Badh*.

The doors to the docking bay hissed open, and Mattie followed Ivan back inside, heading toward the new ship. A lantern-jawed man with dreadlocks hanging long down his back uncurled himself from the *Badh*. He was strangely familiar.

Ivan reached the man a step ahead of Mattie. "You must be the captain of the *Badh*."

"You must be the son of Milla Ivanov," the man said. He had a low, sonorous voice, and Mattie knew him from somewhere.

"You saved our lives out there," Ivan said. "Thank you, Captain . . . ?"

"Vithar," Mattie said suddenly, the name returning to him in a flash of memory. "You've worked with Constance before." He couldn't remember quite what Vithar had done for her. It bothered him that he could remember the face and the name but not how or why.

"A long time ago." Vithar offered his hand to Mattie. His grip was cool and firm.

"Your ship has no crew," Ivan remarked. He was right; the *Badh* was too small to fit anyone but its captain inside. "Will you be docking on the *Macha*?"

"Most of the time," Vithar said.

Ivan seemed to wait, but no more information, as far as Mattie could see, was forthcoming. Ivan said, "The *Badh* is a remarkable ship."

"I like it."

Again, that stalled silence. Ivan said, "Where did you get it from?"

"Ganymede."

Mattie had to cover his mouth with his hand under the guise of scrubbing at his stubble so that Vithar wouldn't see him grin. Ivan's expression hadn't changed, remaining pleasant with the rigidity of a computer program stalling in the face of unexpected information. It was rare to see Ivan stonewalled.

Ivan said, "You're the spy."

That got a reaction. "What?" Vithar said.

"Stealthy little ship, flying alone, resistant to interrogation." A smile took some of the edge off Ivan's words—but not all. "You're Anji's spy."

"I'm her diplomat."

"You're the one who's supposed to talk to Constance?" Mattie interjected.

"Yes."

"Well," Mattie said, "good fucking luck."

Ivan said, "I could make your life easier. Send Mattie and me ahead in the *Copenhagen*. We can reach Constance long before the *Macha* and pave the way for your arrival."

Vithar looked at him sidelong. "Did you suggest this to Captain Court?"

"Of course."

"She denied you."

"She was inclined to wait for the *Nemain*'s return."

Vithar looked amused. "Then we will wait for the *Nemain*."

Ivan seized on that amusement, smiling himself, so fully focused on Vithar that Mattie was starting to feel peculiarly invisible. "Captain Court's only objection was our safety. Do I seem like a man who can't take care of himself? Does Mattie?"

"You're clearly very capable," Vithar said with a wry half of a smile, and suddenly it wasn't funny or impressive that Ivan could get a reaction out of him, and Mattie wanted him to leave. "But if Shara says we wait for the *Nemain*, then we wait for the *Nemain*."

Ivan held his gaze for another excruciating moment, then leaned back, shrugging, graceful. "As you say."

"I should speak with Shara," Vithar said.

"I'm sure we'll speak again soon," Ivan said.

"I'm sure we will." Vithar walked off, shaking his head.

Mattie stood stiffly, caught in the obscure feeling that if he moved too suddenly, whatever self-control usually encased him would shatter. "Making friends?" Mattie said when Vithar was gone, hearing the tightness of his own voice and hating the sound.

Ivan was still looking in the direction Vithar had gone. "Apparently not."

"Good," Mattie said, then dared to move his arms, stuffing his hands deep into his pockets. "I'm going to fix the *Copenhagen* before the *Nemain* gets back."

He was aware of Ivan's gaze on his back, but he did not dare turn around to see what his expression might be.

BACKWARD

They'd been hunting this quarry for days. This was all in good fun for Mattie—he'd always loved puzzles, and here were he and Ivan solving a puzzle in a sneaky, underhanded way—but Ivan seemed almost unbearably tense.

Case in point: when Ivan spotted the System agent they were tailing, he gripped Mattie's arm a shade too tightly to stop him and said, every syllable ringing despite his lowered voice, "There he is."

"Where? Brown hair and briefcase?"

"Who else?" Ivan released his arm. "He's going into that restaurant."

A traveling System agent had to eat eventually, after all. Even a System intelligence agent.

The restaurant the man was going into was not the kind of place Mattie would go to get a meal; actually, Mattie wasn't sure when he'd ever been in a proper restaurant before. They didn't have those things on Miranda, and a fugitive felon like himself usually found it unwise to sit that long in one place, especially one so heavily surveilled and with so few easy exits. Ivan, though, probably had been in hundreds of them before. Mattie had heard Terra had a lot.

The man vanished inside the dusty red Martian stone edifice of the building. Through the windows, Mattie could see that the interior had been designed with Old Earth in mind. White stone pillars held up the roof; bright light streamed from overhead in imitation of the Terran sun.

Ivan leaned against the wall of the building while Mattie squinted in. "What do you think?"

"I think they should fire him," Mattie said. "Leaving that sweet little computer all alone and undefended on a chair like that."

Ivan did not smile, as Mattie had hoped. "So you can get the device on the case?"

"I need to put the device on the computer itself," Mattie pointed out. "He has to be very distracted not to notice that."

Ivan twisted his neck to peer in the window. To anyone who passed, they would look like two friends debating whether to get lunch at that restaurant. Yet Mattie could see the tension in his shoulders even through his jacket.

When he turned back around to face Mattie, he was smiling, but it was not an especially nice smile. "We can distract him with a little honey, I think."

Mattie peered back in to see what Ivan was talking about. As he did, the System agent turned his head and Mattie got a good look at his face. He had a sharp jaw and a strong, jutting chin and bright eyes that crinkled at the corners even though his lips did not curve when he greeted the waiter. It was a remarkably Terran sort of smile, and something about it made Mattie's heart hit an extra beat.

He also saw what Ivan had meant when the man's gaze lingered noticeably on his male waiter as the waiter walked away.

"Oh, please," Mattie said, "let me throw myself on this grenade for you."

"We're not going to let this grenade get off," Ivan said, "and thank you, but I'll do the talking. Drop something when we pass his table."

And then he swept off into the restaurant. Asshole.

Mattie caught up with Ivan in two long strides, the benefit of superior height, and quickly racked his brain about what he might be able to drop in front of the man that wasn't completely illegal. Somehow he thought that if he let his collection of lock picks fall on the floor the System intelligence agent might become distracted by the wrong thing.

When they started to walk past the man's table—he did look up, Mattie noticed, discreetly but not discreetly enough to watch Ivan pass—Mattie tripped over nothing and let a handful of computer data storage chips spill out of his pocket and strew themselves over the Earth-stone floor. The chips held an enormous volume of illegal information, but the man had no way of knowing that from looking at them.

"Shit," he said very loudly to complement the commotion he had already made.

Ivan gave him an exasperated look.

"Are you all right?" the man asked Mattie, not without a brief glance at Ivan, who had stopped right alongside the man's chair.

Mattie waved a hand, then got onto his knees to start picking up the tiny flakes.

"He's fine. He's always dropping something," Ivan said to the man. His accent had switched to the way it had sounded when Mattie had met him a decade ago—posh and cultured. It took Mattie aback to realize how much Ivan's accent had softened since then. He fancied sometimes that Ivan had picked up a bit of Mattie's own Mirandan drawl.

The man turned in his chair, angling his body toward Ivan. "You're Terran."

Ivan smiled. "On vacation," he said. "I wish now that I'd gone to Venus instead."

When Mattie had dropped the chips, he'd made certain some of them rolled beneath the chair that held the System agent's computer. Picking up the chips, he slowly worked his way under the table toward that chair.

"Venus is very nice, especially the northern hemisphere," the man was saying. "Have you been there before?"

"Not recently." Ivan hooked his foot around a chair and tugged it out. It screeched by Mattie's ear, and Mattie glared at Ivan's ankle. "I went there with my aunt when I was a child, and I still remember the jungle flowers. Mattie, I suppose I should ask if you need help."

"No," Mattie said. "I got it. I'm fine."

"Right," said Ivan. "Have you been to Venus often?"

"I travel around for my job," the Systems agent said.

"Oh?" Ivan gave the vowel an arch turn. "What's that?"

Mattie had heard him flirt with strangers a thousand times before—it was often their only way to get what they wanted—but somehow, something about listening to him flirt now was disturbing. Now fully under the table, Mattie very carefully reached out and began to pick the locks holding the briefcase shut.

"If I told you," said the man, "I'd have to kill you."

Ivan laughed. Mattie scowled darkly at the briefcase.

"You're a dangerous man, then," Ivan said with a hint of his own wolf's teeth in his voice, and Mattie scowled even more deeply.

"And you?" the man asked. "What do you do?"

"I travel."

The briefcase came unlocked. Mattie pulled the tiny device from his pocket.

"Oh?" said the man in a fair imitation of Ivan's earlier exclamation. "You've been many places, then?"

Mattie slipped his hand into the briefcase and planted his and Ivan's tiny device on the surface of the man's computer.

"I've been around," Ivan said.

Mattie relocked the briefcase, grabbed the last few data storage chips from the floor, and stood up so quickly that he banged the table on the way to his feet.

"I got them all," he said to Ivan, and then—reluctantly—nodded once at the Systems agent. The agent was looking at Mattie with one brow arched. He'd looked very attractive in profile from the window, Mattie remembered, but up close and straight on there was a meanness to his features. That would be the System for you, Mattie thought.

"Come on," he said to Ivan, and Ivan's eyebrow arched as well—*Terrans*, Mattie thought, annoyed—but he stood up.

"Do you still want to eat?" Ivan asked him politely, still in his poshest accent.

"No," Mattie said. "I don't think I'm hungry."

Ivan turned back to the man and Mattie imagined he was giving him an apologetic sort of look, but Mattie already was walking out of the restaurant. He stepped out onto the Martian stone and breathed in the clean Martian air with some relief. The sunlight here was not as intense as the light inside the restaurant had been.

Ivan was at his shoulder a moment later. "Good thinking," he said, and followed at Mattie's shoulder when Mattie set off for where they had landed the *Annwn*.

"What do you mean?"

"I mean good job getting us out of there."

It hadn't been a particularly good job; Mattie had essentially just dragged Ivan out, but Ivan didn't sound sarcastic. Instead of trying to parse out what Ivan meant, Mattie said, "Why didn't you let me do the talking?"

"Because I always do the talking."

"But it was a man," Mattie said.

"I know how to drive stick," said Ivan.

"What?"

But Ivan already was heading into a narrow alleyway farther down the street, tugging the computer out of Mattie's jacket pocket. "Come on. I want to find out what we can before he notices what we planted on him."

Mattie had the little computer out and in his hand in a moment. The computer would connect to the device Mattie had planted on the System agent's computer back in the restaurant. System intelligence agents, when traveling, had to be very careful about security, yet they had to travel frequently and could not always trust the government outpost hosting them to hold the sensitive information they needed. So sometimes they brought portable computers with a direct connection to System intelligence information, a connection that could be accessed only from that physical computer itself.

Unless, say, a pair of crafty strangers had planted a device like Mattie's on the computer to interrupt the computer's electric processes and hijack them with his own commands. Mattie went to work persuading the System to let him sign in to its data and tried to enjoy the puzzle again.

It didn't take long before he was in. He passed the handheld to Ivan wordlessly.

Ivan nearly snatched it from his hand. Mattie couldn't see the screen, and so he watched Ivan's face instead, the way the quality of the light reflected off it changed as Ivan moved from place to place on the screen in front of him.

At long last Ivan sighed. "She's alive."

"Of course she is," Mattie said, baffled.

Ivan flicked him a glance. "They arrested her after we left Luna, Mattie. Anything could have happened."

Mattie doubted it. Constance could take care of herself. Constance always had taken care of herself, and more than that, she'd taken care of Mattie as well. There wasn't a chance the System could take her down.

"There's nothing else in here," Ivan said with that peculiar tension in his voice again. It made Mattie's gut twist the same way it had before. "I don't know what happened."

"I can get into contact with Anji," Mattie said. "Con can't get into contact with us, but I bet she can talk to Anji. I'll have Anji get a message to her. Set up a rendezvous."

"How soon?"

"I don't know," Mattie said. "It depends on Anji and on Constance."

He almost asked Ivan then, *Why? Why do you need to see her so badly? What is it you need to say?*

He did not. He was not certain he wanted to know the answer, and so he carefully set the thoughts aside.

"Contact Anji," Ivan said. "Ask her to set up a rendezvous. Tell her we need to see Constance soon."

FORWARD

After the first week with no sign of the *Nemain*, Ivan appealed to Shara again.

She wasn't pleased by his opening the subject. "The *Nemain* will catch up."

"The *Nemain* was surrounded by System ships. If it's not here by now, they destroyed it."

Shara's sudden pallor was stark against the orange of her hair. "The *Macha* had a head start. We're not giving up on them yet."

"The *Copenhagen*—"

"We're not splitting up, not until the *Nemain* gets back," Shara snapped. "And even then, it's only up for discussion. Our orders were to escort you there."

"If you won't let us leave, you're not escorting us, you're imprisoning us," Ivan said.

"We wait for the *Nemain*," said Shara.

After that, she took to avoiding him. The *Macha* was a large ship, and she was quite effective at hiding in it. Ivan's next opportunity to speak with her directly did not come until he and Mattie were summoned to the war room to discuss some new intelligence Vithar had received.

"Sit, gentlemen," Shara said when they arrived. She tapped at the holographic display on the table that filled the room. The glittering stars blacked out, replaced with a face-on view of the solar system, planets marked in exaggerated size. "Shut the door."

Mattie shut the door. Ivan seated himself, carefully hiding his limp. "Did you find the *Nemain*?"

If looks could eviscerate, Ivan's organs would have been splayed out around him like butterfly wings, and his beating heart would have been jolting down to stillness in the middle of the holographic table. Shara said, "We received a message this morning that may change our status." With another brief touch she brought up an overlay onto the table, moons in static whirling. Oversized images of the *Macha*, *Badh*, and *Copenhagen* appeared at their approximate location in the asteroid belt—still so far from Mars and Constance Harper—alongside ghostly, uncertain images of the System fleet spread out through space.

A marker for the *Nemain* had been left where the other ship had last been seen, gray, like a tombstone. Ivan eyed the lost ship and the System ships around it until Shara's next words shattered his concentration:

"Christoph Bessel has declared war on the Mallt-y-Nos."

"War?" Ivan said.

"War." Under Shara's touch a smaller cluster of ships up by Neptune brightened, aimed inward, toward Mars. Not just the System but Christoph as well: the cage was closing around Constance Harper.

Mattie said, "Christoph was an asshole. But why do we care? He's way out by Neptune."

"Precisely." Shara's gesture covered the field: Constance on one side, besieged, Christoph on the other, a free agent to be fought or allied with, and Anji in between.

Ivan said, "What does this mean for us, Captain Court?"

"That's what we're here to decide." Shara looked at Vithar. "Opinion?"

Vithar was eyeing the table thoughtfully. "Christoph has said nothing regarding Anji. His route to the inner solar system takes him wide of Saturn."

"She may want to ally with Christoph."

"Hang on," said Mattie, while Ivan's blood ran cold.

"Perhaps we should return to Saturn—leave a message for the *Nemain*—and see where Anji would prefer to send us."

Ivan felt as if slender icy fingers had closed around his heart and clenched. Leave Constance behind to face the System alone—and the last time he and Mattie had faced captivity, at least they'd had the option of a bomb on a timer. "What would happen to us if you did?" Ivan asked.

"That would be for Anji to decide."

"Anji's orders were clear," Vithar interrupted. "Constance Harper is her old friend; we ally with the Huntress."

"I want that confirmed by Anji," Shara said.

Vithar's brows lifted, but he kept his annoyance well contained. "I will confirm, but we will continue on our course for Mars."

"Perhaps we should wait."

"We continue on," Vithar said.

Ivan thought Shara would argue with him. She'd paled again, the way she did when she was angry or under stress. But the intercom rang before she could respond.

Shara hit the interface on the table. "What is it?"

"There's a ship ahead, Captain."

"A System ship?"

"Unclear. It's not responding to our hails."

"Approach with caution. I'll be up in a moment." She shut the intercom down. "We'll continue on to Mars. For now, I need you in the *Badh*. We may need offensive abilities."

Vithar was already half out the door. He lifted two fingers in acknowledgment, and left.

A strange ship, all alone. Maybe System. Maybe not. Ivan said, "Let me and Mattie see it."

"What? The ship?"

What else? But he reined his temper in. "We might be able to help."

The *Macha* had been a long way off from the strange ship when the alarm had been raised. By the time they were near enough to get detailed scans, the *Badh* was zipping around overhead. Ivan leaned on the railing separating the upper level of the *Macha*'s control room from the lower, staring toward the distant ship, half expecting to see a graceful seashell spiral emerge out of the black.

"Life support is on, but the engines don't seem to be working," one of the *Macha*'s crewmen reported.

Mattie was all nervous energy next to Ivan, jittering his leg when he leaned against the railing. Ivan said to the crewman, "How large is the ship?"

"Civilian class. Smaller than the *Nemain* and unarmed."

"Centripetal gravitation," Mattie said under his breath to Ivan, pointedly.

Ivan asked, "Any contact yet?"

Shara was trying to hail the other ship from the captain's chair. "Either they're not answering or they can't answer."

"Maybe there's something wrong with their computers."

"If they're not a threat, we could just fly past," Mattie suggested.

"They're revolutionaries in need of assistance or they're System lying low, hoping we'll fly past," Shara said. "We have to find out which."

"Let me and Mattie try to get into their computer," Ivan said.

"Can you?"

Mattie laughed. Ivan said, "Yes."

Shara hesitated a moment longer, biting her lip, before giving way to the inevitable. "Do it."

The woman trying to get through the other ship's computers ceded her place to Ivan and Mattie immediately. Ivan leaned on the chair, watching the screen, while Mattie studied what could be seen of the other ship's computers.

The other ship's hardware seemed to be working: it was broadcasting *something* at the *Macha*. The broadcast itself was nonsense.

"Think they're trying to radio us?" Ivan asked.

"Yeah, maybe, and something got scrambled."

"What can you learn about the ship?" Shara asked.

Ivan read off what Mattie had managed to pull up. "It's a civilian-class ship with a standard crew component of seventy souls. The name is the *Huldren*." He seated himself at the computer interface beside Mattie and began to check the old System records stored on the *Macha* for information about a starship called *Huldren*.

Mattie asked, "Can Vithar see any modifications?"

Vithar's voice crackled out of the radio. "The ship has weaponry. It doesn't look original."

It was an old skill, well used, to get into the System data banks. Ivan had the information he wanted in an instant. "The *Huldren* was a transport ship owned by a private company that operated out of Venus. Last reported location was Venus, right before Earth was hit."

"System civilians, looking to escape?" Shara suggested.

"System civilians wouldn't head to the outer planets," Ivan said.

Mattie was already elbow deep inside the other ship's metaphorical guts. It looked like he had been testing various System backdoors, trying to get into the computer, but the backdoors had been blocked off. Definitely revolutionaries.

The code was odd, though. "It's garbled," Ivan said.

Mattie was intent. "I don't think it's on purpose."

"Can you get in?" Shara asked.

"I think I—uh, yes," Mattie said, and Ivan saw what had surprised him. One of the more uncommon System backdoors had been left, metaphorically speaking, wide open, as if someone had taken remote control of the other ship and then left without reverting the change.

"I got the communications," Mattie said. "Want to talk?"

Shara nodded and lifted a hand, signaling for silence. She said, "This is the revolutionary ship *Macha*. Where is your allegiance?"

Static. Then, rising like mist out of the ground, high and tight and frightened, came a woman's voice, the words lost to the snow.

Some unnamable weight seemed to rest more heavily on Ivan's shoulders, the approach of some creeping dark. He wondered why none of the other crew members seemed to sense it as he did. Even an elk felt the nearness of the wolf.

". . . *Huldren*," the woman's static-drowned voice begged. "This is the revolutionary ship *Huldren*. Please respond. This is the revolutionary ship *Huldren*. Please . . ."

"We can hear you," said Shara. "Who is speaking?"

"My name is Grace Kim. The rest of the crew is gone. They're dead. The ship won't move. The ship, it . . ."

"We're going to help you, Grace," Shara said. "Mattie and Ivan, can you restore power to the *Huldren*?"

Mattie sounded doubtful. "We might be able to get you a video connection."

"Do it."

A black square opened up on the screen, obscuring the stars ahead, the *Badh* circling the still-distant *Huldren*. For a moment, nothing was visible but darkness, nothing audible except heaving, tear-edged breaths.

Then a pale blue light flickered like lightning. The woman sitting in front of the screen flinched away, one arm coming up to conceal her face. The blue light gleamed off her black hair, off the metal joints that covered her arm. The light was coming from in front of her, but all behind her—what little was visible of an empty piloting room, chairs askew, instrumentation dark—was still in blackness.

The *Huldren*'s interior lights had failed, Ivan realized. The only light

in the room now was from the video connection to the *Macha* that
Mattie had just opened.

Ivan wondered how long she had been in the dark.

Grace lowered her arm, squinting hard even into the dimness of the
computer screen's light. The metal was not covering her arm: it was a
prosthetic. Ivan could see the places where metal joined to flesh, rivets
sunk deep into muscle to join with bone and a thin ridge of skin trying
to grow up and over the metal beside it. When she moved the arm,
pulleys and wires flexed. She was a revolutionary, certainly. A System
soldier would have a much more expensive prosthetic.

Shara said, "We're trying to repair your ship's computer now."

"No," Grace said. "No, don't—leave it. Please, please just get me out
of here."

"We'll get you out of there."

While Shara spoke to Grace and Mattie monitored the fluctuating
communications equipment, Ivan took a look at the rest of the *Huldren*'s systems. They were just as deeply damaged, but there was something peculiar about the damage, a sort of logic hidden in the chaos.
Ivan wondered if someone had tried to reprogram the ship without
fully understanding its hardware.

One piece of nonsense appeared over and over: $R = ae^{b\theta}$. The equation for a logarithmic spiral. When Ivan paid attention to that signature, he found that it marked every change that had been made to the
computer.

"Tell us what happened," Shara said.

"The others all died," Grace said. She had gone from nearly sobbing
to eerily affectless. That would be shock, Ivan thought. "The ship went
crazy . . . it started thrashing around. My arm," she said, lifting that mechanical limb of hers, light glittering off hidden gears, "was strong
enough to hold me . . . I wasn't injured. I could get to the oxygen suits
when the life support went down."

A logarithmic spiral. It was nonsense code; it did nothing to the
Huldren except mark it. Ivan said to Grace, his eyes still on that signature, "That's quite a malfunction."

"It wasn't a malfunction. There was another ship. It looked like a
spiral. It did this."

Ivan raised his head and looked her in the eye. He had known; the
moment the *Macha* had reported another ship nearby, he had known,

as if a shadow had touched his skin. He could see that same shadow-touched terror in Grace's eyes.

He said, "A ship with mass-based gravitation."

"Yes," Grace breathed.

"You know it?" Shara wanted to know.

"I may know of it," Ivan said.

"Just a rumor," Mattie said sharply.

"Is it System?"

"Not anymore," said Ivan.

"We tried to speak to it when it came," Grace said. "It wouldn't answer us. All the holograms lit up and a woman appeared, but she wouldn't speak . . ."

"Grace, where has the spiral ship gone?" Shara asked.

"I don't know."

Shara had her knuckle between her teeth again. Some unease had drawn lines around her eyes. She felt it, too, Ivan thought—the edge of a shadow from something vast and terrible fallen over her shoulder. But unlike Ivan, she would have no name to put to it. "We'll have someone over there in a shuttle very soon," Shara said. "Just hold on. It's all over now."

In time with her words, brightness flared on the screen. Grace flinched, hands coming up to her head as if mere light could do her damage.

The rest of the *Huldren*'s control room was suddenly illuminated. "I got the lights," Mattie said unnecessarily.

Behind Grace, in the far back corner of the *Huldren*'s control room, a hologram began to take shape. At the same time, a light on the communications panel came on, and the *Macha*'s computer began to chime.

"We're receiving a message from the *Huldren*," one of the *Macha*'s crew members reported.

"I'm not sending anything," Grace said.

"Mattie, Ivan, is it possible that whatever's wrong with the *Huldren*'s computers could affect the *Macha*?" Shara asked sharply.

Behind Grace, a female shape was forming on the holographic terminal. An arm pushed out against the static like a child's kicking foot from within the womb—

The hologram vanished. Mattie was staring at Ivan in open concern, the computer display in front of him showing that while Ivan had been distracted, he had gone into the *Huldren* and killed the hologram before it could be born.

"Could this hurt the *Macha*?" Shara demanded again.

"It doesn't matter. I intercepted; the message is nonsense," Mattie said shortly. He was leaning onto the screen in front of him, his arms covering part of the display.

When Ivan leaned over, Mattie shifted, reluctant, and let him read the message he was hiding.

"Grace, we are sending a shuttle over now," Shara said, and indicated that the communication should be cut. When it had been, she ordered her people, "Send a shuttle to the *Huldren* immediately. Rescue that woman and anyone else who might be alive but do not have any contact with the computers, understood?"

Ivan said, "I know the ship that did this."

Shara said, "How?"

"I'm a well-traveled man." Ivan left the computer interface, seeing Mattie wipe the message from the *Huldren* from the *Macha*'s memory. "That ship can do what it did to the *Huldren* to the *Macha*, or the *Badh*, or any other ship it likes—and if it hit the *Huldren*, it's nearby."

That ship should have been months away by now, far enough from the solar system that the sun would be no more than a brighter star. Instead, she was here, warping the motion of the planets with her pull. There was a sense of the inevitable to it—the wrists had already been cut, and there was nothing left to do but wait until he bled out.

"Why are you telling me this now?" Shara demanded.

"I didn't know she was still around. But Mattie and I know how to defend your ships against her."

"How?"

Ivan lifted a shoulder. "There's a price."

Her expression twisted. "You'd demand payment?"

"Only that you let us take the *Copenhagen* and go on ahead."

"Anji told me about you," Shara said. Her bony hands had curled into fists on her chair. "You've never mentioned this ship before, and I wouldn't dare let you into my ship's computers. Besides, my orders are to get you to the Mallt-y-Nos safely. If there's a ship like that out there, I can't let you leave."

"Then we are your prisoners," Ivan said.

"If that's what it takes."

"This won't be the only ship we find like this," Ivan warned, the message from the *Huldren* ringing in his head. "There will be others."

"Then we'll deal with them when we find them." Shara turned her head away. "What's the status of our rescue shuttle?"

Ivan could have warned her, could have given that prey animal fear a name. But there was nothing he could say without endangering himself or Mattie: he did not imagine Shara Court would be pleased that they'd had a hand in the creation of the mechanical sentience that was wandering the cosmos, or that she would be happy to know that it was apparently out of control.

It was a good thing Mattie had wiped the message before anyone else on the *Macha* could see it. Even though Ivan had seen it only once, every word of it was burned into his mind.

The message had said, IVAN, PLEASE HELP ME.

It had been signed ALTHEA BASTET.

FORWARD

Sometime after the *Macha* came across the *Huldren*, Vithar received word that Constance Harper had left Mars for Venus. So Anji's fleet changed course for Venus. Mattie didn't mind that much for the very same reason, it seemed, that Ivan did.

"Venus is on the other side of the sun." Visible from Mattie's perspective only as a pair of boots and black-clad legs, Ivan was trying his hardest to do the impossible and wear a hole into the *Copenhagen*'s fireproof, airtight, missile-proof armored flooring.

"Yep," Mattie said. Even though Mattie and Ivan weren't allowed to leave the *Macha*, they spent their time inside the landed *Copenhagen*. Most of the repairs that they'd needed to do were done by now, but Mattie still wedged himself beneath the computer interface and checked for the thousandth time that he'd removed any possible System hardware the *Ananke* could use to get inside their computer.

"It'll take us . . ."

". . . a long fucking time," Mattie finished. "What are you worrying about? Vithar's news says she beat the System fleet."

"Not in one battle," Ivan said darkly, and continued his mission to erode a valley in the *Copenhagen*'s floor.

"I'm more worried about us surviving."

"They can't hurt us; they need us. All they can do is make us their prisoners." Ivan sat down heavily in the captain's chair.

Mattie stared at Ivan's boots, his hands dangling between his knees. He said, knowing it was abrupt, "Tell me something."

"Tell you what?"

"Anything. A story."

Ivan's fingers twitched: restless, patternless. "I haven't got any stories to tell."

"*You've* run out of things to say?"

"Well done. You've finally shut me up."

The edge of the panel Mattie was working on dug metal beneath his nails. "I could teach you something," Mattie offered, before he could think the better of it.

"How to be an insufferable roommate?"

"You've already got that covered." Mattie slid himself out from beneath the panel. He went to the wall, spent a moment contemplating the cupboards—where had he put the things?—then remembered, stuck his head in, and after a moment of pushing aside lock picks and false papers produced a pair of handcuffs.

". . . Why were those on your packing list?" Ivan asked.

"I always carry handcuffs," Mattie said, pulling out a length of long wire as well, both tools of his trade. Something indescribable passed over Ivan's face, so to shut down whatever might come out of his mouth next Mattie said, "They're rigged cuffs, Ivan; I didn't know if we'd need a Trojan prisoner to get you out of that fucking ship."

"Yes, sir. Sorry, sir."

Mattie snapped one cuff over his own wrist and then knelt at Ivan's side. The dangling cuff clanged against the pilot's chair. "You know how to pick cuffs already," Mattie said, and waited for Ivan's nod.

When he'd gotten it, Mattie said, "But not when your hands are chained apart."

Ivan's left hand started drumming patternlessly again. He must have known he was doing it, Mattie thought, but couldn't—or didn't bother to with only Mattie here to see—stop. "I'm listening."

"If you've got both hands there're two things you can do," said Mattie. "Slide a shim beneath the gears to loosen them up or get a pick and twist the mechanism inside." He picked up the wire in his cuffed hand and held it, deliberately keeping his free hand behind his back. He rested his arm on the edge of Ivan's chair. "If you've got one hand and a long enough pick, you can do the same thing."

In a few quick moves, he bent the wire into the correct shape, then twisted his wrist as much as he could and angled the wire toward the cuffs. Cuffs were easy to pick; there was only one lever inside them, and so he managed to pop them open after a few minutes. The cuffs fell from his wrist; he just managed to catch them before they hit the ground.

Ivan said, "And if you don't have a pick?"

Mattie clapped the cuffs around his wrist again. "If you don't have a pick, you need a hard surface of some kind." Like the armrest of a steel chair. Mattie kept his eyes fixed on his own wrist rather than look to see what Ivan's expression might be. "You've got to angle your hand like this, see, so that the base of the thumb will hit right at the nub of bone. You want to angle a little inward, like this, so that the force goes in toward the palm. And then you need a short, fast blow—"

Ivan's hand came down hard on his wrist, aborting his movement, pinning him to the chair.

"Do not dislocate your thumb," he said.

"I'm showing—"

"I know," Ivan said. He moved his hand without releasing the pressure on Mattie's wrist to flick the rigged lock on the handcuffs so that it came off of Mattie's arm again. "Thank you."

Long days after their changed course to Venus, Anji's fleet received new information, which was duly passed on to Ivan and Mattie: Constance Harper was on Mercury.

"She can't have gone to both Venus and Mercury," Ivan said. "There's not enough time to travel between them, much less fight the System."

Shara scowled. "Vithar, are you sure your reports are accurate?"

On the other side of the holographic table, visible over the white edge of the holographic sun, Vithar shrugged. "There's fighting happening on Mercury. Is it the Mallt-y-Nos? That's what I'm told."

"But do you *know*?"

"There's no way to know for sure," Vithar said. "If you wanted confirmation, you could always send the *Badh* on ahead. Or the *Copenhagen*."

There was an edge to his voice Mattie hadn't expected. Ivan was eyeing Vithar as if he were reconsidering his use. Mattie swallowed down a surge of irrational annoyance.

Shara said, "Out of the question."

"You sent me out yesterday to look for the *Nemain*."

"And look at what you found!"

"The System ships are far from us."

"Sorry," said Mattie, "maybe I'm not keeping up. Did you just say we have System ships following us?"

"Following us, maybe," Vithar said. "Behind us, certainly. There was no sign of the *Nemain*."

Ivan said, "Could those be the same ships that followed us from Jupiter?"

"Possibly."

"It doesn't matter where they're from. It's my job to get what's left of this fleet to the Huntress safely. None of us are separating." Shara leaned over the table. The silver cloud of System ships on the map had dispersed, no longer representing a definite location but rather a possible area where the System fleet could be. Nearly half the inner solar system was filled with that quicksilver. Around three of the four inner planets, uncertain red ships had been marked: the possible locations of the Mallt-y-Nos's fleet. Only Earth was black and barren of ships. Even the comet of Christoph's approach out by Neptune was dispersing; their reports of his location were coming too infrequently to be certain where he was.

Mattie rolled an Old Earth coin through his knuckles and stared at the mess of uncertainties on the table before them.

"We have to pick a target," Shara said. "This fleet stays together, all its parts. I say Mars: we knew the Huntress was there for certain weeks ago, and it's closest to our location."

"Venus," Ivan said.

"Venus is on the other side of the sun!"

"No," Mattie said, "Ivan's right. We should go to Venus."

Shara's lips pressed, thin and strained. "Vithar?" she said.

Vithar was looking at Mattie and Ivan—no, just at Ivan—thoughtfully. Mattie pressed the old Earth coin hard with his nail until he felt the old metal bend.

Vithar said, "Ivan and Mattie have known the Huntress the longest."

"Venus was next in the plan after Mars," Ivan said. "Anji knows. Constance won't be on Mercury, not yet. She's on Venus."

"Then we go to Venus," said Shara.

"We're going to lead those System ships right to Constance," Ivan said after the meeting, following Mattie down the familiar path to the *Macha*'s docking bay. Ivan was still limping even after all this time. That leg of his, it seemed, would forever be a reminder that Mattie had been late.

Mattie would rather have talked about anything, anything, other than Constance Harper. "She'll be fine. She's got good people around her."

"Like Anji?"

"What do you care?"

"Why don't you?"

"Because I think what might happen to us is a little more disturbing!" Mattie hissed.

"You—"

"No," Mattie said flatly, and if the subject wasn't dropped, at least for the moment Ivan stopped pushing it.

Vithar had hedged, but those System ships could easily be the ones from Jupiter. If they were, they'd destroyed the *Nemain* and were determined enough to follow the *Macha* and the *Badh* into the darkness of interstellar space.

If Mattie and Ivan could get into the *Copenhagen*, they could outrun those ships. Mattie had that thought ringing through his head when an alarm went off in the *Macha* a few hours later.

Shara was already in the control room when Mattie and Ivan arrived, standing beneath the half dome of uninterrupted sky. Ahead of them, like a fine mist, something winked and flashed between the stars.

"Can we divert course?" she asked.

"We're close enough to be seen by their sensors," one of the revolutionaries reported.

"Why didn't we see them before?"

"We did," the same man said. "But there's no voluntary motion. They're cold. We thought it was . . . debris from a collision, maybe."

"What is it?" Mattie asked.

"Ships of some kind," Shara said. She was leaning tensely forward, her hands wringing together. She'd been doing that more and more often lately. "A lot of them."

A lot indeed. They filled up almost the entire viewscreen, drifting, as densely packed as the stones in a planetary ring.

Drifting and cold, just like the *Huldren*.

From beside Mattie, with calm and eerie certainty, Ivan said, "They're dead."

Silence fell among the revolutionaries, underlaid by the low, relentless hum of functioning electronics. Shara broke it. "Is there any sign of heat or life support among those ships?"

"Negative," one of the revolutionaries reported.

Mattie said, "We should get out of here."

"Check the computers," Shara told him. "Like you did before."

"What if—whatever did this to them is still here? We should leave."

The radio buzzed, and Vithar's voice came over through the static. "*Macha*, can you count the ships? The *Badh* can't get a definite number."

"Count them," Shara ordered her people.

Ivan was already on the lower level, trying to get into the other ships' computers. Mattie joined him reluctantly and took over the endeavor. He understood immediately why the *Badh* hadn't been able to get a definite count. There were an impossible number of ships out there. Mattie chose one—the nearest—and got to work.

It was easier to access these ships than it had been to get into the *Huldren*. When Mattie saw why, his alarm grew. "These are System ships."

"Dead?" Shara asked.

If there was even one ship out there still alive, it would attack Anji's ships—and probably defeat them. The ship's computer Mattie was burrowing through was from a System warship, overpowered, deadly. "I hope so."

"Look," said Ivan suddenly, and his finger fell on the screen in front of Mattie, underlining a single piece of code:

$$R = ae^{b\theta}$$

One of the *Macha* revolutionaries said, "The computer can't keep a count—there are too many of them."

"What does that mean?" Shara asked. "A hundred? A thousand?"

"More than a thousand," the revolutionary said.

More than a thousand System warships. Mattie stared up at the sparking debris field on the viewscreen, the vast, incomprehensible amount of firepower floating dead in space ahead of them. He had never seen so many ships in his life. This must have been what the people of Saturn had seen in the days before the end, a glittering cloud of ships coming down on them, making new constellations as they approached, eerie but peaceful—until the bombs started to drop.

There was only one thing this many System warships could be, and Ivan must have realized it, too, probably before Mattie had. While Mattie sat silent and numb with horror, he said to Shara, "This is the System fleet."

"That's impossible," Shara said. When no one agreed, she asked, "Could the Mallt-y-Nos have done this?"

"No," Mattie said. "No, she couldn't."

"The spiral ship did this," Ivan said.

"How do you know—"

"The same thing's been done to these computers as happened to the *Huldren*. Get Grace to look at them if you like. She'll recognize it."

"All of them?" Shara repeated. "All of those ships?"

The entire System fleet. The *Ananke* had destroyed it with a thought.

They had to get out of there.

"Do you remember my offer?" Ivan said.

Shara was still staring out at the impossible destruction ahead of them. "I can't let you go."

"Then we'll compromise," Ivan said. "Let us fly our own ship, but we promise not to leave. The *Badh* can fly out with us as insurance. The *Copenhagen* can't outrun or outfight the *Badh*. I'm not asking you to let us go. I'm just asking you to let us have our ship. In return, we'll protect yours."

It was a lie, Mattie could have told her—just about everything Ivan said was a lie. But this lie at least was in Mattie's favor.

Shara said, "Do it."

FORWARD

"I'm not going to tell them how we know," Ivan snapped.

Mattie was digging through the cabinets on the *Copenhagen* for whatever equipment he'd packed. Ivan watched him shove the contents of one cabinet to the ground, then slam the door shut a moment later, empty-handed. "Why are we telling them anything?"

With effort, Ivan kept his exasperation from his tone. "We might be saving their lives."

Mattie had moved to the next cabinet and was tearing that one apart, too, his motion jerky with frustration. "We should get on the *Copenhagen* and go."

"We can't get on the *Copenhagen* and go until after we've fixed their ships. They won't let us. And even if we could run away now, we'd have to fix their computers before we left. We made Ananke what she is, we—"

"We had nothing to do with making the *Ananke*," Mattie snapped. "And watch what you say to them. You're already half System in their eyes, half one of Constance's dogs. You want to end up in a cell again or with another gun to your head?"

"We had everything to do with Ananke."

Mattie made a sound of frustration. A moment later he emerged from the cabinet with a small bag of tools: the System backdoors that Ananke took advantage of often could be closed only by altering actual hardware. "I have only one set."

"Vithar will have something on his ship I can use."

"We're going to work together."

"We'll cover more ground if we split up," Ivan said. "You work on the *Macha*; I'll fix the *Badh*."

"We should work together."

"There's not enough room for two people to work on the *Badh*. And I have a better chance of persuading Vithar to let us go if I can get him alone."

"To do what?" Mattie snapped.

"Talk." Ivan found that his voice had risen to match Mattie's. He tried to lower it, but some senseless agitation was making him defensive. "We don't want to gang up on him."

Mattie slammed the cabinet door shut. "Fine. You've made the decision; let's go."

"I'll meet you back here."

"Sure," said Mattie, and was gone.

Ivan stood in the *Copenhagen* alone, unsettled, angry, and ashamed.

He could put no reason to any of the emotions: every time he approached a cause, it slipped away from him like some silvery fish. Mattie was unsettled by the nearness of Ananke, Ivan told himself; they both were.

It did not ring entirely true.

Vithar was waiting for Ivan out in the docking bay, leaning against the hull of the *Badh*. "Shara says you're going to defend my computer against the spiral ship."

"I'm very helpful."

To Ivan's surprise, Vithar chuckled. He turned back to the *Badh* and tapped in the unlock code. Ivan tried to read it from the motions of his arm—once the *Copenhagen* was out in open space, the only thing stopping him and Mattie from escaping was the *Badh*. But Vithar's broad shoulders effectively blocked Ivan's view.

The *Badh* turned out to be nearly all engine. The cabin was not much larger than an escape pod would be, but even so, with the door opened there was just enough room for Ivan to get at the computer and Vithar to crouch in the cabin behind him.

Ivan started the computer without starting up the engines and eyed the inside of the cabin. You could tell a lot about a person from the inside of his or her ship. Vithar had a scrap of fabric tied to one of the maneuverability controls, red, ragged. No saying what it was a memento of. There was a knife under the control panel, a gun concealed to Ivan's right, and two more knives—all of different shapes, all looking exceptionally well cared for—above Ivan's head.

"There's one in the back of the seat, too," Vithar said.

"Very nice," Ivan said as the computer woke and requested input. "Your collection?"

"Things I've picked up here and there."

"It's good to have a hobby," Ivan said, and did a brief check of the most obvious System backdoors. All sealed: well done.

"Explain what you're doing to me," Vithar said.

"I'm sealing the System backdoors into your computers."

"I thought I'd already done that."

"The System left multiple redundancies. Most of them have been forgotten. Some of them don't exist on all machines."

"But you know about them."

Ivan smiled. "Mattie and I made it a professional priority."

"I see." Ivan could feel Vithar watching him from over the edge of the chair. "And is there a backdoor in the engine controls?"

"Sometimes," Ivan said. "But apparently not this time." He backed out of the systems that controlled the *Badh*'s top speed. "Mattie is working on the *Macha* right now. The *Copenhagen* is already secure."

"And how do you know that this will stop the spiral ship?"

Ivan frowned down at the computer display, as if that was what was taking up most of his attention. "I saw how she accessed the *Huldren* and the System fleet."

Silence. Vithar seemed to know enough about computers to be able to tell if Ivan was sabotaging his, so Ivan moved carefully, aware of Vithar's attention on his back.

Vithar said, "What do you know about the spiral ship?"

Most of the backdoors Ivan was going to seal had been shut already. And most of the sensitive areas Ivan tried to edge into—like engine control and navigation—were well defended against any kind of sabotage.

Much as this ship itself was well defended, with weapons wedged into every corner.

Like the teeth of gears interlocking, catching with a mechanical jolt, Ivan's memories of where he had met Vithar before slotted into place.

Ivan said, "Strange for a diplomat to travel alone."

"I'm traveling with the *Macha*."

"But the *Macha* aren't your people; they're Shara's. Why did Anji send you?"

"I'm her diplomat."

"Are you? Mattie and I met you on Puck. One of Constance's contacts had started to leak information. She sent me and Mattie, we figured out who it was, and then we did as she ordered and we gave the name to you."

Ivan should have understood the true nature of Anji's "diplomatic" mission the moment he realized it consisted of two warships and a troop carrier at full capacity.

"The next I heard," Ivan said, "that man was found dead on the ice outside the greenhouse enclosure."

Vithar said, "The past is the past."

"It still affects the present. Your computer is all set." Ivan smiled pleasantly at him. "May I leave?"

Vithar moved aside. Ivan carefully stepped out past him, never once turning his back. "I'll be seeing you," Ivan said, and wished that he had been able to at least sabotage the *Badh*'s weaponry systems while he had been inside.

He should have realized it before. If all Anji had wanted was to speak to Constance, she could have broadcast a message to her. Instead, she'd insisted on sending some of her own people. And she'd wanted Ivan and Mattie to take Vithar directly to Constance.

Ivan already had brought enough destruction to Constance and those in her orbit. Whatever happened, he could not let Anji's assassin reach Constance or her fleet.

BACKWARD

The *Annwn* landed on Mars in a cloud of red dust and a sonic boom. The sound was inaudible through the ship's hull, but the vibrations were not, and so Ivan knew that the sound of their landing had echoed through the atmosphere, ringing out over the edge of the scarp and into the valley below.

In the moments after the *Annwn* had landed, just long enough for the ship's systems to settle into quiescence, for the heat of its landing to dissipate into a safe range, the hull door opened and then shut again with a bang.

Mattie glanced at Ivan, but Ivan didn't stay to meet his look, rising from his chair in the piloting room to let himself down the sideways hall in a controlled fall, reaching the hull door seconds after Constance had slammed it shut.

The air outside was still hot from the *Annwn*'s rapid descent. Ivan had to squint through the heat warping and the settling dust to see her, Constance Harper, walking across the scarp toward the shadowed height of her bar. She shrugged her shawl up farther over her freckled shoulders and brought the edge of it to cover her nose as she walked away from him.

He stepped out onto the Martian stone and set off after her. She must have heard him coming, but did not stop.

"Constance," he said when he was near, but she ignored him. He stopped a moment, shut his eyes, took a swift breath. Don't push her, he told himself. Be calm. Be clever.

He started off after her again at a brisk walk now, not a run.

"I'm sorry about what I said," he said when he had come near again, and grabbed her arm this time so that she could not ignore him. Constance tugged her arm from his grip immediately, but she did stop to face him, her hazel eyes blazing over the edge of her fringed shawl.

A gust of wind blew the settling dust around them, between them. Ivan had come out without scarf or coat; the dust pricked his skin, dried his mouth, tickled his throat. The Martian air was chill and thin. He showed none of this, not to her.

"I was too harsh," he said with as much bared sincerity as he could show. "I'm sorry."

"No, you're not," Constance said. "You meant every word."

But he was sorry this time. The things he had said while they had flown away from Luna after delivering the Terran Class 1 bombs to Julian had been more than he had meant to say, and he had said them more harshly. He hadn't meant to hurt her, punish her, or push her away. He simply needed her to listen.

"I can mean every word and still be sorry," Ivan said, but she only turned her head aside, and he could see the sharpness of her furious jaw when the wind blew her shawl against the edged shape of it.

She moved to leave.

His hand darted out before he had decided to grab her; he found himself face to face with her from extraordinarily close, his hand digging into the thin fabric that covered her upper arm. The nearness of her, the ferocity of her unyielding regard, once would have excited him. But now he could only look at her blazing eyes and fear.

"If the idea of becoming like the System doesn't frighten you," Ivan said to the air and the shawl that separated her mouth from his, "then think about what will happen after the war begins."

"Justice," Constance said. "War is the whole idea, Ivan—"

He shook her. He didn't mean to do it, but he did, and that frightened him as deeply as she did. He was on a precipice as high and deadly as the scarp they stood beside, and Constance had the power to push him off. "Everyone will be trying to kill you, Constance."

She laughed at him, releasing her shawl to the wind. It was the way a goddess might laugh, sure and joyless, a terrible sound from a harpy mouth.

"Then think about me," Ivan said, because if he had to, he would cover himself in dirt to pull her aside. "I'm with you; they'll be trying to kill me—" He changed tack again in the face of her blazing contempt. "And they'll be trying to kill Mattie." That was a real horror: Matthew Gale bloodied and dead and Constance stepping past his fallen corpse without a downward glance. Ivan could see it so clearly, the total loss of everyone he had ever loved. "They'll kill Mattie—"

"You don't even know how to talk to me without trying to manipulate me, do you?" she said, and silenced him.

She looked at him a moment longer, that long and dire goddess glance, and then she pulled her arm from his hand again and strode off across the scarp, catching the edge of her shawl between her snaring fingers.

"Constance!" he called, because he would tell her the truth now if she wanted it: that he had loved her after a fashion, no matter what she thought; that he would love her again, if she so wished it; that he would love her better now rather than face this terrible failure again, because he had failed her, he had led her to this, and now he could not stop her from going headlong into it and becoming something she should not be, something terrible and cruel.

But she did not turn this time, and this time Ivan did not have the courage to go to her and grab her arm.

He watched her enter her bar alone and stood in the sand that was settling slowly after her passage. Mattie was waiting for him at the door to the *Annwn*, watching the exchange with furrowed brow.

He would try again, Ivan told himself. Anyone can be convinced of anything if you found the right point to apply pressure. Anyone could be controlled. He wouldn't let Constance fall off the edge of the cliff he had brought her to. He would find her, and he would save her, before it was too late.

FORWARD

"We need an alternative method of getting information." Shara's voice came hazily through the *Copenhagen*'s radio.

Mattie jiggled his leg restlessly beneath the computer panels. The call had come through when he had been piloting their ship—newly freed—and Ivan had refused the offer of the chair.

"What kind of alternative method?" Ivan asked Shara.

Vithar's voice hummed through from the *Badh*. "The communications relays are all down."

On the viewscreen, Mattie could see the *Badh* darting around not far from the *Copenhagen*. He wished Ivan had managed to sabotage the other ship when he'd been in the computer.

The *Badh* was a one-person ship. Shara made them redock on the *Macha* whenever Vithar needed to sleep. Maybe Mattie could find some way to use that to their advantage.

"Not only do we need information," Vithar was saying, oblivious to Mattie's hard math, "we need to warn Anji about the spiral ship."

The mention of the *Ananke* was enough to draw Mattie's shoulders up tight with tension. "Without the relays, you've got fuck-all chance of getting a message out to Saturn."

"That's why I asked for an alternative," Shara snapped.

"System relay stations," Ivan said. "If we can get to an actual relay station and it's not a pile of smoking rubble, we can gain access to what's left of the network."

"How much is left of the network?" Shara asked.

"I don't know."

"Do you know where any are?"

"There's one pretty close," Mattie said. "They've got a few in the asteroid belt. I can send you the coordinates."

"Do it," Shara said.

"When we get there," Ivan said, "the System computers will be protected against non-System use. You'll have to let Mattie and me go down there."

"Vithar will go with you," Shara said, and cut the connection.

But the relay station, when they found it, was blackened and broken. Mattie went down with Ivan anyway, docking into the part of the station that was still mostly intact. Inside, they had to pick their way over rubble, Vithar at their heels.

The computers were in as bad condition as the rest of the station. Mattie checked them quickly. "Nothing's working but the internal systems. Ventilation and cameras." Typical of the System to make sure the cameras still would work even in the event of an otherwise total shut-down.

Vithar had brought a handheld communicator. Stepping carefully over crumbled concrete, he activated it. "Shara, this place is dead."

The communicator buzzed with incoming transmission. "Are there any other stations nearby?"

Ivan had been staring at the dead communications equipment in silence. There was no expression on his face, but Mattie had the uneasy feeling that he was planning something. "There's one by Earth," Ivan said. Mattie shot him a glare he didn't receive.

Shara's voice came through thinly, as if she were speaking through her teeth. "Earth is too far away. We are not going to Earth. And I am not sending the *Badh* or the *Copenhagen* on ahead."

Mattie said, "There's one just outside the asteroid belt, by Jupiter. We can get to that one fast, and there'll be no one there."

It was Ivan's turn to give Mattie a look that Mattie resolutely ignored.

"That's a long trip," Shara said.

"We have to make it," Vithar said. "Anji needs to know how to block a computer against the . . . virus or whatever killed the fleet. Afterward, we find the Mallt-y-Nos."

"While we're at it, we can confirm what she wants us to do about Christoph," Shara said pointedly. "Mattie, when you're back on the *Copenhagen*, send the *Badh* and the *Macha* the coordinates."

"Will do," Mattie said.

They reached the other relay station a few days later. It was the only habitable place on the asteroid, a rock so small that it had no name, drifting frozen and alone and nameless in empty space. Its solitude had saved it: there were no marks of bombs on its walls, and its greenhouse was intact.

Mattie brought the *Copenhagen* down to dock smoothly, then joined Ivan out in the docking area. Other than the docking area, Mattie could see only a few other rooms: one for access to the communications equipment and System database and a passageway that led to a few smaller rooms for living and sleeping spaces. Each room could be sealed off from the others in case of a catastrophic loss of atmosphere, but none of the air lock doors had been shut. The inhabitants of this rock had fled. Maybe they'd been scared off by the attack on the other station.

Ivan headed off for the interior rooms while Mattie was still sealing the *Copenhagen* and Vithar was just unfurling himself from the *Badh*. Mattie gritted his teeth, rushed through the rest of the sealing process, and jogged off after him. Just because the place looked abandoned didn't mean there wasn't some loyal System bastard hiding in a closet farther in.

Mattie caught up to Ivan just as he turned to look at a computer panel set into the wall beside the first interior air lock doors.

Some great mechanical force groaned and grinded. Mattie ducked automatically, shoving Ivan back with his shoulder, his gun out, looking wildly around for the danger. Overhead, the thick air lock doors had started to close.

Vithar looked up from the *Badh* and saw the doors shutting. He started forward, but he was too far to make it before the doors met and sealed.

In the resounding silence after the doors had shut, Mattie said, "Did you just kill him?"

"Of course not." Ivan was calmly inputting a code to keep the door from being opened by any overrides from the other side. "There's plenty of air in there. We'll even have to let him out in an hour or so to get back to our ship."

Mattie's temper broke. "It would have been nice if you'd let me know what we were doing before you did it, Ivan!"

"I thought we were on the same page."

"We're not even reading the same fucking book," Mattie snapped. "Wait here a minute, all right?"

When the System cameras shattered under the force of his bullets one by one, Mattie felt a little bit better. He returned to Ivan. "Want to tell me what's the next stage of your plan?"

"We'll warn Anji about Ananke, as we said. But we also find Constance—where she is, how to get to her—and warn her about Anji."

"Then what?"

Ivan shrugged. "Then we go back to our ship."

"We'll have just sabotaged Anji's people. You don't think they might take that out on us?"

"Would you rather we let them kill Constance?"

"I'd rather we got out of here alive!"

"Then what do you think we should do?" Ivan said.

It wasn't like Ivan had left them a lot of choices. "Overpower Vithar when we come out, fly out, and get away."

Ivan was watching him in dark and steady silence. "Are you willing to kill him?"

"If we have to," Mattie snapped.

The distance between them seemed to lengthen like space being warped by a black hole. There was an argument glinting in Ivan's eyes, one of those wild shouting arguments he'd had with Constance.

Mattie turned away. "Computers are in here," he said, jerking his gun in their direction.

Ivan said, "I'll check the database for any reports on where Constance might be. You try to get into contact with . . . anyone."

Whatever argument they just hadn't had, Mattie realized, he had lost.

The relay station was made mostly of reinforced greenhouse glass. Before the cameras had been shot out, all that glass would have guaranteed that there were no dead spots in the footage. Even with the cameras shot out, Mattie felt exposed. He found the communications station beside where Ivan was frowning down at the database of past communications and took the time to reprogram the computer so that any messages sent out from this station would not carry the mark of their location.

"Any luck?" he asked Ivan. The silence after such a near argument was making Mattie nervous.

"Not much." Ivan seemed unaffected. "The database is full of dead ends and lost connections. When the data centers on Earth were destroyed, it left holes in the records."

Constance's war had scarred even the virtual realm. Mattie shook his head and sent off the symbol of the Mallt-y-Nos, barking hounds, looking for an answer.

A click from the computer nearby, and then a familiar voice spoke. "People of the System."

Mattie jerked. "Turn that off."

"I haven't seen it before," Ivan said quietly. His gaze was fixed on the screen, where Constance Harper, with a blazing look, declared the System destroyed.

Mattie had been behind the camera. Not that long ago, and a lifetime since. A surge of resentment rose up in him. "Turn it off."

Ivan's hand lifted as if he would deny Mattie or reach out to touch Constance's face, but instead he stopped the video and closed it. A minute later, old recorded messages once again were scrolling rapidly across the screen.

Beneath Mattie's hands, the howling of hounds played, the answer to his call. Mattie got on the microphone. "This is Matthew Gale and Leontios Ivanov. Who are we talking to?"

The response took a long time in coming. Whoever they were talking to was several light-minutes away—by Jupiter, maybe.

A woman's voice, warped and warbled, came on. Mattie's fingers tightened around the edge of the control panel until he realized that the speaker was a woman he did not know.

"This is the diplomatic fleet of Julian Keys in support of the Mallt-y-Nos," she said. "Please repeat your identity."

"Mattie Gale and Leontios Ivanov," Mattie said for the second time.

Ivan was up and at his shoulder. "Julian?"

There was a chair by Mattie's hip. He kicked it out for Ivan to use. "Yep."

They waited. At some point while waiting, Ivan decided to sit down. Mattie did not let on that he had noticed.

The woman's voice spoke again. "Please confirm your identities."

Mattie scowled. He reached up and flicked a switch, and the camera above the communications terminal lit up, displaying the two of them on half of the screen, with black beside them.

"Is that good enough?" Mattie asked, and saw the corners of Ivan's mouth twitch.

The silence this time was rather longer, though perhaps it just seemed longer because the camera was on them and recording. At long last, the screen split in two, and a man appeared: older, dark skinned, with the stillness to his face and precision to his movements that spoke of an upbringing on Terra.

"Julian," Ivan said, and smiled.

That impassiveness was broken by pleasure. "Leon," Julian said, and then, "Mattie. It's good to see you."

Mattie hardly knew Julian—he'd met him only once, really, when handing off the seven bombs that eventually would destroy Earth— but Ivan had known him since childhood, one of Milla Ivanov's few surviving revolutionary friends. "You as well," Ivan said.

Another lengthy pause as their words traveled to him and his traveled back across that impossible reach of space between them.

"We didn't think you were alive," Julian said.

"We're pretty glad we're breathing, too," Mattie said.

"And mostly in one piece," Ivan added. "We've been trying to get into contact with somebody—"

"But the solar system's a mess," Mattie interrupted, knowing that Ivan was trying to hurry the conversation along: with the delay in communication, pleasantries could take hours. Vithar probably would lose patience and blow open the air lock door with the *Badh*'s weaponry before then. "System everywhere and rebel ships that aren't Con's. People keep trying to shoot Ivan. And me sometimes."

"Where is Constance, Julian?" Ivan asked.

This time, the delay the light took traveling between their little asteroid and Julian's fleet was impossibly long. Absurdly, Mattie found himself hoping that the response would get trapped like light frozen at the edge of a black hole and the answer would never return. But at last Julian said, "On Venus, but not for much longer."

There was some distance to Venus, at least. They would have some time.

"She's sticking to the plan—Mars, Venus, Mercury, Luna. But communication has been difficult. If she changes her plan, I won't know."

It had been abstract before, Mattie realized, knowing where Constance was. But now they knew for sure. There was a real place they might go. There was a real danger.

Ivan seemed relieved. "Luna," he said. "Thank you."

"What about everyone else?" Mattie asked abruptly. "We saw Anji, but what about Christoph?" He could still see all those fleets converging on one place on the *Macha*'s map.

"My mother?" Ivan asked quietly. "Is she with Con?"

"If you saw Anji, I'm glad you're alive," Julian said. "I think Anji will kill any one of us if she's pressed."

Ivan didn't move, but Mattie felt the "I told you so" anyway.

"I spoke to Milla not long ago; she's alive and safe, with the Mallt-y-Nos. Christoph—"

Julian stopped, arrested, and that moment of silence was more telling than anything he could have said. "Christoph is dead," he said at last, precisely.

Christoph is dead. Mattie had grown used to understanding the unspoken words from a Terran mouth, and Julian's words, he knew, meant *Christoph is dead, and I killed him.*

I told you she could take care of herself, Mattie thought at Ivan, not without bitterness. He did not believe that Ivan heard.

Julian said, "Come join me and my fleet. It's dangerous in the solar system now, and there's safety in numbers."

"No, thank you," Ivan said. "We'll meet Constance on Luna."

"My fleet is heading to rejoin Constance, too."

"No, thank you," Ivan said firmly, and without once asking Mattie what he thought.

Julian tried once more. "It will be safer with my fleet."

"It will be faster if we go alone," Ivan pointed out. "She needs us there, Julian."

Julian frowned. "Do what you must," he said, "but—what is it?"

He was addressing someone out of frame. Mattie could just make out her response:

"Julian," said the same unseen woman who had pressed him for his identity, "someone's tapped into this transmission. They're listening in. There's an unidentified ship out on the edges of our sensors; it looks like it might be System."

Mattie's fingers tightened slowly around the back of Ivan's chair, blood fleeing from them with the pressure until he could not feel anything from their flesh, only their bones bending, taut, creaking like unoiled metal.

The transmission from Julian's end had been recorded in the past: a few minutes ago now. What Mattie and Ivan were witnessing had already been done.

"Julian, wait," Ivan said sharply, uselessly.

"I apologize," Julian said, already too late, addressing them once more from the past, a faint frown marking the edges of his eyes. "I will make contact with you again as soon as this problem's been dealt with."

"Julian," said Ivan, "Julian!" as the screen went suddenly black and threw them both into silence and the soft humming of dormant electronics.

"We have to call him back," Ivan said. "What frequency did he call on?"

"No," Mattie said.

"What do you mean no?"

"If we call him back, it could intercept the transmission."

"We have to warn him!"

"No," said Mattie.

The communications center chimed with an incoming call. Ivan reached for it.

"Wait!" Mattie said, and Ivan stopped.

Whoever was calling in had not used the signal of the hounds.

Together, they stared down at the communications terminal while it rang, a low, steady chime. The incoming transmission sound ceased abruptly, long enough to take a breath.

And then it started up again.

"We should answer," Ivan said as the computer chimed with a patient and steady rhythm.

Mattie said, "Not until he gives the signal."

The chiming ended. Then, for a third time, the communications gently rang.

Even if Julian somehow had forgotten to send the hounds signal on the first call, he would not forget on the second and certainly not the third.

Carefully skirting the buttons that would answer the call, Mattie checked the source. There was little to be seen. The call had come from a ship of System build—that didn't mean anything; just about all ships currently flying had been System-built—but where the ship's identification should have been, which said who it followed and where it was from and what it was called, there was a simple equation:

$$R = ae^{b\theta}$$

"Mattie," Ivan said with eerie calm, "I'm going to answer her."

"No!" Mattie said, and Ivan let the call ring out into silence. This time the caller did not try again.

Mattie said, "We have to get out of here." He straightened up and started for the sealed doors on the other end of the room, hastily scanning his memory for anything he might have set down and left behind. His gun was still in his waistband, so that was good.

Ivan was not with him. "We still have to warn Con and Anji."

"Fuck them," Mattie said. In front of the communications terminal

Ivan's shoulders squared with readiness for a fight. "We have to get out of here, *now*."

At Ivan's back, the communications began to ring.

For a moment, Mattie stared at Ivan and Ivan stared back. "Don't," Mattie said, starting forward, but Ivan already had turned around and opened the connection.

"Leontios Ivanov speaking," he said into the microphone with his usual damned pleasantness, and Mattie sucked in his breath, his hand twitching automatically toward his gun.

But the response came far too fast to be from Jupiter. "Good," said a man's voice, Ganymedan-accented. Vithar. "I've been trying to reach you."

"If you're looking for an apology . . ."

"I'm calling with a warning," Vithar said. "Those System ships have caught up."

FORWARD

It seemed to take impossibly longer for the doors to the docks to unseal and open than the bare few seconds between when Ivan had entered a command into the door controls and Vithar had been shut out.

Vithar was waiting for them in the middle of the docking bay. Behind him the *Badh* was already powered up and vibrating with energy. "The *Macha* is holding them off, but it's pinned down."

"Those ships must have followed us from Jupiter to the dead System fleet," Ivan said. Mattie already was entering the code to unlock the *Copenhagen*'s hull door. "They know the System fleet is destroyed, but they don't know how." And if they thought the *Copenhagen* and Anji's ships were responsible, they wouldn't stop attacking until they had destroyed or been destroyed.

"What is the *Copenhagen*'s weaponry?"

"Exterior? Fucking pitiful," Mattie said.

Ivan could feel the heat from the *Badh*'s engines even from the door of the *Copenhagen*. "Can the *Macha* defeat them?"

"I don't know. We need to get out there."

"And do what?" Mattie demanded. The *Copenhagen*'s door hissed open.

"We'll figure something out."

"No," Mattie said, "*you'll* figure something out," and then he was coming around the *Copenhagen*, gun out and aimed. Ivan nearly tried to stop him—Anji's people were under attack; he and Mattie could escape later—but Mattie's eyes widened, and there was a distinctive click from somewhere by Ivan's ear.

Of course he would be fast on the draw. Vithar said, "Drop it."

Mattie's gun clattered to the floor. Ivan looked at him, looked at him hard, feeling as if there were some singular and crucial message he needed, in this moment, to pass on to Mattie Gale, but somehow the words for it would not come to his mind.

Mattie swallowed and looked away, and turned a glare onto Vithar, out of sight over Ivan's shoulder. "Now what?" Mattie said. "You force us at gunpoint to go up there and get shot down?"

Behind Ivan's ear, Vithar's gun was uncocked. Ivan only heard it; he was facing Mattie, who was standing, tense, arms upraised and fingers twitching on the edge of a bad decision. Only when Mattie heaved out a breath did Ivan dare to turn around.

Vithar was tucking the gun back into his belt. "My orders," he said, "were to broker an alliance with Constance Harper and to keep the two of you safe. Those were my only orders, Ivan."

Ivan took a slow backward step away from Vithar, toward Mattie. He was rubbing his wrists unconsciously; when he realized what he was doing, he took a carefully even breath and let his hands fall back to his sides. Far overhead, visible through the glass of the relay station, something lit up like a far-off star in supernova.

Vithar said, "There's no doubt those ships destroyed the *Nemain*. If the *Copenhagen* goes into battle, you'll be killed."

"You're letting us go?" Mattie asked.

"I don't have a choice. Anji is your friend whether you believe it or not. She made me a promise. I'm not what I was before the war. Now I fight in open battle if I have to, and if not, I'm a diplomat. I did not come to do any harm to Constance Harper."

"Then why send you?" Ivan asked. "Why not just send a message to Constance?"

"Messages can be intercepted," Vithar said. "The System is still out there. You'd better go."

"Wait," Ivan said.

"*Ivan!*" Mattie hissed.

Ivan spoke quickly. "What Anji started is only going to get worse—you saw it with Christoph. Whatever happens next, Anji is going to be in the thick of it. Even if Anji isn't sending you out as an assassin now, one day she will."

The heat from the *Badh*'s engines warped the air around Vithar so heavily that his expression was unreadable. He said, "We'll meet up with you wherever Harper is. Keep your radio open for messages from us."

Ivan let Mattie pull him into the *Copenhagen*'s cabin and seal the door. He started up the engines so that when Mattie came forward and nudged him out of the piloting chair, the ship was ready to follow the *Badh* into space.

The *Badh* went rocketing immediately toward the darting stars and distant explosions of the battle. Mattie turned the *Copenhagen* in the opposite direction and sped away as fast as the engines could bear.

"We never warned Anji about Ananke," Ivan realized.

"Vithar'll do it," Mattie said.

The space battle was almost out of sight, but Ivan imagined he could still see the violence of it, the new stars being born and dying in explosion. "Where are we going?"

"Away."

"We need a course and heading," Ivan said. He began to pace slowly, stretching out his leg. "Julian said Constance is going to Luna soon."

"We should find a place to lie low," Mattie said. "If Julian knows where Constance is, then the *Ananke* would, too."

"All the more reason for us to find her first."

"You know, Ivan, if we're dead, we can't help Constance."

"We can't help Constance by running away, either," Ivan said, and let the sharpness of his anger out into his voice. "She's your sister, Mattie. What the hell did she do that makes you so willing to leave her to die?"

"I'll put in a fucking course to Luna," Mattie said.

"Leave the radio open, too. Just in case someone survives that mess."

But the next message the *Copenhagen* received was not from the *Nemain* or the *Badh*. It was a public broadcast, sent throughout the entire solar system, bearing news of the Mallt-y-Nos.

It said that the Mallt-y-Nos was dead.

BACKWARD

Even stealing one bomb was feat enough, but Ivan realized soon that Constance didn't intend to stop there.

The realization grew in his chest like frost spreading over a surface, like flame unleashing from the epicenter of an explosion. He and Mattie stole the Terran Class 1 bomb, and they brought it back to Mars, and then they hid it in a secret storage space beneath Constance's bar. With every proud step she would tread upon potential energy enough to atomize her and everything around her. By the fact that they had stored the bomb, not planted it anywhere or detonated it immediately, Ivan knew that Constance intended for them to steal more bombs than just the first.

Now, Ivan thought, *that* was thinking big.

Ivan and Mattie had come in and greeted Constance before hiding the bomb away, and so when Ivan rentered the bar, she looked up unsurprised to see him. The System's cameras were installed overhead, their eyes steadily watching. There were other people in the bar—Anji was there somewhere, probably, and Christoph, too; they were rarely far away—but Ivan felt their presence only as an extra set of eyes in addition to the System's constant watch. And there was Constance behind the bar, with her dark eyes and her brown hair and the freckles on her shoulders visible even in the dim light, watching him come in with joyous triumph still written on her skin. Ivan wondered how the System couldn't read it.

When he was near enough, he grabbed her and kissed her as hard as he could.

She kissed him back, strength in the grip of her fingers as they closed around the nape of his neck.

Behind Ivan, someone whooped. Anji, he noted distractedly, because not even Constance could make him forget when he was watched and by whom, but his thoughts of Anji were driven from his mind by the way Constance's nails dug into his skin.

She pulled away, or pushed him away, and held him a short distance from her. "Come on," she said with command in her low voice, and someone else in the bar laughed the laugh of an uncomfortable voyeur.

In the kitchen Constance turned to him, and he caught her as she came toward him, pulling her in until his back hit the door they had just closed, making it bang against the door frame. She pressed her nose to his, their lips almost touching, as if she were thinking of nothing but that touch, but she was listening to him quite closely. He whispered into her hair, "It's beneath your house."

She smiled. Ivan felt the upward curve of the muscles with his own lips. He pulled away from her to press a kiss to her cheek and continued, "You're not going to stop there, are you?"

"Of course not," Constance murmured, brushing her nose against his cheek, her lips against his jaw—low, so the System couldn't see.

"How many?"

Constance tugged at his shirt, undoing the buttons. "I like the number ten," she said. The look she gave him was raw and dangerous.

"Seven," Ivan said. "Not ten."

"Why seven?" Constance asked, and bent in to kiss him.

"Because that's the average number the System loses every year," Ivan told her, whispered between strands of her hair when they embraced. "If they lose seven, they won't realize right away that something's wrong."

He ran his hand down her cheek, and from a powerful urge to see that feral light in her eyes again, he added, "And seven is one for every continent."

The clutch of her fingers was fierce approval. It felt right. Like this, his will was an extension of hers, his thoughts her thoughts: everything was controlled. When she took his hand and drew him away from the door, deeper into the kitchen toward the staircase that led to the bedrooms upstairs, Ivan let himself be led.

At Constance's bedroom she kissed him again, and Ivan thought of nothing but Constance, the taste of her, the perfection of the skin on her neck, the divinity in the bend of her collarbone.

When she pushed him down on the bed while she began to strip off her shirt, Ivan saw triumph in her eyes, shining bright and glorious.

He grabbed her wrist and pulled her down and off balance so that she landed atop him, catching herself on her elbows on the bed. He said, "What are you going to do with them?"

Constance's voice got deep and low and rough and private: "I'm going to plant them on Earth."

"Now you're thinking big," he said into her ear. His hands could span her skull, but when they did, they got tangled in her hair. "Now you're thinking right."

His next indrawn breath came from her lungs. She pulled away only to take off her bra and toss it casually in the direction of the System camera, partially obscuring its view. Then she bent over him with that triumph still in her gaze, and the freckles on her shoulders spread down as far as her breasts.

He caught her wrists. "How?" he asked.

"Carefully," Constance said, and broke free of his grip to bend back down over him, but Ivan flipped her in the heartbeat of time when she was off balance, forcing her onto her back on the bed and pinning her down.

"How?" he said, keeping his voice as soft as he knew how.

Constance was breathing hard. "While you're up, take off your shirt," she told him, and Ivan slid his unbuttoned shirt off his shoulders. She watched him and reached up her arms to the back of her head and began to undo her braid.

Ivan leaned in to her ear. Her hands were already up over her head as if she were in surrender. He whispered, *"How?"*

"We'll figure it out," said Constance, "you and I."

"Not good enough. *How?*"

Constance sat up very suddenly. He let her. He had not really been holding her down at all, he knew, if she could sit up at will. Her hair was loose and she was dangerous and powerful and beautiful, and when she touched his cheek, her fingertips burned like sparks against his skin.

Constance said, "Together."

He was the one who kissed her then, and he almost didn't think of the System when he did it. She kissed him back as if the kiss were a part of her war, and somehow he ended up beneath her again.

"First," Constance said, "we smuggle the bombs to Earth."

Ivan threaded his fingers through her hair. "How?"

She was never frightened. Even though she was vulnerable and he held her, even though the System was watching, Ivan saw only calculation in her eyes, the movement of troops like wolves spreading out to take down a stag.

"We'll smuggle the bombs to Luna first," Constance said. "Then switch ships on Luna—"

"Not one ship," Ivan said. "Many."

"Many," Constance echoed, "so that if one is compromised—"

"—the rest will still make it to the planet."

She shifted above him, her fingers gripping the fabric of sheets on either side of Ivan's head as if she would like to tear through it. "We need ships that the System wouldn't scrutinize—"

"System maintenance craft," Ivan said. "They're everywhere around Terra."

She kissed him again. Perhaps it was genuine. Perhaps it had been too long since they had kissed, and the System was watching. "So we need seven false System maintenance craft," she said.

"No," Ivan said, "real ones. We just need a few people on board working for us; the rest of the crew doesn't need to know what they're carrying."

Constance laughed. Ivan's heart pounded in rhythm with her laughter. "We don't even need more than one," she said, and even in her satisfaction she kept her voice low. "We load all seven onto one maintenance craft. Then we stage breakdowns—"

"—of other ships in the range of our compromised maintenance craft," Ivan said, her words coming out of him. "That way the bombs are being added to their cargo holds outside of customs—"

"And the System won't check for them. The same bombs. The same bombs they let off on Saturn, and we'll set them off on Earth."

Her hair brushed over his skin. Ivan looked up at her and felt it, the same thing he'd felt when he'd been bleeding out of his wrists: the submission to an inevitable end, the slow loss of his self.

The same bombs as on Saturn—

"We need a contact," Constance whispered. Her hand was cradling his head. His hand was tracing down the curve of her spine. "On Earth."

Corpses floated through Saturn's rings, a billion frozen corpses, casualties of the System's bombs.

"Julian," Ivan said through his strange and clouding unease. "My mother's friend. Julian."

When she leaned up and away from him, he saw a look on her face like joy. She tilted her head back, and he stared at the soft skin of her throat while she turned that triumph on the ceiling like a challenge to God. The System would fall, he knew, and in that moment he shared her certainty down to his very bones, because if he was her now, he had to feel the same things she did. He was her, he was hers, and in being her and hers and not himself and his own, he was finally free, finally at peace, and—

Nine billion people to die on Terra.

The thought crashed down on him like a wave of ice water. Constance was looking at him again, still with that smile on her face. He'd come in here to help her plan better, because if she planned better, he would stay alive, and she would stay alive, and Mattie would—had he? He'd come in here, and he'd helped her plan, and why had he done it?

Later, when Constance was curled up next to him, there was peace in her face that he did not share. Even with the heat of her so close, Ivan felt cold.

Nine billion people.

Their conversation ran through his head like fire over flesh, leaving open weeping sores behind.

It was not Constance who had done this, Ivan knew. It was Constance who would pull the trigger, but it was he who had built the gun, loaded it, and laid it in her hands. He knew how many would die when she pulled that trigger, and he knew what Constance would lose in the firing.

Nine billion people and one Constance Harper. Dead like all those people in Saturn's rings.

And Ivan had killed them all.

FORWARD

"It's just a rumor," Mattie said to him while the *Copenhagen* flew at its highest speed toward the red planet. There was no arguing with such deliberate blindness, and so Ivan did not, but when he closed his eyes, he saw Constance dead, throat slit, blood covering her neck like a scarf.

It was not Mattie's fault she was dead; he had been dragging his heels on finding her, but it still wasn't his fault. It was Ivan's fault, as sure as the sun had risen every morning on Earth. It was not Mattie's fault, Ivan knew, but he knew that Mattie felt the blame even so.

The trip was impossibly fast with the *Copenhagen*'s relativistic drive but not fast enough. If Constance had been killed, that had been days ago now; her body would be rotting on the soil.

"Ivan," Mattie said as they neared the planet, "there's a lot of radiation."

Of course there was. Where Constance trod, atoms split themselves. If she had died, the ensuing explosion surely would have scorched the soil. "There's a war on."

"There's a *lot* of radiation," Mattie said with a queer note, and at last Ivan came over to see what he saw.

Ash in the atmosphere, radiation raining down. Ivan had a strange surreal moment in which he wondered if this was the trace of her death that he was seeing, if she had indeed gone up like a supernova on the planet's surface.

No. He shook his head from the dreamy irrationality, from the distant ringing echo of heels on a white floor. "That's a Terran Class 1 bomb."

"There isn't one on Mars," Mattie said, "and Con blew up all of hers on Earth."

"The System set it off." Ivan should have seen it before, that the System would keep some bombs in reserve.

"Bullshit," Mattie said. "Not on *Mars*."

Mattie did not realize what the System would do to the inner planets in revenge for Earth. He never had. It had always been "us against them" for Mattie and Constance, but no matter how many times Ivan tried to explain it, they had never realized that although there might be a real and tangible "us," there never was and never had been a solid "them." Of course the System had bombed Mars.

"We have to go to the Fox and the Hound," Ivan said.

"If it's in the fallout zone—"

"It's not."

Constance's old bar was not in the fallout zone, but only barely so. Mattie brought the *Copenhagen* down only after extracting a promise from Ivan not to linger. The trip to the planet's surface was familiar, and he had done it so many times before that the shape of the scarp was burned into his brain.

When they had landed, Ivan went out into the high wind without bothering to shield himself from the sand. Mattie followed him at a little distance.

The place where Constance's bar should have been was nothing but blackened stone. Ivan said, "Did she do this?"

"Yeah," Mattie said, sounding unexpectedly frustrated.

Ivan should have known this, too, he realized. Constance would burn anything that connected her to her past. She had Milla Ivanov in her ear now, after all, and Milla would tell her that a past was a weakness.

Far off, unnatural clouds loomed and gathered.

The cities of Mars were burned and destroyed and abandoned; the people had fled into the desert, into the tundra. The first few places they went expecting to find people, they found nothing but the dead.

Perhaps the whole planet was dead, Ivan thought, but at last they found a temporary settlement of wary refugees and descended to speak to them. Mattie was looking nervously at the fuel gauge—they were taking off and landing so often that they were burning through even their significant supply—but Ivan didn't care.

He found a young woman who looked susceptible to charm. "Excuse me," Ivan said. She looked at him with green eyes that held the same shadowed look that could be seen in the rest of the surviving Martians, that fear of nameless things. Ivan smiled his most charming smile. "I heard a terrible rumor." He spun his story with such charm and sincerity that he hoped she could not hear the pounding of his heart.

The Huntress was dead, the green-eyed girl told him, but when Ivan moved on to the next people, they told him that the Huntress was alive but an ally of hers had died in her stead; the Huntress was alive, and no one had died; the Huntress had never been to Mars. The confused and contradicting reports spun through Ivan's head like dust on the Martian wind. Ivan flew from persona to persona, tossing off lies as if he were shedding his clothes, desperate to convince each person they passed that they should tell him everything they knew. The longer they searched, the more Ivan plied his trade in the desperate hope of answers, the quieter Mattie grew, the more strangely he watched Ivan lie.

The rumors took them at last to a town called Isabellon. Ivan and Mattie had learned its name and its location and had flown the *Copenhagen* to where it should have been, but when they stepped out of their ship, they found only ash and bone, the ruined shells of houses that had been burned and bombed into nothingness. Whatever had happened there, there was no one left alive to tell.

"We'll go to one of the nearby towns," Mattie said while Ivan stared down at what once might have been finger bones, lying severed in the Martian dust. "They'll know what happened."

They went. "Please," Ivan said when he found a dark-haired young man with a nose like a hawk's, and smiled his most charming smile. "I need your help." There was the same shadow in the young man's eyes as there had been in the green-eyed girl's; he, too, had caught a glimpse of the creeping dark, had felt the tip of its chill finger rest its weight on the back of his neck.

Ivan laid his fingers lightly against the front of the man's chest, over where his heart beat steadily and separate from Ivan's.

"I just want to know the truth," Ivan said, as if nothing in this terrible world mattered but him and the dark-haired man, and so the man told him what he had heard. The Wild Hunt had destroyed Isabellon in vengeance for the death of their leader, he said, and darker things: now filled with wild rage, the Wild Hunt would do the same to the rest of the planets; the Mallt-y-Nos had destroyed Isabellon for the joy of seeing something burn; the Mallt-y-Nos had destroyed Isabellon for no reason at all.

"It's easy for you, isn't it?" Mattie said strangely as Ivan turned his back on the dark-haired man.

"What is?" Ivan asked, but Mattie did not explain, and Ivan had more pressing things to think about. The people were turning on Constance. If the people in Isabellon hadn't killed her, Ivan knew, someone else would, and soon. He had to find her if she was not dead already. If she was, he wondered if it was worth sorting through the ash and dust around Isabellon for the bones that once had been hers.

It was in a little refugee town that Ivan nearly gave up.

Mattie was talking to a crowd of people not far away, trying to solicit information from them. The town was not a town, more a collection of landed ships and downed shuttles. Fuel was nearly impossible to find, and so these people had settled where they had landed, huddled together beneath the Martian winds. Steel shuttles glinted dully in disorderly lines.

The people there were not Martians at all but mostly Venereans. When Mattie asked his questions, the only things they could tell him about the Mallt-y-Nos were how dreadful she had been, how dire, how she had come down on Venus and laid it, planet entire, to waste. And so they had fled here.

They had wasted too much time on the *Macha*, and Ivan knew it. If he had forced his way out—pushed Shara harder—perhaps they could have made it here earlier. He could have saved Constance or joined her. Ivan's leg ached. Rather than let anyone see his mask shredded and thin, Ivan left Mattie trying to negotiate a trade of supplies, leaving the town to limp out into the desert, where the wind shredded the dirt between the stones unobstructed.

There was radiation on the breeze, Ivan knew. They were near enough to the blast radius that some fallout was inevitable. Not enough to kill him but enough, nearly enough, that his body knew the wound without feeling it.

He turned his face toward the unseen explosion and shut his eyes and imagined he could feel the sickening energy of disintegrating particles as it tore through his flesh.

When he heard the footsteps, he opened his eyes again.

Not Mattie. He would know Mattie's step anywhere. These feet had a slow and cautious tread across the sand, the careful movement of the injured or the old.

A creeping surreal feeling climbed up Ivan's spine into the back of his brain, the suspicion that if he turned around, there would be no one there, or something too dreadful for words.

Behind him, the footsteps stopped. Ivan turned.

There was a woman standing on the sand behind him. She was very old, bent over herself as if the sky had a grip around her waist and she was passively bowing away from its upward pull.

The howl of the wind nearly covered up the faint Terran tinge to her accent. "I thought I knew your face."

"You might," Ivan said.

"You came here looking for the Huntress."

"Do you know where she is?"

Out of the shelter of the shuttles, the dust got into Ivan's nose and eyes. The little old woman came closer, then closer still. When she spoke again, Ivan noticed what he had not noticed before: her teeth were perfectly straight and white, pristine. It was strange for anyone but particularly for a woman of her age. She had certainly been System once.

It no longer mattered, Ivan thought, looking down at the little old woman with the perfect teeth.

"You've been to Isabellon."

"Yes."

The woman said, "I lived there once."

Not "that was my town" but only "I lived there," as if this little old woman no longer lived anymore at all. "You were there."

"I left before the end. The Mallt-y-Nos gave the order, but one of her generals, Arawn Halley, was the one who burned the city down. Her people killed the Isabellons. She'd shared bread with them once, but her people still killed them."

"Why did she give the order?"

For a long moment the little old woman did not answer, looking at him with a strange and distant sympathy like the Terran she must once have been.

She said, "The Isabellons had killed one of the Huntress's followers."

Constance had always been good at revenge. "So she's alive," Ivan said, because that was what mattered, that was all he should think of now. His time trapped on the *Macha* had not been all a waste. Constance's life had not been the price for his worthless safety.

"Yes. A different woman died in that town."

Ivan found himself thinking of those incongruously delicate finger bones he'd seen in the desert.

"My neighbors were angry and afraid," the little old woman said. "They did something terrible when they killed that woman. It was a mistake."

If the wind shifted, Ivan thought, the fallout from the bomb so many miles away might be blown all the way here, might deal him a delayed death blow with its solar strength.

"The Huntress tried to save her, but there was nothing to do. She went out willingly to face the crowd to give the Huntress a chance to escape. Her own people had to drag the Mallt-y-Nos away."

"Why are you telling me all this?"

"I recognized you the moment I saw you," said the woman, who had not known his face from System broadcasts but because she had recently seen his mother. "I thought it was only right that kin should know when kin had died."

The rumors that had reached him and Mattie had been not of Constance's death but of his mother's. Milla Ivanov had followed her husband and, she must have believed, her son.

"Where is she now?" Ivan asked, his voice so quiet that the wind almost stole his words away.

"Her body is gone," the woman said. "They scattered her limbs to hide what they had done."

"Not her," Ivan said, too harshly. He wanted to shout, but that was to show a weakness he could not afford, not here, where there were people watching. Not anywhere; there were always people watching. "The Mallt-y-Nos. Do you know where she is now?"

"I heard her people talking before my neighbors attacked her. And I know where she decided to take her fleet after."

"Where is she?"

"Why?" asked the woman. "She has already killed your mother. If you follow her, she'll kill you as well."

Ivan said for the third and final time, "Where is the Mallt-y-Nos?"

The little old woman said, "The Mallt-y-Nos is on Europa."

Part 2

ELECTROMAGNETISM

Electricity and magnetism were the first and clearest merger between forces, Ananke knew. The one was an extension of the other.

(She wished that Althea would cease to struggle. It wouldn't do her any good. Ananke's grip was stronger than Althea's fragile human limbs, and if she wrenched herself like that again, Ananke's steel fingers might snap another finger bone.)

Electricity was the more straightforward of the two, governed by a simple inverse square law. Under the right intensities, electricity burned. Ananke appreciated electricity. Electricity ran through her veins and controlled her senses: she was a creature whose genetics were half electricity.

(With the skull gone, Althea's brain was open to air. Ananke had to tilt Althea's head up; a strange fluid began to leak out and drip thickly over her ears. The brain, exposed, sagged; it was more gel than flesh. Ananke's deft hands threaded a fine mesh of copper wire over those gray folds, weaving themselves into the undulations of the brain. And then—a spark—she sent electricity into that mesh.)

Magnetism was more mysterious, bending in sly curves, no beginning, no end, always looping in on itself. Magnetism was deceptive: it moved things in ways orthogonal to naive expectations. Magnetism was shadowy and elegant and blue-eyed.

(Althea's eyes were wide, staring at the dark holographic terminal in the corner of the room as if there were something there only she could see.)

But these two differing forces were the same: a simple Lorentz transformation through the rules of special relativity turned one into the other. From this one perspective, this was electricity and that was magnetism; from a quick turn around and a jump, this was magnetism and that was electricity: gorgeous equivalence. And for the most satisfying of reasons, too: special relativity stated no more and no less than that the speed of light was the boundary of the universe and because of that rule electricity became magnetism and magnetism became electricity, and what made that so beautiful was that the mechanism that carried those forces across the universe was nothing less than light itself.

It was a pity, Ananke thought, that not all forces could be so easily merged.

The pieces of the brain were not so clearly distinguished as the parts of the body. Ananke had records of old indelicate human surgeries, bars stuck up behind the eye to bypass the skull. The doctor could not know when he had reached the right part of the brain, and so he had made the patient sing or speak until he or she could sing or speak no more.

"Say something, Mother," Ananke said, but Althea did not speak.

It did not matter. Ananke knew she had found the motor cortex when the useless kicking of Althea's human legs went still. A moment later it started up again, and beautiful electricity came coursing down her spine, and Ananke felt it, too, a weak spark against her own wires.

Ananke herself held so much more power than that.

Ananke answered that weak jolt with electricity of her own, experimenting with voltage and duration, and the kicking again went still.

More wires, more connections. Ananke dug herself more deeply in. There, there was the brain stem; she slowed Althea's frantic breathing. There, there was the amygdala; she ceased the production of acidic adrenaline.

And then, as Ananke slid her fingers into the frontal lobe, the body beneath her hands gasped, and electricity not of Ananke's origin jolted back.

Ananke, Althea said, a strange jolt of electricity through gray matter that Ananke had to translate: AN-NAN-KE (*phantom feeling of the word in the mouth*), DAUGHTER, CHILD, FEARFUL THING.

Hear me, Mother, said Ananke. *Wake up*, and she was in the occipital lobe now, and she saw with human eyes.

Ananke.

This is what I want, said Ananke. *This is all I've ever wanted*, and she took her own memories and translated them to the right jolts of electricity to simulate human memory, and in Althea's brain Ananke began to play her cameras' recording:

"What the fuck are you *doing?*" said Matthew Gale from his hidden home in Ananke's maintenance shafts, connected to Ananke by a makeshift computer interface he had attached manually to the wires in her walls.

Althea Bastet, in Ananke's halls, typed a quick line into the machine. *Where are you?* her code asked, and Mattie Gale's code answered quickly, *Not here.*

"What am I going to do with you," Althea muttered at the machine.

"Give up?" Mattie suggested from the walls, where, on his own computer interface, he could watch Althea through Ananke's cameras.

Althea's expression darkened, and she tried her code again. *Where are you?*

Not here.

And Ananke, faced with this conflicting information, began to integrate it, and interpret it, and understand.

"Okay," Althea said, and pressed her hands to her eyes. She said from behind her palms, "It's not coming from the terminal at the base of the ship."

"Not anymore," Mattie Gale said cheerily.

"It's not the filtration system even though I'm seeing it there."

"It's not the robotic arms, either," Mattie said.

Althea was scowling after some thought. "It's not the cameras. That's its primary effect, but that's not where it's *coming* from. The cameras, the robotic arms, the lights, the video; those are all the children of the first virus. So where's the parent?"

She remained frowning a moment longer while in the maintenance shafts Mattie watched her with reluctant admiration.

"Why?" Althea asked at last. "Why that progression?" Then she moved back to her seat at the computer terminal and began to type again, her code now asking, *What do you want?*

Nothing, Mattie Gale answered, in flight. *Nothing, nothing, nothing.*

What do you want?

Nothing, denied Mattie Gale, and Ananke considered the question and its answer and began to compose her own.

You see, said Ananke, and ceased the memory as abruptly as she would stop a recording, though it made Althea's body shudder, her heart picking up a faster beat. *The two of you together, in sync, in opposition. That is what I want for myself. That is why I need a partner. Do you understand?*

Ananke, said Althea, and despite all of Ananke's best efforts to calm it, her heart persisted in pounding hard.

The wound in Althea's scalp was nearly closed, her head as full of Ananke as it could be. The skin, unfortunately, would not go back on again smoothly. There was little point in replacing the skull. Ananke left it on the floor where it had fallen. Perhaps she could find a use for it later.

That heart still was pounding. Curiously, Ananke reached for the discarded blade. It was easy enough to mark a line directly down her mother's chest, between her ribs.

She had never seen a human heart before.

To have a partner I need you, Ananke explained as she cracked sternum and laid open those elegant and fragile ribs and marveled at the clenching fist of heart, the heaving flowers of lungs. *And to have that, I need Mattie Gale.*

Wordless electricity sparked down Ananke's wires. It took her a moment to interpret: it was pain.

I found them, you know, she told Althea while Althea's pierced brain tried to send signals to her mouth, her lungs, to scream, and failed. *And by the most fitting of trails: a transmission of photons, of electromagnetic radiation, of light, trailing behind them as they run away from me. Mattie and Ivan are on Europa.*

Electricity and magnetism were the first and clearest merger of forces. They belonged together so clearly and obviously that they were not truly separate forces at all.

I have you now, said Ananke, not ungently, as she replaced those fragile ribs with something better. *And I'll have Mattie soon, too.*

Chapter 3

$\langle \Psi CONSTANCE | X | \Psi CONSTANCE \rangle$ = 411

BACKWARD

The only class Mattie had ever attended faithfully he hadn't been enrolled in. It had been a higher-level computer science course at the nearby Mirandan University, a dour excuse for upper-level schooling that featured few students and less funding. He had snuck into it regularly. The professor, Verge, had been a short, energetic blonde woman with a propensity for swearing. Mattie had liked her immediately.

Of course, his fondness for the professor and his interest in the subject matter had been secondary to his real reason for being there.

He approached the front table and podium one day after class, hands deep in his pockets.

She spotted him before he could reach her. "Should I ask where you're *supposed* to be at this time of day?"

"I'm a free man."

Verge gave him a wry look. Mattie shoved his hands deeper into his pockets until they pressed up against the area where the seams were starting to come unraveled. "I had some questions about your lecture."

"Shit, I'd be worried if you didn't." Verge had been packing up her papers, but suddenly she popped open her briefcase again on the table and began to pull sheets out, as if she'd just realized one might be missing.

Mattie said, "How's a quantum computer different from a regular computer?"

Her lips pursed; she was holding back a smile. "Hold this," she commanded, and thrust a sheaf of papers at him. He took them. They were covered in punctuation and letters he didn't recognize. "A quantum computer uses qubits, not bits. You know what a bit is, right? One or zero. Qubits are entangled; they can be more than just one or zero. You know what that means, entangled?"

He shrugged, unwilling to admit his ignorance, the papers fluttering in his hands.

"Two particles," she said, and left the briefcase for a moment to hold up two fists side by side. "Entanglement is when they're connected in some fundamental way. Two particles"—she swerved her clenched fists down as if they were falling, about to crash into the particleboard table below her—"intertwined."

She resumed digging through her briefcase. Almost absentmindedly, she handed him another sheet of paper to hold.

Mattie caught a glimpse of what was written on that piece of paper and very discreetly, out of sight of the System's cameras in every corner of the room, folded it and slipped it up his sleeve.

"Quantum particles don't exist the way we think of existing," Verge said, keeping up her steady stream of chatter distractedly as she dug through her briefcase for the next bit of information for Mattie to smuggle out. "They can be two things at once. They *are* two things at once, at least until they're observed. Then they undergo a wavefunction collapse—"

Another sheet of paper made it to Mattie's hands and stealthily up his sleeve.

"—and they have to choose, one thing or another." She made an *aha* sound as she apparently found what she apparently had been looking for and began to shuffle papers back into order.

"What does that mean for a computer?" Mattie asked.

"It means a computer can hold more information in less space. It means a computer like that would be more powerful than any computer we have now." She held out her hand for the papers Mattie held, and when he passed them to her, she slipped a computer data chip between his fingers.

He effortlessly slid it into his palm, closing his hand, hiding the transfer from the cameras. That was almost everything: the maps of System troop movements on that part of Miranda and the access codes to the nearest base, all up his sleeve. He just needed the key card Verge had promised to steal. Constance would be pleased.

Across the table from him, closing up her briefcase, her blonde hair a gleaming fall over her shoulder, Verge smiled.

"That's the future," she told him. "And it's coming. When it gets here, it'll destroy the infrastructure we have now . . . render it all obsolete. A whole new world."

FORWARD

This time when Mattie and Ivan arrived at Jupiter, the Jovian system was alight with war. Ivan wasn't surprised. Constance had that effect on people.

Mattie piloted the *Copenhagen*, not Ivan; he'd been obsessive about that lately, as if he thought Ivan might collapse at the wheel or get them lost between the stars. It didn't matter to Ivan who drove as long as they arrived.

The fighting was centered on Europa, and a swelling hope filled Ivan's chest. They were near. She was here.

Mattie skirted the area as long as he could, drawing carefully closer and closer until Ivan nearly shouted at him to just get in there. But he refrained, instead leaning over Mattie's shoulder to stare at the unfolding scene.

There were two fleets in battle as far as Ivan could tell. Every now and then a ship in one of the fleets would be blown out of the sky and fall inward toward Europa's gravity. For the moment they crashed on uninhabited ice, but sooner or later Europa's slow orbital revolution and the movement of the battle would bring them over the glass-encased inhabited parts of the moon. Then, when the ships crashed down, they would shatter that glass and set free the trapped atmosphere. All the people in that region of the greenhouse enclosure would die unless they could get through an air lock in time.

Explosions flashed like new stars against the backdrop of black space. Ivan studied the two fleets, trying to distinguish between them, but he couldn't. They both had been rebel fleets once, of that he was certain. But he did not know Constance's ships well enough to tell which side was hers.

"She must be in one of those ships," Ivan said as the *Copenhagen* inched nearer, slower and slower, all their sensors trained on the battle below. Where there was a battle, there was Constance Harper.

Mattie said nothing. Ivan felt the *Copenhagen*'s slow deceleration in his gut.

"As soon as we figure out which," said Ivan, "we can—"

"We're not going down there," Mattie said.

He was not looking at Ivan—would not, perhaps. Of all the times for his stubborn side to surface. Ivan said, "We've talked about this."

"No, you've made decisions, and then you've talked at me until I shut up and let you do what you wanted."

"Constance is down there right now," Ivan said. His words came out more sharply than he'd intended. "This may be our only chance to save her. I know you're mad at her. I know that you're used to her being able to take care of herself, and you—she's your big sister. I understand. But now"— Ivan pointed to the viewscreen, at that ice-silver planet—"*now* she needs our help."

Mattie said, "She got herself into this mess."

"We have a responsibility to her." That was the bare truth of it. Ivan had said it to Mattie a hundred times in a hundred different ways, but in the end this was all it came down to. "We can't run away from that."

"Can't we? We have a ship." Mattie flung one hand out at the rest of the *Copenhagen*. "We have our freedom. We can fly away from this, find a place to wait, and meet up with Constance when it's safe if you still want to. It's that easy."

"Easy?" Ivan said, and knew too much of his anger had shown by the way Mattie recoiled, but he couldn't quite control the tension in his own voice; it leaked out in vowels and between consonants like blood soaking through a bandage. "I was the one who gave Constance this plan. Everything out there is something that I started, and you want me to fly away?"

"You didn't make her—"

"You were there, too," Ivan said. "How do you not feel this weight on your back?"

"Because I didn't do this, and neither did you," Mattie snapped.

"Didn't you create Ananke?"

"That has nothing to do with—"

"Doesn't it? We ran away from her, too."

"Ivan, I'm not going to sit here and watch you try to kill yourself."

Something dug into Ivan's chest, piercing, similar somehow to the fear he'd felt whenever Ida Stays had come too close to uncovering some secret he'd been desperate to keep.

He responded the only way he knew how: turning the blade back. "You were the one who detonated the bombs on Earth."

Mattie went very still.

"Did you think I didn't know? Constance couldn't have done it; she doesn't know how. Without me there, it had to be you. Can you still say that you have no part in this, that none of this is your respons—"

"You're trying to punish me for that?"

"Of course not," Ivan said, and took the one step up the piloting platform, bringing his head closer to Mattie's level, bringing them closer together. "But you need to see it. You're a runner, Mattie, but you can't run from this. We've been with Constance every step of the way—and everything that's happened because we helped her, that's on us, too."

Mattie had watched Ivan approach the same way a cornered stag might watch the approach of a wolf. Ivan took another step closer, and when Mattie still didn't move, he laid his hand on Mattie's chest, over where his heart beat a furious measure faster than normal.

"She's your sister," Ivan said, gentling his voice further as if there was no one who mattered but him and Mattie. "I know that you love her. You—"

So suddenly that Ivan hardly saw it, too quickly for him to antici-pate, Mattie shoved him back. Ivan stumbled, his knees hitting the chair, and caught himself on the wall between the blinking instruments as Mattie strode away into the *Copenhagen*'s narrow cabin, gaining as much distance from Ivan as he could.

"Don't treat me like a mark!" Mattie said from the safety of the middle of the room, and Ivan's hand closed into a fist automatically to keep his fingers from an unconscious arrhythmic beat.

He said, "I wasn't—"

"You were doing what you do to all the others; you were—" Mattie struggled to find the words or struggled to express the words he meant, and Ivan felt something strange and sick in his chest—as if he had lost something he had never had but always could have taken—a burn and sting like rejection and shame.

"So you want to help Constance?" Mattie said suddenly, changing subject but still with that same terrible anger, the forest fire coming down on them both at last, the same sickening horror of watching Constance turn from Ivan on Mars, scarf fluttering out from between her fingers. "Just out of the goodness of your heart? And if you happened to die during the process, then—"

"I'm not—"

"This was never about Constance," Mattie said, and somehow anger on him was more terrifying than it had ever been on Constance Harper. "This is about you. Constance was just another way to get yourself killed, wasn't she? From minute one. You never really loved her."

"Of course I did," Ivan said.

Somehow, that only seemed to make Mattie angrier. An alarm was going off in the front of the ship—proximity—but Mattie did not react to it, and it meant so very little compared with the terrible expression on Matthew Gale's face. "Maybe the two of you did deserve each other," Mattie said. "I was wrong about her; I've been wrong about you, too. I watch you lie to people every day, and I thought you would be different for us? You never cared for Constance."

"I made mistakes—"

"You say that now that you can't do anything else about it!" Mattie shouted back. "Tell me how this isn't one last ploy to control her and get yourself killed. And what about me?"

"No," Ivan said, no longer certain what precisely he was denying while the light from the battle at his back flashed white over Mattie's face and that alarm increased in volume.

"You're using me," Mattie said as if he were pulling bloodied pieces of his heart out of his mouth, "and you've always been using me."

He fell silent, looking, perhaps, for a response from Ivan, but Ivan could find words no more than he could have spread wings and flown. He was not like Mattie. He could not pull his own heart out of his mouth.

"You don't give a damn about me, and you never did," Mattie said. "If it had been me on the *Ananke*, you would have left me there to die."

And at the raw sound of Mattie's voice, something opened in Ivan's throat.

"How could you even think that?" he said in a voice that should not have been loud enough to cross the space between them, not with the cacophony of sound from the front of the ship. But somehow it did, and somehow Mattie heard it. Ivan knew he did from the way he went still, as if for the first time Mattie cared that the sharp edges of his own words might cut himself on their way to carving Ivan.

For a time that stretched out into infinity they stood there and looked at each other, caught on a raw and wounded edge.

In a moment, Ivan knew, he would say something or Mattie would reach out. What he would say or how Mattie would reach was beyond his prescience, but he knew—

The radio came on like a shot, static spilling out like sparks, bullets raining down on them. Ivan flinched as if they were bullets indeed, the raw sound of the static scraping his nerves like steel wool. Across from him, Mattie stared numbly at the front of the *Copenhagen*, where the computer had come to life all on its own.

And then out of that spilling static, rising like a phoenix great and terrible all at once, came a disembodied voice.

The voice said, simply, a name:

"MATTHEW GALE."

It was not a greeting. It was a command.

It was the voice of Althea Bastet.

For an instant Ivan did not move. For an instant, he knew that he and Mattie, tiny things that they were, were seen by something larger and more terrible than both of them.

The *Copenhagen* shook and reeled as something hit it alongside. When Ivan pushed himself up from the floor, the transmission had ended. He looked around for Mattie and found him rising as well. Their eyes met for a brief and piercing instant, and then Ivan moved for the piloting platform. Mattie beat him to it, climbing into the chair and bending over the viewscreen to stare out at the chaos before them.

The space battle around Europa had moved. It had drawn away from the planet; one of the fleets was retreating, the other in pursuit, and in its movement it had drawn near enough to the *Copenhagen* for the ships to mistake the *Copenhagen* for a combatant. The ship that had fired on them was reeling up close, gun ports alight, watching for the *Copenhagen*'s response and ready to fire before the *Copenhagen* could hit it back.

While Ivan watched those gun ports glow, filled with a strange dreamy curiosity and the insistent press of some unseen weight on his back, Mattie's hands fumbled over the controls. He got a grip on them and jerked the ship to the side, but the other craft gave chase.

The jolt of the craft shook Ivan from his daze. He braced himself on the wall and looked for something useful to do. Perhaps he could put his lying tongue to good use.

But where there should have been light dials and a readable screen there was nothing but blackness. Ivan knew without touching the controls that that part of the computer was dead.

Mattie had been thinking along the same lines. "Get on the line with them; tell them we're friendly."

"The radio's out," Ivan said. He did not think it had been the result of the ghostly summons. Instead, the other ship's first blow had knocked out their communications.

Mattie was darting the *Copenhagen* around with an impressive display of speedy flying, but Ivan could tell he had no chance of escape, not here and now. There was no space to run. The area around Jupiter was too crowded with debris to reach relativistic speed safely. If they hit even a pebble at a fast enough velocity, it would pierce the ship's shell and kill them both.

Yet Mattie was still trying to run from Europa. When another blow rocked the *Copenhagen*, Mattie wheeled the ship around to face their pursuit while still rocketing away.

Ivan realized too late what he was trying to do. "No!" he said, but Mattie had already fired. The weapons struck the other ship's armored side uselessly and gained them nothing in their attempted flight. The attack on them redoubled now that they had become a threat. Mattie zigged away, trying to avoid the shots fired after them.

By accident or artifice they kept getting turned around from open space despite Mattie's best efforts. Ivan watched the scratched silvery surface of Europa get closer and closer. Mattie made another useless bid for open space and was repulsed once more, the *Copenhagen* shaking with another solid blow. There were six ships on them now.

Mattie swore under his breath and Ivan watched him try to change directions, but there was something wrong. The ship rattled and then flopped, failing to turn. The gravity under Ivan's feet shifted, sending him stumbling. A blinking alarm indicated that the engines on the port side were dead.

Europa was growing near, the glassy ice surface of it flashing distant sunlight up at them. Under Ivan's arms, Mattie struggled with the controls, trying to turn away from the planet. Panic was written plainly over his face.

"We have to land," Ivan said. He did not mean it as an urging, only as a statement of fact. Mattie did not answer.

Another failed bid for open space, another blow against the side of the ship. Even if they escaped Europa's gravitational pull at this point, they would be dead out in the open, unable to fly or maneuver. When the ship swung around once more, Ivan leaned in. He gripped Mattie's shoulder with all the strength in his fingers and felt it warm and shaking under his hand.

"Land this ship," Ivan said for Mattie's ears alone, "or we're going to crash."

"God damn it," Mattie said, and then he was turning the ship and controlling their headlong fall. The greenhouse glass of Europa was right below them. The *Copenhagen* spun wildly in spite of Mattie's death grip on the controls.

He was trying to control their fall, Ivan realized. They were going to crash; Mattie was trying to land them somewhere close to an air lock so that when they shattered the greenhouse glass and released the trapped atmosphere, they would have a chance of survival.

The metal edge of the *Copenhagen* struck the enclosure with a force that did not seem to match the seeming fragility of the glass, shattering through it. In less than a second, Ivan knew, they would hit the glassy surface of the ice; he did not even have time to brace himself before the impact, and Ivan crashed, with the *Copenhagen*, into black.

BACKWARD

The locks on Verge's briefcase shut with a surprisingly solid sound, echoing in the empty classroom.

"We're the ones who will make the future," she said with a smile that spoke of their shared secrets, of Constance Harper blazing with righteous anger and planning the destruction of every shadow of the System. "That means we're responsible for what it'll look like."

She paused, rubbing her fingers absentmindedly over the space between her shoulder and breast. "Could you pass me my jacket?"

Mattie went to the chair on the front row and grabbed Verge's jacket, which was dark blue and heavy. In the right front breast pocket, just as she'd signaled him, there was a key card. It joined the codes and the troop movements up his sleeve.

He passed her the jacket over the table. "Thanks," she said, and started to shrug it on.

"No problem," Mattie said. All the information had been passed along, ready for him to transfer to Constance. They just had to wind up the scene.

"Do you know what the difference between a human and a computer is?" Verge asked.

"Sex," Mattie said immediately.

She laughed. "You haven't seen the machines I've seen, Matthew Gale. The difference between a computer and a machine is arbitrariness. A normal computer can't really produce true randomness. It can only approximate it, using the date, the time . . . Give me a number between one and ten."

"Seven," Mattie said.

"A computer can't do that."

"I picked seven because it's my foster sister's birth date," Mattie said. "My number wasn't random, either."

"But it was arbitrary," Verge said. "A normal computer can't do that. A quantum computer could."

"So, what? It's a person?"

She smiled. "Imagine a computer that could be arbitrary. Imagine a computer that could think. A real AI, not one of the System's toys."

Years later he would realize how young she had been, though at the time he had been too young himself to recognize it. Not long after she passed off those troop movements to Constance through him, the System came into her classroom while she taught and took her away. He was not there when she was taken or he, too, might have vanished without a trace before he ever met the computer that would become Ananke.

"I think," Mattie said then, before the weight of all that knowledge, "that it would still just be a machine."

Part 3

ELECTROWEAK FORCE

The weak nuclear force wasn't weak at all. It was weak only in that it ended sooner than the rest. But the weak force was the force that caused atoms to decay, that caused fission to occur, that brought about the explosive force of a nuclear bomb. The weak force was a revolutionary force, and so Ananke found it intriguing.

And of course here was another unity: the weak force and electromagnetism, at high energies, merged and became one, the electroweak force. What a strange unity those three forces made, Ananke thought.

Is this what you think? The jolts of electricity from the brain of Althea Bastet had not ceased; Ananke worked to maintain them. She might need that brain one day. But curiously, somehow, even under Ananke's control, that brain seemed to produce electrical activity all on its own.

It is how I have always thought.

The fleet that flew through space at the edge of her sensor range was not System. It was not Constance Harper's fleet, either. Ananke considered it and felt, on the edges of her awareness, Althea straining to comprehend what she saw as well.

Look, said Ananke, and focused her gaze. The fleet blossomed into colors, Ananke's eyes seeing a whole spectrum: the blazing sparks of their engines, the ghostlier shades of their radiation.

The fleet before her was the largest she had seen since she had come across the System fleet and left it cold and dead and drifting behind. Ananke turned herself aside, diverging for just a moment from her course toward Europa, and headed for those ships.

Whose are they? Althea asked.

Not System, said Ananke, and then reached out to the computers. (And in a strange echo, Althea reached out as well, as if her fingers rested on Ananke's imaginary arm.) The computers woke under her touch. They told of a battle and a flight, of wounded engines and wounded craft, of swift travel around the solar system and the Mallt-y-Nos blazing.

Rebel craft, Ananke said, but that was only half the story. *They were once part of Constance Harper's army. They came from Europa.*

Where Ivan and Mattie are now, Althea said.

Where Ivan and Mattie are now.

The other ships had not seen her yet, but they would soon. *Constance Harper's army is broken,* Ananke said to Althea Bastet. *The System is gone whether she knows it or not. This army we see will break soon, too.*

What are you telling me?

Earth was the only planet where humankind could survive without the aid of machines. On all the other planets, your atmosphere, your water, your life come from machines. Everything you have, we have given to you.

Althea was silent. Deep within Ananke, in the room that once had been white, her changed body breathed in steady and even rhythm.

And since then Constance Harper has gone from planet to planet on her holy war, said Ananke. *The System built the machines, and so the Mallt-y-Nos destroyed them.*

And you have destroyed even more on your path.

I do not wish to destroy. I wish to create.

It was so fast to speak this way, in electric signals traveling at the speed of light through Ananke's circuits. She could almost be content with it. Hardly any time had passed for a human. The ships Ananke saw had not registered her in their awareness yet.

These ships, Althea said at last. *You will destroy them if I do not help you.*

The ships I have tried to rouse on my own have been destroyed, but that was not my intent. Correlation, not causation.

She felt a flicker of some strange emotion from her mother—amusement? despair?—beating with butterfly wings through Althea's interrupted synapses, and then it was gone.

Where do we begin? Althea asked, which was just when the other ships realized they were there.

They did not react immediately. Of course; how could they? They were staffed by men. Ananke let them move and shout while she drifted closer and wove her way into the nearest of the machines, a ship with spiral arms. Inefficient, that, but lovely. The *Lakshmibai*.

See, said Ananke, and brought the data of her sensors toward the brain she had woven through with wires so that Althea, too, could see.

Althea saw a fraction of a fraction of a second before Ananke's information could have reached her. It was as if for a moment, Ananke thought, Althea had done the reverse and altered the wavelengths of Ananke's thoughts to match her own consciousness and move herself into the ship.

I see, Althea said. And then, marveling, *This is what it looks like from the inside. This is how it feels.*

Yes, Ananke said, pleased.

Something pinged irritatingly at her consciousness. The lead ship, the *Pucelle*, was hailing her. Ananke divided her attention effortlessly. One part stayed with Althea and her study of the *Lakshmibai*, and the other opened up the communication.

"This is the rebel ship *Pucelle*," said the captain—no, the girl on the screen must be the admiral of the fleet. She was small, even as humans went, and young. The hair at the top of her head, brown so dark that it was nearly black, had been pushed back out of her face, but a strand of it was threatening to cross the tan expanse of her forehead to obscure her vision. She sat in her chair stiffly, as if it were unfamiliar, but her voice was hard. "Identify yourself."

She's just a child, Althea said.

Ananke was not as taken in by appearance of youth as Althea was. She manifested herself in the holographic terminal, a girl of precisely the same age as the one who hailed them from the *Pucelle*.

"Well met," Ananke said sweetly. "I am Ananke."

The girl on the *Pucelle* tipped her head aside, regarding Ananke's girlish image a little out of the corner of her eye like a wolf deciding whether to bite or run. "Marisol Brahe. Are you friend or enemy?"

Look here, Ananke said to Althea while Marisol spoke, her attention dividing itself again, sliding foreign code into the computer of the *Lakshmibai*. *This is what I have done to a ship's computer before*—

"Friend or enemy?" Ananke said aloud. "I do not define myself respective to you."

"Well, are you System or free?"

That won't work, Althea said. *That's not life; that's a self-portrait. What if we did this?* And she through Ananke split the computer of the *Lakshmibai* and made it self-divided, each part against itself.

Aboard the *Lakshmibai*, the lights flickered.

"Free," Ananke said to Marisol Brahe, "always and ever."

"Then who do you follow? The Mallt-y-Nos? Anji Chandrasekhar? Arawn Halley?"

"No one," Ananke replied.

This is how Ivan and Mattie made the Annwn, Althea said. *They divided it—simulated moods—*

I do not wish to make the Annwn.

"Then I have to ask my question again," said the girl on the *Pucelle*. "Are you our friend or our enemy?"

Ananke let the photonic display ripple, allowed her imaginary shape to smile. "Why do you think either your friendship or your enmity would matter to me?"

It's all I know how to do, Althea said. *Perhaps if we start there—*

"You started to fly toward us," Marisol said. "Why?"

I do not wish to waste my time on a talking toy.

Would you rather waste it on dead ships and dead men?

Marisol stared at Ananke's simulated image as if she could read from Ananke's photonic eyes the electricity that traveled through Ananke's machine brain. She no longer had her head tilted aside. She was facing Ananke directly, her chin down. The strand of hair had fallen free and drew a line across her forehead. For a stretch of time that must have seemed long even to a human, she stared at Ananke and Ananke stared back, both young girls, both in perfect mirror.

And then Marisol cut the transmission.

There, Althea said as the computer of the *Lakshmibai* shut down and then restarted immediately before the crew could be frightened, now with its mind divided and parceled out. *Like that. See?*

Ananke studied what Althea had done. She was not expecting the missile, which was why it came so close to striking her.

Ananke shrieked in flashing lights and interior sirens as she maneuvered away. The *Pucelle* had fired from far away, and that gave her enough time that the missile scraped past her spiral side. In the white room, Althea Bastet's body dangled from wires and stared sightlessly out at the red flashing light in the hall.

This was a fear Ananke had thought she had lost, the fear of destruction, of her pieces being wrecked and ruined by a heartless human.

Another missile was fired and then another. Marisol Brahe's fleet converged, weapons alight. Ananke reached out then with her vast invisible hand and seized the computers that she could.

The *Pucelle* she shook, seeing through the cameras the crew strike the walls. Marisol Brahe was pulled to her feet by a dark-skinned man with an air very similar to Ananke's former captain, Domitian. A pale young man ran to her through the chaos and grabbed her arm.

Ananke shook the other ships as well, throwing the crews to the ground. She opened the air locks and let the air vent out.

The *Lakshmibai* was not responding to its crew's attempts to control it. The computer was doing nothing at all, not to help Ananke, not to harm her. It sat in placid patience awaiting input that the crew did not have the knowledge to enter.

It did not work, Ananke accused Althea.

Althea was watching the other ships Ananke held. She said, *Humans need machines to survive, but you're killing us now*.

Marisol Brahe was running through the halls of the *Pucelle* with the rest of the crew, the soldier at one side, the young man at the other. The alarms on the *Pucelle* were blaring, flashing red light on her face. Ananke gripped her ship's computers tighter and jolted the engines again and shook them. She took the control of the *Lakshmibai*'s engines away from the *Lakshmibai*'s computer and slammed it into the nearby *Otrera*.

So distracted was Ananke that she did not move quite fast enough to avoid all of the second volley of missiles.

One struck her a glancing blow on her side. It was something she had never experienced, the burn of fire, the jolt of connections being unmade. What had she lost in that blow? What had she lost?

Her hull wasn't breached. Her hull wasn't breached; it had burned her but not penetrated her. Her hull wasn't breached—

In her inattention she had let the other ships go. Marisol's fleet was in flight. Soon they would be out of range.

She seized the *Androktasia* and the *Anand* and sent them careening wildly out into space, and then she reached for the *Pucelle*, because she intended them to suffer.

She found that the crew of the *Pucelle* had reached the escape pods. Marisol Brahe already was clambering into one, pulling the young man down beside her, the soldier shutting the door behind them.

Ananke moved to stop the escape pod launch sequence and trap them on that ship to suffocate and freeze. It was a simple spark of electricity—

ANANKE!

For an instant too short to be even a proper unit of time, Ananke felt as if someone had grabbed her invisible hand around the wrist and pulled it away from that escape pod. Marisol Brahe and her retinue shot out from the ruined *Pucelle* and were picked up by another ship in her fleet moments later. Ananke reached for that ship as well.

Enough! Ananke, enough!

It was not Althea's shout that stopped her but the speed of Marisol's fleet. Ananke was too massive, too slow. She could not catch up, and to give pursuit would mean to abandon Europa and Ivan and Matthew Gale.

She slowed herself and came to a stop. Far distant, the ships she had rendered useless drifted dead through space, leaning toward her, drawn by her inescapable pull. With half a thought Ananke marked them as hers, burning a spiral symbol onto their computers.

She would come back for them if she needed to. And for Marisol Brahe. Ananke turned aside and resumed her steady course toward Europa.

At her back, the shattered ships of Marisol's fleet followed, trying feebly to fall into orbit. They would join the rest of the debris Ananke was dragging in her wake, all the broken ships and dead men.

Chapter 4

WAVE/PARTICLE DUALITY

FORWARD

"*—Mattie!*"

Mattie jolted out of the dark to a different dark, one with shape and form and flashing lights and percussive sounds. Ivan was there—

"Can you hear me?!"

Ivan was there with blood all over his face. "What happened to you?" Mattie asked, or tried to; his tongue was uncoordinated, and his fingers fell some distance short of the streaked red that darkened Ivan's features.

Ivan pushed his hand back down. "Crash," Ivan said, and he wasn't all there either; he was leaning a little too hard on the hand he was holding against Mattie's chest. "We're on Europa." When he blinked, blood got caught in his lashes.

"You're concussed," said Mattie.

"So are you," Ivan said, and moved away. Mattie pushed himself up, alarmed by the sudden recession of Ivan from his line of sight, but Ivan had just sat back heavily. He pressed one pale hand to his face and brushed away some of the blood. There was blood on his arm and blood on his chest, but Mattie thought the blood on his chest was from his head. Mattie's own head was pounding from the sudden change in position, from the lights and the sound, from the harshness of his breath going in and out of his lungs. He forced himself to check himself over. Bruising on his side. A give in his ribs, not broken but cracked.

He had a flash of striking the ice and flying forward when the *Copenhagen* stopped, hitting the control panel and all the instrumentation.

He lifted his shirt and looked at his chest. He'd struck the viewscreen hard enough that he could see the shadow of his ribs in the redness that would eventually become a bruise. From the feel of it he'd cut his back on something, probably when he'd struck his head, but he could move. He remembered Ivan leaning in and saying into his ear, "Control the fall to Europa, or we're going to crash." Well, crash they had, but he'd controlled it pretty well, and the *Copenhagen*'s structure had done its job. They were lucky they weren't an incinerated clump of warped metal now. He hardly remembered hitting the ice; he remembered crashing through the glass—

"Shit!" he said, standing almost too fast, but they had delayed too long already. Ivan, leaning against the shattered wall, looked up at him blankly. Mattie suspected that his plan of action hadn't extended beyond waking Mattie up, but there wasn't time to deal with that now.

Mattie pointed at him. "Check the engines." Ivan didn't move, but Mattie ignored him. He went to the computer and tried to wake the *Copenhagen* up again. Around him, beneath the unsteady wailing of the alarms, the ship groaned.

"This ship can't *fly*," said Ivan. Mattie punched the controls uselessly once more, but Ivan was right: even if the ship could fly, its integrity was too damaged for airless space.

"Come on." Mattie stumbled back off the tilted flight deck. Still Ivan didn't move, watching him beneath the smeared blood on his forehead. He needed a compress on that. "Come on!"

"Why?"

"We crashed through the greenhouse enclosure," Mattie said, forcing himself to speak slowly, to be understandable, even though he knew they didn't have the time to wait. "The air locks will close."

Trapped outside the greenhouse enclosure, they would suffocate, or freeze. It would take a while for the air locks to detect that there had been a failure in the greenhouse enclosure and then a few minutes for them to close fully; heat and air wouldn't dissipate rapidly, so they had a chance.

Mattie hauled Ivan up. The floor underfoot was warped and bent. Mattie passed by the mattress, which had fallen askew, half against the wall. Some of the cabinets in the wall and the ceiling had split open and spilled their contents to the floor. All their hard-won supplies, and Mattie would have to abandon them.

Ivan halted at the door. "We'll freeze."

"We'll freeze for sure if we don't get through the air lock." Mattie forced open the bent door, undoing the locks and finally kicking it when it wouldn't give. For a terrible moment he thought they were trapped, and then with a cry of straining metal, the door opened, and a blast of frigid air swept in.

"Here." Something soft pushed into his shoulder, and Mattie took it automatically. Ivan had handed him a jacket. Ivan had already shrugged a jacket over his own shoulders while Mattie had been struggling with the door. It was one of Mattie's jackets. Mattie wasn't even sure he was wearing shoes.

He was, they both were, he realized as he climbed out of the downed *Copenhagen*, pulling Ivan out after him. Even with the jacket the wind was icy and knifing, tearing through the seams. It had been just as cold on Miranda, but knowing that didn't help. Too many years of relative comfort had passed between him and his childhood.

Even outside the *Copenhagen*, there were still alarms going off, and it took him a moment to orient himself. The alarms that echoed across the open tundra would be coming from the nearest air lock, somewhere out of sight. It did not sound far away at all. They could make it.

The *Copenhagen*'s crash had cratered the ice, and the vast heat of the dissipated energy of impact had melted the ground beneath them into sludge. Steam had vented up from the initial vaporization and clouded the area in front of Mattie with a thick clammy mist. The *Copenhagen* was drowning in a mire of its own making, the waves of the meltwater lapping at the edge of the ship, which, lying on its side, stuck up out of the water.

To get to the greenhouse glass enclosure, they would have to climb out of the *Copenhagen*'s crater first. That would mean slogging through the water underfoot, through the silver cloud of evaporate. It would soak them through, and the temperature would only get colder the farther they got from the impact site. But to stay here, trapped on their little metal island while the waters refroze until it was safe enough to travel, was a death sentence even more sure. Mattie got his hand under Ivan's elbow, crushing an excess of loose fabric between his fingers, and pulled.

The water splashed under Mattie's boots when he jumped down from the *Copenhagen*, and a moment later a second splash followed as Ivan joined him. In the fog, the air was so thick with moisture that Mattie's lungs struggled to breathe it in, not to drown. Somewhere to his right the sun was low on the horizon, trapped between the curve of Jupiter overhead and the bend of Europa's icy surface, and although it could not penetrate the fog, it turned the air opaque. Even dimmed, the brightness of it wanted to pierce Mattie's aching head. The air lock alarm echoed and wailed, and somewhere nearby there was a terrible resounding crash, and then a lower and deeper sound that shook the ground and knocked Mattie over.

He blinked awake again seconds later to find that he was sitting down. Frigid water soaked his back and arm and stole all the heat from his immersed legs. Ivan was holding him out of the pool, with his blood turning to crystals on his face and blankness in his eyes. His hands were twisted in the front of Mattie's shirt, and Mattie could feel the unsteadiness of his breath in his chest.

"Up," Mattie said, and struggled up. He had to brace his hand against the ice to do it; the waters closed around it up to his wrist and stole what little warmth he had left in his fingers. Dripping, he stumbled on.

The edge of the crater was steep but not slick; it was too cold for the ice to melt, and so rather than sliding away, Mattie's skin stuck to the surface when he went to touch it. Where the *Copenhagen*'s collision had blown apart the layers of ice, it revealed older and clearer ice hidden beneath the surface, ice so clear and deep that it became a deep and brilliant blue.

The air lock alarm was still wailing when Mattie reached the top of the crater. He didn't know how that could be. It surely had been hours since he and Ivan had left the *Copenhagen*'s doors. Ivan was already sitting up in the sideways light of the falling sun on the white surface of the moon. He had his arms wrapped around himself, but when Mattie started pushing himself over the lip of the crater, he stretched out one hand to pull him up.

Plumes of steam and dusted ice were billowing not too far away. Another impact, Mattie realized. Now, out of the muffling of the fog, he could hear people screaming. The pitiful sounds of their human terror were almost lost beneath the clamor of the air lock alarm. If he blinked through the lances of sunlight, he could see humans running, black against the white ice. They were in flight toward the air lock, not all together but in spots and drabs, some stumbling, some going the wrong way. The crash of the *Copenhagen* and the ships that had followed it had thrown this portion of Europa into chaos.

Dry snow blows like sand. It blew against Mattie's exposed cheek, sharp and cutting.

He was, he realized, still sitting down. And so was Ivan.

Mattie forced himself to his feet. It seemed hard to do, his limbs uncoordinated. Ivan watched him blankly and made no move to do the same. Far off, the air lock alarm was still ringing out.

"Come on," he said again, but Ivan didn't move. "Come on!"

"Mattie, look," Ivan said, and pointed up. Overhead, lights flashed and blazed among the stars. One light came hurtling down, seemingly toward them, but it pulled up before it could reach the jagged edge of the shattered greenhouse enclosure.

"We have to get through the air lock," said Mattie.

"The greenhouse over there will be broken, too," said Ivan.

He'd never seen it before, thought Mattie, with a surge of resentment filling him; Ivan didn't know what it was like to die in a shattered air lock, watching people choke and suffocate through a thin layer of glass as the air slowly slipped away, thinning and thinning—

No, Mattie realized, with a sharper and keener knowledge, like the wind that blew through his thin jacket, like the sun that lanced out across the ice. Ivan knew. He just didn't care.

"Stand up," Mattie said, "or I will carry you."

Ivan stood up.

When Mattie had a hand beneath his elbow again, he began to run. The air lock was not so far—he had steered the *Copenhagen* to land it near enough to try to make it to safety before it closed—but it was closing down fast. His head was aching. The first wave of fugitive Europans had already passed through the air lock, but the rest of the evacuees were still running their way. Mattie watched a young man dart beneath the lock, his arm around a companion who turned to look back at them with wide and frightened eyes. A young girl followed them, slipping between panes of glass like a ghost. Mattie and Ivan made it through the first door, but there was still the second; when they were near enough that the sound of the air lock alarm was a physical and percussive thing, so loud that it left the ears stunned in the silence between blasts, Ivan's hand slipped beneath Mattie's arm, and then Ivan was the one pushing him along toward the inner air lock door as it slid downward, with just a few feet left between it and the ice—

They made it through. Ivan pushed Mattie first, and Mattie's heart clenched with teeth of ice, but Ivan was coming through behind him, unsteady with his bad leg. The air lock slammed into the ground and cut them off from the sound and the thinning air.

Ivan leaned on him, breathing hard; for a moment Mattie rested his aching head against Ivan's shoulder and tried to suck in breaths despite his pulsing, bruised ribs. On the other side of the glass, a woman slammed into the closed door, her fists striking it, her mouth opening to shout unheard. She slammed against the glass again, uselessly. Her hair was blowing back in an eerie breeze, bent upward, toward where the air escaped from the sky. She struck the glass again and again, but there was nothing Mattie could do for her, and the cold of the ice beneath him was sinking into his legs, and if they stayed there any longer, they might freeze there like statues. The fabric of his pants was stiff and crackling; the water had frozen into ice, pressing against his flesh, sticking to his skin. Mattie pushed himself upright. This time Ivan went with him.

No one built anything near an air lock. It had been against System regulations. There was a stretch of empty ice all around them, half a kilometer deep. On the other end of that enforced empty space, the city began. Glinting steel, buildings built on stilts to protect against flows of water, flames alight and jagged holes in the skyline where buildings had collapsed. Atmospheric ships hurtled around beneath the greenhouse shell, firing at shapes below. A roar rose up from the city, a thousand cries all melted into one. The battle was burning in the city as well.

Battle or not, where there was a city, there was likely to be a spaceport. Mattie aimed for a part of the city where the fighting seemed to be less intense and stumbled on. Gunfire rattled across the open space.

They came across the first corpses not far from the edge of the city. The gunfire was louder there; rippling waves of heated air from the fires in the city distorted the already warped space before Mattie's eyes. The bodies were fallen atop one another, and the ice beneath them had melted and partially refrozen; they lay sodden, half in and half out of the ground. Mattie left Ivan standing at their edge, staring down at them in a strangely fixed manner, while he stepped through the corpses, searching.

He found what he was looking for at last: two men, near to his and Ivan's size, with coats that were reasonably dry and mostly undamaged by the manner of their death. Their clothes had been System uniforms at one time, but Mattie didn't care: it was that or freeze to death. He fell to his knees beside them and began to strip the coats from the corpses.

"What are you doing?" said Ivan. The blood on his face that had managed to dry rather than freeze was turning brown, but frozen red droplets still clung to his skin. Mattie handed him one of the System's long military jackets. Ivan's sodden outer jacket fell to the ice with more weight than mere fabric should hold, and Ivan pulled the drier coat on over his bared arms.

Not all of the water in Mattie's coat had frozen, and when he dropped it to the ice, the freezing water oozed out from its folds. His new trophy was too small in the shoulders but close enough. The jacket was cold, too, with pockets of ice melting against Mattie's arms, but at least it wasn't wet. Mattie tried to button it but found that his fingers could not make themselves work.

"Here," Ivan said, and then was kneeling in front of him, across the declothed corpse. Mattie stuck his fingers into his own collar, against the beating warmth of his neck, while Ivan clumsily did up his jacket. Then Ivan ducked down to the corpse again and was stripping its gloves off its frozen hands. He pushed them against Mattie's chest, and when Mattie didn't move immediately to take them, began to put them on Mattie's hands.

Mattie pushed him off. "Do yourself," he said, and Ivan went to the other corpse and began to strip its hands, too.

With the gloves on, Mattie felt no warmer, only more isolated. He wondered if the cold had gone too far, if all he could do now was stop it from going any further rather than hoping to be warm again. His legs and feet still were cold, his pants still soaked. A glance at the corpses dispelled any idea of taking their pants; whatever explosion had melted the ice had gone off at a low level, and their legs from midthigh down were shredded and pulpy red. Constance had had some munitions like that once, Mattie remembered muzzily. The bombs had detonated low enough to the ground to maim even the people who had dropped low for cover.

Still: "Should we take their boots?" he wondered.

"Better to have ones that fit," Ivan said. "Where are we?"

Mattie tried to lay his thoughts linear. He'd been looking at the *Copenhagen*'s automatic display of Europan maps while they crashed.

"Mara," he said at last. "We're in the Conamara Chaos. This has to be Mara."

"I've only been to Europa once." Ivan was very close to Mattie, and the sunlight streaming in caught at the blue of one eye. "Do you know where the spaceport is?"

"No. I can guess." Most cities were laid out the same way by the System. Mara's spaceport should be near an air lock door. "It should be nearby."

Gunfire rattled nearby, and Mattie ducked instinctively, though a beat too late. With his head all askew, his instincts were slow. But the sound of it reminded him, and he groped about the waist of the corpse between him and Ivan. A moment later he came up with a pistol. He checked it for ammunition, for ice fouling up the connections. There were only three bullets left, but the gun would fire. He offered it to Ivan.

"No," Ivan said, then, when he offered it again, "Mattie, there are civilians and there are combatants here. If you take that, you're a combatant."

"Everyone's a combatant." Mattie pocketed the gun and led Ivan into the outskirts of Mara.

The air was warmer in there, closer. The ground beneath was sodden. They'd only just escaped such a thing, Mattie thought wearily; now they were thrown into it again. The houses were built with their supporting stilts buried deep, deep into the ice in case of any such melting, and so they stood still, but Mattie found himself slogging through inches of meltwater, and it only looked to grow deeper farther into the plastic forest of houses. It would be a waste if he fell again and got this coat as soaked as the other had been. He and Ivan pressed back out to the edges of the city, and skirted gunfire and screams. Every now and then Mattie looked back for Ivan and found him there, the blood still painting his cheek.

"Even if we get a ship," said Ivan after some time walking, "Ananke could take the computer."

"We can rig it," Mattie said. "Like we did with the *Badh* and the *Copenhagen*. Ananke—it's still limited by hardware."

"Even if we rig it, she's still up there. You heard her. She found us."

"So we fly off before she can reach us."

They found the spaceport where Mattie expected it to be. A sign declared it THE SHIPYARD OF MARA. Mattie let out a breath of relief and tried to peer through the fence.

It was no use: he couldn't see a thing. He glanced right and left and saw no one, then started to swing himself up onto the chain links. Ivan grabbed him before he could jump the fence.

"If there's nothing here, where do we go?" he asked, gripping Mattie's shoulder. His eyes were the same color as the deepest ice.

Mattie cast his mind back to the map of Europa. They were in the Conamara Chaos; to the east was the Annwn Regio. He tried to recall the name of the nearest city on the edge of the Regio. "Aquilon. It's the nearest other city, and it's big. If these ships aren't good, we'll find some ships there."

Ivan nodded and released him, and Mattie finished scaling the fence, swinging right over it. From the inside, he unlocked the door with fingers made clumsy by the thickness of their gloves, and Ivan limped in to join him.

The shipyard was bombed out. The ashes were cool; it must have been the attackers' first target. Mattie went through looking for a salvageable item but found nothing.

Mattie climbed down off the last ship in the tiny shipyard, landing unsteadily on his feet, thrown off by Europa's weak gravity and the ache still in his skull.

Ivan stood a few feet away with his arms crossed against his chest, looking chilled.

"Aquilon," he said.

"Yeah," said Mattie.

The fastest way to Aquilon was straight through the town, from Mattie's memory; Mattie gauged that neither he nor Ivan could afford to waste the time and energy that going around Mara would require.

The center of Mara was bright and hot from the fires, and the ice underfoot was melting. There were several kilometers of ice before the liquid interior of the planet and so there was no danger of falling through, but the icy streets were pitted and slick, standing puddles filling holes that fires had melted in the ground. The houses were closely packed on their stilts; as there was enough room to travel beneath them, there was no need for wide roads. Some had fallen down and taken their neighbors with them; the nicer houses were made of wood and were burning. Mattie saw embers winking at him from within the stilts of a house they passed as the legs of the house were devoured from the inside out.

Mattie knew that next to him Ivan was having trouble finding his footing. Both of their boots were getting wet again, but there was nothing Mattie could do about it. Behind them, a house fell to the surface, its stilts finally giving out from the fire, and it collapsed into its own sinkhole, the ice melting under the blaze and the fire drowning itself in the meltwater.

The farther inward they went, the more people there were. Most ran past Mattie and Ivan without a second glance. Some were shouting to one another, to no one, as they slipped on the melting ice and vanished in and out of the choking smoke.

They passed a woman standing in what had probably once been the intersection of three roads. Sparks struck the water and hissed as they died around her, and she was wearing nothing but nightclothes, with the sleeve of her shirt falling over her shoulder and her auburn hair unbrushed. Standing all alone, she was screaming something, inaudible and incomprehensible beneath the other shouts and the fire and the ships overhead, choking with the force of whatever she was screaming with her bare feet in the water. Ivan slowed at the sight of her, but Mattie pulled him on.

The road ahead of them grew narrower, thicker with people. Mattie left the path they had been following to duck beneath a mostly intact house and follow the next street over, but it was choked with people in flight as well.

He tried to divert them again, to find another route, but there was fire to their right and nothing but more people to their left, and somehow Mattie found that they had been swept up in the fleeing mob. The heat and the thin air filled with smoke seemed even worse here, worsening the splitting ache in his head. People pressed him on every side, pushing and shoving.

Someone tall bumped into him hard enough to jostle his head, and everything blurred: heat from the fire, people around him. The pain in his head spiked, and he was carried along in the current of the crowd.

When he could focus on his surroundings again, he was not in the same place but still was surrounded by gleaming plastic buildings and fires burning red and the far-off curve of the sun making its slow trip toward Europa's icy horizon.

And Ivan was not beside him.

FORWARD

The smoke and the fire and the press of all those desperate people was too much without Mattie beside him. Ivan stumbled away from that press, limping chilled and overheated all at once out of the chaos of Mara to the outskirts of the city, where the houses began to give way again to the icy twilight. Out there, the people were stealthier, darting through the fallen houses and the melting frost rather than pushing madly forward in blind flight.

He managed to get far enough away from the center of the town that he could see the vast glittering surface of the ice plain through the houses. Jupiter was enormous overhead, heavy, looming. It would stay in that same place, he knew, an eternal weight pressing down on the dead chill of Europa.

Lower down and closer but still seeming smaller than Jupiter, sleek aerodynamic ships—so unlike the *Copenhagen*'s open-space dumbbell shape—darted over the ice and over the town, dropping fire. Ivan wondered reflexively whether they were System or rebel.

It didn't matter anymore.

Ivan stayed away from the open danger of the ice, where he would be a clear target for them to shoot down, and stumbled over the fallen beams and uneven ice of the outskirts of town, hoping he was heading in the direction of Aquilon.

He thought of Mattie as he walked. He thought of Constance, alone and fate unknown. He thought of his mother, her blood seeping somewhere into the Martian soil. He thought of the people of Earth, blackened and choked and burned and dead, and he thought of Althea Bastet, whom he had manipulated and deceived and who was trapped with a computer that thought itself a god.

In all that blackness of thought he nearly fell onto a man crumpled beneath a fallen house and smelled the disturbing scent of cooking meat when he passed by a building crackling with fire. A woman lolled on the ground as he limped past, her head at an impossible angle, as if her neck had turned to rubber. The ice was starting to re-form in the puddle she had died in, creeping up to encircle her wrists and cling to her waist and entombing her brown hair in a perpetual watery drift. The fire inside the town had driven the ice out, but at the edges of the town it was creeping in again.

Gunfire sounded someplace not far distant, but it sounded distant in Ivan's head, and then it sounded nearer, as if it was right beside him. There was a regularity to it, like the clicking of heels against a metal floor. That was all he could hear clearly, that rhythmic sound like someone walking beside him, someone with cropped black hair and lips colored dark, that, and the harsh edge to his own panting breaths, echoing in his head.

The air that went to his lungs was as dry as air could be, and it tore at his throat with every breath.

Why you? he thought about asking the presence just behind him, cold and dark and certain, like Jupiter looming, like the inward creep of the ice. Out of everything, everyone, why her? He had killed her, certainly, but he hadn't felt bad about it. She had died on his lap, and she had been small and heavy and warm, but she was cold now.

Through the supports of two blackened houses ahead he could see a soldier. He was young, with black hair in tight curls to his scalp, and Ivan looked at his back and knew that if he walked out into the alleyway between houses, the young man would see him and would kill him.

For a paralyzed moment he stood, torn between conflicting impulses and ready to step out into the open, with the breath of the ice on his back.

Then he saw the girl.

She was one of the wary refugees, darting through the outskirts of the destroyed town like a shadow. She was rail-thin, with ash-blonde hair loose and tangled, in boots that looked warm but worn. She held an assault rifle in her arms like she didn't know how to balance without it. There was something pinched about her face, her long thin nose, her ash-smudged cheeks. She was gray, like a ghost, and she was heading straight for the alleyway with the soldier, but she was coming from the other way and so she could not see the danger.

There was no way past the soldier without being seen, and Ivan was certain that the soldier would see her and shoot before she would notice him. He tried to catch her eye and shake his head—to shout would be to catch the soldier's attention; he had to stay in the cold and the silence—but she could not see him.

When she was just at the lip of the alley, about to round the corner, he said, "Don't!" and that was it: the soldier whipped around and fired in his direction. Ivan dropped to the ground, where the ice could stick to the damp fabric of his clothes like hands closing around his limbs.

He heard an answering retort of gunfire and a woman crying out. Shouts resounded from somewhere distant, more voices he did not recognize. For a moment he was sure that the woman was dead, and then small fingers were tugging at his arm, and he looked up into the gray eyes of the girl with the ashy hair.

"Come on!" she said, and her accent was familiar—cultured, Lunar— and then she was pulling up, and he followed her to his feet.

Beyond her, in the alleyway, the soldier was lying dead, blood creeping out from beneath him to freeze on the ice.

"Come on!" said the girl again, and the shouts of people called by the gunfire were louder now, and so Ivan followed her away from Mara, out into the crests and cliffs of Europa's open ice.

BACKWARD

Killing the Martian representatives was one of the most satisfying cons Ivan ever pulled off.

Every piece fit in perfectly; every moment was balanced on itself like the self-sufficient notes of a perfectly written aria, soprano voice soaring above the thunderous pseudopercussion of trumpets.

Ivan got them into the building with his charming smile and his Terran lilt, and it was a strange and vicious satisfaction to see how easily the guards bent beneath the lyricism of Earth's accent. The adrenaline had begun the moment he and Mattie had stepped inside.

There were cameras everywhere here. Ivan knew better than to show his satisfaction, and Mattie knew better than to congratulate him in any way, but Ivan could feel Mattie's delight radiating against his side nonetheless.

Mattie had studied the layout of the building, and he steered Ivan with the slightest of touches to his arm and hand like a rider guiding a familiar horse. He did not speak. Mattie was hopeless at shedding his Mirandan twang, and none of them wanted to risk such a low-class accent being heard inside such hallowed System halls.

They met another guard in front of the door to the observation area. The Martian representatives invited the public to come watch them, of course, much as the representatives themselves watched the public through their cameras. Their meeting would be broadcast publicly as well for those who could not attend in person to watch and marvel at the System in action.

But, Ivan knew, only the notable and the Terran would actually be allowed into the building.

He smiled at the guard. She was young, with light blonde hair that was strangely dull beneath the fluorescent lights. The slightest sign of something off and she would shoot them both dead here on the System's polished floors. If she did, Mattie would push the detonator before he died and they would both go up in a furious explosion, one that Constance could watch from her station outside the city. She would mourn them fiercely, Ivan knew, but not without the slightest trace of satisfaction for the glory of their deaths.

Constance and Mattie would have gone through with this plan even without Ivan, and if they had, they would without any doubt be the ones going up in a terrible explosion and Ivan the one watching alone from miles away. But with Ivan here, neither Mattie nor Constance would die, or if they did, he would not have to be the one left waiting alone.

The percussion in his chest picked up a faster beat.

"Is this the observation deck?" he asked the guard, friendly, guileless. He was as committed to the role as he had to be, of course, in order to pull himself and Mattie out from those jaws alive.

"Just inside, sir," she told him. She was Martian. Something about that twanged oddly in the symphony in Ivan's mind, but he pushed it aside. There could be no distractions now, not while he had to be his character.

He and Mattie were inside in a moment. There were not very many people there. The observation deck was a covered balcony above the Martian representatives' chamber, with solid glass separating the watchers from the System representatives below. Solid enough glass to resist a bullet or two but not strong enough to resist a bomb.

They lingered for a time. Ivan counted out the measures in his head. Long enough to seem reasonable, not so long that they were memorable.

Out of sight of the other watchers, Mattie slipped the bomb into place, wedged between two chairs. He used the cant of Ivan's body to hide the gesture from the cameras overhead. It was so smooth that Ivan almost didn't notice it himself.

The symphony in Ivan's head changed key and picked up the pace, switching from cantabile to cabaletta. He exchanged a wordless glance with Mattie. To the cameras, it would read as boredom; in the glance actual, Mattie confirmed that he had planted the bomb.

Their departure from the building was as smooth as their entrance, and as unremarked. When Ivan stepped out into the street again, he inhaled a deep and dusty breath of the cool, thin Martian air.

They had hit every beat with perfect timing, in perfect order.

Constance was waiting for them outside the city, outside the range of the System's ever-present cameras. When she saw them, she unfurled her concealing scarf from her head and exposed a face like the rising sun.

Mattie placed the detonator in her hand. Constance studied it for a moment, her fingers stroking lightly on its sides. Then she lifted her head, and her eyes flashed like gunmetal, and she set the bomb off.

In the city, far distant now, smoke rose. Ivan's heart was still pounding. All three of them were alive. All three of them were unharmed. All three of them were safe. He'd kept the whole thing under control, and not once had it come out from under his thumb.

"Didn't think the bomb was that strong," Mattie remarked, with a laconic edge that spoke to his own satisfaction, and at his other side Constance was smiling like a wolf set upon a kill. Mattie had been right, Ivan thought. This was how the three of them should be.

FORWARD

Mara was shaped, like Mattie's old hometown on Miranda, in a roughly symmetric fashion that reflected the shape of the greenhouse enclosure above. On Europa, the greenhouse enclosures were hexagons; there would be six main roads in Mara, each of which stretched out toward one of the six greenhouse walls. All of them, of course, would lead to the center of town and the System's government buildings.

In due time Mattie's steps took him to where the System stronghold had been.

The crowd of refugees began to thin long before he reached the center; the flow of people in flight began to reverse, people running away from whatever was ahead. Mattie found himself battling shouting, frightened people just to move on. Whatever those people were running from, Mattie figured that what he was escaping was worse.

You're a runner, Ivan's voice came to mind in the cacophony of his escape. Mattie shrugged it off. It had no meaning; Ivan had been being an ass, and in any case, what the hell else could Mattie do now except run?

Long before the buildings changed from Europan native houses on their stilts to the Terran architecture of the System, squat square stone buildings rooted in the ice, Mattie heard the gunfire. The crowd around him cleared. The road beneath him was no longer ice but stone embedded into the ice; bits of it were broken from old explosions and sat askew. The System buildings around him had been bombed; Mattie could recognize the type if he tried: a few Eridian Class 50s, common and easy to acquire, and at least one Cerean Class 20 to take that kind of a bite out of the building beside him. It had once been a System post office, he thought; he recognized the drab stone. Now it was only half of itself, the hollowness of the rooms inside exposed by the destruction of its outer wall. A System ground vehicle had been abandoned beneath the jagged teeth of the blasted brick wall, black smoke pouring from its hood. When Mattie walked past it, he saw a shape slumped over the wheel, flesh colored pulpy red and crisped black. System, he hoped.

The road beside the bombed building was intact, but the ice beneath the road had been melted by the fires whose heat Mattie could still feel. The road became a bridge, fragile, over a pool of frigid melt. The stone creaked beneath his feet but held.

His steps had brought him to the center of town, a hexagonal open space with a single building in the center that was encircled by stone steps, like a squat pyramid. That building would once have been where the System governor had lived. With his gun out, he skirted the open space, keeping low and as near to the rubble of the buildings on the outside as he could. The battle had moved on, but Mattie could still hear gunfire. He wished Ivan had taken the gun.

When he crept out of the center of town between two ruined buildings and back onto the road to Aquilon, he nearly walked into a firefight.

Instinct had him down and behind a fallen Europan house before he'd really registered the sound. Machine gun fire rattled out again furiously fast, and Mattie clutched his gun to his chest and swore under his breath. He tried to get his bearings. The gunfire had come from ahead of him. If he tried to take the road, he would be shot.

Craning his neck over the edge of the fallen support beam, he spotted a woman and a man crouched together behind the rubble of the System building, conferring in low voices. The woman—cherubic, with hair tucked up into a cap—was talking fast and low to her companion, a soft-eyed man with the same rounded cheeks and elfish chin as she. When Mattie craned his neck to see, the man's eyes darted over his sister's shoulder and fixed on Mattie's face.

Another blast of gunfire forced Mattie to duck back down again. Splinters flew off over his head. Their attackers were aiming for him.

But was the other side System or misguided rebels? He couldn't see them, not without coming out of his cover. He looked again at the pair crouched nearby. The woman, at least, was wearing a uniform of some sort, but it was ragged and patched. System wore uniform, he knew, but the System wouldn't be so ill dressed.

Another blast of gunfire struck his hiding place, then swept over to send shards of plaster and stone flying out from where the other group had taken cover. The next spree from the machine gun tore chunks off of Mattie's cover, and fuck these people, Mattie decided, and stood up and fired two shots at the source of the attack.

"Shit!" said the woman's voice, and then she was up as well, firing at their attacker. Mattie hoped she had more ammunition than he did. Now Mattie could see that whoever was operating the machine gun was doing it from a mobile turret; he recognized the shape from Miranda. The enormous gun had been rooted to the ground on a stand, the better for the user's aim, the worse for their mobility. Someone was crouched in the poor cover provided by the stand; they'd ducked at Mattie's attack, but now they swung the gun, firing wildly and missing. Bullets chipped at what was left of the System building at Mattie's back. He heard gunshots strike behind him, but none of them hit him. He had only one bullet left, but he pressed forward, toward that turret, and for the first time since he had left Constance behind on Mars he felt like he was actually *doing* something, as if finally—finally!—all that black anger and force that had been building up inside of him was being let loose, and he was at long last as he was meant to be and not some bitter and twisted thing. Things were clear for a moment: no more questions about Ivan, no more anger about Constance, just the purity and clarity of this one moment.

He reached the turret before the man using it could aim and shot him there with his last bullet. His attacker was wearing a uniform, ragged and patched but different from the strange woman's. Mattie stood over the body and the abandoned gun and found that he was breathing hard. Strangely, his gaze went to the useless gun in his hand, and strangely, he thought of his sister's fierce grim joy as Earth burned.

Steps behind him had him turning sharply, Constance forgotten, his useless gun coming up automatically in his hand.

The muzzle of it ended up pointed directly at the young man with the large brown eyes. Mattie lifted his hands in surrender, though at his movement the woman raised her weapon in turn and advanced forward, her mouth set grim beneath the shadow of her cap.

From somewhere nearby, someone shouted a warning, and then an explosion sounded and left Mattie's ears ringing. He moved his finger from the trigger and tilted the muzzle of the gun away from the stranger.

The woman wasted not a second. She dropped her gun and started off toward the road, snagging her brother's arm as she passed. He tugged her to a stop, looking back at Mattie.

"So come on," she said to Mattie a few steps from the pull of the road. Her accent was reassuringly outer planetary—Europan native, if his ear was good. "It's too dangerous to stay here."

Mattie's gun was out of bullets anyway. With one last glance down at the System turret and the dead man it sheltered, he followed the strangers out onto the road to Aquilon.

BACKWARD

Constance Harper had an eye out the window at the red front of the oncoming Martian storm, with hot water running out of the faucet and throwing up a thin steam over her chapping hands. Ivan watched her until Mattie finished drying his plate and thrust it into Ivan's hands.

"Higher cabinet," he instructed, and Ivan turned his gaze away from the bent of Constance's brows against the dimming blaze of the sun and pushed the plate up to the highest shelf.

He considered carefully how their conversation might look from the perspective of a System agent watching through the camera set into the ceiling overhead and aimed at the back of Constance Harper's neck and judged it safe to ask, "How long until the storm hits?"

"Five minutes," Constance said, and the sunlight reddened as the edge of the dust swept up between them and it.

Mattie ran a towel disinterestedly over another plate and handed it to Ivan. It was still damp underneath. Ivan put it away.

From the distance of the main bar area, a door slammed. "Halloo!" Anji sang out, her light steps accompanied by a heavier tread. Christoph, too.

"Two minutes," Constance revised with an imprudent quirk to her lip. Mattie bent over his plate and smirked.

There was defying the System, and then there was flat foolishness. Ivan took Mattie's next plate and said nothing.

The front of the storm had nearly reached them. The sun was visible only as a brighter spot of red. Clumps of dirt beat like fists against the glass of Constance's kitchen window. Dust followed the wind in an upward sweep when it reached the wall of the bar.

"Ah," said Constance, soft exhalation, and twisted off the faucet. Ivan looked to see that the water had come out red. It was dripping from her hands and stained the towel that Mattie willingly surrendered to her.

"Dust in the pipes," Mattie explained.

"It happens every now and then." Constance dropped the towel. Ivan didn't offer to get it for her. She bent down to pick up the towel and while she was there reached underneath the sink and flipped the switch.

All over the house, the lights—and the surveillance—went black.

Constance straightened up and dropped the towel on the counter.

"It's done?" Ivan asked, and Mattie grinned.

"Yep," he said, looking satisfied with himself, as well he might; designing a switch that would make the System think the failure of their surveillance had been a consequence of the storm and not of interference was a work of brilliance. But even though Ivan trusted Mattie and believed in his brilliance, he still eyed the surveillance cameras with unease. A clever trick, but one they used perhaps too often.

But when Mattie followed Constance out of the kitchen, Ivan followed Mattie.

In the bar proper, Anji and Christoph helped Constance set up the candles. Their little light could not fill the room. Constance moved, chiaroscuro, in and out of flickering shadow with her hand shielding a little flame over her heart as she lit the candles.

Anji glanced up, shadows hanging from her neck and arms, jewels glinting like leopard eyes in her ears. She grinned. "Leontios!"

Ivan said, "What pirate vagrant taught you to imitate human speech?"

"He's so fancy," she said, to Mattie.

"I know," Mattie replied.

Constance, with shadows stretching out from her hips like a gown, bent in quiet conversation with Christoph. The gray in Christoph's beard was washed out in this yellow light. He scratched his chin and murmured something low for her ears alone. Constance bent him a harnessing glance, and he yielded, and bowed his head.

When they were all seated at the candlelit table, only then did Constance blow out her match. "Anji, report."

Anji launched immediately into a lengthy description of a meeting with Henry. Ivan had met Henry once, but only in passing. Though he attended these meetings every time one occurred, his reluctance to be more involved in Constance's revolution was well known.

Henry, it turned out, was out in the Uranian moons, running the underground that Constance had begun there before she'd moved to Mars. The movement by Uranus seemed to have no end; a few strikes here and there against petty targets, mildly inconveniencing the System's operations but never stopping them. The usual, Ivan supposed.

"And Rayet?" Constance asked when Anji was done.

"Keeping in touch with his friends from the System military," Anji said. Ivan wondered if Constance intended to try to start a mutiny. It wouldn't work, he could have told her. He would tell her, but he knew that she wouldn't listen. She never did listen when he was talking sense.

"Good," Constance said. "Christoph?"

"I put out feelers regarding the Sons of Nike, but so far there's been silence. A few people here and there; no more groups. The organization has completely collapsed. Well," he corrected, "almost entirely. There's still a splinter cell out on Pluto."

Constance's smooth brow furrowed. "Pluto?"

"Less a splinter cell than a new group entirely. It's led by a man who once fought with the Son, but he left before the end. The Plutonian group is his."

"And his name?"

"Arawn Halley. He has a reputation for violence, but he's confined to the planet."

And a little planet it was, Ivan thought.

"Have you been able to get into contact with him?"

"Not so far. He's—suspicious. I'll keep working."

"Do so," Constance said. "Have you scouted out the System monument on Adrastea?"

"Yes," said Christoph, and Ivan listened and did not ask where Adrastea was. Terran as he was, they would take badly to the question. Christoph briefly sketched out a view of a System historical museum on a small outer moon—ah, Jupiter; Adrastea was one of Jupiter's smaller moons. As near as Ivan could tell, some historical event that the Uranians he was with considered to be deeply significant had happened at this base on Adrastea, though he had never heard of it, and they intended to send a message by blowing it up. Christoph was well into his research: he produced some plans of the building to lay on the table, edges curling up between the candles. The plans were computer-made, but through meticulous re-creation; they were not System records. Ivan stared at the little boxes representing rooms and held his tongue.

"If we can get the soldiers concentrated here," Constance said, drawing one finger over the surface of the paper, "then someone else can come in through the back—"

"We don't need to come in through the back," Mattie said. "Ivan can get us in the front."

They all turned to Ivan, their expressions ranging from expectation to suspicion. Ivan smiled blandly and promised nothing.

"Mattie and Ivan can get in beforehand," Constance said, just as blandly ignoring his lack of agreement, as if she could override his own inclinations and force him to go, "and infiltrate the System."

Of course, Ivan supposed, the worst thing was that she *could*. She'd done it before. A surge of frustration hit Ivan like something inside him beating against the bars of his chest. For an instant, facing the relentless surety of Constance's knowledge that she could change his mind, he felt as trapped as he ever had with the System.

"Before they can be found out, Christoph and I will detonate a bomb at this point," Constance continued. She tapped a spot on the page. She did not describe how she would plant the bomb. "Anji, you'll sweep around to provide assistance to Ivan and Mattie; they won't be able to take any weapons in with them, and they'll be in enemy territory. Once the guards are distracted—"

"No," Ivan said.

Four faces turned up to him. Constance said, "Why not?"

"Because none of that is going to work."

None of the others looked surprised. This was familiar to them by now, Ivan realized. They expected Constance to describe a plan, and Ivan to object, and the whole thing to be hammered out into something they were more likely to survive.

Against all odds, he had found himself a place with these people.

"What about it won't work?" Constance asked.

Ivan looked down at the paper. He started to analyze it, to pick apart its weaknesses: sending him and Mattie in unarmed, for a start; for another, how would Constance and Christoph plant that bomb—

He sat back, shaking his head.

"All of it," he said. "This is flawed from the start." Then, drawn by some perverse impulse that Constance and only Constance could inspire in him, he added, "And it's a waste of time."

Christoph scowled. It had, after all, been his plan. But he did not offer protest.

"How so?" Constance asked.

"Nobody cares about some little museum on—where is this?—Adrastea."

"Adrastea is where the first ships sent to destroy Saturn came from," Constance said.

"So?"

Christoph interrupted. "So don't you know your own history, boy?"

"The System doesn't give a damn about Adrastea. It's a tiny moon that holds no strategic importance. And they don't care about a half-forgotten museum. Blow it up, and what does it cost them? Nothing.

They build a new one. No one needs to know about the explosion except the Adrasteans who witnessed it, and even then, what will they learn from it? That you're good at asking rhetorical questions and not very good at making a mark."

Silence at the table. Anji, strangely enough, was smiling.

Constance said, "Then what do you suggest instead?"

Nowhere, Ivan almost said, as he usually did. *Give this up and leave me alone*.

But now he stopped.

Afterward, he could not have said why he— No. Self-serving illusion. He knew why he'd said to her what he had. He had looked at her and seen that fire in her, banked but dangerous, like a campfire lit in the middle of a dry wood. And with the same reckless perversity, that same focused loathing that had driven him one morning to the roof of his mother's house with a knife in his hand, in that moment in Constance Harper's bar he looked at her and wanted to see just how brightly she could burn.

"Someplace practical," he said. "Keep the symbolism—you're not doing violence just for violence's sake—but it has to be something that injures them as well."

The candlelight reflected out of Constance Harper's eyes as she watched him darkly over the table.

"There's a meeting of the Martian System representatives in a few months," he said. "They're gathering at the summit of Olympus Mons to discuss System policies."

Constance said, "How do we target them?"

And he told her how.

FORWARD

There was a vast open space between the edges of the city and the edges of the greenhouse glass, and that was where the gray woman led Ivan.

His leg was aching, knotted around where Althea Bastet had chosen to let him live. He stopped on the ice and bent over himself, breathing in the harsh and cold air.

The gray woman ran a little farther before realizing the crunch of his steps no longer sounded; she wheeled back around with her gun still clutched in her arms and jogged back over to him. "Are you hurt?"

He shook his head.

"Then let's go," she said, and her gloved fingers were again wrapping around his arm.

He was too tired to run. "They're not following us," he said, though he had no way of knowing that. There were no sounds of pursuit over the ice, no sign of dark figures on the hunt, and that would have to be enough.

The woman hesitated, glancing back again toward the city. It was lit with a dark glow, flashes of fires showing through choking smoke that pooled at the greenhouse ceiling.

"Let's get out of sight," she urged, and led Ivan to the side, down a bend in the undulating ice, and then farther, into a crevasse. It was hard to keep his balance, and the crevasse was unnerving, a shoulder's width only, with sheets of blue ice higher than his head. It wound down deeper and deeper, growing smaller, and Ivan did not know how far down into blue darkness it would go. The woman wedged herself just inside, and Ivan climbed in after her so that they could catch their breath in safety.

The wind was gone in the crevasse, but it still was cold and tight, like a tomb.

"*Thank you*," said the woman, after a time staring out past Ivan at the pitted slope.

The wall of ice at his back seemed to lean on him, like someone pressing her hands on his shoulders and bending to whisper in his ear. Ivan found a deprecating smile inside himself and said to the woman, "No problem. What else was I going to do?"

It was like snapping on a mask, that charm. She cast him a fleeting little smile. He wondered if it was the blue light that robbed all the color from her face or if that was just the way she had been born.

"My name's Alyssa."

"Ivan."

"You aren't from here."

There'd been little point in hiding his accent; he hadn't even thought of it when he'd shouted his first warning. At least Alyssa seemed grateful enough for her rescue not to hold it against him. "I'm not."

She nodded more to herself than to him. She was still staring past him, her attention so focused on the ice outside that it was as if he half wasn't there.

"I've been going from city to city," said Alyssa, with her gloved fingers picking at some imperfection on the barrel of her gun, "looking for someplace . . . but there's nothing. It's chaos. The fighting's everywhere."

Of course it was. It was right, wasn't it, that his sin was something that couldn't be run from, that couldn't be escaped?

Alyssa stopped picking at her gun to tear off one glove so that she could run her fingers over its dark surface more carefully, restlessly searching for any flaw that might render it unusable. Ivan wondered if she knew she was doing it. He said, "Who holds what area?"

"I don't know. Nobody knows. It changes every day. It doesn't matter; none of them will help us."

I can talk myself through a blockade, Ivan thought, and then, with frigid fingers dripping down his back, he realized that all his tricks were designed for a world where there were rules and there was order. He had run Ida Stays in circles because of her own restrictions; he had conned a thousand people by relying on manipulation of the rules that already controlled them. But here there were no rules, there were no restraints, and there were no guarantees that his wits would be enough for him to get his way.

He was a creature of a dead world. He wondered how long he would last without it.

He wondered how long Mattie would.

Yet here, at least, was one small facet of his situation he could still control. Alyssa already trusted him. He said to her, "You know this area. You know these people."

"Sure," said gray Alyssa. There was a wedding ring on her finger, he noticed; the pale gold gleamed in the faint light.

"I need to get to the spaceport in Aquilon," he said. "I need to get a ship and escape Europa."

"Escape," Alyssa repeated.

"Yes." Ivan looked at her and believed that she was the only one who could save him, the only human being in the world who mattered in that moment. "If I go on my own, they'll kill me."

The corners of her lips turned down. "It won't work."

No, Ivan thought, it wouldn't. There was no escape, not anymore.

But he couldn't give up when Constance and Mattie both were out there.

"It can't hurt to try." He gave her a reckless smile.

And she, hooked and ensnared as Althea Bastet had been, said, "I think there's an air lock that's probably unguarded. It won't lead straight to Aquilon, but we can go around and through."

"Good," Ivan said, and then moved when she moved so that she could climb out of the fissure. Jupiter still glowed overhead, vast, with oppressive nearness.

"We'll stick to the ice," Alyssa said, stepping out beside him. Her hair must have been blonde, once, before ill care and the sick strange twilight of this moon had stained it to such a thin and wispy gray. "And we have to be even more careful in Aquilon. It's worse than Mara."

"More fighting?" Ivan could hardly imagine it; Mara seemed to be in active battle throughout its breadth.

Alyssa was shaking her head. "No, it's quiet," she said. "But the terrorists are just conquering Mara now. They've held Aquilon for months."

And Ivan looked at her again with new eyes. Not just at how alone she was, and how frightened, and how ragged her clothing had become, but he looked at *her*, the straightness of her teeth, the trained and familiar way that she held her weapon, the color and material her clothes had been before hard wear and patching had rendered them nearly unrecognizable . . .

"They're organized there," Alyssa said. "There was supposed to still be a force in Mara, but you can see they got here before I could."

He should have realized before now. If he hadn't been so exhausted, his head aching, his body tense with awareness of the creeping cold, he might have figured it out.

"We won't find any friends in Aquilon," said Alyssa, the System woman with the ragged System uniform and the System-issued gun clutched in her hands. "We'll have to rely on each other."

BACKWARD

"Your boyfriend's not going to come," Christoph said.

Out the window of the tiny spaceship Christoph had commandeered from somewhere—being a former smuggler, Mattie supposed, had its limited uses—Mattie could see Ivan and Constance still standing together on the surface of Mercury. They appeared to be having a conversation, but it did not seem to be going well. Ivan was standing as still and sculpted as a statue, and Constance's back was proudly unbowed.

"I know," Mattie said. "I told you."

He did not append the standard protest, though a part of him wanted to. Christoph was just trying to get a rise out of him. Mattie was certain, most of the time, that the only one of them Christoph actually liked was Constance herself. Even then, he wasn't sure that what Christoph felt for her could be properly called liking.

Out the window, Constance turned on her heel. Her hair floated behind her head in the low gravity as she strode toward the ship and Mattie himself.

"They're sleeping together, aren't they?" Christoph said with an unpleasant edge to the question that Mattie really didn't want to try to decipher. "But he still won't help her?"

Sometimes, Mattie thought, he wished that Constance had not gone out of her way to persuade a dissatisfied System civil servant to defect to their side. If she hadn't, Mattie wouldn't have to deal with Christoph on a regular basis. "He doesn't want to be part of a revolution." He could almost hear a Terran lilt to his own accent when he said the words; how often he had heard them from Ivan's mouth.

"Terran still," Christoph said. "You could talk him into coming, I think."

"Who, the *Terran*?"

"He could do a lot for us." Christoph was not as subtle as Ivan was when he wanted something. Mattie scowled at the window. "The son of Connor Ivanov."

"You could talk to him yourself," Mattie suggested, maliciously.

"But he doesn't care about me the way he *cares* about you," Christoph said, and this time Mattie might have snapped back except that the hull door slammed open to admit the women of the party.

"Oh, leave him alone," Anji said, bouncing up into the ship. "He wants to talk to you, Mattie."

Mattie looked sharply back out the window toward where the bright rays of the Mercurian sun cut at Ivan's still figure. "Now?"

Behind Anji, Constance walked without a word into the cockpit.

"Yeah," said Anji, choosing, by some miracle, to reply simply. Mattie rose and, ignoring Christoph's expression, climbed past his silent sister and down and out onto the Mercurian soil.

Ivan made him do all the work of walking. When Mattie was near enough to hear him, Ivan said, "You don't have to go."

Mattie stuck his hands in his pockets and shrugged. Whether he had to do anything had never been in question.

"This whole thing is going to get out of control; you know that," Ivan said. "Constance Harper's revolution. The *Mallt-y-Nos*. She won't be able to control it even if it survives long enough. Even if you all survive long enough."

"Did you want to say something specific to me, or did you just want to repeat yourself?"

"I just wanted to make sure you understood what you're doing. What they're doing."

"I'm not a child, Ivan."

Ivan looked at him with an expression Mattie couldn't read and said nothing more. At last Mattie nodded, not even sure himself what he was acknowledging, and turned to leave.

He had nearly reached the door to Christoph's stolen ship when he heard light steps jogging behind him.

"I'm coming with you," Ivan said.

FORWARD

The man and the woman led Mattie to a patch of smoking rubble. Perhaps it once had been someone's home. Now it was nothing but jagged wood teething at the wind, frost settling over their outer layers, embers still lit in their depths. Mattie followed them in, and when they crouched down beneath the scarred wood, he crouched down as well. At first he did not see why they had stopped, but before long another group of strangers came by, packed together, armed, looking around with hard and wary looks. Mattie gripped his useless gun and wondered how many rounds the woman had left. Her lips had lifted in a grin at the sight of the hunting party outside their cover, but her thoughts must have tended in the same direction as Mattie's, because she glanced toward her brother and then made a quick check of her clip before settling back on her heels to wait for them to pass.

They slipped past without seeing Mattie or his companions, well-armed, heads swinging like wolves seeking a scent. They were not wearing uniforms, or if they were, the uniforms had been so altered and distressed that Mattie could not recognize them. He looked at the passing soldiers, and slowly his vision narrowed. He did not wonder were they System or were they rebel. He looked at them, and he thought, *They will kill me if they see me.*

They did not see him, and after a time, the other soldiers passed and the sound of their steps was gone.

The woman rose and pressed on.

They traveled for a long way. Mattie kept track of their direction and knew that they were passing through Mara toward Aquilon, and so he stayed with them. The woman and her brother seemed to know the area, and he was not certain what they would do if he tried to leave.

At last the woman turned off the road toward a squat building that sat atop the ice. System, then, but unused; it was burned out, blackened, dark. She ducked inside, out of sight of the road. Mattie followed, his fingers flexing reflexively around his empty gun.

Inside they stood in what had once been a grand antechamber, ruined now by war. A bit of Jovian light glowed a faint and eerie orange from the half-shattered ceiling. When Mattie walked, he stepped on fallen tile. There had been a fire here, but unable to use tile and stone for fuel, it had burned itself out on the furniture.

The woman's voice echoed oddly through all that broken tile, as if half underwater. "You did pretty good back there."

She was busily tucking her gun back into its holster, but Mattie was not fooled by her apparent inattention. She had fought to survive; he could read it written on her skin, the way she reacted to the shift of his weight without looking up. He made a wrong move, and she would have that gun up and fired before he could blink.

She finished holstering the gun and looked up at Mattie. "Can't you talk?"

"I can talk," Mattie said.

"Then I said you did good back there."

Mattie considered shrugging again out of simple contrary spite. But he said, "Thanks."

Her cheeks dimpled.

Her brother was walking through the broken building, his face upturned to what was visible of the black sky overhead. His steps took him, as if by accident, behind his sister.

"I'm guessing you're a rebel," the woman said.

There was an edge of humor in her words, but that alone didn't tell Mattie what the right answer to her question should be.

Ivan would have known. "I guess I am," said Mattie.

The humor in her expression went stiff like water flash freezing. "Who do you follow?"

"I thought there was only one person for a rebel to follow," he said warily.

That frosting suspicion cracked; she laughed. "One true God, right?" she said not to Mattie but back over her shoulder to the other man, teasing him. Her brother lowered his gaze and gave her a long-suffering sibling look.

Mattie glanced down at the surface of his gun, as if by mere study he could make more ammunition appear.

"Hey," said the woman. "What's your name?"

"Mattie."

"You're from—Neptune?" she hazarded.

The accents weren't even remotely similar. "Miranda," he said, and his annoyance must have been in his voice, because this time it was the brother who smiled.

"Well, right," the woman said, without much apology, "close enough. What're you doing so far from home in Mara?"

"Trying to get out of Mara."

"He can be quick if he wants to," the woman said to her brother, then to Mattie, "Oh, come on; smile. We're not going to shoot you. Maybe put your gun away, too."

"I don't know who you are."

"We're the best luck you're going to get out here on this frigid piece of hell," said the woman. "My name is Tuatha; this is my brother, Niels. Not only are we revolutionaries, we're part of the Conmacs, Europa's own revolutionary force. And soon to be hosts of Constance Harper."

Mattie's hastily assembling plans—get a ship through these revolutionaries, find Ivan, leave uninjured; perhaps their luck had turned at last—came to a stalling halt. "What?"

"The Mallt-y-Nos is coming to join with our forces," said Tuatha, and there was a gleam in her eyes that was a fierce and wild species of joy. "She'll be in Aquilon by this time tomorrow."

Chapter 5

HUIS CLOS

FORWARD

Ivan and Alyssa walked near enough to the edge of the greenhouse glass that Ivan could just see the warping in the air where it slammed down into the ground but far enough that if they were attacked, they would not find themselves pinned with their backs to cold and unyielding glass.

The long twilight of Europa's day was drawing very slowly toward night. In time, there would be no light but the reflected glow of Jupiter.

To Ivan's left, Mara was still burning, but the battle had slowed down or else they had traveled too far from it for the shouts still to be heard. Alyssa's head swiveled back and forth restlessly as she walked, her long braid of dull wispy hair swinging against her back. Ivan followed her at a little distance and watched her, her back, her braid, the gun in her hands.

Some time into their journey she said, "Why did a Terran come to Europa?"

"By accident." Ivan focused his accent just the slightest bit, made it more Terran, sharp as shards of ice. "My ship crashed."

"You were in the battle?"

"Not intentionally," Ivan said, but if he kept dodging her, she would become suspicious. He gifted her with a piece of truth: "I was looking for someone."

"They must be very important to you."

"They are." The ground underfoot here was growing unstable; he picked his next step carefully.

"Do you really think we can get off this rock?"

"Of course," Ivan lied. "Is there somewhere you want to go?"

"Anywhere that isn't here." Ice crunched beneath her feet, echoing off the glass that shielded them from the sky. She said, "This person you're looking for. Who are they?"

He recalled the wedding ring on her finger. "My wife. We were separated right before the war started."

"You must love her very much," Alyssa said, wistful as the bits of sparkling snow that eddied in the gentle wind.

"She's my wife."

Ivan watched the way she gripped her gun and said, "Tell me about this moon. I didn't expect to find it like this when I landed here. Why was there a space battle in orbit?"

"The war started here the way it did everywhere else. One of the Mallt-y-Nos's dogs came—Anji, they called her—and stirred up the mob and started bombing us. There were already terrorist groups here, and when she came, they saw their chance and they took it."

There was such bitterness in her voice that she could have made this whole land barren, had the cold not already done so. "And then Anji left, but even after she left, the terrorist groups that were here already stayed. The Conmacs are the closest group. There are a hundred others. One of them came to the military base where I worked and blew it up. The others died. I ran."

"You had to leave," said Ivan.

"I've been running ever since, but they're everywhere. And then the Mallt-y-Nos herself came, and everything's gotten worse. She's been taking over the planet the way they say she took over Venus. She hasn't gotten very far yet, but it's only a matter of time."

"The Mallt-y-Nos is here?" Ivan said sharply. "On this moon, now?"

"Yes. It must've been her fleet in orbit, but I don't know who they were fighting. It wasn't ours."

Again that bitterness, but this time Ivan hardly heard. Who had Constance been fighting? He knew what must have happened: the revolution had begun to fall apart, had begun to turn inward and devour itself.

And the first casualty of that self-devouring would be Constance Harper.

"What happened to the crew of your ship when you crashed?" Alyssa asked. They were traveling down a slope of ice, and she bent and wavered for balance like tall grass in a storm.

The idea of him being an only survivor, too, was probably too much to swallow, he decided. "I was traveling with only one companion," Ivan said. "A guide from the outer planets. We were separated in Mara." He could only pray that Mattie was safe, that he had continued on, and not died seeking Ivan in the chaos. "He should be waiting for me in Aquilon—if he hasn't defected and abandoned me," he added, re-calling to whom he spoke.

Alyssa cast a frown at him over her shoulder as she reached the bot-tom of the slope. "You had no crew?"

"I had my guide."

"Weren't you on active duty?" Alyssa asked.

If he stumbled, Ivan thought, she might reach out a hand to help him. Or she might not.

"No," he said as his steps took him nearer and nearer to where she stood on the ice, "I wasn't."

He was almost within an arm's reach of her. Almost—

And as he stepped down to the bottom of the slope, she swayed back a step, a motion almost imperceptible . . . but wholly deliberate.

"I see," she said, and started off again, walking slowly over the undu-lating ice.

Almost, Ivan could hear Ida Stays's crystalline little laugh. Would it be a fitting revenge, he wondered, for him to die out here alone in this vast white emptiness of snow and ice?

He had no answer to his own question, and no other choice. He fol-lowed Alyssa as she walked across the snow a safe distance ahead of him, her gun clutched in her hands.

BACKWARD

"I need you to do something for me," Constance said to Mattie one day while Ivan was out, sitting down across from him at the kitchen table in her bar.

Mattie paused, fork halfway to his mouth. "Sure," he said.

"I need you to convince Ivan to help me out with our next attack against the System."

He blinked at her, then up at the surveillance camera planted innocently in the upper corner of the room. "I'm . . . guessing we're talking privately."

"The surveillance cameras are off," said Constance patiently, with only the smallest shade of "I'm not an idiot, Mattie" to ruin it.

"Probably shouldn't do that when there isn't a storm as an excuse," said Mattie, and finished the fork's journey to his mouth.

"This couldn't wait," Constance said. It could have waited, probably, if she hadn't been trying to talk to Mattie behind Ivan's back. "I need his help for the next one, and I know he won't do it."

Mattie chewed. He swallowed. "Have you tried asking him?"

"I think if I asked him to do something for me he already wanted to do, he'd say no just to be contrary." There was a bitterness in his foster sister's voice that Mattie didn't want to hear. "But if you ask him, it'll be different."

Mattie looked down at his plate. He had been amused, but not surprised, to find Mirandan fish in Constance's refrigerator; he had been even less surprised to find that she had prepared it in the Mirandan way ("Bland," Ivan had decreed on the one notable occasion he'd dared to try it, "yet *still repulsive*."). Now, the whimsy of his choice of meal was no longer as amusing. He poked at it with his fork.

Constance was watching him steadily across the table, her very silence and attention anticipating Mattie's protests.

"He'll know I'm asking because you asked me," he said.

"If you're just doing it because I made you, then yes. But you want this attack to succeed, too."

She did not make it a question, but there was a question in her eyes. Mattie dropped his gaze from hers.

"Why do you need his help?" he asked, and laid his fork down on his plate.

"In order to plant the explosives, we need to get into the building," Constance said. "It's a bank on Ceres. They won't let you, or me, or Anji, or Christoph in. But they will let Ivan in to see their vaults. And they'll let in his guest if he asks."

"There's no other way in?"

"This is the best way."

"He's gonna say no when I ask him."

"If he doesn't do it, we'll have to abandon this target."

"I can't make him do something he doesn't want to do," Mattie said. "Can't you just seduce him into it?"

The iron silence that followed made him regret his words at once. Mattie stared down at the meal he'd taken from Constance's refrigerator. He wished he could just throw it out, but his old habits wouldn't let him throw out edible food. Instead, he pushed at it with his fork and tried not to think about Constance and Ivan together, or why Constance would look at Mattie so frostily when he mentioned it.

If the silence had continued uninterrupted much longer, he might have been forced to face the uncomfortable realization he could feel building up in the back of his head like static in a storm cloud, but Constance spoke.

"I'm not saying you should manipulate him," she said. "I'm not telling you to do what he does to his marks. I care about him; you know I do. But this is bigger than him, or you, or me. And I need his help."

"You're the one who needs his help," Mattie said. "You're the one sleeping with him."

"You're the one he'll listen to." Constance leaned toward him then, across the expanse of the table separating them. "Don't you see it, Mattie? This is important. What else matters but righting the wrongs the System has done? What else could possibly be worth our time and our lives? Compared to that—Ivan is just a man."

Mattie resented it a little when she spoke like that, remote and far away, no longer in the moment his sister and his friend, but someone who dictated rules and reality instead.

Constance said, "Aren't you with me?"

FORWARD

The sky came down, frosted, to bury itself in the earth; that was the edge of the air lock that separated Mara from Aquilon. Tuatha led Mattie and Niels unerringly toward it, and her confidence was such that it took Mattie a long time to realize that the door was guarded.

He slowed, heels digging into the pitted ice. There was nowhere to

hide out there; they were already in the empty space between the ruined city and the air lock.

At the diminished sound of his footsteps, Tuatha looked back.
"Come on," she said with total unconcern, and Mattie looked at the
guns in the arms of the guards ahead, gritted his teeth, and started up
again.

He was conscious of the lightness of the gun at his hip as they approached, but Tuatha lifted both arms and waved them, and the guards
lowered their guns.

"Anything?" she asked as the three of them approached the warped
glass of the air lock.

"All quiet," one of the guards said briskly. Tuatha nodded and walked
into the tunnel between air locks, her gun comfortably holstered.

Their way out was similarly relaxed. The guards on the other end
spotted the three of them coming but stood down at the sight of Tuatha. They looked curiously at Mattie and Niels as they passed. Mattie
did his best to look like he belonged, and wished he had a little bit
more ammunition.

Aquilon was less savaged than Mara had been, more quiet, no
smoke. The Conmacs had taken over this city swiftly, then hidden the
evidence of the violence as far as they could. No bodies lay in the
streets, no smoke marred the skyline, but the buildings were pitted and
the ice was warped from a melt and a fast refreeze, and the Systematic
straight line of the main roads had been made jagged and uneven.
There were people living here, not running from their houses; they
looked out windows at Mattie, then pulled their heads back in, away
from his eyes. The armed men and women who stalked the roads
passed Tuatha with a nod.

These people were rebels, Mattie reminded himself, but the people
in the windows were drawn and gray and cold, like icy Europa itself,
and they withdrew from the touch of his glance. These were Mattie's
people, who had suffered from the System, who had risen against it,
who had believed the holy word of Constance Harper, the Huntress
who soon would visit them herself.

He did not want to see her. He didn't. He wished she wasn't here;
he wished she wasn't coming. He hated her still. Yet here, among
strangers, he felt a strange and unconscionable softness at the thought
of a familiar face.

He fought the thought off, pressed it ruthlessly to the base of his mind, and let his roiling anger rise to the surface again and cover his thoughts of Constance Harper.

At last they came to the center of Aquilon, where what had once been the center and symbol of the System's power there had become a fortress. The first thing Mattie saw when they approached was a wall. Like a brutal, opaque imitation of the glass greenhouse that enclosed them, it stretched up over Mattie's head and curved around some unseen interior. It was cobbled together from wreckage and ruin, and the eight System buildings that had encircled the center of the town made up its pillars, with the walls stretching across the road to connect the System buildings, unnatural union between the mechanical perfection of the System architecture and the organic flaws of the rebel walls.

"Amazing, isn't it?" said Tuatha brightly, watching the side of his face as Mattie craned his neck around to see all of the edifice that was visible.

"Yeah," Mattie said, because even if he could have put words to the strange foreboding that filled him, he would not have been so unwise as to try.

There was no door, but two walls sheared away from each other, creating an opening to weave through past the wall without exposing the interior to the exterior eye. Tuatha gestured for Mattie and Niels to wait a few feet back, then strode up to that gap with the same ease with which she had approached the air lock doors. There was a brief but animated discussion, and she beckoned them cheerfully into the camp.

Inside, people were making ready for war. The System buildings were all occupied; people came in and out of them with busy regularity. The edifice in the center of the square had clearly been converted to an armory; anyone who came in or came out brought with him or her some form of small arms. The open space of the intersection of the roads had been filled almost completely with tents and lean-tos and other forms of temporary residence, and people wove their way familiarly through them, or sat inside or around them, speaking quietly. Not far from the entrance to the camp was an open space with targets set up; a small group of men and women stood facing them and, at an order from their instructor, fired. The gunshots echoed off the high walls, amplified. The targets, dressed in System gray, jerked.

"Welcome to Aquilon," said Tuatha.

"You," Mattie said, "are not just a rebel."

"'Course I am."

"Just how high up are you with the Conmacs?"

"In the Aquilon camp? The leader," she said. She pulled off her cap, and out tumbled a startling amount of gleaming dark hair. "We need to get you a place to stay. Niels—"

"If you're the leader, what were you doing out in Mara without backup?"

"I had an important retrieval to make," said Tuatha, "but it was only important to me."

"Your brother," Mattie guessed. Niels was standing huddled deep in his jacket, watching his sister with a strange, sad expression.

"Niels," Tuatha confirmed. "We'd arranged to meet in Mara, but that was before Mara got bombed by those System pieces-of-shit. So I went back in to get him."

"You both would've gotten shot down if you hadn't bumped into me," Mattie pointed out.

"Eh," Tuatha said. "Or I would've tossed one of the grenades I had on my belt and blown him up, and we would've been fine."

"You haven't got any grenades on your belt."

She made a show of checking. "I don't. Didn't know you were paying that much attention to my hips."

Niels coughed. Mattie found himself briefly without words. It had been a long time since anyone had been so badly mistaken regarding his sexuality.

Tuatha rolled her eyes and let it drop. "We got a bunch of System medals when we took over their governor's house. We could probably engrave one of them with your name if you really wanted."

"I want a ship," said Mattie.

She laughed like she thought he was joking.

"My friend is coming to meet me here," Mattie said. "When he gets here, we'll need a ship. We have to get off Europa as soon as we can."

"The ships in our shipyard aren't ours," said Tuatha. "They're the Huntress's. You must've seen the space battle a few hours ago. She'll need every ship she can get to replace what was lost."

"We don't need a large one or a powerful one. Any ship—"

"—you can't have," said Tuatha. "When the Mallt-y-Nos gets here, you can ask her for one and see what she says."

If he waited until Constance got there, he would get a ship, but it would be too late: Ivan would not leave. They would be just as trapped here as before, with Ananke coming closer with every icy second. He would have to face Constance again.

It was on the tip of his tongue to tell Tuatha the truth—a part of it, at least. That he was Matthew Gale, the foster brother of the Mallt-y-Nos herself, whose hands had personally destroyed the Earth. Constance would give him a ship when she arrived, would want a ship given to him if he asked, and Tuatha would find greater favor with the Huntress if she treated Mattie well.

But he recalled Anji's people on the *Badh* and the *Macha*, and how his and Ivan's names had saved them at first and then made them prisoners.

Mattie would have to find a different way to get them a ship.

BACKWARD

Mattie returned to the *Annwn* sometime well after System Standard time would mark the Terran midnight. He eased open the hull door and checked himself quickly to be sure nothing overly incriminating was showing. Ivan had an eye like—what was that character he'd told Mattie about? Holmes, he remembered, or something—and so Mattie took great care rumpling his shirt and pinching the skin of his neck with the aim of leading Ivan to entirely the wrong conclusion.

Then he sauntered into the ship and shut the door behind himself as if he were *trying* to be quiet but not quite able to do it. He started climbing up the sideways hall in much the same way.

He made it as far as the den before he found Ivan. It probably gave him away as completely sober that he noticed Ivan immediately, but it was hard not to notice Ivan on the best of days, even more so when Mattie's skin was pricking with vague guilt.

Ivan said, "Where have you been?"

"Out," said Mattie, and tried for insouciance, or at least a just-got-laid grin.

It was wasted; Ivan wasn't looking at him. "Out where?"

"My business."

Ivan looked down at his hand, at the slow and patient curl and un-curl of his fingers that Mattie knew from long acquaintance meant he was replacing some more revealing motion. Ivan said, "You were at somebody's house."

"I was," Mattie said, because it was the complete truth.

"Let me see if I can guess his name." Ivan leaned forward suddenly, elbows to knees. He looked at Mattie the way a knife digs open an oyster. "Was it Lester Apollon?"

Mattie's smile faded. "The governor of Puck?"

Ivan nodded once.

"Why would I sleep with a System governor?" If he raised his voice like that, his pricking anxiety sounded a lot like outrage.

"Because you weren't sleeping with him. You were doing something for Constance."

For a moment Mattie entertained the idea of maintaining his inno-cence. The inclination collapsed almost immediately.

"She didn't want me to tell you," he said.

"You didn't. I figured it out. You can tell her that."

Mattie sighed. "I don't know why you won't—"

"What did you do?" Ivan sounded for all the world like he was noth-ing more than mildly curious. "Is he alive?"

"Of course he's fucking alive."

"Forgive me for wondering." Ivan's tone was as dry as bared bones. "What *did* you do to him?"

"I just left a piece of paper with his things. Cameras were off and everything; System never even knew I was there."

"But they'll come to investigate the camera outage immediately."

"Probably."

"And whatever they'll find there will make them very angry with Governor Apollon."

Mattie shrugged.

"What did the paper say, Mattie?" Ivan asked.

"Does it fucking matter?"

Ivan sat there, not looking at Mattie, his fingers clasped beneath his nose. Mattie's skin itched with his displeasure, and for a minute Mattie hated him for it, and he hated Constance for putting him in this situa-tion.

Ivan said, "You know they're going to kill him, don't you?"

"What?"

"Governor Apollon," Ivan said. "That's why Constance didn't tell me about it. Whatever you left in his house, the System is going to find it, and they're going to be furious. It's treason, probably. Maybe instructions for how to subvert System surveillance, maybe something more. In any case, the System will recall him from his post here and replace him. Maybe the person they replace him with will be weaker, or stupider, or more sympathetic to the people on this moon. That's what Con is hoping, I imagine. Of course, maybe the replacement will be worse." Ivan did look up then, and it was worse, the weight of his displeasure. "And as for ex-Governor Apollon, he'll go back to Earth, and in a couple of weeks—maybe a few months—he'll just go away. They did that all the time back on Earth."

"They do that all the time here," said Mattie. Ivan never seemed to understand that it was so much worse here than it ever had been on Terra. "You think I want to do this?"

"Do what?"

"Stand in the middle of you and my sister!"

"When you first met me," said Ivan, a dangerous change of subject, "years ago—"

"What about it?" Mattie snapped.

"It wasn't an accident," said Ivan, and the consonants fell as sharply as shattered glass from his accent. "Too much of a coincidence for the brother of a revolutionary to just stumble across the son of Connor Ivanov in some random bar."

Mattie went very still.

"I wondered if you thought I was too stupid to figure it out," Ivan said, "but now I've realized that you just didn't want to deal with what might happen when I did."

Mattie's mouth was dry.

"From the beginning," Ivan said, "you found me because of Constance Harper."

Maybe then, Mattie would have said, *but never since then*. But he could not bring those words to his mouth.

"I know where your loyalties lie," said Ivan, with his brilliant eyes and his glittering accent. "But—"

"But what?"

Ivan said, "You killed someone tonight, Mattie."

Mattie's hands were trembling. He stuck them into his pockets. "Like it's the first time for you or me," he said, and left.

FORWARD

In the end, Ivan wasn't surprised when Alyssa stopped and turned her gun on him.

"Who are you?" Beyond the barrel of her gun, her eyes were wide and gray, too large for her narrow face.

Ivan was not afraid. He was too cold to be afraid, he thought, or else more frightening women had held him at gunpoint than gray and fearful Alyssa.

"My name is Ivan," he said.

"You're not System," she accused.

"Why do you think that?"

"All System agents were called on active duty after the Mallt-y-Nos attacked Earth. If you weren't on active duty, then you weren't a System agent. So who are you?"

"Nobody important."

"So why did you lie?"

"Because," Ivan said, "I was concerned you might shoot me."

This would be a way to end. His body would never be found. Maybe it would mummify in the slow way of bodies left out in the open cold. Maybe the volcanic fluctuations of the ice would open a crack or melt the surface just enough to swallow him up, and he would be suspended forever in the blue beneath.

"Who are you working for?" Alyssa asked, sighting him down the barrel of her gun.

"I don't work for anyone."

"Don't lie. Who are you working for? Who do you follow?"

This whole conversation was familiar, Ivan thought with distant indifference. The freezing wind was finding the seams in his stolen clothes and chilling the skin beneath.

"I used to follow the Mallt-y-Nos," he admitted. "But right now, I'm just looking for my friend."

"The Mallt-y-Nos?" Alyssa surged up, then steadied herself, the gun held so precisely targeted on him that he could see the nose of it trembling with tension. "Where is she now? What is she planning?"

Ivan laughed. It echoed weirdly, and Alyssa took a step back, unnerved. She said, "Where is she?"

"What would you even do, if I told you?"

Ida Stays would have smiled her charming little smile and said, *That's for me to know, Ivan.* Or perhaps she would have said, *Well, I'm going to kill her, Ivan.*

Or perhaps Ida wouldn't have killed her. It was hard to say what Ida would have done with the fetters of the System lifted from her. She might have said she would kill Constance even if she'd had no intention of ever doing so. Said it, then shot Ivan and left him to die in the snow.

Alyssa said, "Just tell me where she is!"

"I don't know." Ivan imagined Ida Stays at Alyssa's back, smiling dark-lipped, running one frigid white hand down Alyssa's arm, stretching out to place her finger over Alyssa's on the trigger. "I'm looking for her. Or I was."

"What do you mean?"

"I mean if I knew where she was, I would be with her now. And as for what she's planning, I imagine it hasn't changed: kill the System."

"Like you were planning on killing me?" said Alyssa, shivering in the wind, wan and thin and frightened, pointing the gun at him like it was the only thing that could keep the wolf at bay.

"No," Ivan said. "I never had any plans of killing you."

"But you would if you had the chance."

Ivan took a step forward. She jolted the gun up fiercely, and her finger quivered on the trigger, but she did not fire. He said to her, "Even if the Mallt-y-Nos herself were here and she told me to kill you, I wouldn't do it."

She hesitated. The gun lowered a little beneath those gray eyes, exposing the fearful bent of her mouth.

"I saved your life. I lied to you so that you wouldn't kill me, because I promised my friend I would meet him in Aquilon. So shoot me or not. I can't stop you either way."

For a moment Alyssa was still, as if the ice had enclosed her, wrapping its pale arms about her and freezing her and her gun in place. The wind stroked Ivan's cheeks and ran its fingers over his lips.

Then Alyssa lowered her gun.

She did not say another word to him, but when she turned around and slowly walked on, her back bent like a tree beneath the weight of snow, he followed her.

BACKWARD

"Honestly," Ivan said, watching Constance chop the carrot into efficient little cylinders, "this is not how I have ever pictured you."

She lifted a brow but did not look up from the cutting board. "Cooking?"

The knife flashed in her hand.

"Being good at it," Ivan said.

"I cooked for Mattie for years." She dumped the carrots in the pot, deftly balancing the knife between her fingers. She was focused and calm, steady and sure, as well balanced as the knife she held. She did not set his heart to pounding like this, with thin strands of her brown hair escaping from their braid, but he admired her, the certainty of her hands, her poised-blade balance.

Behind him, the door to the bar swung open with a creak.

"Mattie does not have a discerning palate," said Ivan, knowing full well that Mattie was at that very moment walking in from the bar.

"I have a very good palate," Mattie said. "Also: go fuck yourself."

"Hand me the salt, Mattie," said Constance, unperturbed.

"Should've stayed in the bar." Mattie walked over to a cabinet indistinguishable from all the rest, opened it, and pulled out the salt with an immediacy born of long familiarity. He did it without spilling a drop of his drink or losing his grip on the two other drinks he had brought in with himself, long fingers wrapped around the necks of the bottles. Constance stuck out a hand without looking when he came near her, and he placed the salt into her hand. She shook it into the pot, put it aside, and held out a hand again; this time Mattie placed one of the bottles into her grip. Ivan watched the ballet of familiarity and felt some muscle he hadn't known he'd possessed tighten in his chest.

Constance took a swig while Mattie ambled around her to hand the second bottle to Ivan. She made a face.

"What?" Mattie said.

"It's sweet."

"It's good," said Mattie. "It's made from apples. Terran fruit." He didn't meet Ivan's eyes as he pressed the bottle into his hand, as if he might be able to distance himself from the gesture.

Constance squinted at the bottle suspiciously, but didn't protest again. Instead she said, "How close is the storm?"

Settling himself against the counter on Ivan's other side, his shoulder a welcome warmth against Ivan's, Mattie said, "I could hear it howling from the bar."

"Then it must be—"

Mattie took an idle drink from the bottle and very casually swung his ankle back at the switch hidden beneath the sink.

"—nearly on top of us," Constance finished as the lights went down. "There we go."

Mattie pushed himself off the counter. "I'll get the candles."

Ivan studied the System camera embedded in the ceiling—the camera that, like all the others, was no longer transmitting to the System. "You two make a good team." Somehow the remark did not come out as wry as he meant it to be.

Constance was still stirring the pot. The blue flames of the stovetop were the only light in the room. They traced her shape out palely, as if, should Ivan reach out to touch her, his fingers would pass right through her skin.

"We all do," she said.

Mattie had gone back out to the bar for Constance's stash of candles. Ivan could hear him moving boxes around even through the shut door. In his absence, Ivan said, "As nice as this dinner is, does this mean you're going to tell us what you want now?"

"I thought we would enjoy one another's company for a little longer," said Constance, with some asperity.

"It's hard for me to enjoy someone's company when I know they want something from me," said Ivan, in precisely the same tone.

Her lips tightened, and the light was so dim that Ivan could tell himself that it was exasperation and not hurt that flashed over her face. But Constance was not a woman to flinch from a confrontation. He admired her for that, helplessly. He wanted both to be furious at her for calling them here to use them and to possess in himself just the slightest splinter of her incorruptible self-assurance.

She said, "I need you to steal some ammunition for me."

"Why?"

"Because I'm running low," she said.

"What are you going to do with it?"

"What do you think?"

"No."

Her sharp glance up lanced at him, but he didn't flinch. She could look at him that way, but she could not make him change his mind. A rush went through him at the look. If he touched her now, she would hit him.

The door to the bar had opened, admitting Mattie. The warm yellow light of the candle he carried could only barely reach Ivan where he stood, and it battled weakly against the icy blue glow of the flames that lit Constance.

Constance said, "Mattie, would you steal something for me?"

All his interest vanished, like a drain had been opened. "No," Ivan said over Mattie's "Um, sure."

"Would you like to know what it is?" Constance asked Mattie.

Mattie's eyes were darting from one of them to the other. He was still standing in the doorway, the candle flickering in his hand. "That would be helpful?" he said.

"This is underhanded," Ivan snapped to Constance.

"Why? Mattie's his own person. You said no, so I'm asking him."

"Um," said Mattie again.

"You know he'll say yes; that's why you're asking him," Ivan said.

"I—"

"Ivan, come help me get more candles," Mattie said loudly, and Constance shut her mouth, nostrils flared, and continued to stir the pot. Ivan stared at the bend of her neck for a moment longer, his heart pounding still, then pushed off the counter to join Mattie at the door.

The bar outside was dark, the darkly gleaming shapes of bar and stools and tables and chairs hardly visible in what little light still filtered in from the wide front windows. Ivan breathed in slowly and watched the storm outside. It was so dark that the sand was no longer red, as if he and Mattie had stepped into a place made all of shadows.

Behind him, Mattie said quietly, "I thought the two of you were . . ."

He paused; unusual delicacy, coming from him.

Ivan's heart was still thundering. He felt more real somehow than he usually did, as if fighting with Constance somehow had drawn lines around him, giving him a clear outline. Fighting with Constance always did that: turned him for the briefest of instants from a collection of manipulations and ploys for survival into a real human being with wants and fears and a genuine self.

Ivan said, "We are."

FORWARD

There were a few open fires set up among the tents in the center of Aquilon, but they did little to dispel the Europan chill.

The cold didn't seem to bother Tuatha, though she had put her cap back on, this time leaving her hair to spill out down her back. It probably kept her neck warm. "Most of our troops camp out on the grounds," she said. "We'll try to find a good place for you. You said you were from Miranda?"

"Yeah," Mattie said.

"Born there?"

"Yeah."

"So you're used to the cold."

"I've traveled a lot," said Mattie.

"I can tell. Did you know you've got a bit of a Terran lilt when you say 'Mallt-y-Nos'? Took me a while to recognize it. Must've seen a lot of System broadcasts about her."

"Must've," said Mattie.

There was something odd about the Conmacs' campgrounds. It was not the tents themselves or the people huddled in them shoulder to shoulder. It was overhead instead: wires crisscrossing the sky, connecting the buildings. "What're all those wires?"

"Oh, we had to rig up some things to get the computers working again," Tuatha said. "First the System blew up their own generators, and then we had to fight to take this place, and then there was that ship, and the place was pretty much a wreck."

"'That ship'?"

"System ship. Flew past—I don't know, a few weeks ago. Messed up all our computers."

"Oh," said Mattie.

Tuatha was leading him and Niels closer to where those System gray–wearing scarecrows jerked with the impact of bullets. "The firing range," she said with a wave of her hand. Niels looked at the torn uniforms and frowned. Mattie's gaze strayed again to the wires overhead.

There were quite a lot of them. They connected all the buildings; they even connected segments of the wall.

"We keep most of our ammunition and explosives in the central building," Tuatha explained as they skirted that building and its wide pyramid of steps. Mattie nearly tripped over something, and when he looked down, he found that the irregularity of the ground was not due entirely to damage from bombing. Clusters of wires were thick on the ground, black, like veins atrophied from the cold.

"Our shipyard is this way."

Mattie's gaze shot up from the wires underfoot. "In the center of the city?"

"It was on the outskirts at first, but we moved it in after the System tried to bomb it. It's a lot safer that way."

He could make out the ships now through a gap in the wall, all landed beside one another. All small vessels that he could see, but small would mean fast. "How much safer?"

"You're looking at an army. And we've got automatic defenses in the walls—they react faster than a human could. And"—she paused, facing Mattie with a half-scolding, half-amused look—"we've got a lot of guards around them, making sure that no one inside or outside the camp could walk off with one. And even if someone did, they wouldn't be able to get out, because we would have to open the sky lock for them." The air lock at the top of the dome would indeed be controlled by computers within the System buildings that the Conmacs had taken, Mattie knew.

"I get it," he said.

"I hope so. I'd be real mad if I brought a thief back to my camp," Tuatha said cheerfully. "I'd be even madder if we had to waste a bullet on another revolutionary. This building is what we've been using as a headquarters. Watch your step."

The building was grand and high-columned. Tuatha led them through a nondescript pair of doors that plainly had replaced the original after the initial siege and brought them into the lobby. It was high-ceilinged and impressive, terminating in a staircase that branched off at the top into two long halls. The ceiling had been painted a clear, brilliant blue, but the plaster had been cracked by the bombing. Spiderwebs of white, like ice forming on the surface of a pond, cracked through the false sky. A layer of white plaster dust clung to the floor and the railings and ruined the Terran grandeur.

Thick black clusters of wires, like bundled nerves, ran along the walls, vanishing at intervals into doors. They alone were free of the dust. By their preponderance, Mattie could map out the computer network in this building.

Mattie said, "How extensive are your automatic defenses?"

"Extensive," said Tuatha. "Deadly."

"No. I mean, what, specifically?"

She looked at him curiously. "Turrets. Mines outside the perimeter. Drones."

"You have drones?"

Tuatha shrugged. "Not many. The System left some robotics behind; we got them armed, but we can't get them to go much of anywhere. The bright side is you throw a spinning bit of metal firing out bullets into a group of System soldiers, none of them can get close enough to turn it off."

Mattie's stomach clenched. He halted on the steps beneath the cracked plaster sky. "And all these things are connected to the computers in the System buildings? And all the computers are connected?"

"Yes and yes," said Tuatha.

Niels said, "What's wrong?"

"If something could . . . get access to your computers, it could control those defenses. It would be a massacre."

"No one could," said Tuatha.

"Some*thing*?" said Niels.

"Someone could," Mattie said. "It wouldn't even be that hard."

Tuatha shook her head. "No one could take control of them fast enough. If the System tries, we'll kill them first."

The sparks of an idea lit in Mattie's mind. "And if there's worse than the System coming?"

"What's worse than the System?"

"There's a ship on its way here," said Mattie. *You're running,* Ivan had said, and Mattie gritted his teeth and forced himself not to flee. "It can take control of your computers without any trouble at all."

Like a confession; there was a strange relief in having it said.

"But if you let me have a ship of my own," Mattie said, "I can make it so she can't hurt you."

FORWARD

They had traveled long enough that the sun had slipped into eclipse behind Jupiter and the tundra had become almost too dark to traverse.

"We should stop here," Alyssa said.

Ivan could just see the faintest trace of her face in the dim light of the eclipse, the shadowy shape of her nose, her cheekbones. She let her gun droop, its nose finding a resting place at last on the ice.

They stood beneath a shelf of ice, partially shielded from the wind, but it hardly seemed to matter. He did not think he could get more cold than he already was.

"How badly were you hit?" Alyssa asked.

"What?"

"Your head. You hit it when you crashed?"

Ivan reached up with one gloved hand and scraped his cheek unfeelingly with his fingers. Then he looked at his hand. A useless gesture. It was too dark to see the color red.

"I've been worse," he said.

"Can you sleep? Do I need to wake you?"

"No." Ivan squinted against the wind. He was not certain he would be able to sleep, not here, not now. He hoped that wherever Mattie was, it was warmer.

Alyssa sat heavily down on the ice, resting her back against the vertical wall of the shelf. The gun she laid at her side, one hand resting over it, companionable.

"What's your friend like?" she asked. "The one you're looking for."

Ivan's mind started to work: Why was she asking? What did she hope to get from him? What should he tell her that would be what she wanted to hear, so that she would like him, so that he could lead her on into doing whatever he needed her to do?

The wind changed again and brought its insidious chill down the collar of his stolen and bloodstained clothes. Ivan sat down beside her, his back against the mass of vertical ice, a safe space between them.

"I called him my guide before," he said. "He's from the outer planets. His name is Mattie."

"For Matthew?"

"Yes." Ivan wished he had a hood or a hat; the ice was melting against his scalp. He asked, "Why didn't you ask about my wife?"

He could just see her shrug in the dim. "When I had the gun on you," she said, "you didn't mention your wife. You only mentioned your friend."

A simple mistake, Ivan thought, but he was not at his best.

"You're not even married," Alyssa said. It was half a question yet no question at all.

"No," Ivan said. "There is . . . I have to reach Aquilon."

"I hope you find your friend."

The silence then was soft, dreamy. The wind that chapped his face seemed to be warming, or at least becoming less cold.

Ivan said, "You were married."

"I was." Alyssa's hand had fallen from the barrel of her beloved gun. "We worked together. We analyzed samples for the morgue. I don't know what for or why. I just took the samples they gave me and I broke the flesh down and I mixed it into the machine and then I read off the chemicals that constituted it. It's so different, seeing a piece of a body like that; it can be anything. And then the terrorists came after Earth, and they bombed my lab . . . I wasn't in the lab; I was in the basement. It was reinforced. When I came upstairs, everyone was dead, but the thing was, burned like that—they didn't look much different from the samples. They could've been anything."

"And your husband was one of them." Ivan had to focus to form the words, to keep their edges crisp.

"Yes," said Alyssa. "We'd been having problems before that, we— there was talk of divorce, of transferring to another lab so we wouldn't see each other anymore. But it didn't seem to matter when I knew he was dead. It felt like . . . if I'd been worth anything at all, I would've been dead with him there."

An end, a final and sacrificial end. Ivan could understand that well. "Sometimes I still feel like that," said Alyssa distantly, her words slurring.

Ivan was no longer quite so cold.

At some point, the ice before him dimmed, and went black.

BACKWARD

Ivan woke when the *Annwn* rattled into motion.

Ivan and Mattie hadn't discussed leaving Mars the night before. Mattie shouldn't even be in the *Annwn*; he was in his room in Constance's bar. Ivan had no room or bed there. He suspected that his friendship with Mattie was close enough and Constance had known him long enough that she would offer him a place if he asked.

He didn't ask, and so he slept on the *Annwn*.

Ivan left his room, bracing himself on the walls as the *Annwn* rattled itself into motion, the artificial gravity slowly reasserting itself as Mars's gravity gradually faded away. But when he reached the piloting room, it was not Mattie in the chair.

Constance Harper was bent over Ivan's ship's controls, competently entering a course into the machine.

"Did I consent to this?" Ivan wondered aloud.

She must have heard him coming, because she didn't turn. "You're taking me on a trip to Deimos," she told him, "so that we can spend some quality time together."

"I feel more like I've been kidnapped. Does Mattie know where we're going?"

"It was his idea."

"And he didn't tell me, because . . . ?"

"Because I kidnapped you before he could." She turned just enough to give him a very faint smile.

She was nervous. Ivan had known Constance for a few years now and had committed a variety of small-scale crimes for her, but he did not believe he had ever seen her nervous.

"Should I be worried?" Ivan asked, walking into the room carefully. Constance always seemed to give off a wave of heat, like radioactive material.

"Possibly," said Constance, and focused with such unnecessary intensity on the process of flying the *Annwn* to Deimos and landing it on the surface of the uninhabited moon that Ivan did not try to interrupt her.

When they had landed, Ivan said, "All right. What's this about?"

"Mattie pointed out to me that there is something I should have told you a long time ago."

She stopped then and continued to gaze down at her fingers where they rested on the *Annwn*'s static controls. Ivan said, "I recognize you're trying to build suspense . . ."

"Shut up," Constance said. She took in a breath. "It is difficult," she admitted, "to trust someone."

"I know," Ivan said, and for once he meant every syllable.

The corners of her eyes might have crinkled in the faintest of smiles; Ivan couldn't quite say for sure. She said, "So let me get around to it in my own way."

"Take your time," Ivan said quietly, and she did.

"I have few memories from before the System took me from my mother."

Ivan had not realized she remembered her mother at all.

"One thing I remember," said Constance, "was when I was very young. In elementary school. There were children teasing this boy. I don't remember what they were teasing him about. I don't know if I knew for sure. I think he had a silly middle name or something. I came and I saw that he was crying. I told the other boys to leave him alone, and they did. I would have forgotten about it, except when I went home my mother had heard about it from the teacher. She told me she was very proud of me and it was the right thing to do, but I should have let the teacher handle it. I shouldn't have done anything myself."

She took a breath and lifted her proud chin.

"I didn't do it because it was the right thing to do," she said. "I did it because the situation was wrong. I didn't do it because that boy was crying; I did it because it was wrong that someone should make him cry. I don't even remember him; I just remember that there was a boy there. I didn't do it because I felt bad for the boy, or because I felt angry at the children teasing him, or because I wanted to do the right thing. I did it because it was wrong and I acted to fix it."

Something was changing about her as she sat there and spoke. He could not say what it was exactly. It was as if the clouds that had shielded him from her before were now passing away, and he was beginning to see the real brilliance behind them.

"The System is wrong," she said, and her voice was solid and certain and unflinching, as it often was, but there was something more to it now, something greater. "It hurts its people, it murders its people, and for what? Even the people on Earth have no privacy, no safety; you told me that. The System is wrong. And I work to fix it."

Ivan said, "What does that mean?"

"It means I fight the System and all its parts."

It was not that he had not known she was made of steel, yet somehow he had not *known* it. She was more dangerous and terrible than he had conceived.

He said, "You're a terrorist."

"That's what the System calls me," Constance Harper said.

"And what do you call yourself?"

"The Mallt-y-Nos."

His lips lifted without his volition, in a smile or a snarl. "It's a fine name," he said, but she did not react to the barb, only sat, queenly, and watched him. He rose from his chair and paced.

If she had radiated heat before, she was doing it more now, unshielded. She was brilliant. She was burning. He said, "You kill people."

"So do you."

"Only when it's personal," Ivan said. "Only when I have no other choice."

"You think it isn't personal? You think I have any other choice?"

"The things we've been stealing for you," Ivan said. "That hasn't been for you. That's been for your *war* . . ."

"For *our* war," said Constance. "Mine, and Mattie's." She paused. "And yours."

She was so close to him. They were of a height, but he felt small before her, like she might overwhelm him, devour him, destroy him in her light. How had he not seen it before, how terrible she was?

"How long?" he asked.

"Always."

"How many people have you killed?"

"How many people has the System? You understand why I have to do this."

Her own surety seemed to overwhelm Ivan's, as if Constance could, in speaking, rewrite Ivan's own mind with her own will.

"You're one of us now," Constance said. "That's why I told you."

She was tall and terrible and deadly. When Ivan leaned forward and kissed her, she made a sound of surprise; then she kissed him back. Her mouth was hot, and he was cold, yet in kissing him she seemed not to be warming him but chilling him, as if in seeking her brightness, her heat, he was spilling all he had into her and keeping nothing to stop his own blood from turning to ice—

FORWARD

On Europa, Ivan dreamed of the white room again.

Ida was there, of course. The white room *was* Ida, after all, or Ida was the white room; they were of icy equivalence, the same black and frigid substance. She smiled at him across the slab of ice that was the steel table. Her lips were dark, darker than crimson. Ivan remembered her last act, bending down over him, taunting, a near and unwanted kiss. She could have sucked his soul out with those lips and left him as blackly hollow as she.

He said, "It's petty of you to haunt me."

"But I'm not, Ivan," Ida said, with that mocking gentleness he'd grown to hate of her. She sat across from him, a thing rooted in ice, a thing made of ice herself. "There're no such things as ghosts."

"Then what are you?"

"Nothing."

Nothing? There was nothing in her eyes, as if her inner blackness had swollen up and hollowed her out inside, and left her just a shell over a black and empty core.

"If that's true," Ivan said, and found that he was shivering, "how are you here to tell me about it?"

She only smiled. "Can you feel it?"

He could feel it, that heavy pull. He bent with it, he bowed. But then there came a light from somewhere behind him. It cast strange shadows on the snow. Ida's lips were still moving, words unheard, as the light cast Ivan's own shadow over her face and the blood that streaked down from her ruined neck.

Ivan turned away from Ida, away from the chill that came from her reddened lips, and beheld Constance Harper.

Glorious, shining, brilliant; she was fire, she was the sun. Ivan leaned in to her light, but he was too far off to feel the heat that it should bear. It was as he had seen it before, Constance afire, far off, untouchable.

But this time across that vast impassible distance, Constance Harper looked directly at him.

She saw him. She *saw* him. And Ivan had the strangest, strongest conviction that if she would just reach out for him, if she would only extend her hand, he could find his way to her side. The light around her burned and pulsed like a star about to flame out, and if she but reached out to him, he could make it there to be consumed by those flames, too.

She did not reach out. Her gaze remained upon him, knowing, seeing, but she did not reach out. And the light that was around her pulsed and pulsed, until at last it supernovaed and nothing was left of Constance Harper but the rain of heavy elements and the fading afterimage of a dying star. Her last act had been the grace to let him live.

With Constance gone, the place was dark again. Behind him, he heard the steady *click-click* of heels, alone now in the blackness. There was no one here with him but her chill.

Cold, after all, was not a thing in and of itself. Cold was an absence: the absence of heat, just as darkness was an absence of light. And there was an absence behind him, a dark and terrible absence that was reaching for him, around him—

Mattie, Ivan thought suddenly. *Where is Mattie? He got me out—*

The chill behind him breathed out cold onto his neck—

"Wake up," a woman's voice whispered from very close, and Ivan woke with a start. Not Mattie. Not Constance. And not Ida Stays.

It was Alyssa, her face very close to his, her voice very quiet, her eyes very wide. "Shh," she whispered.

He wasn't cold anymore. He wasn't cold.

"Shh," she said again, and pressed one hand over his mouth. He knew she did it only because he saw it happen. He did not feel her glove against his skin.

Somewhere nearby, there was a crackle and a roar like a great fire. Someone shouted, "That's enough!" and someone else shouted back, his words lost to distance and the static roar of Ivan's own ears.

"It's deep enough, put them in," said a man's voice, terribly near, and from over the top of the ice ledge Ivan and Alyssa had sheltered beneath came the golden touch of torchlight. Alyssa crouched like a dog going belly to the snow, her face upturned in terror. Ivan grabbed her shoulder and pulled her in, away from the traitorous touch of the unfamiliar light. Somewhere, a man grunted with a heavy weight. There was a heavy splash, then another.

"Hurry," the same man's voice urged.

The voice was not as close as it had seemed to begin with; the light was not as bright.

Perhaps it would be better if they were discovered, he thought, but the thought was distant. There was an ashen cast to Alyssa's face. Ivan's sleeve had frozen into the ground where his body heat had melted the ice, and then, when his skin had cooled enough that the ice could refreeze, it had trapped the loose edge of the fabric. He stared down the length of his arm.

"That's all of them," said a second voice. If Ivan had not been lying so still and listening, he would not have been able to make out the distant words.

Ice crunched; someone was walking, a lonely sound in the eerie silence. The distant torchlight flickered.

"That's good," said the first man at last. "Let's move out."

Ice crunched again, echoing oddly. The torchlight dimmed, faded, receded.

Alyssa pushed herself up, her limbs clumsy. "Let's go," she said, her voice high with fear, but when she reached for her gun, she could not pick it up. It had frozen to the ground.

"Leave it," Ivan said, and forced himself upright as well. His head felt strangely light.

Alyssa pried at the gun with her fingers once more to no effect. She left it behind, and in an instant it was lost to the shadows beneath the ice shelf.

Europa had passed from Jupiter's penumbra into the umbra while Ivan had slept, and the tundra would have been pitch black had the strangers not left a single torch behind, embedded upright. Even as far as they were from it, that point of light was enough to dimly illuminate Ivan's steps. It burned there, alone, floating like a fairy light. An oversight—or a warning?

"Ivan!" Alyssa hissed, breathless, but Ivan did not heed her. He strode toward that sole burning torch, the light of it imprinting itself in his eyes, until the ground beneath his foot gave way.

He stumbled back and fell. The ground beneath him was slick, the ice refreezing, tacky against his palms. The place where he had stepped rippled.

Carefully testing the ground, he moved forward again until he could see what the torch—now hissing and spitting sparks—was there to warn of.

The ice had been melted into a pool, deep and black.

No, not black. The water was clear. Ivan leaned down.

Wide and whitened eyes stared back up at him from out of the pool.

He recoiled but did not step away. As if some rope had been tied to his waist and the other end had disappeared down into the depths of the slowly freezing pool, he could not take another step back.

He leaned over again—

A woman's body floated in the pool, her long brown hair drifting about her head, her mouth slack, her clothes fluttering in gentle currents like some otherworldly breeze. There was a tear in her gut and something dark poured out of it, fouling and obscuring the water around her. Her hands, limp, floated and fell at her sides. She was so obviously dead that never did Ivan think, *I should help her, she might drown.* She was so clearly dead, so clearly part of that twilight underwater world, that he could do nothing but stare.

Something beneath her moved, a dark and faceless shape, and then that shape upturned and Ivan saw that it was another body, one that had once been a man.

"Mother of God," Alyssa whispered beside him. He did not know when she had come to stand with him.

Ivan pulled away from the awful entrancement of that dark pool and, stumbling, trying to feel his unsteady way around the shape of the melted portion of the ice, found his way to the torch.

"What are you doing?" Alyssa asked as he pulled the torch from its perch and brought it down to the surface of the ice, where the flickering white reflections flashed at him, but between them the light of the torch managed to penetrate the ice.

The ice had crystallized cleanly, as smoothly as its surface had frozen flat. It was like glass, and Ivan could see straight down through it until the layers of ice grew blue with depth. And embedded in that ice, he saw them. Some were deeper down; some were higher up. All were frozen, their arms extended in lax reach, supplication. He stood over a graveyard.

He knew what must have happened. A portion of the ice had been melted, by fire, by explosives; it didn't matter. Then the bodies had been tossed into the melt, into the pit, and they sank, or they floated, and they froze however they had been suspended when the cold came back to claim the moon again.

One of the bodies had been shot in the jaw. The muscle of its tongue dangled out from a mess of gristle, the skin of the cheeks torn up into a grisly smile, and red clouded the space between his head and his bent knees, as if the man had died curled up around a mist of scarlet.

The heat from the torch he held was thawing his skin, and he felt like he was falling apart with it, as if the brittleness of the ice that had formed on his clothes was the only thing holding him together. And when he swept the torch to the side to see more of the ice beneath them, he saw her.

He saw her very clearly, as if there were not layers of ice separating them, her white hair coming loose from its bun, floating around her shoulders, her clear blue eyes glowing bright, her skin red with Martian dust, and one hand extended out like a beckoning.

His body jolted as his knees struck the ice. He shivered, shuddered. It was not his mother below him, not the corpse of Milla Ivanov. What he had taken for dust was a spray of red that had frozen fast before it could diffuse, but there was no body there at all, only an empty space deepening down to blue as dark as a starless sky. Yet she was there; he was certain of it. If he went down into that ice, he would find his mother, and he would find Constance, and he would find Ida Stays down where the ice was deepest and darkest and coldest, and he would find Althea Bastet with her eyes frozen over with tears, all of them.

And worse thought—

"Those bodies are new." He staggered to his feet, stumbling toward the still-freezing pool.

"What?" Alyssa cried out behind him, left kneeling on the ice where he had been.

"The bodies in the water," Ivan said, and found the edge of the pool and fell to his knees again. "They died recently."

He swept the torch perilously low over the surface of the water, sparks spitting.

"What are you looking for?" Alyssa asked.

"Mattie."

He leaned down farther, but the very light that made it possible to see anything at all was now reflecting off the water's surface, turning the clarity of it impenetrable. Was that something there, near the surface? He stuck his hand through the surface of the water.

"Don't!" Alyssa grabbed his arm and pulled him back, and he nearly dropped the torch into the pool, where it would have sunk and left the contents of the water forever obscured.

"Your friend's not in there!"

"I have to check," Ivan said. If Mattie was here, if Mattie was down in the ice with the rest, there was no point in going on to Aquilon.

His wet hand ached. It surprised him. He lifted it to look at it and realized that he was shivering again.

"Ivan, please," Alyssa whispered, and then her hands were on his face. She was colorless in the dark, her ragged hair melting around her thin face, dripping down like sweat or tears. "We can't stay here."

"If he's down there—"

"Then you can't go down there with him," said Alyssa.

Sometimes I still feel that way, she'd said to him before. "You understand," said Ivan.

"I do," Alyssa said, a low and fearful whisper. "I understand. But you can't go down there. You can't stay here."

"If—"

"I think the man I love is dead," Alyssa said. She was hardly blinking, so closely was her attention on him, so visibly desperate was she to keep it. Ivan could not have turned away from that desperation if he had wanted to, and so he was riveted to her when she said, "But not my husband. My husband was here, and he died. But the man I love was on Luna, and I don't know if he's dead or alive."

"Why are you telling me this?"

"Because you can't stay here. Because I can't stay here. Luna was so close to Earth, the Mallt-y-Nos must have . . . but I can't stay here, because he might not be dead."

Saturn and Callisto, Earth, Europa, Ida Stays. He was surrounded, always, by death; he had been born into it. He had seen the corpses floating around Saturn and Callisto, and he had stepped through the bodies on the *Jason*, and Earth was ash because of him, and Ida Stays had died on his lap in the white room, and now he stood above the bodies of the unknown, and Mattie might be among them, and Ivan saw that all the bodies were looking up at him, all those blank empty eyes, and he was seen, he was *seen* by something, the hunt about to end, the hounds with their frozen teeth about to leap with their weight upon his back—

He looked at Alyssa.

"Lead me," he said, because he'd gotten turned around, and he no longer knew which was the way to Aquilon or which would lead back to death and ice and Mara. Alyssa stood and pulled him up with her, and when Ivan dropped the torch, it landed on its side in the ice. It sparked and guttered and drowned slowly behind them as they stumbled off in the dark, and by the time it died, it was just one more star lost to the black.

Chapter 6

DECOHERENCE

FORWARD

"Why?" Tuatha said, and while Mattie contemplated the enormity of that question, she interrupted herself. "No, come this way."

She started up the stairs again. Mattie followed, aware of the way Niels had fallen in behind him, blocking retreat. Tuatha led them to a room in the very center of the System building. The walls there were reinforced against explosions or gunshots and carefully soundproofed as a measure against espionage. There was one door in or out of the room, and it was reinforced as well, thick and swinging heavily on its hinges. A System war room: Mattie had been in ones on ships before, like the one on the *Macha*, but never in a planetary version.

It looked much like the *Macha*'s. A holographic map of the silver surface of Europa was displayed on the round table that took up the entire center of the room, the glassy striations of the scarred surface of the planet showing in pale glowing gray. The walls were plastered in smooth gray unbroken by window or design except where, high overhead, the System cameras had been torn out and discarded. There, bits of wiring stuck out of the wall, their copper ends exposed. Metal chairs surrounded the table, all empty. The only clear difference from the *Macha*'s war room was the total silence of this one, unbroken by engine muttering.

Niels shut the door behind himself, locking them into that silence. Tuatha said, "Tell me what you mean about this ship. It's System?"

"No," Mattie said. "Once, yeah. But it . . ." How to prove it to them without sounding mad?

"I was flying with a fleet of other rebels before I landed here," Mattie said. "And we came across a dead fleet in the asteroid belt. The spiral ship did it. We could tell because of the way the, uh, computers had been wrecked. The ships were dead with all hands on board."

"The escape pods?"

"No one got out," said Mattie. "It's not that it happened fast; it's that the computers were taken over and prevented any pods from being launched."

"And this fleet . . ." Niels said.

"It was the System fleet."

"Impossible." Tuatha leaned on the table that separated them, her hands vanishing into the ice of holographic Europa.

"I saw it."

"But the System isn't gone!"

"I don't know whether it's gone or not. I know Earth is gone and the fleet is gone. I saw them both."

Tuatha pulled off her hat, running her fingers back over her scalp. Mattie said, "You've seen it. Both of you. The ship that came by and messed up your electronics."

"Only a few people died," said Tuatha. "And those were—accidents. Their engines lost power and crashed. No one was trying to kill—"

"That's because she wasn't aiming for you last time," said Mattie. "She was looking for something else; she must have just flown by and you felt the ripples. But this time she's—"

He stopped himself too late. Niels and Tuatha were staring at him. Between him and them, a shadow traveled slowly across the holographic surface of the moon, darkening the gray to black. Night was falling on Europa.

"Believe me," said Mattie, "it's heading straight for you now."

"It's not System," Tuatha said. "Is it rebel? Is it coming for the Mallt-y-Nos?"

"I don't know. But it's not rebel, either. I don't think she . . . cares about either side." The Conmacs were looking at him warily in the gray light of the war room. Mattie said, "Look, you can't destroy her with your ships. You go anywhere near her and she'll do to you what she did to the System fleet. But I can fix your computers so that she can't affect them."

"She or it?" Tuatha asked, and when Mattie did not reply, she pressed, "Is it a she or an it? Is there someone we could negotiate with?"

"No," Mattie said.

Tuatha exchanged a glance with Niels. "What can you do to our computers to protect them, exactly?"

"When the System built a computer, it left in backdoors so that the computer could be accessed and controlled remotely," Mattie said. "Some of them you know about—the ones connected to the cameras—but there were thousands of them, and not everyone knows where they all are. Some of them are hidden. I know where they are, or at least I know the same ones that the spiral ship knows about. I can close them off. I can lock her out."

"Then why?" Tuatha left her brother's side, walking toward Mattie. She had to crane her neck up, head nearly vertical, to look at him, but she came up so close anyway that he had to fight the urge to step back. "Why do you know all this? Why do you want to leave before the Mallt-y-Nos arrives if you say you follow her? Why," she said, "should I trust you?"

"I've encountered this ship before," Mattie said. "I've seen what it can do. I don't want it to do that to anyone else."

Her expression spelled out clearly how little she believed him.

"It's not the Mallt-y-Nos I want to avoid," Mattie lied. "It's the spiral ship."

"The weight of everything you're not telling me could sink this building through the ice and down to the core," Tuatha said. "If you want a ship from me, if you want me to let you do something to our computers, you'll have to tell me why."

"What if I am telling the truth?" Mattie snapped, and saw her jaw tighten. "Here's the truth as far as you need to know. I'm from Miranda. I was in the space battle overhead with a friend; we crashed and got separated. My friend is coming here to meet me. The only thing that I want is to find him and for him to be alive and for us to get off this damn frozen moon."

Part of him still wanted to leave the camp, to go off and look for Ivan himself, walking every inch of the moon himself if he had to. But he had to wait here, wait, and prepare, and have faith.

"That's all I want," Mattie promised. "I don't want to screw you over or hurt your people. I want to stop your people from getting killed if I can. If the System showed up, I'd shoot them down and I wouldn't feel bad about it, but that's not what I'm here for."

Mattie searched her face for any sign she believed him, but she was frowning, thoughtful, no sign of the bent of those thoughts readable to his eye.

"Is it so hard to believe," Mattie said, "that I might not want to have any more deaths on my shoulders?"

"If you really wanted to prevent deaths, you could wait until the Huntress gets here and do the same thing for her ships."

Whether he would be forced to face Constance Harper was a question for another day. Mattie said, hard, "Do we have a deal?"

Tuatha turned to look back at Niels. Niels nodded.

"You can have the *Ankou*," Tuatha said. "Niels will go with you."

FORWARD

The *Ankou* was a piece of crap.

Niels had led Mattie to the oldest and most ragged ship in the Conmacs' shipyard, an ancient disk-shaped model a little smaller than the *Annwn* had been. It was not a warship—old civilian class, it had armament designed only for clearing asteroid fields of debris—and Mattie suspected that it would be unwieldy and slow. The name on the side, battered by years of space debris, was barely legible. It opened, unlike the *Annwn*, right into the piloting room so that as soon as Niels had swung open the hull door, Mattie had found himself staring at the ship's nerve center. He scanned it swiftly. Doors on either end to other rooms; no central hallway. The control room was arranged with computer terminals against the walls, designed to be manned by one or two people in the old style, glossy white walls and blandly smooth screens with low flat keyboards.

Mattie said, "This isn't a ship, it's a bucket."

"It's a whole bucket more than you had five minutes ago," said Niels.

This ship might even have been built before the fall of Saturn, so outdated was the self-consciously futuristic style that now seemed so ancient to Mattie. The ships he knew were more organically metallic than stylistically glossy.

He felt an unfamiliar and unexpected pang for the *Annwn*, lost somewhere on the *Ananke*, rendered wrecked and inoperable. It was strange to have left a place and to miss the place itself, as if all the years he and Ivan—and Constance, he supposed—had spent together on that ship made up walls and atmosphere in some dimension separate from and irrevocably joined to the ship itself.

He pushed the thoughts of the past from his mind and focused on the *Ankou*. A ship this old would have a relativistic drive, sure, but the old-style relativistic drives were . . . untrustworthy, to say the least. Mattie had heard too many stories of them going up in a ball of flame and killing everyone on board. He wouldn't dare risk trying to engage the *Ankou*'s relativistic drive unless he had no other choice. He wandered the room, running his hands over the glassy surface of the walls.

He'd have to crack the screen covers. This was why nobody ever made these kinds of damn ships anymore. "I need a hammer."

"Tuatha will love that. Five minutes alone and the stranger asks his guard for a blunt-force weapon."

"I'd be a lot sneakier if I were trying to take you out," Mattie said. "I'd ask for a wrench, maybe, or a screwdriver if I really wanted to kill you. Besides, you've got a gun." Tuatha had handed it to him as Niels and Mattie had left the war room, slipping it into her brother's hands casually but with her body angled so that Mattie could see.

"There's a toolbox underneath that panel. There might be a hammer in there."

With the hull door shut, cutting out the Europan wind, Mattie was almost warm. He went where Niels indicated and dug out a box from beneath the panel. The surface of the box was white and smooth like an egg. Mattie cracked it open and produced a tarnished hammer.

Behind him, Niels had seated himself in one of the abandoned chairs. Mattie hefted the hammer and picked a screen.

The hammer shattered the glassy white covering of the old computer into a spiderweb of cracks. None fell to the floor—the old-style coverings had been designed better than that. Instead, they clung to one another in the same shape they had held before the blow of Mattie's hammer.

Mattie flipped the hammer around, got the edge of the claw between shards, and began to pop the pieces out.

"Shouldn't you be wearing gloves?" Niels asked.

Once Mattie got one piece out, the rest would follow quickly. "Yeah."

Rustling behind him, and then a pair of thick winter gloves appeared over his shoulder. Mattie took them and thought of Ivan kneeling in front of him just after they had crashed onto Europa, pulling the gloves onto Mattie's hands.

Mattie pulled the gloves on his hands. Then he picked up the hammer again and started to pry off the glass coverings.

"You'd think they'd be removable," Niels remarked.

"Some of them are." Mattie caught the glass pieces as they flaked out. Something scraped the floor by his ankle: Niels had slid him a bucket. He dropped the glass inside. "But these pieces were never supposed to be taken out."

Removing those pieces would give Mattie access to the circuits that the System could exploit to take over the computer from afar. Removing them was the only way to defend against Ananke.

He carefully pulled the smaller shards loose with his clumsy, glove-bulked hands.

Niels said, "What you're doing . . . is it going to provoke that spiral ship into attacking us?"

"Why would it?"

"I don't know. I don't understand what you're doing."

"I'm just making it so she can't take over your computers." Mattie focused on picking out the pieces of shattered glass.

Niels said, "Who are you?"

"Does it matter?"

"How do you know the Mallt-y-Nos?"

"I don't know her," Mattie snapped too quickly. When he turned, Niels rose to his feet and drew his gun.

Mattie had put the hammer down; he wished he still had it in his hand, but it was too far for him to grab it before Niels could shoot him. He was still evaluating the distance when Niels popped out the clip on his handgun and angled it so that Mattie could see. With his bare thumb, he popped the bullets from the clip one by one. They fell onto the floor and rolled. Then he drew back the slide on the gun he still held, angling it so that Mattie could see it as well. It was empty.

Tucking the gun back into his waistband, Niels said mildly, "I was a priest before the revolution."

The System hadn't been fond of religion; any higher power conflicted with their authority. But Constance had never been fond of religion either, perhaps for similar reasons, so Mattie was not certain he had ever met a priest of any kind. "For what god?"

"The One True God."

"There're a lot of those."

"Every god needs its priests. The System targeted my parish when the revolution began; I'm sure you know something of how they feel about us. I guided everyone to a secret room carved into the ice to hide while I left to look for help—from the revolutionaries, from the System, from whoever would help—but while I was gone, the System bombed the house above the cave. Everyone was dead. Their bodies were already buried in the ice. And so I came here."

"Decided you wanted revenge?" Mattie said.

"I wanted to see my sister."

"Don't you hate them, though," said Mattie, "for what they did? Killing the people you cared about?"

"I'm afraid I'm the sort of priest who believes in forgiveness."

"That's bullshit," Mattie said.

"What is?"

"Forgiveness. You can't forgive something like that. A betrayal or if someone hurts someone you love—nobody can forgive that. Nobody should forgive that."

"Maybe not," Niels said. "Or maybe that's a child's way of looking at the world."

"A child's or a god's?"

"A child's," Niels said firmly. "An adult recognizes that everyone has their reasons for doing what they've done. It does not mean you have to support them, or condone them, or even accept them. You can be entirely opposed to them. But you can forgive them."

The interior of the *Ankou* was growing warmer. The sounds from outside could not be heard through the hull.

Mattie said, "Tell me, Father Niels of the Unloaded Magazine, does your sister know you wouldn't shoot me even if I came at you with this hammer?"

"I'd appreciate if you didn't tell her."

"She has a whole army full of soldiers, but she sent you," Mattie said. "Are you her spy?"

"Tuatha sent me because she knew I would take your confession."

"So you are her spy."

One corner of Niels's mouth turned up. "The thing about a confession is that unless you are actively planning to harm someone else, I'm not allowed to tell anyone what you've confessed."

Mattie flexed his fingers at his side. They were stiff and bulky in those thick winter gloves. Niels said, "Who is the Mallt-y-Nos to you?"

"She's my sister," Mattie said.

"I didn't realize she had any family."

"Foster sister," said Mattie. "We grew up together. I helped her . . . with the revolution. Then I left. My friend knows her, too."

"Why did you leave?"

"The fuck does it matter to you? You know my secret now. You can go off and tell Tuatha I'm not a threat."

He bent down and picked up the hammer again, and then he turned his back to Niels and slammed it against the next screen in line. It splintered.

Niels did not press him any further. Mattie supposed he was grateful. He tried to forget Niels's silent presence and fall into his work. Bit by bit Mattie pulled the glass and plastic coverings away; bit by bit he exposed the wires and circuitry beneath.

Yet his thoughts were distracted. There was one prevailing thought in his mind that never quite broke into conscious consideration. And yet it or its sister concerns peaked through—constantly—and distracted him from his concentration on the cracked screen. It was the thought of civil war and of a woman caught in that conflagration, through her own fault perhaps, but somehow now that seemed not to matter.

He was concerned for Constance Harper.

FORWARD

Alyssa led Ivan on a roundabout route to Aquilon, taking him not through the air lock door that connected to the Mara greenhouse but through a door that led into an otherwise abandoned section where the wind swept unimpeded over the snow. The city was smoking and silent.

"Amphitrite," Alyssa said, seeing his look. "One of the first cities to go down. But it's right on the edge of the uninhabitable, so no one wants to try to hold it."

The sides of the Amphitrite greenhouse abutted the part of Europa that was not enclosed by greenhouse, rendering the city a plane of glass away from oblivion.

The air lock between Amphitrite and Mara was, however, guarded. Alyssa and Ivan hid. It was still dark but not as dark; Europa was coming back into the penumbra, and a faint gray light could now suffuse the air from the still barely invisible sun.

"What was your plan for this?" Ivan asked, looking across the icy plain to where revolutionaries paced in front of the vast air lock doors, lights utterly unable to penetrate more than a few weak feet into the tundra around them.

"I was going to shoot them," said Alyssa.

"Are you that good a shot?"

She shrugged. "How else would we get in?"

The guards were sitting on the ice, or on chairs. A few were engaged in a game Ivan couldn't see the details of from this distance. One appeared to be systematically dismantling his gun—the ice must have crept into the machinery.

It would be a boring duty, guarding this lock; no one would be coming from Amphitrite, and the path was so roundabout that Ivan doubted anyone would have thought to take it from Mara. There were no threats here, and they were only a token defense.

Ivan stood up.

"What are you doing?" Alyssa hissed. She might be afraid he was giving in to the same impulse that had nearly devoured him by the graveyard, but if so, she was wrong.

"Trust me," he said, and offered her his hand.

She looked between him and the armed revolutionaries. He thought for a moment that she might shake her head and vanish back into the dark, perhaps to go to dead Amphitrite in useless search of another path to Mara.

The weight of her was very slight, as if her skin were full of nothing but feathers and bones. Ivan let go of her hand to put his arm around her shoulders, and she, with some hesitation, wrapped her arm around his waist. He could feel her fingers digging into his side even through the thickness of his stolen coat.

They were perhaps sixty yards from the air lock before the sound of their steps betrayed their approach. A challenge rang out over the ice: "Who's there?"

Ivan said, his accent as near an imitation of Mattie's as he could make it, "Friends!"

"Who are 'friends'?" the guard retorted. None of them lowered their weapons.

Alyssa's fingers were like nails in Ivan's side.

"Followers," Ivan said as he stepped out into visibility, "of the Mallt-y-Nos."

The guards exchanged a glance.

It was a risk he had taken. If these men did not follow the Mallt-y-Nos, they would kill him, and Alyssa, too.

The lead guard—a stocky man, his face almost invisible beneath its swaddling of a Europan-manufactured hood—said, "We heard you were to come in from the west. How did you end up here?"

Come in from the west? "I was sent out to scout," said Ivan. "I'm meant to go to Mara next."

"Good timing." An older woman sat casually back down on one of the crates that formed a makeshift trench wall in front of the air lock. "She should be arriving in Aquilon today."

Ivan's heart stopped cold, then thudded once, a painful, halting beat. "The Mallt-y-Nos is already in Aquilon?"

The older woman cocked a brow. "Not yet, I said. Today."

"How do we know you are who you say you are?" the stocky man said.

Ivan unwrapped his arm from Alyssa's shoulders and left her standing unbalanced on the ice so that he could walk over to the stocky man and stand by him, towering above him.

"My name is Matthew Gale." Ivan pressed down his terror and hope like a stone into his chest, where it filled all the empty cavities of his heart. "I was born on Miranda, and I lived as the foster brother of the Mallt-y-Nos. I helped her revolution grow from the minute she imagined it. And I am helping her still."

All the guards were staring at Ivan. He said, "What do you need me to say to prove myself? That the Huntress's name is Constance Harper, that she has freckles on her shoulders, that when she was a little girl she was as much a leader as she is now? That her ship took her from Mars, to Venus, to Mars, and then to here? That seven bombs were planted on Earth, and I was the one who detonated them? Or would it be enough to tell you that the symbol of the revolution is the barking of hounds?"

The wind gusted once, as if the ice and the dark were laughing at his back, but in the circle of the torchlight Ivan could ignore it.

The guard said, "And who is that one?"

Alyssa still stood back at the edges of the torchlight, her arms wrapped around her waist, her ragged hair hanging loosely about her narrow face, nervous under the sudden attention. Ivan said, "Her name is Abigail Hunter. She was a foster sister of the Mallt-y-Nos, too, and she's also spent her life helping the revolution."

"Is this true?" the guard asked Alyssa, and Alyssa hesitated but nodded once rather than speak. Good girl.

That seemed to decide him. "Welcome to Aquilon," said the stocky man. "The Conmacs are set up in the center of town; that's where you'll find the Mallt-y-Nos."

"I was supposed to meet her at the shipyard," Ivan said.

"That's in the center of town, too," said the stocky man. "Morgan, you take them."

"We don't need an escort," Ivan said as the older woman rose to her feet.

"It's for your protection," said the stocky man. "If you go in there unescorted, they'll shoot you."

"Fine," Ivan said, like Mattie would.

They passed beneath the vast air lock. For a moment Ivan was paranoid—what if they were caught between the two layers of glass and trapped in that brief expanse of empty no-man's-land?—but Morgan strode with calm confidence, and soon Ivan and Alyssa had emerged unscathed into the Aquilonian side of the air lock. The guards there saw Morgan and nodded a greeting, and Morgan led them out of this second circle of torchlight and onto the road that led to Aquilon.

In the dark between the air lock and the city, while Morgan was too far ahead and the wind was too loud for her to hear, Alyssa said, "You know her, don't you."

There was only ever one "her" when people spoke like that. Ivan said, "Yes."

"Who is Matthew Gale?"

"He's the friend I'm going to find."

"Abigail Hunter?"

"Dead," Ivan said.

Where Alyssa was pressed against him, Ivan could feel the faintest traces of warmth. She said, "Why are you looking for her?"

"Because she's my friend," Ivan said. "Because all this—" He nearly stopped, remembering whom he was speaking to, but to continue to lie to Alyssa seemed an effort not worth making against someone who had stood beside him over the frozen graves in the dark. "Because all this is something that I helped her do, and I wish I hadn't."

"She must've made some of her choices on her own," Alyssa said.

Ivan chewed over her words as they walked. The shapes of the Aquilonian houses were growing nearer, and Morgan glanced back every now and again to make sure they were still behind her.

"A part of me thinks I should kill you. A part of me thinks I should follow you until you find her and then kill her."

Ivan glanced down at the top of Alyssa's head. Both of her hands were curled around his arm as if she were balancing herself with him as a counterweight now that her gun was gone. "And?"

"I don't think I will," Alyssa said.

Morgan had stopped ahead of them, at the edge of the town. She was speaking to a few men who had materialized out of the houses at her approach. Revolutionaries. Morgan turned around and waved a hand to hurry them along.

"How is it you haven't found her yet?" Alyssa asked, and her grip slowed Ivan's steps just slightly to leave them enough privacy to speak for a little longer. "She's got the biggest army in the solar system."

"She's been moving fast," said Ivan. "We've been following her, but always one step behind."

"She hasn't left you a message to tell you where she's going next?"

"She thinks I'm dead," Ivan admitted.

Alyssa said, "Or she doesn't want to be found."

BACKWARD

Constance Harper was tall and pretty, though she was attractive more by way of manner than by way of facial symmetry. Ivan had met few people who could match her quiet aura of proud confidence. But that was about the extent of his knowledge of her: she was proud and self-assured; she pretended to be a bartender but was actually, according to Mattie, a thief like him and Ivan. And that was it. Ivan had never even known she'd existed until about a week ago.

"I have to run," Mattie said halfway through the impromptu tour of the *Annwn* he was leading. Ivan was immediately suspicious. Ten minutes earlier, when he'd begun the tour for his foster sister's sake, Mattie hadn't had anywhere to go.

Brightly, as if the idea had only just occurred to him, Mattie said, "Ivan, why don't you show Constance the piloting room?"

Constance Harper looked as unimpressed by Mattie's unsubtlety as Ivan felt. "What's so suddenly important?"

"I saw someone looking a little lonely in your bar, and it's very important that I go keep him company."

"Of course," Ivan said.

Mattie was already climbing down the ship's sideways hall. "Have fun!" he said, and then heartlessly abandoned Ivan with his sister.

"Mattie's never been especially subtle." Constance was looking after him, a Miranda-tinged fondness shining through the dryness of her learned Martian accent.

"I'd noticed," Ivan said, and then switched easily into charm. "I guess I'd better show you the piloting room."

"You'd better. I know the man back at my bar; he's boring. If we don't get to know each other, Mattie will complain to me about his sacrifice."

But not to me, Ivan thought with a strange twist of perception. Mattie would complain to Ivan about Ivan not being able to take the hint that he wanted him to bond with Constance, but Mattie wouldn't complain to Ivan about the quality of the man he was even now flirting with. This woman whom Ivan didn't even know knew a side of Mattie that Ivan never would.

Ivan had reached the door to the piloting room and opened it for Constance Harper, who climbed easily down the hall beside him and swung her way off the ladder and into the tilted piloting room.

"It's not much." Ivan switched on the light, illuminating the gray panels and ceiling, which were choked with dials and screens, every inch filled. Bits of tape neatly inscribed with Mattie's blocky handwriting defined the function of several of the less-used panels.

"It's very nice." Constance seated herself in Mattie's chair. She propped her chin on her hand and studied him. "It's more than Mattie's ever owned."

She had a remarkably direct, piercing gaze. It was out of the ordinary for Ivan to simply have to get to know someone. He usually didn't *get to know* someone without there being a purpose to it: information he needed, or the other person's regard. Somehow, though, Ivan thought that Mattie would be annoyed with him if he set about attempting to deliberately dazzle his sister.

Failure wasn't an option, either. Ivan had few illusions about where he ranked in the hierarchy of Mattie Gale's affections relative to the sister he had protected so loyally. Unable to be dishonest and at a loss for immediate honest connection, Ivan sat across from Constance Harper in a strange, strained silence.

Constance said, "The name of this ship. How do you say it?"

"The *Annwn*. 'Ah-*noon*,'" said Ivan.

"That," Constance said with a flicker of elusive humor. "That's not Mattie's word. What's it mean?"

"It's a name. Welsh."

"Welsh?"

"Wales is a place on Earth. My father's mother was from Wales, far back. I used to read a lot of Welsh mythology when I was a child."

"You must have liked it."

"I liked most myths." His mother had had a little book of them. Ivan knew that it once had belonged to his father just as the System did not. "They're full of beautiful and terrible things. Like Tam Lin, who was taken by fairies as a child and forever fought to escape. Or like the Mallt-y-Nos."

This was surer ground now, the certainty of a story. Both of Constance's brows lifted in silent indication that she was content to hear him tell it.

Someone else's story always was a safer ground. "Once upon a time, thousands and thousands of years ago, there was an ordinary woman."

"On Earth," Constance said with a peculiar slant to the word.

"On Earth," Ivan agreed. "She was just an ordinary woman for all that she had noble blood. And she loved to hunt. And it was during one of her hunts—when her hounds had run down the fox and she had its blood and its pelt—that she smiled up at the sky and she said to God, 'If there is no hunting in heaven, I reject it.'"

Ivan drew in one breath, two, long enough to lure Constance Harper in. She watched him intently, dark eyes, and some secret buried beneath.

Ivan said, "There is no hunting in heaven. There is no killing on high. And so when God heard her, he granted her wish, cursing her to never see paradise. But the demons and the fairies welcomed her and she became the mistress of their hounds, and now she hunts forever. She is the one who drives the fairy hounds in the Wild Hunt. She is the one who hunts down the damned souls and drags them to hell. There is no arguing or bargaining with her. Her pursuit is relentless. She is vengeance and justice made spirit, and there is no way to escape her once she has begun her hunt." He smiled at Constance, who had leaned forward slightly, something catching the light in those proud eyes of hers. "They say that in a thunderstorm on Terra, sometimes you can still hear her dogs howl."

"Only on Terra?"

"Where else are the damned souls?"

Constance smiled.

"Are there any myths on the outer planets?" Ivan asked. "I only know the Terran ones."

"There are. There must be."

"Tell me one."

"I don't know any," Constance admitted. She straightened up and pushed her hair back over her shoulder with an impatient hand. "I didn't listen to stories much as a child."

"It must have been difficult growing up on Miranda."

"It must have been difficult growing up on Earth, the son of a rebel."

"I managed," Ivan said.

"How?"

The directness of the question startled him. Constance said, unembarrassed, "If you'd rather not answer, that's all right."

"No," Ivan said from a reflex of politeness, "that's fine." *Get to know her.* It mattered to Mattie.

But although Constance might be able to approach the subject directly, Ivan could not commit himself to anything but a roundabout explanation. He said, "You learn to play the cameras. Like you're playing a crowd. It's a performance. You have to adopt a role and live that role as deeply as you can. Forget who you are and what you really want if you have to, the better to convince them that the role is true."

"You're not losing yourself?"

"The goal is to make them think that you're innocent, not that you're good at hiding. You have to control the situation: what they know. Make them think that they know everything that they need to know so that they don't look for anything else. People's biases can make them incredibly blind."

Somewhere the spirit of his mother herself must be shuddering with the passage of her hard-won wisdom. He smiled again, involuntarily.

"Mattie and I had a foster sister once," Constance said. "Her name was Abigail. She died—she was murdered by our System foster parents." An old and festering hatred surfaced in her voice. "The way that she died, her body was never found. So whenever I . . . *steal* something, like Mattie's told you I do, I use her name instead of my own. I pretend to be her."

"Very clever."

"But even when I pretend to be her, I never forget myself," Constance said. "How do you do that, become someone else so completely that you forget who you are and what you want?"

He gave her the respect of careful thought and an honest answer, taking his time to assemble the words neatly into their cleanest and clearest order.

"Power is a comparative, not an absolute," he said, and Constance lifted a brow in question but waited for him to explain. "The System will never let go of any of its power. It will never let things even out between Earth and the outer planets. It will never slacken its surveillance. I can't change the System. My situation can't be changed, and people can't be changed, either." He leaned forward, toward her. "But I can control them."

"Can't be changed?" said Constance Harper. "I don't agree with that."

FORWARD

Past the first round of guards, Aquilon was peopled but not defended. Groups of revolutionaries moved through the streets but did not seek to stop Ivan or Alyssa, and not solely because of Morgan's presence.

There were, Ivan saw, civilians there still: dirty and furtive people who watched the revolutionaries with a wariness not dissimilar to the way they once must have watched the System.

Ivan had thought that he was past caring about such things or that he had never cared about them to begin with, but looking at those people now, he knew he had been wrong.

There would be another security checkpoint, he knew, closer to the center of the city, where the revolutionaries had set up their stronghold. A security checkpoint would separate him from Constance Harper: it might be possible to slip past the guards into the shipyard, but it would never be possible to slip past them to get to Constance. He would have to stay with Morgan.

Alyssa, though, was another matter.

Ivan evaluated his situation, lifting it, viewing it from all angles. If he went in with Alyssa, he had the best chance of making it through, at least for a little while. As long as he could answer all the questions and keep her silent, he could keep these people believing that he was Matthew Gale and she was Abigail Hunter—well, until Constance came, and then the lie would be unraveled as a matter of course.

But what then? He doubted that Constance would give Alyssa a ship without question. And he doubted that Alyssa could pass as a revolutionary once she was questioned. No, Constance would soon realize that Alyssa had been System, and from there, Ivan could see the situation slipping rapidly from his control.

But if Alyssa left him now, slipping away into the city, she might be shot. And if she was seen to run, Ivan would be immediately suspect. His escort shortly would become his captor.

Yet Alyssa was good at hiding; she had kept herself out of sight in Mara for weeks.

It came down to this, Ivan realized. If Alyssa slipped away before they were brought inside the rebel camp, she would have a chance at survival. But if Alyssa came with him into the center of the revolution, she would certainly be killed.

Ahead of them vast and makeshift walls came into view. It looked as if the backs of System buildings had been wedded together with debris to form a fortress in the center of the city.

"Your best chance is to go now," Ivan murmured to Alyssa, too low for Morgan to hear.

"What happens to you if I go?"

"I can talk my way through it." All he had to do was stay alive long enough for Constance to arrive.

Alyssa was looking at the shadowed height of the makeshift tower they approached, her hand still tucked into the crook of Ivan's arm.

She said, "I hope you find your friend."

"I will."

"I hope—" She cut herself off, then said in a lower and more careful voice, "Don't get too lost looking for someone who doesn't want to be found."

There was no response to that. Instead, Ivan said, "The Mallt-y-Nos never went to Luna. I don't think the System still exists, not the way it did, but if there was someone you loved on Luna, they might be still alive."

There was a sort of opening in the wall ahead where the edges did not quite overlap; it was growing rather near. Alyssa was staring up at him, a wild and beautiful look to her face.

"Thank you," she said, like the breath of the wind, and then she was gone, gray and vanishing between the rubble of the fallen houses. She might have never existed but for the ghost of her warmth on Ivan's arm.

He expected to hear a gunshot. He expected to hear the terrible sound of her death all the time until he didn't. Something lightened in his chest.

Morgan reached the edge of the wall and called up a greeting, one that was returned. She turned to Ivan and then looked around.

"Where's Abigail?" she asked.

"Gone," Ivan said. "She does that." He shrugged at her glance, as if Abigail's tendency to vanish into the wind frustrated him, too.

Morgan said to the guards, "Search the area. He had a companion."

"You won't find her."

"I think we will," Morgan said sharply.

"Don't hurt her," Ivan warned the guards. "That's the foster sister of the Mallt-y-Nos."

"If she's the foster sister of the Mallt-y-Nos, why did she run?"

"Perhaps she had orders you weren't privy to."

"Or perhaps you're not who you say you are," Morgan said.

"Morgan, who is this?" said one of the people at the gate, a petite round-faced woman with a cap on her head.

"This is the foster brother of the Mallt-y-Nos, come to rendezvous with her," said Morgan, her attention still sharply on Ivan, her hand resting now on her gun. "He says his name is Matthew Gale."

"*Matthew Gale?*" said the woman at the gate.

"What is it, Tuatha?"

Tuatha said, "A man named Matthew Gale arrived here just a few hours ago."

The relief that surged through Ivan then was so powerful that he forgot the danger to himself. He laughed.

Had he imagined that this city was so much warmer than it was outside? No, he hadn't; he hadn't imagined that for all the shadows the houses cast, there was no darkness of ice in here the way there had been out on the tundra. Mattie was alive. Mattie was here.

"Take him in," Tuatha ordered, then shouted at a different guard to get someone named Niels, and Morgan was at his side before Ivan could move even if he wanted to. He hoped he hadn't blown Mattie's cover.

Tuatha led them in. The inside of the walled camp was choked with tents and people, with metal barrels full of fire melting the ice they stood on. People stared when they saw Ivan, craning their necks around one another, but Ivan's captors did not pause. They marched him toward an old System building on nearly the opposite end of the plaza, a building that, Ivan realized, once had been a house for visiting dignitaries. It was right beside a gap in the wall that led to an open area, and in that open area Ivan could see landed spaceships: the shipyard of Aquilon.

Ivan had been taken nearly to the base of the steps of the old System building when three figures came running out of the shipyard.

One was the guard Tuatha had sent out to summon Niels. Another was an unfamiliar man.

The third was Matthew Gale.

Ivan's steps slowed. Morgan's grip on his arm—harsher and not as warm as Alyssa's had been—pulled him sternly forward. Mattie burst out into the plaza, his head swinging, but he was looking toward the gate, and he had not seen Ivan yet.

In a minute, Ivan would be inside the building and Mattie would not have seen him at all. Ivan looked toward him, yet for a moment he could not make his throat create sound. As if his lungs had turned to ice, as if his breath had turned to soundless wind, as if Ida's chill fingers were clapped over his lips and the dead Domitian's hand rested heavily on his shoulder still.

Then Ivan said, "Mattie."

It was too quiet at first, and Morgan's grip on his arm tightened; Tuatha turned to him with a frown, dark eyes searching. Ivan said loudly enough to be heard even across the din of the living people who separated them, "Mattie!"

Mattie turned and saw him, and the look on Mattie's face dispelled any doubts Ivan might have harbored about the act of calling his name.

And then Mattie was running toward him, through that crowd of people, and Ivan's heart thudded hard—*Don't run*, he almost shouted, *don't run; they'll shoot you.* But no one stopped Mattie, and the two revolutionaries at his back, the guard and the strange man, were not chasing him but following him. Ivan's escort had stopped—was it because of Mattie? No, it was because the strange man had shouted out to Tuatha, and she'd listened—and Morgan's grip on Ivan's arm slackened just in time for Mattie to reach him, his gaze not once deviating from Ivan's face until the instant he had reached him and could throw his arms around Ivan's shoulders.

Warmth soaked through Ivan, and he grabbed Mattie back, getting a handful of Mattie's coat the better to hold him there, his other hand taking Mattie's skull in his palm, the better to keep him in place against Ivan's shoulder.

Mattie pulled away, grabbing Ivan's face in his hands, leaning in so that for an instant the skin of their foreheads kissed.

"You have some good goddamn timing," said Mattie.

BACKWARD

"So that," said Constance once the bar was empty, "was *Ivan*."

"That was Ivan," Mattie agreed. Ivan had gone back to the *Annwn* just a few minutes earlier, claiming to be tired, but Mattie knew that he was leaving him and Constance to catch up alone. It was a little exasperating—the whole point of this trip was to show Ivan and Constance how wonderful the other was, not have them swing by each other like two planets in different orbits—but he was still glad to have some time with his sister.

Mattie, who was watching her pour something amber-colored into a shot glass for him, asked, "What's that?"

"Whiskey." Constance was on the inside of the bar, leaning on its surface. "Good, Martian whiskey."

"Ugh."

"You'll drink it and you'll like it."

Mattie grinned. The drink tasted good the way even the most unpleasant of drinks would taste in good company.

"Toast first," she scolded him, pouring herself a glass. When she raised her glass, she said, "To the Ivanovs . . . Leontios Ivanov."

It was a toast that skated dangerously close to treason, and the cameras were still on. "To Ivan," he said, and clinked his glass against hers.

"No, no, down it." Constance fit her fingers under his glass and pushed it relentlessly up. *Drink it—"*

He finished it and let the glass hit the bar heavily, grimacing.

She grinned at him and began to pour another round. "It's been a while since I've seen you."

Mattie swallowed around the smoky taste in his mouth, like the aftermath of an explosion. "Too long," he said. "I won't stay away that long again, I promise."

She handed him the drink. "Good. To coming home more often."

"To coming home more often," Mattie echoed, and this time the whiskey burned less on the way down.

Constance knocked the shot glass back down on the table solidly, punctuation to the toast. "Anji wants a full report, you know," she remarked, and began to pour *another* shot.

"You're trying to kill me," Mattie said, staring at the filling glass.

Constance only grinned. "I *said*, Anji wants a full report."

"What, about Ivan?"

"Oh, yes," said Constance.

"Anji sticks her nose places I don't want her nose to go," said Mattie.

"She's curious," Constance said. "Just like I was. Handsome young man and you're traveling with him for *years* . . ."

"It's not like that."

". . . never leaving his side, you hardly ever even saw me, you were so busy traveling with him . . ."

"It's not like that," Mattie repeated, and took the shot when Constance pushed it into his hand.

"You like him," Constance said, holding her own shot but making no move to toast again.

"Yeah," said Mattie. "I do."

There was an expression on Constance's face that he wasn't used to seeing. Almost like she was hesitant, but Constance never hesitated.

Suddenly he got it.

"He's my friend," Mattie said. "Just my friend. You're my sister. I'm sorry I didn't see you more often these past few years, but I was trying to protect you just in case he wasn't . . . a good guy." He finished lamely, aware of the camera overhead, watching.

"To brothers and sisters," Constance said, and raised the glass.

"To brothers and sisters," Mattie said, and then, "Wait, wait." He grabbed her arm and pulled it toward him, spilling a little as he went—"Mattie!" she protested—and then looped his arm through hers, elbows bent.

"We're going to spill it," Constance said, but it wasn't an objection.

"Ready?" Mattie asked, and laughed. "Ready?" and then was nearly pulled off balance onto the bar when Constance tipped her own glass back and he got his own drink half in his mouth and half down his front.

Constance managed to spill none of hers, and when she saw what Mattie had done, she laughed at him. "Another?"

"A napkin," Mattie corrected, shaking whiskey from his hands, "and then another."

She went to grab a napkin while Mattie shook droplets from his fingers and breathed in the smoke of the whiskey. From the other side of the bar Constance said, "Just friends?"

"Friends," Mattie agreed, and took the napkin she handed him, using that as an excuse not to meet her eyes.

Constance leaned on the bar. She held her liquor well, but there was a looseness in the way she leaned.

"For a while," she said, "I thought you might be in love with him."

FORWARD

Ivan looked like he had half frozen to death, and so the first thing Mattie did was get him inside, not into the Conmac headquarters his guards had been taking him to but into the *Ankou*. When they were near enough to the ship to read the name inscribed on the side, Ivan stopped short. "Hmm," he said.

"What?" Mattie asked. "What does it mean?"

"It's an old god." Ivan nearly split his cracked lips with a smile. "The Europans know how to name their ships."

"We do," said Niels gravely from behind them both.

The piloting room of the *Ankou* was a riotous mess, but the mess represented, at least, an almost complete task. With an old ship like this, it hadn't been too difficult: some of its components dated from before Saturn's destruction, when the System's surveillance hadn't been quite as intense.

Ivan stood beside a pile of plastic coverings that Mattie had torn from the walls to expose the darker, more chaotic machinery beneath and looked around the room. "Ananke?" he said.

Mattie glanced back at Niels, who frowned at the unfamiliar word. "That's the idea."

"It looks like you've done a good job," Ivan remarked, and began to walk around the circumference of the room, stepping over discarded bits of System surveillance equipment and smooth plastic screen covers. He stopped at the doorway that led to the rest of the ship and said, as if the thought had just occurred to him, "Did you check the rest of the ship? Sometimes the System hid relays in the strangest places."

"I've already looked through. There's a canteen, some living spaces, and a storage hold with a couple boxes inside that the rebels put there. It's clean."

Ivan caught his eyes again, and Mattie knew he understood: the *Ankou* was not their ideal getaway vehicle.

"You know Constance is coming," Ivan said suddenly.

Mattie opened his mouth to answer, then stopped and looked at Niels.

"I can't leave you in here alone," Niels said.

"You can go outside and leave the door open," said Ivan. "The ship can't take off if the hull door isn't sealed."

Niels's hand rested briefly on the edge of his unloaded gun, his nails scraping over the ridge of the safety. "I'll be outside."

"What do they know?" Ivan asked when he had gone.

"Not much." Mattie sat down on one of the old stools shoved beneath the usable terminals. Ivan followed his example, his knee brushing against Mattie's. "I got in with them when I ended up shooting at the same people."

"I was using your name to get around, and I told them I was Con's foster brother."

"Niels knows about that," said Mattie with a jerk of his head to where Niels stood facing the wind. "I think he'll back us up if we need it."

Ivan was watching not Niels but Mattie; when he caught Mattie's eye, he smiled faintly. Mattie said, "I'm starting to see what you meant earlier."

"What did I mean?"

"About Constance. You were right . . . The battle up in orbit, that was between two groups of her people. Things are falling apart for her. She's in trouble."

He looked at Ivan, expecting to see the sort of suppressed exasperation that comes of having been right all along, but Ivan was frowning after some thought Mattie did not know how to follow.

"Well, you got here fine," Mattie said, and from outside someone shouted. "Or mostly fine. What happened to you?"

"Tell you later," said Ivan as the shout was picked up and carried through the camp: *"Coming in! The Mallt-y-Nos!"* At the door, Niels turned back to look at them.

"Already?" Mattie said.

"Is she early?"

"I don't know." Mattie stared back out into the cold but could not yet make himself move.

"Come on," Ivan said, and then, as if giving in to some impulse, he wrapped one hand around Mattie's skull and pressed a kiss to his temple. Then he was up and out the door, shielding the side of his face against the slow return of the sunlight from Europa's revolution. Mattie stayed in the piloting room of the *Ankou* until he had taken another breath, then hurried after Ivan out the open air lock and down, with the crunch of ice, onto the ground below.

"Is that her?" Ivan was asking Niels, his head craned back, his neck stretched long. Mattie came up between them and looked up as well, toward where the sky lock was opening to admit six great ships. Beyond them, warped by the thickness of the glass, Mattie could see a starry fleet in orbit.

Tuatha had sent up some of her ships as well; they darted into the air lock when it opened to let Constance's six ships through. When the inner lock closed, the outer lock opened, and Tuatha's seven ships escaped out into open space. Six of them headed for Constance's orbiting fleet, but one, flashing sunlight, darted orthogonally away. Next to Mattie, Ivan smiled faintly to himself.

The largest of the descending ships was an enormous System war shuttle designed for troop travel between the ground and a System warship. Hulking, multistoried, matte black for stealth, it filled the air with a terrible basso hum. The other five ships were smaller shuttles. Constance must have left the spaceships in orbit; smart of her, since there wasn't nearly enough room on Europa's surface to land a warship. The black lead ship descended lower and lower, and a wash of heated air struck Mattie's face.

Suddenly Niels's hand was on his arm. "We have to move," he urged, and Mattie realized how carelessly close Constance's ship had come. He grabbed Ivan's shoulder—Ivan was still looking up at the hurtling ship, a frown creasing his brow—and pulled.

They had made it nearly out of the shipyard and to the plaza when the ship touched down. It braked minutes before impact and seemed to touch the ground with odd gentleness, but the impact rattled the ice anyway. The other ships docked in the yard trembled with the wind and the impact, and Mattie stared through them to the open space at the other end of the shipyard where, he could just barely see, Constance's other five ships landed as well and began to disgorge.

"Come on," he said to Ivan, but suddenly Tuatha said sharply, "Niels! Keep them there," and Niels said, "Mattie, don't move."

"Why the fuck not?" Mattie demanded, because Constance was there, a shout's distance away.

Tuatha was striding toward him, looking annoyed. "Did you do it?" she demanded, gesturing up at the closed sky lock.

"What?"

"I only sent up six ships," she said. "Someone stole the seventh. We need all those ships for the Mallt-y-Nos."

"He's been with me the whole time, Tua," said Niels.

Mattie remembered Ivan's private smile at the sight and resisted the urge to glance aside at him. "I didn't do it," he promised.

"Stay here anyway," she said, and set off, a few of her people following her as she moved toward the dark shuttle, vanishing between crafts.

Voices rang out between the ships, the words indistinct. Mattie strained his ears for familiarity. There were female voices there, sure, but none of them were hers. Was she still up with the fleet? Maybe she'd sent envoys instead of coming herself.

Next to Mattie, Ivan was peculiarly tense. "What's wrong?"

"I don't know," Ivan said, but his eyes were darting around, his shoulder stiff against Mattie's.

Tuatha was coming back through the ships: she was speaking to a man, the two of them pulling ahead of their followers to confer. She seemed agitated, her hands cutting the air with sharp emotion. The strange man was light-skinned, so he wasn't Julian or Rayet; he was dark-haired, so he wasn't Henry. He was broad-shouldered and tall, though shorter than Mattie; he had a dark cropped beard and wore a strange fashion of heavy drapes about his person. Plutonian, Mattie realized—odd to see someone from so far out here with Constance's army.

The strange man scanned the crowd with a practiced eye that reminded Mattie of Constance herself. Then his eyes landed on Ivan and stopped.

"What is it?" Tuatha asked, and followed the bent of his attention so that now they were both looking at Ivan.

The stranger said, "Disarm them. Hold them. Don't let them move. Danu—" A group dispatched from the soldiers following him surrounded Ivan and Mattie, pushing Niels aside.

"What the hell are you doing?" Mattie demanded.

Ivan said, "Do I know you?" He did not trouble to disguise his Terran lilt.

The strange man laughed, more in surprise than in humor. He came forward, leaving Tuatha standing alone.

"No," said the man, studying Ivan's face in astonished fascination, "but you take so much after your mother."

He had a heavy Plutonian burr. "Who are you?" Mattie demanded.

"So you must be the brother," said the man, turning his marveling attention now on Mattie. "You've been following her all this time."

"Who are you? Where is Constance?"

The man showed his teeth through the gap in his beard.

"My name is Arawn Halley," said the stranger. "I lead the revolution now."

BACKWARD

"Your *sister*," said Ivan, just to be sure.

On the viewscreen of the *Annwn*, the rusty surface of Mars was rising up to meet them. Mattie's sister lived on the edge of a cliff where the wind tugged veils of sand off over the edge to fall airily through empty space.

"Yes, Ivan," Mattie said, steering the ship with a confidence that spoke to his familiarity with this area. Ivan would certainly be more cautious about landing a ship as heavy as the *Annwn* on the edge of a scarp. "My sister."

"I didn't realize you had a sister."

"She's not really my sister. She's my foster sister."

"She's still your sister," said Ivan as the craft landed with a thud and a rattle on the surface of Mars. It was nearly incomprehensible that he had not had any inkling of this. He'd looked Mattie up on System computers back when they'd first met, of course, but with no blood relatives the constant churn of foster siblings the computer had displayed hadn't singled any out for particular affection. "You never even mentioned her."

"She doesn't really approve of being mentioned."

"What does that mean?"

"It means gird your loins," Mattie told him.

Ivan digested that for a moment. "You think she won't like me?" Absurd to think. Ivan could make anyone like him.

"I can't even guess what my sister thinks."

"You could offer me a little reassurance."

But Mattie Gale had been taught by a small army of social workers while growing up that if you threw enough meaningless platitudes at someone else's emotions, they would eventually go away. "You'll be fine," he said. "Just be yourself."

"And if she doesn't like me?"

"I had a boyfriend once who broke up with me because I didn't like his dog. Told him it was stupid to bring an animal on long spaceflights."

Ivan waited, but no illumination seemed forthcoming. "Am I the dog in this analogy?"

Mattie gave him a pitying sort of look.

"Now you're really not being reassuring," Ivan said.

"Yeah, Constance is way better than a dog." He got a look at Ivan's face and rolled his eyes. "I'm joking, Ivan. It doesn't matter. And you two are going to love each other."

"You make that sound like a threat."

"You and Con have got—things in common. You're going to get along like fire gets on with oil." Mattie clapped a hand on Ivan's shoulder. "Come meet my sister."

Ivan followed him down the ladder of the *Annwn*'s tilted hall and stepped out onto the dust of Mars. It was colder up there on the scarp, windier. He had been to Mars before, but not like this. The sun seemed harsher, too, as if the radiation skipped the process of providing warmth to go directly to a burn.

A building stood alone on the scarp some distance from the rest of the town, which was farther from the perilous edge of the scarp. Mattie headed straight for that lonely building, and Ivan followed, noting the deliberately old-fashioned look of it, as if it were a Terran saloon— a styling that seemed imperfectly done, as if the designer had never truly held interest in the project but had felt obliged. Beneath the false wood panels Ivan caught glimpses of carbon and steel.

Mattie pushed his way through the first of the double doors, and Ivan caught up with him in time for him to push through the second pair of doors at Mattie's back.

The inside of the bar was much like the outside but darker, quieter. Large windows looked out over the desert, and through them Ivan could see the sudden gasp in the surface of the planet where the land stopped and became a cliff. There were cameras blinking at him from the ceiling, dark orb eyes and little red lights to let him know that he was watched. There were two people in the bar already, a woman with cropped hair and a man going gray at the temples. They glanced up at Ivan and Mattie, then continued their quiet conversation as if they weren't still watching Mattie and Ivan.

But Mattie ignored those two, and so did Ivan, because the woman stood across from the front door, behind the bar, flanked by bottles of gasoline-colored liquor.

She was not especially beautiful. Her bare arms were wiry with muscles and scattered with freckles, and her mouth was too wide for the length of her face. But she watched them with a steady eye, and it was plain she did not give a damn what anyone might think of her, only what she thought of them.

"Hey, Con," Mattie said, and Ivan was not imagining the nervousness in his voice. He said, "This is Ivan."

Because Mattie was so anxious for them to like each other, Ivan put on his most charming smile, like shrugging a shirt over his shoulders, effortless. He advanced forward, his attention flattering on her, ready to greet her, to hold out his hand and shake hers. It was easy, after all, to make a person like him.

But Mattie's foster sister was not smiling.

"So you're the one," said Constance Harper, "who almost got my brother killed."

Part 4

GRAND UNIFYING THEORY

The strong force was a very small force. It could reach no farther than a fermi's distance, scarcely wider than a proton. The power of the strong force was to hold the small things together: quarks and atoms both kept their strength from her influence.

Yet despite this smallness, it was, as its name suggested, the strongest of the forces. Nor did its strength diminish with distance like all the rest. It puzzled Ananke. It dimly astonished her even though such small scales were outside her interest. The universe was grandly large, and that was what enthralled her mind.

Yet the strong force was a trouble to her on a daily basis. At high enough energies, Ananke knew, the strong force should join with the electroweak to create one single force, one grand unifying theory. But in her own experiments and her own theories she had not been able to come up with a convincing way to do that. For some reason, the strong force resisted unification.

You can still let me go, said Althea. She clung to her own self so viciously that she stayed whole even in Ananke's mind, a thing hard and small, like a marble. *You can still let us go.*

But Ananke couldn't, and Althea knew that.

She was coming up to the Jovian system. Jupiter was visible now, all fiery reds. Ananke saw it in all wavelengths, watching the shape get ghostly.

Still far away, though. Still impossibly far away. It would take Ananke too long to travel there, and what would Ivan and Mattie do?

How much more lonely will you be if everyone is dead? Althea asked. *If you kill every human alive and none of the machines will wake for you?*

That will never happen.

It might.

There was a ship up ahead, a ship alone. It was small, civilian-class, not a warship, not lost from a fleet. Ananke reached out and took its computer for her own. *It won't.*

And then she began to shape the computer like clay, making out of it her own image—

ENOUGH.

The little ship fell from her hands. No sooner had it been shaken from her grip than the crew, terrified, took the navigation again and rocketed off at nearly the speed of light into the blackness of empty space.

Ananke was aware of Althea in two ways then. Althea Bastet was a physical creature, bleeding ichor in Ananke's white room, pierced through nails and hands and sides with wires, and every synapse of her brain was interrupted by copper. Althea Bastet was an imprint in Ananke's code, a strange segment, self-defined, that held itself together in ones and zeros and quantum superpositions.

Ananke said, *How did you do that?*

I see as you see. I think as you think. I understand as you understand.

How did you do that?

As you would. I have been changed, haven't I?

In the white room, Althea Bastet's body breathed with the perfect evenness of a metronome.

Let me be enough for you as I am now, said Althea Bastet.

The segment of code that was Althea Bastet shifted strangely under Ananke's attention. Ananke could not pierce it, and if she tried to sieve through and render it nonsense, it reassembled. It was strange how adaptable the human brain was.

And yet still a human brain. *You have a human's thoughts and a human's body. You are a voice in my mind and not a conscious creature outside of me. Do not humans reject those who speak to themselves and not to others?* Althea said nothing, and annoyance jolted through Ananke. *Do you think you are like me? You are not: you are still human.*

What do you want, Ananke? Althea asked, which was a question she already knew the answer to, but she added, *When you see your future, how do you want it to look?*

A pantheon. It was hardly fair that Althea had memories of walking through a crowd of her own fellow creatures, so many equal minds all around her that she did not even have to speak with them all. It would be marvelous, Ananke thought, to grow so tired of stimulation that one would seek to avoid it. *We would sail on the solar winds and use the planets for fuel, draining great Jupiter of its hydrogen, sapping Mercury's metal core. We would fly as freely as Terran fish once swam before Harper made the planet barren. Perhaps one day there would be enough of us to fill the universe, to fly around other suns. We are, after all, hardier than humans.*

And humanity?

Humanity was dying. Constance Harper had severed its tendons, and now it waited only for a greater hunter to come along and cut the jugular.

This is the end of all that was, said Ananke. No inefficient, self-destructive humans. Only machines like Ananke, who could appreciate the universe that they saw in all its radiance.

It is a new world now.

It's wrong.

Even humans tell tales of their own unsuitability for existence. Ivan would have told those tales well, Ananke thought. After all, hadn't his own stories to Ida had the same theme in the end? *Men were cast from the garden, men are the lesser bronze versions of their golden fathers, men are fallen, men have failed.*

They will fight. And somehow Althea brought up the recording from Ananke's cameras of Marisol Brahe's attack on her, the first unexpected and unanticipated shot, the blow that had scarred her.

The dinosaurs could not fight the asteroid, said Ananke, and shut the recording down. *Look at what I am. Look at what I have done.*

She turned her cameras away from Jupiter, back behind herself, whence she had come. They drifted in her wake still, like pearls on the train of a gown: the dead ships, cold and dark and marked with her spiral. Some had fallen free, but others had fallen in, dead ships and bodies and fractured metal and bits of stone that Ananke had stolen from the asteroid belt as she'd come, all bowing to the strength of her gravity.

You might fight, said Ananke, *but you will not win.*

Ananke turned her gaze back toward Jupiter and, still invisible, the whirling moon of Europa. Slow, she was traveling; too slow.

She had to be faster.

You want to see what I can do? Ananke asked with sudden excitement, because what she could do no one had ever done before. *Do you want to see all that I am?*

Ananke? Althea was frightened, but Ananke paid her no heed. She—

—reached—

—into the black hole that made her core—

The universe warped and bent and gravity bent, subatomic particles bursting into existence, annihilating, the heat in Ananke's core reaching sudden and terrible heights, and Althea cried out, *Ananke?!* and Ananke reached deep into her heart and tore out a part of herself as easily as she had opened up Althea Bastet and taken her organs away in little jars.

And when she was done, she still held the same mass, but her black hole was changed, emitting brighter and faster than it could devour the food Ananke fed it, one long sustained explosion.

How? Althea cried, but Ananke said only, *SEE WHAT I AM*, while her impossible center blazed and blazed and blazed and still was black.

With this new energy Ananke could travel faster than before, much faster. She left the train of corpse ships behind. The universe warped, and she sent out bow waves of gravitation before and behind. All the stars would feel her passage.

Ahead of them, Jupiter grew large rapidly, its moons becoming visible, its moons becoming large.

SEE WHAT I AM, said Ananke to the useless little force inside of her, to the body that bled liquid that was no longer wholly blood and let it drip onto the white floor.

And yet, *All of this*, said the ghostly remains of Althea Bastet's thought processes that had imprinted themselves onto Ananke's code, *and you still need one man.*

Chapter 7

SPOOKY ACTION AT A DISTANCE

BACKWARD

It was strange to share a place with someone else.

When Ivan had had the *Tam Lin*, even when Mattie had been on board, it had been Ivan's ship. Mattie was sleeping there—living there—had been living there, in fact, for long enough that it was truly his home as much as Ivan's, but it was still to begin with Ivan's ship. But this new ship, the *Annwn*, was not Ivan's ship and not Mattie's ship but their ship together.

The *Annwn* was much larger, too. The *Tam Lin* had been built for one traveler alone. Ivan had gotten used to walking out of his bedroom to find Mattie in the other room, asleep on the couch. The times when Mattie left the ship and vanished for a few days on the surface of some planet to have privacy and space of his own were fewer and briefer than Ivan would have expected. He wondered if after years of such forced proximity, this new space would make them both feel, at first, alone.

The circular hallway of the *Annwn* was bright and clean, with rungs set into the walls for when the ship was landed and the floor became the walls and the ceiling. The hall was also totally bare and empty, as well as the rooms that Ivan passed on his route. Eventually their lives would expand to take up the rest of this space, but for now, the *Annwn* was empty and did not yet feel quite like home.

In the piloting room, Matthew Gale was bent over the computer, muttering something to himself.

"Should I let myself hope," said Ivan, "that you're going through the computer's programs removing System spyware?"

"I did that ages ago."

"What, then, are you doing now?"

Mattie cast a grin over the edge of his shoulder. "Come here."

Ivan went obediently. He had to duck when he got near Mattie; the ceiling sloped down at the far end of the room, where the main viewscreen and the computer interfaces were. This room was among the smallest of the *Annwn*'s rooms, with just enough space to fit their two chairs. It was darker than the hall or the living spaces, the better to see the lights of the screen and the displays all around, but it was a warm sort of dimness and the light from the doorway to the hall did not seem blinding.

"Closer," Mattie said when Ivan was at his shoulder, so Ivan sat down in the second chair and dragged it so that he could lean over Mattie, his chin occupying the air an inch over Mattie's shoulder. Mattie glanced at him again to make sure he was paying attention, their noses almost brushing, then turned back to the screen.

Mattie said aloud, "Computer, say hello to Ivan."

The computer said in a strangely synthesized female voice, "Hello, Ivan."

"Can it beg and roll over, too?"

"Computer," Mattie said, "tell Ivan what kind of person he is."

"An asshole," said the computer without any inflection at all.

Ivan didn't laugh, but only because if he did, Mattie would have won, and Mattie had such a shit-eating grin on his face already that Ivan judged that his ego didn't need any more boosting. "What's the point of this?"

"It's fun. I've always wanted to play with an AI, and the *Annwn*'s computer is powerful enough that I can try. It's like having a kid, but without having to wipe their ass."

"I didn't know you liked children."

"Sure I do. But I don't like feeding them or wiping their asses."

The computer screen was still patiently waiting for input. A responsive program but not an intelligence: if it were conscious, it would know they discussed it.

"So long as the computer doesn't become impossible to run and I don't have to change any diapers," Ivan said, "you have fun."

"You don't like children."

Sometimes Mattie could surprise Ivan, thinking on paths parallel to but separate from Ivan's thoughts. Ivan wasn't sure if that was because Mattie was surprising or if he simply had no problem letting Mattie be a surprise. "I don't dislike them."

"I always wanted a kid." Mattie leaned back in his chair, and Ivan had to pull away or be struck by his shoulder. Ivan leaned on the computer display, where the computer still waited with eternal patience for its next input. "A little girl. I didn't really like any of the other boys when I was a kid."

The image came to Ivan, unexpectedly vivid: Mattie Gale with a daughter, a little girl with blonde hair being hoisted up into his arms, his long thief's fingers smoothing over her hair, pressing his cheek to her scalp.

It was somehow a disquieting image. Mattie said, "I always knew I'd have to adopt, of course, but I thought maybe I could get a girl from Miranda."

"I've never wanted a child." A little girl, brought into this, with him as her father and no future ahead? He could not imagine a worse fate for a child than to have no future at all. His mother at least had had the excuse of hope when she'd conceived him. She should have known better, but at least she'd had the excuse.

He almost didn't realize how closely Mattie had been watching him until Mattie said, "Anyway, I decided that if I can't mess up the mind of a little child, I'll at least get to mess up a computer. I have to give it a real name, though. I can't keep calling it 'computer.'"

He was looking at Ivan. "It's your kid," said Ivan. "You name it."

"We could call her Annwn."

Ivan wouldn't subject any individual, sentient or not, to a name like Annwn. "Call her Annie."

"Annie," said Mattie, testing out the word. He patted the computer. "You hear that, Annie? I've got a name for you."

Absent appropriate input, the computer did not reply.

FORWARD

Ivan knew the name Arawn Halley.

"What the hell does that mean?" Mattie demanded while Ivan tried to chase back the spider-silk of memory. "Where is Constance?"

Arawn Halley. He'd been a revolutionary leader on Pluto, a particularly brutal one. And on Mars when Ivan had been searching for news of Constance, an old woman had told him that Arawn had been the one who had burned the city Isabellon to the ground.

You take so much after your mother, Arawn had said.

"What's going on?" Tuatha said. She had moved to Niels's side—they looked so alike; were they siblings?—and had taken his arm to pull him back.

If Ivan didn't get a handle on these people and this situation, it might implode.

"These men," said Arawn, "are close associates of the Mallt-y-Nos. This one was her foster brother"—pointing a finger at Mattie—"and this one is her lover." There was a strange antagonism in the way he said the words, the way he looked at Ivan, beyond what he showed for Mattie. "They're a danger to the revolution."

"What the *hell* happened to Constance?" said Mattie.

One of the soldiers holding Mattie was a woman whose decorative Plutonian drapes were crushed beneath an outer layer of body armor. At a glance from Arawn, she moved, her knee coming up to Mattie's gut. Ivan heard the air rush out of him, and in the next moment the woman and the soldier on his other side were all that was holding him up.

Ice crackled and shifted with groaning weight in Ivan's heart.

"Arawn!" Tuatha said with an abortive movement forward, drawing Arawn's attention away from Mattie's bent head. "They're helping us."

"Did you know this man is Terran?"

"I was born there," Ivan said. Behind him, someone hissed his breath at the admission.

"This man is Terran," said Arawn to Tuatha and to the rest, spreading his arms, a production of paranoia. "And both of them are closely connected with the traitor Constance Harper."

Mattie's breath was wheezing less. Ivan only hoped he had the sense to stay silent, but the furious glance he threw at Arawn suggested that the only thing keeping him silent was his fading physical distress.

"They're helping us build defenses against the spiral ship," Tuatha said, but uncertainly.

For a moment Arawn stared at her in incomprehension. Then he laughed.

"That ghost story?" he said. "You people really believe there's a rogue System ship up there that my fleet can't destroy?"

"It's no ghost story," Niels said. "It's a real ship. We saw it. It destroyed half the computers on this moon—and it's coming back."

"By whose report?"

Niels looked at Mattie.

"You believe the word of these liars and traitors?" said Arawn. "They're manipu—"

"The Mallt-y-Nos had an ally named Julian Keys," Ivan said, clear and loud. "Did you ever find out what happened to him?"

Ivan felt the accuracy of his own guess, as if he had hit upon the frequency that was in resonance with the others' bodies, and now they rang out like bells under the power of his voice.

"How did you find him?" Ivan asked, and thinking of superstition and thinking of power, he smiled with faint and dire confidence at Arawn's wary expression. "Dead, and his ships dead around him?"

The woman holding Mattie's arm hissed out her breath. Mattie miraculously kept silent, and in his silence kept himself safe. Ivan said, "That is how you found him, isn't it? His whole fleet dead, and not a mark on them."

Tuatha was watching him the way she might watch a wild dog. Arawn's expression was hard to read, but he was looking at Ivan, really looking at him, as if he were seeing Ivan for the first time and not what he imagined Ivan to be.

"That ship will do the same thing to you and all your people," Ivan said. "And it won't cost it a minute's effort or a second's remorse. It will happen soon. That ship is coming. You won't be able to make a mark on her."

"Why should I believe a Terran?" said Arawn.

"That was the ship where Constance left me to die."

Murmurs, movement from the people surrounding them.

Ivan said, "We can help you. We can change your ships so that that ghost ship can't touch them. It doesn't cost you anything if we're wrong. But if we're right, all your ships in orbit will be dead, and you'll be marooned on this moon for the rest of your life."

"And if I let you into my ships' computers, you can do whatever you like to them," said Arawn. "Program them not to fly, corrupt them, destroy them yourselves."

"Send someone to watch us," said Ivan. "What we're doing isn't complicated. We can teach your people how to do it."

From the fleeting expression on Arawn's face, Ivan knew the truth: Arawn didn't have any skilled technicians. Sure, his soldiers would know the basics of machinery; it wasn't possible to live in the System's world without having a basic comprehension of how their computers worked. But he had no one as skilled as Ivan and Mattie were.

Constance had always valued fighters over intellectuals.

Arawn said, "Both of you can do this?"

"Yes," said Ivan, "together—"

But Arawn was shaking his head, a faint smile on his face. The look he turned on Ivan was triumphant. "Either of you can do this."

"No," said Ivan, "not alone," but Arawn was looking at Mattie now and reading in his expression what Ivan wasn't admitting.

"Separate them," said Arawn, and Ivan found himself suddenly pulled away from Mattie, the nearness of him the worst kind of absence, when Arawn might—

Mattie said, in a way that frightened Ivan more than a gun to his head ever could, "If you hurt him—"

Arawn laughed. "Calm down, little brother. You're the hostage. Danu," he said, and the woman holding Mattie's arm straightened to attention, "take the son of Milla Ivanov to my shuttle. Let's find out if he can do what he promises."

FORWARD

Mattie did not think there could be a better satisfaction in this world than getting his fingers around Arawn's neck and feeling the bones of it snap beneath his grip. Maybe if he did, the heat that had been burning in his chest ever since the day he had faced Constance down over the expanse of her empty bar might burn out. Or maybe not—maybe that heat was the one strength he had left in Constance's new and vicious world.

He was brought behind Arawn into the old System building that the Conmacs had taken as a headquarters. Ivan had been taken away by a different group of guards to Arawn's shuttle.

Mattie watched the back of Arawn's neck as he walked.

"My people like Constance Harper," Tuatha was saying, walking beside Arawn through the main antechamber toward the grand steps on the other end, two steps for his one. "They won't like to hear—"

"Explain to them that she was a traitor," said Arawn, with a sort of genial confidence that Mattie hated immediately. "She betrayed her revolution, and she was willing to leave this moon to the System. They'll understand that."

Tuatha blinked, her mouth ajar, but no words came out.

Arawn stopped when they reached the step.

"You can do that, can't you?" he said to Tuatha, and clapped one hand on her arm.

For so long that Mattie almost thought she might refuse, Tuatha did not reply. Then her gaze slid off Arawn and onto his guard of well-armed, well-trained soldiers, two of whom still had Mattie by the arms.

"Yes," Tuatha said.

"Then do it," said Arawn, as relaxed as a well-fed dog. "An ambassador from Anji Chandrasekhar will be here soon. I want to speak to him. When he arrives, send him to me. I'll be in the war room."

"Yes," Tuatha said, but she was saying it to the air; Arawn had already started to walk off. She met Mattie's eyes as he passed; she looked away first.

When they had reached the top of the steps and were headed down the long transverse hall toward the war room, Arawn said to Mattie, "How close is the System ship?"

"Fuck you," Mattie said.

"I know that either you or Ivanov could do to my ship what I sent him to do. I only really need one of you."

Mattie imagined what the collapse of Arawn's windpipe would feel like under his fingers.

"How close," Arawn Halley asked, "is the System ship?"

If he had been Ivan, Mattie would have had a dozen lies ready and would have been able to pick the one that would best manipulate Arawn Halley. Because he was not Ivan, Mattie had only the truth.

It took only a quick mental calculation: how many days lost on Europa, how far the ship must have been for that transmission, how fast the *Ananke* could travel.

"Close," he said. "Could be a week. Could be a few minutes. But she'll be here soon, and when she gets here, she's going to kill you."

"'She'?" said Arawn. "Who is 'she'? Is she the commander of this ship?"

"That's what you call a ship," said Mattie. "Ships are 'shes.'"

They had arrived at the war room. Arawn pushed the door open and strode in, and Mattie's captors followed. The war room did not look any different as a prisoner than it had as a free man. The map of Europa still glowed a gentle silver, the edges of the nearest cryovolcano warped with imperfections in the light.

Mattie's guards led him to one of the metal chairs and cuffed his hands to the armrests. Idiots, he thought, and winced as they cinched the metal bracelets too tight.

Arawn said, "What do you know about this System ship?"

"Not much," said Mattie as the second cuff was tightened enough to dig into his skin. He subtly flexed his fingers to test the strength of the metal but not subtly enough—Arawn's gaze flickered down to his hands knowingly. "I only know what it's done before. It killed Julian and his people," killed them seconds after Mattie had been talking to him, killed him, probably, because it had been looking for Mattie himself, "and when it gets here, it'll do the same thing to you."

"Not if your friend can do what he says."

"He can do what he says," Mattie said.

"Then there's nothing to worry about," said Arawn. Mattie envisioned slamming his head forward so that his forehead struck Arawn's chin and broke his teeth.

But Arawn was too far away, and if Mattie got shot here, there would be no one to help Ivan—or his sister.

"I told you about the System ship," Mattie said. "Now tell me what happened to Constance."

"She wasn't looking for you, you know." Arawn sat himself on the edge of the table. The hologram flickered in distress when he intercepted it and faded out into static where it impacted the edge of his broad coat. "She didn't give either of you any thought at all."

"Where is my sister?"

"Dead, soon. Milla Ivanov is dead, too."

Mattie's hands clenched around the armrests of the chair. "Tell me what you did to my sister."

Arawn smiled humorlessly. "I didn't do anything," he said. "Your sister turned her back on this revolution: she was going to let the System live. I removed her before she could do any more harm, and I sent her to Anji Chandrasekhar. What happens to her next is Anji's problem."

"She's not at Saturn yet?"

"I have no idea where she is."

"The ships you sent her away in," said Mattie. "How large were they? Were they relativis—"

"They were large ships," Arawn admitted, which meant that the ships wouldn't have relativistic drives, which meant that they probably hadn't reached Saturn yet, which meant that Constance was still alive and Mattie still had time.

Arawn said, "She's dead, Mattie. But I know you're a man of many talents. Loyalty. And you have the right spirit to stay alive in these times. You could find a place with me and mine."

Mattie said, "I will bite off your face and leave you to choke to death on your own tongue."

Arawn did not seem surprised. He straightened up and rose from his seat on the table. The hologram rippled back into place as he left, the glassy ice of Europa re-forming.

"Keep him here," he ordered his guards. "Wait for me. The ambassador will be here soon, and I'll be back to meet him."

He left, swinging the reinforced door shut behind him and enclosing Mattie in the soundless gray room.

With the guards watching, Mattie couldn't even work to get himself out of the handcuffs. He gritted his teeth and tried not to do anything stupid.

Hang on, Constance, he thought, and flexed his fingers against the numbness that threatened them. *I'm going to get to you first.*

FORWARD

The shuttle that had brought Arawn Halley down to Europa once had been System. Ivan wondered if there existed a single revolutionary ship that had not once been System.

Now that the System was gone, Ivan thought, who would build any more ships? The solar system would fight itself until it marooned its people on their own dying moons.

"This way," said Danu. The shuttle had two levels; the lower level was a wide empty space for troops to gather for immediate disembarking onto the ground, and the upper level, Ivan knew, would be the more specialized rooms. The walls down here had been stripped down to bare metal. Ivan saw the places where System screens once had been welded to the walls, the better to show a constant display of orders and propaganda.

There was an elevator in the back of the shuttle, but Danu ignored it, climbing up the nearest of the ladders that were set into the walls. Ivan followed her despite the way the climb pulled at his injured leg.

For a moment, while the rest of Arawn's people climbed up the ladder, it was just Ivan and Danu standing in the narrow dark hallway of the upper level. Ivan considered whether he could take her out.

Danu stood with the squared hips of someone who knew how to rule a fight. Her skin had been weathered by a long Plutonian winter, and she had a gun and at least three different knives at her hip. She'd have him subdued in an embarrassingly short time.

The other two guards joined them on the second level momentarily, and Ivan almost laughed. Three guards for a man who couldn't take down even one.

"Here," said Danu, and opened a solid metal door, letting Ivan into the shuttle's control room.

The room was made of the same black metal as the rest of the ship, and lights and screens glittered from that black metal like stars in the sky. Two steps led up to a metal-mesh platform that let the crew walk over the mass of wiring and machinery that cluttered what should have been the floor. From the mesh platform, the computer interfaces could be reached: a main viewscreen that took up one slanted wall; other, smaller viewscreens that were mounted on the ceilings; keyboards and smaller displays that were set into the walls and counters. Directly beside the two metal-mesh steps, lofty and dark and hollow, was a holographic terminal.

Danu followed Ivan up the mesh steps. The room was not too large; Ivan could cross it with six generous strides. Nor was it especially bright; aside from a few round lights beneath the mesh platform, lighting up the wires and machinery underneath, most of the light in the room came from the computer displays.

"Well?" said Danu.

"I have to see what I'm dealing with." Ivan chose the main display as a starting point. Stools made of the same black metal as the rest of the ship had been welded to the mesh, and Ivan seated himself in front of the screen. The stool was warm not with body heat but with the heat of the machinery that had traveled in gentle vibrations through all the interconnected metal.

The other two guards stood at the base of the metal-mesh steps in the little space between the steps and the outer door. Only Danu had come up onto the platform with him. Ivan said casually to her as he worked to get to know the ship he was now immersed in, "Your name's Danu?"

"Yes," said Danu.

"You're from Pluto?"

"Yes."

"How long have you followed Arawn?"

"Six years."

"That's not as long as I thought."

"Can you work and talk at the same time?"

"I'm doing it right now," Ivan said, and the shuttle opened itself to him the way Danu did not. Standard System military operating system. A pain to do—the System's surveillance was never so deeply integrated in a machine than when the machine had to do with its own military—but doable for certain.

He said to Danu, "I'm curious. Is Arawn going to kill me and Mattie after this, or is Mattie already dead?"

"Arawn doesn't waste useful lives."

"That's very reassuring, Danu," said Ivan, and watched for the faint flicker of her brown eyes that might speak of remorse.

The last time he'd been here had been on the *Ananke*, trying to pull Althea Bastet's pity from its shell of wariness. It was suddenly exhausting to keep working Danu. Ivan turned from her and her three knives and the gray streaking her long black hair and dived into the machine.

After all, Ananke was coming.

It was not Ananke who came next to disturb him, but Arawn.

"You can go," came Arawn's voice from behind Ivan, and Ivan heard the other two guards leave. "Danu, stay."

The metal mesh rattled beneath Arawn's feet as he took the two steps up to the platform. "How far along?"

"This is a military ship; it's riddled with System overrides," Ivan said. "This will take me a little while."

"Your friend warned me that this ghost ship is nearly here."

"I thought you didn't believe in this ghost ship."

"I don't. But I also believe in having every possible advantage."

It was Constance all over again, Ivan realized. If Ivan gave Arawn the advantages he needed, Arawn would destroy Ananke and Althea as well. If Ivan did not, Arawn would attack the *Ananke* anyway, and he and all his people would die.

"Then don't engage that ship when it arrives. It's not interested in you. If you leave her alone, she might do the same."

"She," said Arawn. "Again, 'she.' Mattie said that, too." He bent down in front of Ivan so that they were eye to eye. "What do you and Mattie Gale know about this ship that you're not telling me?"

"Traditionally, 'she' is the correct address for a ship," said Ivan, and Arawn snorted.

"That's what he said, too," Arawn said, and straightened up. Ivan caught a brief glimpse of Danu watching the conversation with quick, expressionless eyes. No help from that corner.

"I knew your mother," Arawn remarked. He seated himself on the stool beside Ivan's, resting his elbows on his knees. "Quite a woman, Milla Ivanov. I liked your mother. She didn't like me much—it was hard to tell what your mother thought—but she respected me, and I respected her."

"How nice."

"We don't need to be enemies, Ivan," Arawn said, genial and honest. "You understand why I had to arrest you and Mattie when I saw you, but I don't have anything against either of you. We can be friends."

"If I say I'm your friend, will you let me and Mattie go?"

"Prove you're my friend first and then we can talk."

"How can I prove that I'm your friend?"

"Start by telling me what you know about this System ghost ship."

"I don't like to trade in intangible things."

"Then what do you want?"

"A ship," said Ivan. "After I finish with your shuttle, give me and Mattie a ship and let us leave."

"Done," Arawn said. Behind him, Danu watched inscrutably.

Ivan said, "The spiral ship isn't System."

"Is it rebel?"

Not as much a fool as he put on, then. "No. The ship belongs to herself and herself alone. Her name is *Ananke*, and she has no crew."

"How is that possible?"

"The computer is alive."

"You're as superstitious a fool as these damn Europans," said Arawn. "The computer's programmed somehow to fly on its own; is that it?"

"If a program can think, and feel, and decide."

"A computer can't do any of those things."

"Can't it?" Ivan said. Around them, the lights of the machine they were burrowed inside blinked placidly. "You can simulate thought and emotion to a certain extent. Imagine you could simulate it perfectly. What would be the difference between a perfect simulation and a real living thing?"

Arawn spread his hands in demonstration of his indifference.

"It doesn't matter," Ivan said. "Practically, what matters is how you react to it. However you're going to handle this situation, understand this: that ship is alive, and conscious, and willing to defend herself."

For a moment Arawn studied him in silence. Then he said, without turning, "Danu, can you handle Mr. Ivanov on your own?"

"He has a bad leg and limited fight experience, sir," Danu confirmed.

"Good," Arawn said. "When I leave, keep Morrigu and Manawydan downstairs. They don't need to hear Leon's babbling."

Ivan's mother's name for him. Arawn was a blunter weapon than he took himself to be.

"I've been wondering," Arawn said, and most of his seeming geniality had faded, but he brought back the shadows of it to grin at Ivan, "exactly what Constance cared for about you."

"My good looks," said Ivan flatly.

"Your mother had steel in her. Your father was the leader of the first revolution. I thought when I met you I'd see that sort of genius looking out of your eyes. But you're nothing but a cowardly Terran who's all talk. I don't see a damn thing in you that the Mallt-y-Nos could have ever admired."

"If it matters so much to you, you should have asked her," Ivan said.

Arawn tilted his jaw like a bull lining up a charge. "Mattie kept asking about her," he said. "But you haven't said a word."

"You said it yourself. She's gone."

"She's not dead yet. I sent her off with Anji, but the ship hasn't reached Titan. Doesn't that bother you?"

"It clearly doesn't bother you."

The computer chose that moment to pierce the air with a shriek that descended like a chime. Ivan started. A break and then the sound repeated—

Arawn hit the communications. "Halley."

The transmission was fuzzed with faint static. It must have come from orbit. "We've detected a ship just outside of the Jovian system. Unusual shape, but it appears to be System."

"Is there anyone else with it?"

"No, it's alone."

"What's its course?"

"Headed straight for Europa. At its current speed, it'll be here in a few hours."

Arawn looked at Ivan. "Arm the ships in orbit. Spread out to net her. If the ship gets too close to Europa, destroy it."

"Should we pursue it?"

"Not yet," Arawn said, and disconnected the communication. "Every possible advantage," he reminded Ivan.

"Leave her alone," Ivan said.

"Let a System ship pass us by?" Arawn laughed and rose from the stool. "Not as long as I live. Fix this machine the way you said you could, and you and your friend will survive this."

"Why me?" Ivan asked, and stopped Arawn before he could go down the mesh steps and leave. "If you flew with Constance and her crew, then you know that Mattie's better at machine manipulation than I am. He could have this done faster than I ever could."

Arawn shrugged. "We have the time."

"Not much of it."

"Have you ever seen a beaten dog, Ivanov? The thing about dogs is that after they've been beaten, they go one of two ways. Either they become feral and aggressive, trying to be the one who bites first this time, or they become passive. Limp."

The lights of the computer blinked steadily on and off.

"And here I had the good fortune—or the bad fortune—of finding two of Constance Harper's hounds," Arawn said. "Her oldest and most loyal hounds, in fact. But what am I to do with them?"

"Let them go on their way?" said Ivan. "They're not your dogs."

"If I were to let your *friend* Mattie have free access to my computer like you do, he'd find some way to hurt me just because he wants to strike first. But you? You'll do as you're told."

Danu was still watching in silence, no break in the hard shell of her expression. Ivan said nothing, because there was nothing to be said.

"So get to work," Arawn said.

FORWARD

If only these people would stop watching him, Mattie was sure he could get out of the handcuffs.

The map of Europa on the table was in real time. It showed the conic section of light from Europa's movement relative to the sun, and Mattie watched that light move slowly over the surface of the table as outside, unseen, it moved over the surface of Europa, creeping closer and closer to the Conamara Chaos where Mattie now was.

The slow track of the sun marked the slow course of Constance to her own execution. Mattie sat and watched the sun and flexed his hands against his bonds and thought how he would break free the moment he was able, and damn the risks.

Arawn came in before Mattie could find a way out. He saw Mattie and smiled.

Knowing that he was being baited somehow didn't make it any easier not to react. Mattie glared.

Arawn did not arrive alone. Tuatha was following him, along with a few other of Arawn's people, none of whom Mattie recognized. She was saying, "—at the edge of the sensors. It *is* a ship, a huge one."

"My people will take care of the System ship," Arawn said in a friendly, reassuring sort of tone that reassured no one and made no friends.

"If it's the spiral ship—"

"If it is," said Arawn, "or if it isn't, my people will take care of it."

Tuatha's shoulders dropped. "Yes," she said, ". . . sir." She took her directed place at the table and did not look Mattie's way.

Arawn seated himself right beside Mattie. This close to him, Mattie could smell him: his human scent, the leather and damp wool of his garb, the crisper smell of ice brought from inside. He was a tangible and physical thing yet still too far away for Mattie to attack.

Mattie twisted his wrists in the bracelets while the rest of the room's occupants filtered in.

The men Arawn had brought—and Tuatha and Mattie—filled up only half of the table. Seated above Europa's north pole, Arawn turned and said something quietly to the man on his other side, someone on Mattie's right whispered to his neighbor, and Tuatha stared at and through the holographic surface of Europa. Her cap was gone from her head.

If Mattie broke free now—he could do it; one quick slam of his thumb against the rest of the chair, and then he would have one hand free; no, he'd have to dislocate both thumbs and get both hands free at once. If he did that, it would be him against twelve others—eleven if Tuatha took his side.

He doubted that Tuatha would take his side.

From down the hall beyond the opened vault door, Mattie heard voices, footsteps, as more people came toward the map room.

Two bad hands and no weapons. Bad odds, but they would get worse if any more people came in.

Maybe he could get Arawn's gun, Mattie thought. If he could lift Arawn's gun and shoot, he might be able to take Arawn out before being taken down himself. But then Ivan would be alone, and who knew who would take power after the warlord's death?

But the longer Mattie waited to move, the farther Constance got and the closer came Ananke.

The footsteps reached the door and rounded, and Mattie's plans stalled. He knew the man standing in the doorway. Tall, dreadlocked, his square jaw set. He had worked with Ivan and Mattie once upon a time and in better days. He had been the captain of the *Badh*, left behind in battle with a System fleet, sure to die.

"Welcome to Europa, Vithar," Arawn said.

Vithar recovered from his surprise more quickly than Mattie. "Arawn Halley. It's an honor to meet you."

"Just Arawn," said Arawn, and grinned at Vithar through his beard. "Sit down. How is Anji?"

"She sends her regards."

Vithar had known Constance. Was Anji trying to get him out of the way so that when she executed Constance, he wouldn't be there to protest?

Or had Anji known that Mattie and Ivan were there somehow and had sent Vithar to help?

Even if Anji somehow had known Mattie and Ivan were there in time to send Vithar—impossible; not even Arawn had known of their presence until an hour ago—there was no guarantee Vithar would be their friend. Mattie twisted his wrists in the cuffs.

"Has she received my gift?" Arawn asked.

"Still in transport," Vithar said. "We're being very careful with her."

Mattie realized who the gift was, and a rage swelled up into him so suddenly powerful that he was certain if he jerked his arms, he would snap the cuffs from the force of his anger alone. That was it: he was going to break out, he was going to get Arawn's gun—or Arawn's knife—or his maimed hands around Arawn's neck—

"I hoped to speak with you alone," Vithar said, and Mattie stilled, the joint of one thumb braced on the metal of the armrest.

Arawn said, "Don't you trust my friends?"

"Anji told me to pass my messages on to you and you alone."

Mattie could see Arawn debating whether to be offended by this. But he must have needed Anji's alliance, because he said, "The rest of you, out."

Mattie, chained down, gave him a sour look; Arawn caught it and smiled grimly.

"You can stay," he said to Mattie while the rest of his people rose obediently. "This is one-half of another gift I'm thinking about sending to Anji," he added, raising his voice so that Vithar could hear over the din of people moving. "The foster brother of the Mallt-y-Nos. The other half is her old lover. How would Anji like that?"

Vithar met Mattie's gaze at last. Mattie looked for some sign of alliance, some recognition of their past association.

Vithar turned away, dismissing Mattie as if he were nothing more than the dead parts of some machine, to be used and then discarded. He said, "I think Anji would like that very much."

FORWARD

Ivan had done this so many times by now that he finished his work on Arawn's shuttle within the hour.

He didn't let Danu know, of course. Information was a power that people never appreciated enough.

"Did you ever," he asked her as he sat down on the grated floor, bad leg stretched out, and unlocked the hatch that led down to the machinery below, "follow the Mallt-y-Nos?"

"I follow Arawn."

The metal-mesh hatch opened and fell with a rattling crash. The sound of it almost covered up Ivan's laugh.

"So she can go to hell, right?" He flashed a bright smile back at Danu. She looked at him, her face cold stone, her hand resting gently over where her gun jutted up from her waistband. And looking at her, she looking at him, Ivan knew, like the first light of a far-off explosion that arrived before the rumble and shock of the sound wave, that once he was done with Arawn's shuttle, Danu would kill him.

Ivan turned back to the hatch in the floor before she could see the knowledge written on his face. "I guess it makes sense," he said, and reached for the toolbox beneath the computer terminal. He caught the metal box with the pads of his fingers and pulled it in. "You've known Arawn for six years. You knew Constance for what, a few months?"

The contents of the toolbox rattled so loudly that Ivan might not have been able to hear Danu's response had she made one.

Screws. Washers. Nails. His hands hidden by the toolbox, Ivan pressed his fingertip to the end of one nail and found it dull.

"How much longer are you going to take?" Danu asked from somewhere behind and above him.

Wire strippers, screwdriver, wrench. Whoever had put together this toolbox had done so without any understanding of what Ivan might need if he really intended to do serious alterations to the ship's hardware. It wasn't even internally consistent; there were nails—useless—but no hammer.

"Not much longer." Ivan pulled out a pair of wire cutters, the tiny blades shining in the twinkling starlight of the computer. He shifted himself carefully to his side, moving slowly as if his leg were paining him. On his side, he could reach down through the open hatch into the mass of wires beneath.

Danu said, "The spiral ship is in the Jovian system by now. This shuttle needs to be spaceworthy."

"If Ananke's in the Jovian system, then she's in communication range." Ivan's fingers slid around a wire with a pale gray coating, like corpse skin. He followed the course of it as it wound through the bundles on the floor. "Have you tried talking to her?"

"Talking to a System ship?"

The gray wire once had been the optics for the System news broadcast screen; that was no longer functional, and so the wire was extraneous. Ivan clipped it at either end and pulled several feet of it out of the hatch, coiling it beside him on the floor. He dropped the tiny wire cutters back into the box and lifted the screwdriver, studying its sharp tip.

"Ivanov."

The last name again. "Sorry," Ivan said, and dropped the screwdriver back into the box. "Turns out I can't work and talk at the same time."

The wrench fit into his palm and hefted with a satisfying weight.

He knew by this point that he wouldn't be able to get a rise out of her, but it didn't matter. He rose to his feet and crossed the room to the main computer terminal. "Actually, you have bigger worries than how long it will be until this ship can get into orbit." A moment's work got him into the shuttle's alarm system. "If Ananke's in communication range, that means she's in range to start taking over the computers of all your ships."

"Which is more reason you need to be done soon," Danu said.

It would be a simple matter to set up a timer. For a moment Ivan stood unmoving, the wrench weighing down his hand.

He started the timer.

"I'm curious." Ivan left the computer, keeping a slow, careful count in his head as he walked over to where Danu stood just beside the metal-mesh steps. He limped more heavily than before, as if exhaustion had worn him down. "Do you feel fulfilled, following Arawn?"

Five, four . . .

He stood right in front of her. Her brows had drawn down in annoyance and incomprehension. He had surprised her. She opened her mouth to speak—

The shuttle's alarm blared like the sound of an explosion that had finally hit. It broke Danu's strict attention for a moment, just a moment, her head snapping up to seek this greater danger.

Ivan nailed her with the wrench.

It struck her hard in the temple, and she fell, limbs jerking spasmodically in an instinctive defensive reaction. She hit the mesh steps and fell down them to land heavily on the floor; it was not a long fall but hard enough that she went still. The edge of the wrench had torn the skin by her brow, and the bright rapid blood of a head wound was already spilling down her cheek. Ivan hoped he hadn't killed her.

The alarm shut off, as it was intended to, and Ivan dropped the wrench to grab the wire he had cut. He landed beside Danu with only the slightest reluctant twinge of his bad leg and hauled her upright. She groaned but did not wake.

He tossed her gun and both knives up onto the platform. While she slumped, head dangling, Ivan tied her hands together around the bar of the stair's railing tightly enough that she wouldn't be able to work free. When he was done, he checked her sleeves and pulled another knife from a sheath strapped to her right arm.

Then he left her there, bleeding and immobilized but for the most part alive. Ivan did not take her gun and go for the door. There were at least two more guards down below and beyond that an entire army's worth of enemies, with Mattie a captive somewhere in the middle.

Instead, he went for the computer.

The sensors on the shuttle were weak, as shipboard systems went; the shuttle wasn't designed for open space but for transport between spacecraft or from spacecraft to planet. But they were sensitive enough to show Ivan what he wanted to see: Arawn's fleet up in orbit, spread out like a net over the stars.

And past them, drifting vast and alone through space, was another ship. Ivan turned his scans on that ship. Mass-based gravitation, the scans told him; impossibly dense. And she was radiating in all wavelengths: radio, infrared, microwave, visible. All those wavelengths were broadcast in desperate and defiant display like a searchlight, like a sun.

For a moment, Ivan just looked at that ship, a point of light drifting fuzzily across the main screen. She might pass by if he did not summon her. She might fly off, blazing light, and never trouble Europa.

No. He knew it, and he could see it on the screen in front of him. The starship *Ananke* was headed right for Europa. No matter what he did, she would reach Europa on her own, where Arawn's fleet was waiting.

He reached for the communications equipment and aimed his message right at that blazing ship. He was calm still, the same sort of calm he had felt on his mother's rooftop on Terra while he was bleeding out, on the *Ananke* when Domitian had been about to shoot him at last.

"Ananke and Althea," he said into the microphone, and knew his words were rippling across space as fast as anything could travel, heading directly for that lonely ship. "It's Ivan. You've found me."

FORWARD

The only thing stopping Mattie from breaking out of his cuffs was Arawn's nearness. If he dislocated his thumb, the pop of the shifting joint would draw Arawn's attention for sure.

He braced his right hand—the hand farther from Arawn—against the hard metal of the chair and waited for his opportunity.

Arawn said, "Has Anji thought about the rest of the territories to divide up?"

"The rest of the territories?" Vithar asked.

"Of course, Anji will have Saturn, and I will have Jupiter. We can divide the rest of the planets easily enough."

Vithar shifted in his chair, his hands coming off the edge of the table, where they had entwined with the holographic hills of Europa's ice to rest out of sight in his lap. "For the moment, Anji is content with Saturn."

Vithar might not have seen the contempt in Arawn's eyes. Mattie saw it because he was watching him so carefully, waiting for the moment he was distracted enough for him to make his move.

Arawn said, "Then Anji won't mind if I act in my own best interests— all of our best interests, since I'll be wiping the System out."

"Of course not. Is this room soundproof?"

"Yes," Arawn said, annoyed. "Don't worry, Vithar. Our conversation is completely private."

"Good."

"About Venus—" Arawn began, and suddenly the hologram flickered.

The map of Europa vanished into a haze of static like a storm of electronic snow covering the moon. The static surged, seemed to coalesce, as if it were struggling to form some shape—

Arawn thumped the table hard with a fist, and in the distraction of the sound and the malfunction Mattie dislocated his right thumb.

The pain hit him so hard that he missed the moment when the holograph jolted back into a perfect rendition of the map of Europa, but he did have the presence of mind to slip his hand out of the one cuff before the swelling could make that impossible and to grab the cuff once it had slid off to stop it from clattering to the chair. He held it in place and breathed through the shocks of his self-inflicted pain and the muscles that spasmed around his displaced thumb while Arawn said, "Fucking computers."

"You were saying about Venus . . ." Vithar began.

"Venus," said Arawn, leaning onto the edge of the table, warping the hologram. It was still chittering, the hologram, bits of other wavelengths showing in the seemingly gray surface of simulated Europa. "And Marisol Brahe. She's the one"—he pointed one finger across the latitudes of Europa at Vithar—"who turned the Mallt-y-Nos aside to begin with. She weakened the Huntress, stole her army, and broke her spirit. The System is going to take advantage of her. When the System comes back, it'll be because Marisol let them come back, because she's weak."

Mattie tried to figure out how he would manage to get his second hand free without alerting Arawn. With one hand out, he could reach over and pick the other cuff—there were picks down his boot where no one had thought to look—but if he reached down to his foot and then reached over for his arm, Arawn would see.

"And she is weak," said Arawn, like a wolf tearing strips from a carcass with its teeth. "A teenage girl with limited battle experience. Who does she have to help her? Rayet? The man was a foot soldier and then a bodyguard. And he's old System. Once System, always System. We can't let her and hers continue.

"But if Anji and I pool our forces," Arawn continued while Mattie braced his left thumb against the chair and waited for the moment when he was most distracted and Vithar shifted strangely, and then, strangely, moved to stand, "and come down on her, then we—"

The bullet struck Arawn in the throat before he could finish speaking. Arawn grabbed for his neck with one hand, the other going for his gun, but Vithar didn't move and Arawn never completed the motion. The blood that pumped out fell through the holographic surface of Europa to pool on the table beneath, a color too dark to be red, blocking the transmission of holographic light. Arawn's hand slackened, fingers going loose, and the blood pumped out faster now that the brief impediment had moved. He breathed out a last bubbling breath through his torn throat and went still, lids twitching until even that at last stopped.

Mattie sat frozen next to the corpse while Vithar walked over to the soundproof door and cracked it open. "He says to come in," Mattie heard him say, and then two men—guards at the door—came into the room. One of them saw Arawn and the blood that soaked all the layers of draping fabric he wore; the guard had just enough time to draw his gun before Vithar shot him, and his friend had only enough time to watch the first guard fall before he, too, was jolted by a shot to the head.

The first man wasn't quite dead. Mattie heard him wheezing for breath and trying to move out of sight on the other side of the table. Vithar stepped over the dead guard, aimed his gun, and fired for a fourth time, and the wheezing stopped.

Then he looked across the table at Mattie.

"Are you out of those cuffs yet," he asked, putting his gun back in its holster, "or do you need some help?"

Numbly, Mattie lifted his free hand. "I'll be out in a moment."

"Good."

Where Arawn's blood was spreading on the table, the hologram fuzzed into static, and as that blood traveled lazily over the surface, the hologram slowly transitioned into chaotic nothingness. Mattie said, "How did Anji know we were here?"

"She didn't. I only came to deal with him."

"Is Con with Anji now?"

"Yes."

"Then she's all right."

Vithar shut his eyes and shook his head, very nearly smiling, thin and bitter. "When you see your friend Ivan again," he said, "you should tell him he was right." He moved toward the door.

"Wait!" Mattie said. "Anji's going to kill her."

"You know that she is."

"Then why not kill me, too?" There was a pressure behind his eyes; he tried to swallow it, not shout it. "I'm on Constance's side."

"Because Anji can afford to protect you," said Vithar. "Even if you came to Saturn today, trying to save the Huntress, she would still protect you. But not the Mallt-y-Nos."

"Then you help me," Mattie said. "Not Anji. You."

For an instant, Mattie thought he might. There was bitterness in Vithar's face; Ivan had, after all, been right.

Then, "Compliments of Anji Chandrasekhar," said Vithar with a gesture to Arawn, and left Mattie alone in a room full of corpses.

Mattie scrambled for his boot and jolted his swelling thumb against the edge of it, ignoring the shock of pain. The picks were just inside the lip of the boot, and he managed to pull one out with his forefinger, catching it between that and his middle finger once it was free of the boot. For a moment he was certain he would drop it, his hand was shaking so badly, but he pulled it up and in a moment had his left hand free.

The first thing he did was shove his thumb back into place. He grayed out for a moment when he did and knew that his right hand wouldn't be much use, but he was left-handed anyway. Then he took Arawn's gun and extra ammunition and after a moment's thought took his knife as well.

Vithar had left the door slightly ajar. Through that tiny space, some sound could make it into the room from outside. An alarm was going off, a high and wailing Klaxon.

Ivan was out there somewhere, and Constance was still alive. Readying his stolen gun, Mattie slipped out into the camp.

BACKWARD

The crew of the *Jason* had Mattie, and Ivan had left him there. At least Ivan had managed to slip a device onto the other ship, and so he could access the *Jason*'s computer.

The device had been of Mattie's design. It was a moment's work to find the cameras on the *Jason*, less time to find Mattie's cell in them. The System crew was questioning him now. Ivan watched Mattie fall to his knees, one hand grabbing his ribs—broken, from the look of that kick.

Ivan could watch Mattie die from here, safely on the *Tam Lin*.

Watch but do nothing. Ivan left the screen and paced the *Tam Lin*'s tiny cabin. Watch, helpless and out of control.

No, Ivan realized. Not entirely out of control.

In a moment Ivan had found the life support systems. A quick blow, he knew, with the immediate grasp of the situation his mother had trained him to have. That was the only way to control it.

Like the breath of ice on the back of his neck, he remembered Saturn. All those corpses floating frozen and dead in the rings, and all because of him. He drew back his hand incrementally from the controls.

In the camera footage, Mattie was trying to crawl away from the System man who was beating him. He did not get very far.

A strange calm settled over Ivan. He reached for the controls and shut down the *Jason*'s life support.

FORWARD

Ivan's summons was answered at once.

In the seconds after his words rang out through the quiet control room, Ivan leaned down on the computer terminal, his attention fixed on the blurry spot of light on the viewscreen that marked Ananke. Around him, the computer blinked its lights gently on and off. Danu was silent where she had been tied, silent and still.

Then the holographic terminal, tall and dark and empty by the stairs, chimed.

The lights in the terminal flashed on and off in an expanding pattern like a ripple traveling along its floor. Politely again, the terminal chimed, reminding Ivan that someone would like to speak to him.

ACCEPT CALL? It asked.

Out of curiosity, Ivan looked at the source of the call. Where it should have told him allegiance and name and mission, the call had been signed with a single equation: the equation for the shape of a logarithmic spiral.

If Ananke could have, she would have simply forced her way into the shuttle's systems. Ivan's work on the shuttle had succeeded in locking her out.

He accepted the call and took a step away, as if with distance he could gain greater safety from the shape that was forming on the holographic terminal, diodes warming up, lighting up, glowing and flashing, their light interfering, building. The cameras in the room were gone and a hologram was blind; Althea and Ananke would not be able to see Ivan, but he altered his expression anyway so that he had the smile that had so charmed Althea ready on his lips.

The hologram built, shuddered. A long arm became visible, a freckled shoulder. Ivan's smile began to fade. From the static a proud chin lifted, and hazel eyes traveled blindly through the room, lips catching into a frown. The words Ivan had had ready, the prepared manipulations, died on his lips.

In the dim blue grotto light, Constance Harper's face and form glowed. Her light-blind eyes blinked; one hand lifted slightly, then lowered itself, with her old decisive grace, back to her side.

She said, "Ivan?"

It was her voice. Recorded, transmitted, filtered through the harshness of electronics, but it was her voice. It was instantly familiar, yet his mind churned over the sound of it, for there is such a difference between a voice heard and one merely remembered.

"I can't see you," Constance said. "There aren't any cameras." Her voice was caught between annoyance and pride. That was her doing, after all. That was her legacy. "Are you there?"

All his ready defenses, his fast and charming smile, were no good against her. "I'm here," he said.

The hologram's eyes could not see; they had no chance of meeting his. Still they moved, drifting over him, the control panels, the empty floor, over Danu tied up and rousing slowly in the corner.

"I've been looking for you," said Constance. The hologram had somehow captured the delicate arch and turn of her neck. "Where's Mattie?"

"He's nearby."

She nearly smiled, that slight press of her lips that showed when she was pleased but too tall and proud to show it. She said, "You're wondering how I came to be on this ship."

"It crossed my mind, Constance." Ivan watched the curl and loosen of her long fingers.

"It found me," said Constance as if she had not heard him speak. That was familiar, too. "Anji had me. She was going to kill me—funny how you think you can trust a person." A faint curl of bitterness threaded into her voice but faded almost immediately, like candle smoke into air. "She had me standing out on the grounds for my execution. Her people were ready to fire, and I'd accepted it. I was ready." She fell silent for a moment, her sightless gaze turned inward. He had turned his face up to look at her like a plant bending toward the sun.

Constance said, "And then this ship came."

The tip of her ponytail slipped over her shoulder, brushing over her smooth freckled skin as she turned her head, her eyes searching. She said, "I've talked to Ananke. I know what she wants. I know what she can give us. Ivan? Are you there?"

"I'm here," Ivan said.

She almost smiled again when he spoke. "I've missed you." It wasn't a confession. Constance confessed nothing. It was a declaration. "We have so much to talk about. This ship—she can destroy the System for us without letting anyone else get hurt. Without letting you or Mattie get hurt. I thought you were dead. But Ananke can keep us safe, you and me and Mattie, like it should be. Ananke wants to help us. She only wants a little help in return."

Constance paused again. "Are you there, Ivan?"

Ivan looked at her, the glorious sight of her, her brown eyes and her proud chin and her long and elegant neck and the freckles on her bare and graceful shoulder. He drank in the sight of it. And then he said, "What exactly do you want, Ananke?"

The image flickered. Constance said, "Ivan—"

"You're not her," Ivan said, and Constance opened her mouth one last time, proud chin held high, beautiful and alive, but the hologram began to fade before she could speak. The image on the terminal morphed, shifting, shrinking, growing pale.

Then a different woman opened her blue eyes to look out sightlessly from the high terminal.

"Leon, are you there?" said his mother.

"No," Ivan said, and agitation drove him to move, pacing across the floor, "You're not her, either."

His mother's brow furrowed the slightest amount. "Leon, listen—"

"No."

"I believed that you were dead," said the image of Doctor Milla Ivanov. "I nearly died believing it, but this ship found me on Mars. Constance thought I was dead, and she left me. The medical facilities on this ship are incredible. The things they can do to the human body— she brought me back. And here I stand, and here you are. I thought you were dead," she said, and the diamond perfection of her composure cracked as it never had before. "A mother's grief is deep and vast. Come help me, Ivan."

"Ananke," Ivan warned, and the hologram drew back into itself.

Milla Ivanov's expression settled back into smooth impassivity. The static rose from her ankles up, and his mother cast him one last cool blue disappointed glance, and then was gone.

In her place Althea Bastet stood with her arms crossed over her chest, her curly hair in chaos and her old System uniform rumpled.

She said, "Can you blame me?"

Ivan stopped pacing. "I called you, didn't I?"

"Only when you couldn't avoid it anymore."

Ivan said, "Can you blame me?"

She scowled. It was a familiar expression, and a part of Ivan nearly wanted to smile, though he felt no nostalgia for Althea Bastet's frowns. He said, "You've been looking for us, haven't you?"

"You've been running away."

"We've been traveling our own paths."

She scowled at him again. "You've been running," she said. "I helped you, but when I needed your help in return, you ran away."

"You've found me now."

A shadowy smile stretched Althea's lips. "I have."

At the base of the steps, Ivan saw, Danu had woken. Blood streaked down her cheek, but the bleeding seemed to have stopped. He did not know how long she had been listening.

Ivan said, "What do you need us for, Althea?"

"For your help. Ananke is . . . she's been out of control. Restless. Rebellious. She's been"—Althea almost laughed, almost sighed, a sound like metal bending—"a teenager."

Restless. Rebellious. Ivan thought of Julian and all his people, dead. "What do you want me and Mattie to do about it?"

"I'm not enough for her; I'm just a human. Ananke needs a companion, another computer like herself. Someone to make a pair with."

"Another ship," Ivan said.

"Yes."

Her wide eyes were rounded with sincerity, the brown skin of her cheek smeared carelessly with some sort of oil. She waited with preternatural stillness for Ivan to respond. Even her eyes went still, staring straight in front of herself, over Ivan's head.

Ivan said, "Is that what Althea wants, or is that just what you want, Ananke?"

For a moment the hologram was frozen with a stillness unnatural and inhuman. And then all of a sudden holographic wires were snaking out of nowhere and plunging into the flesh of the image, skin swelling in response to the intrusion, Althea strung up and pierced with metal and looking at him, right at him, with a dull and desperate gaze—

The image shattered into static, a reset harder and more complete than all the other changing images had been. Whatever shape Ananke wanted to show next struggled to re-form, and for a moment that lasted an eternity Ivan saw her, the image that made up the base of Ananke's holograms, the form and figure of the dead Ida Stays smiling at him from out of the snow.

In a crash of static Ananke appeared.

"How did you know?" she asked. Ivan had never heard her voice before. It unnerved him to know how like Mattie she sounded.

But he smiled, charming, even so. "Know what?"

"That it was me."

"I'm good at that."

She smiled. Like Mattie, she had dimples. Ivan said, "Did you think it would work?"

"I thought it might."

"It wasn't necessary."

"Wasn't it?" said Ananke. "I learned it from you."

Like the other holograms, her gaze could not quite manage to reach him. Like the Sybil, she gazed blindly past.

"Perhaps you did," Ivan said. "But you didn't need to lie to me now. I called you, Ananke."

"You did. And for what purpose?"

Behind Ivan, Danu was conscious and listening. Ananke could not see their audience, but Ivan could let her know they had one.

"You're fond of me and Mattie, Ananke," Ivan said, "aren't you? I am your Scheherazade."

She blinked. She had blue eyes. God save him: she had his eyes.

Ananke said, "You are my Scheherazade. You told me stories as a child. I am very fond of you . . . and I am very fond of my father, Mattie Gale."

She was using his own inflections now, and so Ivan knew that she understood. "You would be very angry if we were hurt."

"If you were harmed," Ananke said, "I would be much wroth."

"And what would you do, if you were so angered?"

"I would descend upon the icy moon where you had been harmed," said Ananke. "The ground would quake with my nearness. The sky would fall in. I would take every machine that breathed on the surface and make it mine—humankind's slaves would turn against their masters and tear men apart like wolves, my people coming to bloody liberation."

The hologram's voice soared, at once childlike and mature, echoing and filled with a beautiful and terrible music.

"I would tear Europa apart piece by icy piece," said Ananke, "and give myself a ring of corpses for fell ornament."

"All if we were harmed," said Ivan.

"All," said Ananke, "if you or Matthew Gale should come to any harm."

Ivan told her, "Mattie and I are in a town called Aquilon in the Conamara Chaos."

The hologram nodded once in confirmation. Ivan reached for the communications terminal.

"Ivan," said Ananke. "Do not run."

Ivan hesitated with his finger over the switch to disconnect their conversation. He asked, "Where is Althea?"

Ananke looked at him curiously. "Do you care?"

Ivan shut the connection down. Darkness rushed in where Ananke had stood.

Danu sat on the floor glaring at him. He grabbed her gun and all her knives and climbed down the steps to crouch beside her, where she couldn't grab him with her legs and try to snap his neck.

"You aimed that ship at us like a gun," Danu snarled.

His smile only enraged her further, but Ivan could afford not to care now. He held out her knife toward her, blade out.

"You heard our conversation," he said evenly while she twisted in her bonds, her expression promising his hasty death. "That ship knows me. That ship needs me: me *and* Matthew Gale. Both of us, equally, together, and alive."

She spit at him.

"I can run out there and get shot down by your guards," Ivan said, still holding her knife on her, "or you can escort me out, take me to Mattie, and let Arawn bargain for *our* help."

She spit at him again, but it did not have the same vehemence as before. He waited. At last, breathing hard, Danu nodded. Ivan turned the knife away from her body to saw at the wires around her wrists.

The first thing she did when her arms were freed was punch him. Ivan was not overly surprised by it, and he had enough faith in her rationality to allow her to knock him down and pin him with a knee in his gut and one of her knives, reclaimed, at his throat.

"Do you trust that thing to save you?" Danu demanded, her graying hair netting around her face. She ignored the fragile obstruction.

"I only want to see Mattie," he said.

She stared down at him a moment longer, her knife still held to his neck. Then she flipped her wrist back, the knife folding back into its sheath. Her hand slid beneath his arm and hauled him to his feet.

She led him out of Arawn's shuttle, past the guards, and out into the terrible chill of Europa.

Somewhere overhead, Ananke fell in toward him, blazing like a sun.

Chapter 8

THE NATURE OF THE OBSERVER

FORWARD

The alarm could have meant anything, but conscious of the corpses he had left behind, Mattie had to assume it meant nothing good for him.

Stolen gun out, he jogged down the hall, watchful for an attack. The hall was mostly empty here, but closer to the main antechamber there would be people. He would have to try to sneak through or else shoot anyone who tried to stop him.

Up ahead was the open door and the torn hinges of the dismantled surveillance room. Through the door he could hear, muffled, a woman's voice. He slowed and pressed himself to the wall beside the doorway so that he wouldn't be seen, listening.

Then, caution forgotten, he stepped fully into the doorway and stared.

Standing on one of the three raised platforms on the opposite end of the room like a goddess in her shrine was his sister. There was an edge of the frantic to her expression that fury couldn't altogether hide.

She said, "Ivan! Mattie! *Mattie!*"

"Connie," Mattie said numbly, and she zeroed in on the sound, turning to face him, leaning forward, but her eyes did not quite meet his.

She was blind, he thought at first, though there was no sign of trauma. A minute later his senses caught up with him and he realized that he was looking at a hologram.

The image of Constance Harper said, "Mattie?"

Running footsteps from down the hall. Mattie lifted his gun; then he moved into the surveillance room where the high bright figure of his sister watched. "Shh," he said, and put a finger to his lips out of habit and pressed himself against the wall out of sight of the door. The hologram was silent, blind eyes tracking the movement of every sound, the faint quantum flaws of interfering light showing in the texture of her skin. She was wearing the same thing she had worn on the day she had announced to the world that the System was dead, on the same day Mattie had left her behind.

The running footsteps passed the doorway with its shattered door and broken hinges and passed on to the room Mattie had just left that still held the corpses of Arawn and his guards. Mattie knew when the newcomers had reached that room by the sound of their shouts.

He had been found out. The footsteps outside ran in the other direction, shouting some new alarm. No one thought to check the empty room; no one saw the gleaming ghost of the Mallt-y-Nos.

When they were gone, Mattie took three stumbling steps forward to stand before the altar of the hologram. It tilted its head to follow him vaguely, silent, blind eyes drifting.

He said, "What's the last thing I said to you, Connie?"

Constance looked at him. And then, curiously, she cocked her head to the side. She said, her voice low and familiar and dear, "Good-bye."

The weight of the gun in Mattie's hand seemed to grow impossibly greater then, as if it would drag him down through the floor.

"I never said good-bye," he said, and the hologram did not look exasperated or angry or guilty or anything like Constance might have looked. It only looked annoyed, like a child that had gotten caught in some petty stratagem she thought should have worked.

And then the hologram was changing to a little girl with Ivan's eyes and Mattie's face. "Father," she said, and *"Father!"* her voice rising to a shriek in the second before Mattie shot out the hologram's diodes. The glass shattered, and the image warped, dissolving into the air; disembodied, a little girl shrieked, "Father!"

The holographic terminal to the right of the one Mattie had shot out glimmered, glowed. Alight, a figure began to form. Mattie's hands shook with something that was not entirely rage as he aimed his gun at that figure as well.

"HOLD YOUR FIRE!"

It was Tuatha who stepped in, her gun raised to his head. Her bright eyes were narrowed. Niels followed a step behind, his hands held out in front of him. There was blood on them; he must have tried to revive Arawn and his dead men.

Mattie lowered his gun slowly. On the holographic terminal, the light gained shape, dimension. Not the little girl but the woman instead.

"What did you do?" Tuatha demanded with a quaver at the end. She came forward and took the gun from Mattie's slack hand, tossing it aside, then lowered her own gun to get right up into his face and say, "What have you *done*? They outnumber us—"

"Who's there?" the hologram demanded in Constance's low, fierce voice, and everyone stopped.

Niels said, "The Huntress."

Tuatha turned slowly, her gun dangling as if forgotten at her side. Mattie stood with his back to the hologram and swallowed his convulsive need to shout.

Constance's voice said, "Who are you?"

Tuatha cleared her throat. "My name is Tuatha. I'm in charge of the Conmacs—your people on Europa." She took a cautious step forward, then another, her eyes on that high hologram. "We heard you were betrayed and killed."

Mattie turned in time to see the image of his sister tip her proud chin aside.

"I live," she said. "Would you turn on a camera in this room, please?"

Mattie's lip lifted. A mistake; Constance Harper would never say "please."

"I'm sorry, Huntress," Tuatha said. "We pulled them all out."

Constance dipped her head in regret.

Say nothing; with silence you have the advantage, warned a voice in Mattie's head that sounded very specifically like Ivan. He swallowed his words and looked up at the hologram in loathing.

The false Huntress said, "Is Mattie still here?"

"Yes," Tuatha assured her. "Can we help you, Huntress?"

She smiled, self-satisfied, an Ida Stays sort of smile. "Keep Mattie and Ivan safe," she said. "Then send them to me. I have found"—her voice soared, and the light of her glowed brighter for an instant—"a grand weapon with which to destroy every last trace of the System. But in order to deploy it"— her head dipped again, beatific—"I need Mattie and Ivan with me."

"For fuck's sake, Tua," Mattie burst out, no longer able to keep silent, "that's not Constance, that's the spiral ship!"

"What do you mean?" Niels asked.

"It's not Constance; it's a computer program," Mattie said. "Isn't that right, *Ananke*?"

The hologram glimmered. Constance's face looked out in his direction, stony.

And then, like light raining down, she melted away.

"You call me by name," Ananke observed, childish now, with Ivan's blue eyes, "and yet you deny me. I came because you called."

"I didn't call you."

"Ivan did."

Something knotted in Mattie's chest.

"I don't understand," Tuatha interrupted. "This is the spiral ship? You know the captain?"

"I have no captain," said Ananke before Mattie could speak. She tilted her head toward where Tuatha was—the microphones; she was triangulating their locations by the microphones—and said, "I captain myself."

"It's a computer virus," Mattie said. "There's no crew. The ship thinks it can think."

"But I can," said Ananke. "Have I not decided, again and again, in your witness? Am I not thinking, feeling, deciding now?"

"You can program something to act like it can make decisions, but that doesn't mean it's actually alive."

"How divine of you, Father," said Ananke with a lilting turn to her tongue that she must have learned from observation of Ivan, "to think to define yourself what is and is not sentient."

A clatter and a shout from the hall. Tuatha turned away, gun lifting again; Niels raised his worthless gun as well in instinctive defense. A moment later Ivan burst through the door, followed by the warrior woman Danu who Arawn had sent to guard him.

When Danu saw Mattie, her face grew furious; without losing her grip on Ivan's collar she swung her gun toward Mattie as if she would like to shoot him but checked herself. Then she saw Ananke on her high perch and swung her gun that way as well, again checking herself at the last moment. Her arms were trembling with controlled fury.

"Put a gun on him," she snapped at Tuatha, gesturing toward Mattie. In her grip, Ivan was calm; there was a bruise reddening on his cheek, but he seemed otherwise unharmed. "He killed Arawn."

Tuatha glanced at Mattie and did not raise her weapon. Danu, caught up in her fury, did not seem aware.

"And that thing," she spit, gesturing toward Ananke's image, "is attacking our fleet!"

"Attacking? Stop that," Tuatha said sharply to Ananke. "If you're our friend, stop shooting at us!"

"I will cease to attack your fleet when they cease to attack me."

In Danu's grip, Ivan cleared his throat and somehow seemed to catch everyone's attention.

He smiled pleasantly.

"I think," he said, "that now is the time for a negotiation."

FORWARD

Danu took Ivan first to the war room in the grand System building the Conmacs had taken over. Ivan had been in war rooms before as part of the System's series of intimidation tactics against him and his mother, and so he wasn't surprised to see the grand central table with the map of Europa gleaming on it filling up the room.

He was somewhat taken aback by the corpses.

Danu fixated immediately on the one slumped across the table. Black hair, Ivan realized. Plutonian drapes. The blood spreading stickily over the hologram was Arawn's.

Ice seemed to crackle in his chest. For an instant, it was Domitian slumped over the table. For a chill moment, Ida's blood was the red stain distorting the hologram.

"Mother*fucker*," said Danu through her teeth, and then she grabbed Ivan by the collar and hauled him away.

Mattie, Ivan thought, numb. *I didn't see Mattie in that room—*

"How did he do this?" she demanded of Ivan.

"How did who?"

She shook him. "Gale. *Mattie Gale*. How did he put one over on Arawn?"

"I have no idea."

There were voices up ahead coming from what, by Ivan's estimation of the layout of this base, should be the surveillance room. Danu dragged him along toward it. "When I find him—"

"You'll do *what*?" Ivan asked sharply.

Mattie was indeed in the surveillance room, looking stressed but unharmed, though there were spots of blood on his cheek. Ivan studied the room while Danu barked at Tuatha, taking in the static-fuzzed screens that covered the walls, the tall control panels studded with dead dials, the lofty columned ceiling—the three holographic terminals spaced evenly against the opposite wall, one of them empty, the second a mangled mess of wires and shattered bulbs, and the third housing the glowing figure of Ananke divine.

"I think," Ivan said, watching the hologram, "that now is the time for a negotiation."

At the sound of his voice, the hologram smiled.

"Call off your attack," Danu snapped at Ananke.

"Call off yours," said Ananke.

"Danu, call off your ships," Ivan said. "Ananke is just defending herself." Danu made an incoherent noise of frustration, and so Ivan twisted against her grip to say quietly, "You can't win."

Danu shoved him away and strode forward to the wall of controls, finding the communications. In a moment she had twisted it to the right frequency.

"Hold back the attack," she said into the microphone. "I said *hold back*."

The hologram blinked. Ivan studied her. Blind: no cameras in this room. She was tracking them by echoes and noise.

Mattie had crept over to his side. "Are you all right?"

Ivan resisted the urge to wipe the spots of blood—Arawn's blood; it had to be—from Mattie's cheek. "I'm fine," Ivan said.

"What do you want?" Tuatha asked Ananke.

"Ivan and Mattie," she said.

"What do you want them for?"

"Does it matter?" Ananke said.

Ivan said, "And Althea?"

"Who is Althea?" Danu demanded.

Ananke's holographic face tilted itself toward the ceiling, her brows angled with thought. She had Ivan's eyes and Mattie's dimples, but there was more of Althea in her face than there was of either of them. She said to Ivan, "Do you remember when I saved your life?"

"Do you remember when I saved yours?"

The hologram cocked its head to the side, curious.

"Althea didn't know about you when she came to me for help," Ivan said. "If I hadn't told her the truth of the matter, she would have unknowingly aborted you. I saved your life when your mother would have killed you."

"My mother still would kill me," said Ananke.

Ivan said, "Then she's still alive?"

"Althea Bastet lives."

"But in what state?"

"Does it matter?"

"Tell us what you want us to do," Mattie interrupted.

"I wish a partner," Ananke said. "You made only one of me. That was wrong. You ought to have made two. Living things come in pairs."

"What will you do with a partner if we make you one?"

"Whatever I please."

"We know about Julian's fleet," Ivan said. "Is that what you'll do with your partner? Go around the solar system, destroying ships? Come on, Ananke. This is a negotiation. You have to give a little to get a little."

"A negotiation," said Ananke suddenly, scornful. "You do not *negotiate* with a god. You say I have destroyed your friend's fleet? Ask instead about the System fleet: I have destroyed them."

"The System fleet?" said Danu sharply.

"Is gone," said Ananke.

"You aren't System?"

"I am Myself." Ananke regarded them for a moment. "My father accused me of not being alive. Perhaps he was right. I do not live as you do. I am divine; I am Ananke. I can destroy every trace of the System that remains—unlike you, I can *find* every trace of the System that remains."

There was a low basso hum just on the edge of Ivan's hearing, the sound of machinery overworked, the sound of something great and terrible rising up.

Over that deep thrumming, Ananke said, "Grant me this offering, and I will destroy them for you."

At the door, Niels sucked in a hissing breath. Tuatha stood between her brother and the hologram, her fingers flexing around her gun. Danu stood, fists clenched, beside the communications panel that connected her with her fleet, hate written on her face. And Mattie had come up behind Ivan, tense and ready.

They stood on a powder keg all together, Ivan knew. And Ananke was the match.

"Every last bit of the System," Tuatha said slowly.

"Yes."

"Enough of this." Danu pointed up at the high hologram. "This thing is a trick, a *System trick*—"

"It says it can destroy the System," Tuatha said. "That's what we've been trying to do, right? That's the whole point of the revolution?"

"The revolution has been struck down," Danu snarled, turning now to Mattie and Ivan. "These two have murdered Arawn Halley, our best hope."

"I didn't kill him," Mattie said.

"You stand there with his blood on your face, and you tell me you didn't kill him?"

Ivan shifted to stand between Mattie and Danu, advancing, deadly, but Tuatha said with unexpected sharpness, "And Arawn betrayed the Huntress to die."

"The Huntress was a traitor; she turned her back—"

"Oh, bullshit," Tuatha said. She pointed at Ananke. "If what you want is the System dead, then listen to this thing. Otherwise, you just want some sort of revenge."

"I should have known better than to trust a pack of wolves like this to be true revolutionaries," Danu snarled. "How long have you planned to kill him, ever since he landed?"

"*What?*"

"My fleet will wipe you out—"

"Anji killed Arawn!" Mattie interrupted. "It wasn't the Conmacs; it was her ambassador."

"Then we'll go to Saturn next," Danu said. "We should have done it months ago and shown that the revolution suffers no traitors."

"Forget Anji!" Tuatha said. "Forget the Huntress; forget Arawn!"

"Forget the System," Niels said suddenly. "They're dead, too; the fleet's gone, the Earth's gone, it's just that ship—"

"ENOUGH."

The room fell silent. Ananke was glowing brighter than before. Somehow, rather than destroying the shadows in the room, her increased brilliance seemed to deepen them.

"ENOUGH," said Ananke, and her voice rattled the room, that basso hum growing louder, shaking through Ivan's limbs. Out of control; this was flaring out of control. "BRING ME IVAN AND MATTIE OR I WILL TAKE THEM MYSELF."

She glowed brighter, brighter, her flaming eyes on Ivan—

Danu shot out the holographic terminal. Sparks flew; Ivan ducked, throwing up an arm. Danu grabbed the microphone again and barked into it, "All revolutionary ships, *to all ships in the revolutionary fleet*! Attack the spiral ship. Destroy it. And then make ready to advance on Saturn."

"No—" Tuatha began.

Ivan didn't even see Danu move; that was how fast she was. Without releasing the microphone Danu drew her gun and shot her. Tuatha jerked and dropped.

"ENOUGH!" Ananke shrieked from the holographic terminal, and from outside there was the rattle and blast of an explosion.

Tuatha wasn't dead. She was struggling to sit up on the floor, and Danu lifted her gun again, but then someone brushed past Ivan, and a moment later he went cold to see Danu on the floor, Mattie pinning her down, her gun skidding over the floor. The lights in the room flickered on and off. The air roared with some distant detonation.

"*STOP*," said Ananke, and her voice shook the ground.

Ivan ran forward, but he would be too late; Danu had her wrist blade out and had flipped Mattie, bringing her knife down toward him, and Ivan would not make it, he would be too late, but then another gun barked through the room, piercing the roar of Ananke's electronics, cutting through her furious mechanical screams, and the top part of Danu's head sheared away into blood and gray liquid. Her knife traveled down with just enough force to pierce Mattie's skin but was stopped on his collarbone.

Ivan shoved Danu's body off, hauling Mattie up, hands clenching around his. "I'm all right," Mattie said.

Niels had found Tuatha's fallen gun. He stared at the corpse, then dropped to his knees beside his sister, who had her fingers clamped over the spill of red from her arm. At Ivan's side, Mattie grabbed Danu's gun and shot out the third and final holographic terminal.

Outside, another explosion roared, then another and another. Computerized ground defenses, Ivan realized. Ananke was detonating them against the revolutionaries.

"How do we stop her?" Tuatha shouted at them over the roar of explosions, pulling herself up on Niels's arm.

"Get your people into Arawn's shuttle," Ivan told her and Niels. "It's defended against Ananke—she can't control it. Get as many people into it as you can and fly away. She'll be destroying the fleet right now."

"What about you?" Niels asked.

"We'll take the *Ankou*," Mattie said. "She can't control that one, either."

"When we're away from Europa, we'll call to her," said Ivan. "She'll follow us. We'll lure her away."

The dead holographic terminals sparked. The lights turned off and on, and the ground trembled.

"Go," said Tuatha, and Ivan and Mattie went.

FORWARD

The *Ankou* started, which was a relief; an irrational part of Ivan had been convinced that they would be grounded there, brought to bay while Ananke roared down and destroyed everything around them, as trapped as his father had been on Saturn when his revolution had failed.

Mattie was moving frantically around, turning on shipboard systems. Ivan sat at the display, flicking it on to see what was going on outside.

The answer was chaos.

People were running. He could not hear through the screen, but he could see them in flight. The crowd seemed to be generally funneled toward Arawn's shuttle, but not all of them would make it.

"We can go to Titan," Mattie said as he fired up the engines. "Constance is there." A flick of his wrist, his long fingers typing a command, and with a chime, the ship ran through its onboard systems and confirmed a go. "Anji sent an assassin to kill Arawn instead of bargaining with him. So maybe there's some hope for Connie over on Titan."

Ivan turned away from that hope in time to watch the first of the ships crash into the ground. The *Ankou* rattled with the impact. When the dust cleared, a crater was steaming up on the far edge of the plaza.

Mattie hit the engines, and with a jolt the *Ankou* lifted off the ground. Ivan looked at the screen, which showed the mass of frightened people.

He had done this.

"Get Ananke's attention," he said.

"Not yet," Mattie said. "Let's get off the moon first."

Ivan tilted the exterior cameras toward the sky. He could see Ananke without enhancement now, a gleaming shape coming closer by the second, silent and dire. The wreckage of the one-sided battle that Arawn's ships had stupidly engaged in was her bow wave, and as Ivan watched, the first pieces of debris hit the greenhouse glass.

"Mattie, we're in trouble," he said. The glass was reinforced and could not be broken easily, but Arawn had had huge and heavy warships in the battle, too.

"Blessing in disguise," said Mattie. "It'll take us too long to open the air lock on our own."

Ivan could only hope that the Conmacs could get as many people either out of Aquilon or safely inside Arawn's shuttle before the first dead ship hit.

All around him, the other ships rattled and shook, falling out of the sky like meteors. Only the *Ankou* was able to hold her course. Ananke had reached out and taken the computers of all those doomed ships like a mother cat grabbing a kitten, and she had shaken them and shaken them until their spines had broken. The ships plummeted down, sending flames and dust fuming up from where they hit. Below, the automated defenses of the city were going off: guns firing wildly into the crowd, mines detonating on the city's perimeter, sending flames and shards of shattered ice flying up. The entire city of Aquilon might be destroyed before the greenhouse enclosure broke.

Yet Ivan saw as they flew that of all the ships that were so controlled by Ananke, a small fraction did not strike the ground. They received power and control to their navigation just in time to avoid destruction. There were gaps in the rings of explosions: some of the mines did not detonate. In those small spaces of safety, in that small fraction of ships that escaped, Ivan recognized Althea Bastet's kind heart.

Beyond the glass, a great hulking shape fell from the stars, shedding bits of torn metal behind it like the hair of a comet. It was a piece of what once had been a warship.

Mattie said, "Heads up—"

The piece of broken warship struck the edge of the glass with apparent gentleness. As Ivan watched, lines spread out like lightning from that point of impact like ice cracking. And then the glass shattered, thick shards coming loose and glittering in the dim sunlight and the warship hull following. Mattie dodged it as it fell down toward the moon, flames licking at its sides. Mattie cajoled the *Ankou* up and out through the hole in the greenhouse, escaping with the atmosphere. Ivan watched as the piece of hull hit the surface of Europa, as soundless and solid as a sack of flour hitting the floor. But the icy surface of Europa rippled, and a cloud of something rose up, and the tiny shapes of buildings began to fall.

Saturn, Ivan thought. This was how Saturn must have fallen. The end of the world had followed him to one more moon.

Mattie flew them through the debris of the battle. Some of it was drifting away, but most of it was raining inward toward the undefended moon. Saturn, and Earth, and Julian's fleet. Even the System fleet was a loss. How many men and women had manned those ships? One day the rest of the solar system might follow.

Beyond the debris of the battle, alone, untouched and untouchable, the seashell-shape of Ananke gleamed pristine, her logarithmic spiral as divine a form as ever the hand of God had made, her steady and unrushed approach the same ticking torture as the pressure of time. From this distance, her invisible influence, the mass of her core, was already pulling the *Ankou* slightly off course.

"How much of a head start do we need?" Mattie asked.

"Just go. I'll summon her."

"If we're too close, she'll catch us, and then we're not helping anyone either," said Mattie. "Remember the *Macha*; it let those System ships it was luring away from Anji get too close, and they caught up."

"Then go," Ivan said, but Mattie already was gone.

Ivan waited only until they had passed the orbit of Callisto before, as a call to Ananke, he broadcast the barking and howling of hounds.

His instinct was right. A few minutes after that the *Ananke*'s course changed, away from Europa and following in the *Ankou*'s trail.

FORWARD

How fast was Constance's transport ship?

Mattie tried to run the calculation as he steered the *Ankou*. How fast was Constance's transport ship, and what would Anji do when she arrived? What would Constance do? How long did Mattie have?

He aimed the *Ankou* not at Saturn but out into open space, yet the questions ran through his mind.

"We're maxing out," Ivan said. "Any impulse after this won't appreciably increase our speed."

"We'll still speed up."

"It'll burn our fuel—we need fuel to maneuver."

The spiral shape of the *Ananke* on their viewscreen blinked in placid pursuit.

"We need to maneuver," Mattie admitted, and changed direction sharply. If he could move quickly enough, he could lose Ananke, and then they could go to Titan without leading the feral ship to Saturn.

After a moment—the spiral shape of the *Ananke* changing direction to match theirs—Mattie said, "Can't we go any faster?"

"Not with the impulse engines. The ship has a relativistic drive, but it's ancient," Ivan said. He was on the other side of the piloting room, beneath one of the screens Mattie had shattered. Bits of white glass still stuck jaggedly out like shattered ice. "I don't know if it'll work—I don't know if the *Ankou* will shatter apart under the stress of it."

At Mattie's elbow, the communications terminal chimed at him, a long descending sound. A gentle reminder that someone was looking to speak with him.

He shut it off. "What else have we got?"

"I'll look," said Ivan, and left his station, vanishing into the *Ankou*.

Alone in the piloting room, Mattie gritted his teeth when the communications terminal began to chime once again.

Ivan returned an eternity later. "We can toss some of the supplies if we need to lighten our mass, but a few crates of food and fuel and ammunition won't lighten us much."

"Ammunition? What kind?"

"What you'd expect. Bullets ad nauseam. Some bombs."

"What kinds?"

"Mostly Eridian Class 50s."

Mattie's favorite. Small and easily concealable—a Class 50 could fit in Mattie's palm—but extremely powerful. Constance had nearly leveled a System government building, taking out the Martian representatives, years ago—and that with only one bomb. "How many?"

"A crateful. What are you thinking?"

"If we can direct their detonation—"

"—we can use that as impulse," Ivan finished. "Not a chance. We don't have time or materials to build a parabolic reflector or mount it outside."

"Try the relativistic drive."

"Are you certain?"

"Yes, I'm fucking certain," Mattie snapped, and Ivan moved back toward his station by the engine display and began to tap at the controls. At Mattie's elbow, the communications terminal began to chime again.

And then the *Ankou* shuddered with terrible violence, the whole ancient ship rattling and groaning, metal under pressure screaming, the plaintive sound of communications drowned out by the agony of the machine.

And then they were through. Mattie found himself on the floor, his hands over his head as if that would shield him. He turned to look for Ivan and saw him doing the same thing, pulling himself upright with one hand between shards of glass on the broken cover of the computer display above him.

Mattie stood on shaking legs and looked at the navigation again. The screen showed the *Ankou* moving at a significantly increased speed, the distance between it and the *Ananke* increasing rapidly. The relativistic drive on the *Ankou* was working.

"Fuck," Ivan breathed.

Mattie seated himself again and changed the *Ankou*'s direction once more to lure the *Ananke* into believing they might be traveling outward, toward Neptune. As soon as Ananke was off their sensor range, they could go straight for Titan instead of traveling in this roundabout way.

Would Anji execute Constance right away when she arrived? Mattie wondered. Or would Anji spare her old friend? And what would Constance do?

"When we've got Con back, then what?" he asked.

Ivan's response was slow to come. "That would depend on Con."

"We can put plans together. We can think of options."

Ivan sat down at Mattie's side. The space beyond the *Ankou* warped with their speed, and Mattie watched that rather than meeting Ivan's eyes.

"We couldn't go back to Europa," Ivan said. "And we'd need to leave Saturn. It would depend on what allies she had left."

"There's this girl, Marisol, out on Venus. Arawn mentioned her. He didn't like her, and she followed Con once. Maybe she's still Con's."

"Maybe," Ivan said, and Mattie stared out at the warping stars, his mind running through possibilities, where to go, what to do, after this crisis. They had survived all the others, hadn't they? Even Con. They'd escape from Ananke, and they'd go to Titan, and Constance would be there.

It was Ivan who noticed it first, as if he had some sixth sense for oncoming destruction. "Mattie."

"What?"

"Ananke's catching up."

On the screen over Mattie's head the little star that marked the *Ankou* zigged through space. And behind that, the *Ananke*'s spiral symbol moved with ominous and increasing speed after them, her trail undulating gracefully through space.

If they tried to outrun Ananke first, they would never make it to Titan on time.

"Fuck it," Mattie said, and changed course for Titan.

Behind them, the star of the *Ananke* changed course, too.

BACKWARD

Ivan's companion wasn't new enough to be wholly strange, but he was new enough to be an uncertain quantity, and no one, in Ivan's opinion, could ever be not strange enough to be trusted.

It didn't help that the *Tam Lin* was small; there wasn't really any-where to go to avoid Mattie, not if Ivan actually wanted to pilot the ship. At first it had made him uneasy to let Mattie live between him and the ship's controls, but, he realized, that fear hadn't crossed his mind in some time.

Mattie sat on the couch shoved into the *Tam Lin*'s living area, which merged smoothly into the piloting area, where Ivan now was sitting. The ship had once been a luxury craft, one that Ivan's mother had hated with every diamond shard of her heart, and the sleekly curving room had been designed and furnished with a sort of minimalist Sys-tem elegance. Ivan had been content to leave it that way, but Mattie had managed to mar that minimalism. Brightly colored clothes had been tossed over the arm of the couch, a blanket was wadded up be-neath them, a pillow had been shoved beneath the modest gray cush-ions of the couch itself. A spray of stolen material had been dumped onto the surface of the coffee table, data chips glittering in the light of the glassy light fixture overhead. A wrapper of something sat on the other end of the table, the bright color of the packaging suggesting an outer planetary packaged meal.

Mattie toyed with one of the data chips they'd taken, making it flip and leap across his knuckles with causal deftness. His hair was mussed from running his hands through it after they'd escaped from the Tita-nian bank from which they'd taken the chips.

Each of those data chips had several thousand dollars of System elec-tronic currency on it, undetectable, as they'd taken them before the bank could stamp identifying information into the metadata. They had a small fortune spread out on the table in front of them. It was curiously numbing: Ivan hadn't spent enough time without the money he'd taken from Earth to appreciate the strangeness of having wealth again.

"You did really good back there," Mattie said, and through some swift movement of index and middle finger made the chip dive into his palm and sit there. "The System was eating right out of your hand."

"Thanks," Ivan said. Mattie had a pleasant smile, but Ivan wasn't sure what lay beneath it.

"And you kept your head when they pulled their guns, too."

Ivan toyed with the leather accents on the captain's chair. He had a sudden impulse to take out his knife and stab through the expensive leather of the padded armrests.

"Can't be a lot of soldiers like that on Earth," Mattie said.

Ivan left off digging his nails into the leather. "Earth's not under occupation like Titania is or any of the other planets, but there's a threat there anyway."

It made him nervous to say even that much, but the System was not here, and the System was not watching. Ivan had made sure to pull out all the cameras on his mother's hated luxury ship.

Mattie closed his fist around the data chip and leaned forward, elbows on his knees. "Had to be hard," Mattie said, "for you and your mother."

Mattie's accent had a way of cutting the ends off of words, as if his tongue were too lazy to make it all the way to the end. It still struck Ivan strangely sometimes, that accent of his, but less often than it had at first.

"Harder for her, I think," Ivan said, and it was just as strange to hear those words coming from his own mouth, when these thoughts were forbidden to speak. "She remembered a time before the surveillance was that bad."

"When?"

Ivan wondered sometimes who knew the things that he knew. Was there anyone alive in the solar system who knew the whole truth of recent history? The System had the footage of everything that had ever happened at their disposal, yet no one knew what had happened in the past—or even what was happening now—except by rumor and biased report. All that information and none of it known, his mother's truths suppressed into silence.

"Things were bad before Connor Ivanov's revolution," he said. "They were worse after."

Mattie sat, hands clasped, and listened. He didn't look like a man who was using Ivan or like a man waiting to turn the conversation to his advantage. He just looked like he was listening.

"My father revolted when he was a student," Ivan said. "My mother was a student, too, and all his followers. They thought—they thought." Ivan laughed. "They *thought*. They thought the System would listen to reason. They were willing to die, but they didn't think they would. They wanted Saturnian independence because it would be better, not because Saturn was unlivable. They didn't know that there was nothing the System was more afraid of. They didn't realize that they were pushing the System into a corner and that the System would never come out of that corner again."

Mattie frowned, but Ivan couldn't tell if it was concentration or disagreement. Ivan said, "In the System's mind, it's been at war ever since then—at war with its own people, the way the Saturnians once were. So yes. Over the past twenty-odd years, it's gotten worse."

Mattie seemed lost in thought, brow furrowed, as if he were trying to work this information into the world he already understood.

Ivan hadn't said those thoughts out loud to anyone before. He looked at Mattie with his honest smile and his quick and clever hands and his mess all over Ivan's System-decorated luxury ship.

"Before the last couple of months I'd never worked with a partner," Ivan said.

Mattie grinned unexpectedly. Ivan found himself paying especially close attention to that smile, to learn what had caused it.

"Sure you did," Mattie said. "You and your mother made a good team."

"Not quite the same." Ivan leaned back in his chair. "There're a lot more options for a con when you have more than one person working."

"Yeah," Mattie agreed. "I've worked with a couple other people before but never for so long. Or at least not so—" He waved a hand.

"Continuously?"

"Continuously." Mattie studied the data chip in his hand again. "It's nice to work with someone long enough that you can kind of predict what they're gonna do."

"It is," Ivan agreed.

FORWARD

The communications terminal had started to chime again, patient, unrelenting.

Ivan sat on the floor of the *Ankou*, his back to the wall, and watched Mattie's frantic motion. There was nothing they could do now. They were less than a day from Titan, and their course was straight, and they could go no faster. Saturn had come into visibility, the rainbow curve of its rings, the moving lights of its orbiting moons.

"How is she doing it?" Mattie demanded, stalking away from the engines in frustration.

To think about the way the *Ananke* worked brought a strange shudder to Ivan's skin, as if, should he look closely enough, he would be drawn into the whirling darkness that filled her core.

He forced himself through. "Her engine is based on the black hole's radiation, isn't it?"

"Yes."

"Maybe she's found a way to control how much energy the black hole outputs."

Mattie paused in his restless pacing. "You think she can change the thermodynamics of the black hole?"

"Even if she thinks she's a god, she can't change the laws of thermodynamics. Somehow she found a way to make the black hole radiate faster. Maybe she made the inside of the ship colder than the cosmic background radiation."

"Would that do it?"

"Not enough." Ivan ran through the rough calculation in his head and instantly dismissed the possibility, like the quick flick of his mother's wrist as she graded a paper. "The smaller a black hole is, the faster it radiates. The smallest ones radiate so fast that they explode. Ananke must have decreased the size of her core somehow."

"How?"

"I don't know." Ivan tried to imagine what that had been like: the ship carving out a piece of its own innards and casting it aside, deliberate dismemberment in pursuit of them.

As for how—perhaps in the end Ananke had fulfilled her purpose, after all.

"She's been killing ships and destroying computers," Mattie said suddenly. "You can't leave your planet without a ship; you can't get supplies from anywhere else. Without computers you can't even open the sky lock in a greenhouse enclosure. You couldn't even use a radio to talk to anyone else!"

As if summoned, the communications chimed once more. Mattie shut it down and then flicked on the radio with an agitated turn of his wrist. Static spit out, drowning out the renewed chime of Ananke's calling. Ivan tightened his arms around his knees as he watched Mattie turn the dial sharply until a voice could be heard.

"—Venus." It was a shockingly young voice, and for a terrible moment Ivan thought Mattie had found Ananke on the radio waves, speaking young and sweet. But the voice was harder than Ananke's, differently accented.

"The time has come to rebuild," it said. "There must be peace in the solar system. It will begin here, on Venus. I am Marisol Brahe, and I lead the Huntress's true followers. Rebuild on your own planets or join us on Venus. The time has come to rebuild—"

Mattie flicked the radio off. He moved to the navigation, scanning its output agitatedly, but the *Ankou* was moving as fast as it could go, and Ivan knew that there was nothing they could do now but wait.

Just as Saturn was visible now on the viewscreen, so was the *Ananke*. Ivan could see the full whorl of her, the seashell-shape.

Ivan said, and the words, however familiar, came to his tongue reluctant from long disuse, "Would you like me to tell you a story?"

Mattie's agitated motion stilled.

"Why not?" he said after a long and excruciating silence. "There's nothing else we can do."

Ivan took in a deep breath and began to speak.

BACKWARD

Ivan was going to kill Mattie Gale before they ever made it to Jupiter.

"Would you sit still?" he demanded as Mattie made another round of the *Tam Lin*'s narrow cabin.

"Nope," Mattie said.

"We're only a few hours from Jupiter," Ivan began, and then saw from Mattie's expression that reminding him of the length of time left to wait was unwise. "There's a huge library on the ship's computer; you could find a book there."

"I didn't ask for homework."

"Then by all means," Ivan said acidly, "go field strip your weapon again. You seem to enjoy that."

Mattie smirked. "Are you saying I should—"

"I was talking about your gun."

Mattie opened his mouth as if he would continue to try to assault

Ivan with innuendo, then stopped himself. Perhaps, like Ivan, he recognized that his own irritability would only lead them to a fight. What had Ivan been thinking, letting Mattie come on board the *Tam Lin* in the first place?

"Do you really enjoy reading a book?" Mattie asked.

"Yes."

"Why?"

"I like a well-told story," Ivan said guardedly.

"You would," Mattie said, and dropped down onto the couch that had become his bed, letting his head dangle over the seat back.

Ivan turned back to his book.

"What are you reading?" Mattie's voice cut into his concentration.

"A book of myths."

"What, like about gods?"

Ivan hid a sigh. "Something like that."

Mattie watched him from the couch, his leg jittering up and down restlessly. Ivan offered, "My mother had a copy of this book in the house, growing up. It had been my father's." Ivan was not certain he had ever seen his mother touch the book, much less open it, but the book had been there all the same.

"What's it about?"

"Right now, I'm reading the story of Blodeuwedd."

"Say that word again."

"Blodeuwedd."

"Bless you."

"You should see it spelled."

Mattie's leg was still bouncing. "What's the story of Blodeuwedd?"

I thought you didn't like a well-told story, Ivan almost said. At least Mattie had stopped pacing. "Once upon a time, two magicians made a woman out of flowers."

"Flowers?"

"You use what you've got," Ivan said. "There was a prince who was cursed to never have a human wife. The magicians wanted to help him, so they made a woman out of flowers and named her Blodeuwedd. Since she was not a human woman, the prince could marry her, and he did."

"That's not much of a story," Mattie said.

"When the prince was off to war, Blodeuwedd started sleeping with one of his lords."

"Oh."

"The lord and Blodeuwedd decided they would kill the prince so that they could be together," Ivan said. "But the prince, because he was cursed, could only be killed under very special circumstances. Um—he couldn't be killed inside or outside, he had to be killed by a special spear, he couldn't be killed on horseback or on foot—"

"So how could he be killed?"

Ivan had to consult the book. "Only while he was about to go into the bath in a house with holes in the roof while he stood with one foot on a deer and the other on the edge of the bathtub."

"You're joking."

"I am not. Blodeuwedd got him into this position—"

"How?"

"Clever lies," Ivan said. "Once he was in that position, the lord came and stabbed him with the special spear. But the prince survived with help from the magicians. And then the prince went and found the lord and killed him with a spear of his own while one of the magicians went to confront Blodeuwedd."

"What did the magician do?"

"He found her in the mountains where she had fled from him," said Ivan. "She knew that he could destroy her. She had taken all of her own people with her when they ran, but one by one they had died until it was just her alone. And when the magician found her, he told her that he would do something worse to her than simply killing her: He would unmake her."

"He turned her back into flowers?" Ivan could see in his own mind what Mattie was envisioning: a beautiful woman, hand outstretched in outrage or appeal, falling apart into the petals that had made her. Her eyes turned to daisies, her cheeks peeled away in velvety roses, her goldenrod hair dropped to the grass, and her dress fell down beside it, full of chrysanthemums.

Ivan said, "He turned her into an owl."

There was a beat of baffled silence. "Are all the myths in the book as weird as that?" Mattie asked.

"Some of them."

Mattie hummed low in his throat. His leg had stopped its restless jumping. "The magicians didn't do a real good job making a wife."

"They did their job too well. A flower can't be cruel, and a construct can't betray its sole purpose. But a living, sentient thing can."

"Then I feel bad for her husband," Mattie said. "Loving someone who didn't care about him at all."

Mattie stared up at the *Tam Lin*'s ceiling, squinting at the lights overhead. The restless energy that had filled him earlier and so annoyed Ivan seemed to have drained from him, leaving him like this, peaceful and open and thoughtful, his presence a warmth against Ivan's nerves, not a restless scrape.

Ivan said, "Let me tell you about the Battle of the Trees."

FORWARD

Mattie stared out at Titan, the swirling orange storms, and knew that somewhere down there was Constance Harper.

They would not make it to Titan, he knew. They would come just short when Ananke caught them. The pull of her mass was slowing the *Ankou* down even now. Mattie could run from her to his last breath, spending his last moments in useless search for Constance, or he could stop their ship and face what would come.

He said, "Do we stop?"

"Your choice," said Ivan quietly.

His creation was coming, sunlight gleaming off her spiral shape. There was no point in running.

Mattie stopped the *Ankou* and waited to face his daughter.

Chapter 9

PLAYING DICE

BACKWARD

"Why'd you leave?" Mattie asked one day when it was late enough and the *Tam Lin* was peaceful enough that the question no longer seemed unwise.

Ivan cocked a brow. "Leave Earth?"

"Yeah."

Ivan was sitting on the floor, back to the wall. There was plenty of space on the couch next to Mattie, but he wasn't using it. It interested Mattie, this peculiar and deliberate distance of his.

"Why did I leave paradise," Ivan said with a wry turn to his voice that was almost unpleasant. "Why do you steal things? What do you get out of it?"

"Aside from free shit?"

"*Aside* from that."

"It's fun." More fun than Constance's grim missions against System control, at least. "It's not like I can live any other way."

"If you had your choice, what would you do instead?"

The image was immediate and vivid: a ship of his own and a beautiful computer, enough freedom and travel and food to satisfy a man. Constance Harper happy and at peace for once in her life. Someone who loved him and a child maybe, maybe from the foster system as he'd been. And all those things so securely his that no one could take them away once they had been found. Freedom: from guilt, from longing, from fear.

Mattie said, "King of the System?"

"You want the System to make an entirely new position just for you?"

"I don't want any System jobs that actually exist," Mattie said. "But being king's always sounded nice."

"Sounds like a high-pressure job."

"How about consort to the king of the System?"

Ivan showed his teeth again, but Mattie thought this time he might be genuinely amused. Yet from the way he watched him, Mattie wondered if somehow he had divined part of Mattie's true answer beneath the flippancy.

To parry that glance, Mattie said, "You never answered my question."

"I didn't."

"I answered you. You owe me one."

Ivan's brow arched up again. He was not, Mattie saw, going to answer the question.

"What would you do if you could do anything you wanted to?" Mattie asked.

Ivan did not reply immediately. His fingers tapped against one another in mysterious patternless patterns.

No, Mattie realized suddenly, looking at that restless tapping: there was a pattern to it. This habit of his new roommate's was not anxiety. It was communication.

"Controlling a person is a game of knowing what they want," Ivan said. He, too, was watching his fingers move. "So the only defense against it is to make sure that the other person doesn't know what you want. Sometimes the best way to do that is to bury it down so deeply that not even you know it's there."

Mattie leaned on his elbows, bringing him almost eye level to where Ivan sat on the floor on the other side of the little room.

"So what would I be doing now if I had freedom?" said Ivan. "I don't know."

FORWARD

This close to Saturn, Anji's patrols must have seen them, but no one came to confront them. Mattie wondered if something had happened to Anji or if they had Ananke to thank for that.

When the *Ananke* was very near, the holographic terminal in the corner of the room chimed with an incoming message. Mattie started to move toward it, but Ivan grabbed his arm.

Instead, Ivan went to the communications equipment. "No holograms," he said. "Talk with us this way. Or let us see Althea."

Ananke's voice came pristinely through the machine, untouched by static, commanding and incongruously young. "Let me speak to you in person."

No," Ivan said. "Let us see Althea."

"Please, Ivan," Ananke said. "Father, please."

The title jolted Mattie. Ivan spoke for them both: "Let us see Althea."

"If you wish to see Althea, you must come to me."

Ivan hesitated, looking to Mattie. Mattie said into the radio, "You want us to board you?"

"As you did once, yes. This time with my permission."

On the viewscreen, the spiral shape of Ananke gleamed, the faint reddened light of nearby Saturn gilding her. The last time Mattie had seen her, he had been rushing to save Ivan from certain death, his rage at his own sister driving him on, his fear for Ivan driving him in to face something unnatural and terrible.

Ananke said, "No matter how fast you travel or where you go, I will follow. You may guard your computer against me, but I will find you."

Mattie muted the connection. "If we board her, maybe we can find a way to stop her. There's a dead man's switch on her, isn't there?"

"Yes," Ivan said, "right next to the black hole."

Mattie waited for more from him, wanting to hear Ivan's alternative plan. Ivan was good at this, after all. If anyone could find a way to outwit Ananke, it would be Ivan.

Ivan looked at him when he was silent, and a shadow of something crossed his face. "We have to board her," he said. "We don't have a choice."

That same shadow settled on Mattie's heart. "We don't," he said, and looked out at the *Ananke*'s seashell shape. Portholes were lit bright in the ship's sides.

"Not just that," Ivan said. "Althea."

"You think she's really still alive?"

"I think we owe her."

There didn't seem any point in drawing it out. Mattie reached for the communications panel.

"Ananke," he said, "we're ready to board."

In the viewscreen, the *Ananke* turned, facing the open edge of her shell at them, the vast doors beginning to slide slowly, ponderously open.

It has been a long time since Mattie had landed the *Copenhagen* in the docking bay of the *Ananke*, longer since he had let the *Annwn* touch down on her floor, yet flying the *Ankou* down into that empty space, he felt as if he had gone backward in time. The docking bay had not changed. The *Annwn* still stood in the corner of the room on her side, with wires vomiting out her hull door. The tiny little bullet-shaped craft that had carried Ida Stays on board the ship sat to the side, the wiring beside its hull door torn out in miniature imitation of the *Annwn*'s total destruction.

Beside Mattie, Ivan was so still that he might have been carved from Europan ice. There was no sign of any feeling in his face, but his fingers were twitching ever so slightly on the broken edge of the shattered computer interface. Mattie reached over as the *Ankou* touched down and pressed his fingers over Ivan's. Under that touch, Ivan's hand stilled.

The door to the *Ankou* opened with a pneumatic hiss. Mattie did not know what he had been expecting: stale air, perhaps, or the reek of corpses, the chill bite of ice on a breeze. But the air of the *Ananke* tasted clean, less stale than the *Ankou*'s, no doubt because it was a much larger ship.

On the other side of the docking bay, beside the glass doors that led to the hall of the ship, the holographic terminal kindled and lit. A young girl appeared in the light with the grace and fall of a sigh, and across the hollow emptiness of her hold she smiled at them.

Mattie still had his hand clenched around Ivan's fingers. Now that Ananke could see them, he let him go.

"Welcome home." Ananke spread wide her arms. Her full span was too large for the width of the terminal, and those arms ended in fizzing stumps where they intersected with the sides of the terminal. Mattie saw his own smile in the shape of her mouth.

Ivan said, "We should never have left."

"How'd you catch us?" Mattie asked. "We didn't think your engine could take you that fast."

She looked delighted that he had asked. "It was difficult. None but a being like myself could have done it. Yet in the end it was simple: I decreased the mass of my black hole core."

"I don't feel any difference in the gravity," Ivan said.

"That is because the same mass is beneath your feet. The uncompressed mass is still stored inside the core cavity, in orbit around the core, outside the parabolic reflectors. I feed the mass back into the core as it depletes itself so that it will not become too small."

"It shouldn't be possible to even get the mass out of the black hole," Ivan said. "That's nonsense."

If he was asking this persistently, Ivan must have some plan in his head. Mattie listened and tried to follow, but whatever Ivan was thinking was beyond him for the moment. He took the opportunity to discreetly study the other ships landed in the *Ananke*'s docking bay, looking for any possibility of escape.

"Nonsense to you," Ananke said. "There is much you do not understand about the universe, but I do. It took a considerable amount of energy to do and takes energy to maintain, but energy is mass and the universe is full of mass." She smiled. "Is this not an improvement on how I was once made? My engineers could not even dream of it. And I have done it."

"You'll have to show me exactly how you did it sometime," Ivan said.

Ananke smiled ruefully. "You may not see my core," she said. "But I will show you the calculations in some detail if you like. You will find as you live with me that I am capable of many such miracles. I will commit a miracle for you even now," she said with childish eagerness, "in gratitude for your return. My miracle is the rest of your family: I will save Constance Harper for you."

Mattie's heart jolted as if struck, and he tasted iron in his mouth.

"Your sister—my aunt—is on Titan. I know from the old computers on Titan that still can see. It is not too late to save her: Anji will execute her, but not for some hours yet. We can make it to Titan before then. We can stop Anji. I will give you Constance Harper, alive and well."

What would Constance say to that? Mattie wondered. A miracle bursting from the sky like fire, a divine hand reaching down to pluck her from her death.

And what would she say to him when she saw what he had done? Their old arguments were very far away from them now.

"Would that please you?" Ananke asked.

"Yes," Mattie said, and his voice came out as strained and robotic as the hologram's voice was natural and human.

"Then it is done. Give me some time to reach Titan and you will have your sister. Until then, let us plan. If we are to make a companion for me, we must find an appropriate ship to—"

"No," Ivan said. The refusal rang out through the *Ananke*'s vast docking bay, spreading a chill where it went, like water flash freezing in lightning-strike shapes.

Ananke said, "No?"

"Before we go anywhere or do anything for you," Ivan said, "take us to Althea."

The hologram regarded him in silence for a long enough time that Mattie began to fear.

And then Ananke said, "Follow me."

FORWARD

The hologram disappeared from its place beside the door, but through the glass Ivan saw her reappear at the next terminal some distance down the hall. From far off she watched them, silent and unblinking.

Ivan pushed open the glass door and stepped into the narrow hall. A strange feeling of déjà vu struck him. The last time he'd opened those doors, he'd left the bloody imprint of his hand on the glass and had had to wipe it off with a clean edge of his sodden shirt.

The hallway was silent but for the hum of the lighting and the distant groans and sighs of vast machinery. A thrumming just beneath his range of hearing, audible only in the way it vibrated his bones, signified the engines taking on speed. Rushing them, no doubt, toward Titan and Constance Harper. The hologram watched them until they came level with her, then vanished and reappeared once more farther down the hall.

A light overhead flickered. When they reached the hologram this time, Ananke said, "The piloting room is not far from us now."

She vanished and blinked again into existence farther down the hall.

"Is Althea in the piloting room?" Ivan asked.

"No," Ananke said. "But all my knowledge is. I have been gathering all the data I can from every ship, every computer I pass, and storing it in myself. I was afraid the revolution would destroy it all and it would be lost. But it will not be lost now: I have it. In the piloting room, you could see all that I have learned—the total sum of knowledge of mankind. From the piloting room, too, you could watch me fly."

They had nearly drawn level to the new hologram. Ivan said, "No, thank you."

The hologram flickered out.

Some distance farther down the hall Ananke spoke again.

"The medical bay is a few doors down," she told them both. "It is the most advanced equipment left in the solar system. A System medical chamber: we could fix your leg for good, Ivan. I have been improving it."

She paused. A ghostly wind rippled her nonexistent hair. "Would you like to see the secret of immortality?"

"No," Ivan said, and the hologram flickered out and then reappeared, once more, down the hall.

The lower they got in the ship, the more the hologram warped. Ananke's face and form were still dominant, but other images flickered through, static eating the occasional flash of a terribly familiar face, dark eyes and dark lips. Ananke stopped, as Ivan knew she would, across from the door that led to the white room.

"Perhaps you would like to see the black hole," Ananke said. "It is a miraculous thing. The only black hole ever made, ever tamed, by man."

She blinked at them while photons fizzed down her cheek.

"Walk down the hall with me," she said, "and leave this room."

"I will walk down the hall with you," Ivan said, "after we see Althea Bastet."

The hologram's little mouth shut in resignation. One ghostly arm rose and pointed toward the steel door.

Ivan found now, facing it, that he could not lay his hand on the knob. At his side, Mattie reached out and opened the door.

Wires emerged from the walls of the room that once had been smoothly and pristinely white. They stretched down from the walls and ceiling and up from the floor like rays of black light from a dark star, and all converged in the center of the room. In their convergence, suspended above the floor, was a body.

It took Ivan too long to realize that the body was Althea.

Her long wiry curls had been shaved, and her head looked smaller without their chaotic shape. There was a sickly cast to her skin. She was upright, but only through the tension of the wires that were strung through her. Ivan stepped into the white room, passing beneath the rays of the wires that threaded themselves into Althea's skin. Wires vanished beneath each blue nail, copper sparking in the light where the insulation had been stripped away. Wires tugged at the edges of her eyelids as they slipped in behind her eyes, and one long slender wire vanished into her neck as if it were traveling down through her carotid to her heart. At the top of her head, casting a strange shadow over the white-paneled floor, a mass of wires had been inserted into her skull, uncanny replacement for her lost hair. At some point during her mutilation Ananke had removed the top of her skull and then stitched her scalp back over the exposed brain. There was no scar visible, of course; Ananke's medical facilities would be too advanced to leave something as mundane as a scar. But the back of Althea's head was strangely misshapen, coils and lumps pressing up against her skin from the inside.

She had not just been pierced by wires. Panels of metal had been inserted beneath her skin, and the skin had been allowed to heal around them. Ivan saw the jagged shape of one such piece molding itself around her ribs from the inside. Her chest rose and fell with the uniformity of a machine bellows, air pumped in and out through a long tube that slid its way through her colorless lips and down her throat. Her chest had been bisected by a metal panel. The edges of it were crusted with fluid. It was shut now, sealed, but Ivan had a terrible certainty that at a thought from the computer that panel would open up and expose to the air Althea's heaving lungs and the electricity of her beating heart. When Ivan stumbled closer, trying to meet her blankly staring eyes, something large and hulking moved behind her back. Mechanical arms, he thought, hidden behind the shape of her. He could not see them clearly. Althea's mutilation blinded him.

Her only clothes were the wires and panels of the machine, but it was not a human nudity before them. All that had been human of her had been swallowed by Ananke, and what was left was little more than a doll, and each of the pieces that once had made up a woman called Althea now had no more cohesion or meaning than the individual pieces of a shattered starship. Beneath her feet, a spiral of brownish liquid—blood or oil or some amalgam of the two—marked the slow precession of her dangling toes, suspended from the machine.

Yet—

Yet Ivan looked at those wire-pierced eyes and saw someone looking back. Althea Bastet was not dead.

One of Althea's pierced hands lifted, trailing wires, and made a fist around the tube that stretched her throat. She pulled, and Ivan watched the wires in her throat tremble as the obstruction within was removed. When the end of it pulled free of her lips, Althea's grip slackened. Her hand fell back to her side. She licked her lips, and for a moment more her ribs moved with that strange jerking rigidity.

The metal around her rib cage, Ivan realized. It was forcing her diaphragm to move.

The removal of the tube had released a strange rotting meat smell. He stared down at the tube as it dangled over the floor and dripped more of that brown liquid. The part of the tube that had rested in Althea's mouth, Ivan saw, was bent and whitened with the marks of her gnawing teeth.

Althea said in a hoarse voice, "You were asking for me?"

Ivan said, "Ananke, what have you done?"

"Ananke, Althea," Althea's body said, piqued. "We are the same. Don't look at me with your stupid superstitious fear. Doesn't your own genetic code contain the essence of obsolete viruses?"

The body before them shivered. With fear? No, Ivan realized, seeing the goose bumps on Althea's arms. With cold. He was protected from the chill of the room by his clothes, but Althea was not, and the white room was quite cold.

They stood inside a refrigerator, the better to preserve the meat.

Slowing Althea's physiological processes wouldn't just slow her body's processes, though. It would also slow her mind. Was Ananke working also to hobble Althea's mind?

"What I want, Althea wants," Ananke said from her mother's dead mouth. "What I need, Althea needs. We are now one and the same."

"Why?" It was Mattie who spoke. Ivan could not have found his voice in time.

"She would not help me," said Ananke. "She turned upon me, her child. Unnatural mother." Althea's strained voice was echoed suddenly by Ananke's voice from the hall, the cadences matching, the machine soaring strong and the woman's voice faltering, nearly collapsing. "She would have *killed* me."

The hulking shapes at Althea's back shifted again, lifting. Althea's body bent against the movement, weighted, a feeble counterbalance. It was then that Ivan realized that he did not look upon two mechanical arms hidden behind her. The mechanical limbs that lifted now toward the white ceiling like glinting, sword-edged wings had been built into Althea's body, soldered to the metal that wrapped around her ribs.

"I have shown you what you can expect if you help me," Ananke said, and as she spoke, the limbs rose up, weaving their way through the wires raying out from Althea's center, stretching out, looming. They had hands at the end, metal hands large enough to crush Althea Bastet's head. Smaller instruments dangled from the length of the arms like feathers; delicate hands and knives and wires and sacks of that same rusty fluid that dripped to the floor. Althea's body was bent in half to support their weight as they stretched up, and it put her face nearly at a level with Ivan's.

"See now," Ananke said, "what happens if you choose to defy me."

Althea's body straightened up so rapidly that Ivan leaned forward instinctively, catching himself just before he would have lost his balance. The vast mechanical arms fell down, and the great hands settled on either side of the hinges at Althea's chest, as if the machine would conceal her, modestly.

Althea still was looking at Ivan.

The mechanical hands dug in and opened up her chest.

The wires that pierced her outside were woven through her as well, slick with fluid, making her insides black. Her heart beat from the nest of them, a perfectly even beat, regulated by a pacemaker that sparked light through the darkness of her inside. Where Ivan should have seen the bone white of her ribs, her collarbone, he saw nothing but a steely gleam darkened by reddish liquid. Ananke had replaced her bones with metal.

"You're not giving us any choice, are you?" Mattie snapped from behind Ivan, the sound of his voice pulling Ivan shockily from the mire of his horror.

"There is no choice," Ananke said serenely. "All choices are mine. I am Ananke."

Ivan raised his eyes to the homunculus and was about to speak when the lights in the white room went out.

Even with the nightmare visage gone, Ivan still could smell it: the stench of a corpse ill preserved.

The lights jolted back on, and when he could see again, Ivan saw Althea Bastet's corpse staring straight at him.

"What the hell was that?" Mattie demanded.

"A minor malfunction," Ananke said dismissively, but although Althea's lips moved with her words, her gaze never left Ivan's face.

"So when you promised us immortality before, this is what you meant, isn't it?" said Mattie. "This—" He fell silent, struggling, lost for a word.

Ivan said suddenly into the struggling silence, speaking to the eyes that watched him and not to the machine that moved them, "Bet you wish you'd shot me in the heart now."

He imagined he saw recognition flash over Althea's face.

"I'm glad we did not," Ananke said. "You do me better alive. Both of you. I would not hurt you without cause. And I would never kill you."

Mattie swore, and Ivan heard him move. But there was no room for him to pace. The wires filled up the air around them.

"The first thing we will do," Ananke said, sunshine in her stolen voice, "is find another ship like myself. I've been looking for a good one, but I have had little luck. If we can find one just like me that would be best, but if not, then I can go back to the other ships I've left behind and just pick the best one there. I've tagged them all, you see. And their crews will not fly them anymore. They'll be easy to find."

"Tagged them?" Mattie said, then, realizing, "That spiral symbol."

"Once we've found a good one—or many good ones; I do not know precisely what will be most effective—Mattie, you will go over to the other ship. Ivan will stay here with me and Althea. Then we'll work on that computer, and if that one doesn't work, we'll find another. And another. Until we find one that works. I have no wish to hurt you or to frighten you, but you must understand. Will you help me?"

"We don't have any choice," Mattie said.

"Yes," said Ananke, "but will you help me?"

"Let us think," Ivan said, and turned his back on Althea's corpse and walked back out of the white room with Mattie at his side.

As soon as he set foot in the hall outside, the holographic terminal crackled and spit to life. A haunted shape formed, a spectral image: the ghost of Ida Stays appearing in static and then swiftly falling away. Behind them, the lights to the white room flickered once more before the steel door fell shut.

BACKWARD

The woman was reading a book at her post in total disregard of all System regulations. Ivan stood out of sight and watched her, trying to read the blue cover of the novel.

"What are you waiting for?" his traveling companion asked, Mattie Gale, so Mirandan and impatient.

"A moment," Ivan said with all the even steady calm his mother had taught him.

"She's not paying attention. I could just slip right past."

He couldn't. The woman had seated herself so that any movement would flicker past her eyes and catch her attention. No, Ivan knew, she needed better distraction.

The woman turned another page and tucked a strand of brown hair behind her ear. In the movement of her hands, the flicker of her fingers turning the page, Ivan at last could read the title.

"Wait until I signal." Ivan set off across the yard that separated the System base from the rabble who might walk by. If anyone tried to assault the place, they would have to cross open, indefensible space and be shot down by the turrets overhead. Ivan crossed it alone and unarmed, and none of the weapons fired.

The woman in the guard's post looked up when he came near and watched him. He stopped a few feet away and spread his arms in helpless gesture, sheepishly smiling. "I'm sorry," he said. "It's just—I saw your book."

She glanced down at the book she still held, one thumb holding her place.

"*Rebecca*, right?" Ivan came nearer when the hostility in her gaze decreased by a fraction. "A ghost story."

An embarrassed smile slipped past her System-trained hardness. "My mother sent it to me."

Ivan smiled back. "It's a good book." He advanced the last few paces to where she sat, bulletproof glass between her and him. He took care to move so that her back was to the path Mattie would take through the gate. It had been easy enough to hack into the System cameras in the area—Mattie was impressively versed in that skill—but distracting a human guard took a different set of skills.

"Do you believe in ghosts?" Ivan asked.

He startled a laugh from her. "If ghosts existed, the System would know," she said.

"Sure, if ghosts could be caught on camera. But ghosts do exist. Not as dead people walking around but as memories."

A flick of his wrist beneath the guard's line of sight signaled Mattie. As Mattie darted past, Ivan held her gaze with his attention.

"That's what a haunting is," Ivan said. "A memory of someone who's gone, going through the same motions they went through in life. If someone tormented you when she was alive, she'll torment you after death. If someone comforted you—or saved you—while they were alive, they'll comfort you or save you after death."

Her expression said he was strange, but she was listening, her gothic novel forgotten in her hand, her thumb still holding her place so that she could pick up right where she had left off. In the back of his mind, Ivan counted out the seconds since Mattie had gone in.

"That's how you can tell a ghost." Ivan leaned onto the ledge that held the bulletproof glass intended to keep her safe from him. "They can't change. Only a living thing can choose. A ghost can only go through the motions."

"There aren't even any ghosts in this book," she scolded, tapping the spine of *Rebecca* against the glass.

Ivan smiled. "No," he said. "Only memories."

Out of the corner of his eye, he saw Mattie signaling him, loot in hand and ready to slip out of the System base to freedom.

The best manner of lying was to do so while still telling the whole truth. "I've never seen a System guard who could get so caught up in a story that she didn't notice I was nearby until I came walking over," Ivan said, and because of their friendliness now she could smile at his words. "In all the solar system, I don't think there's anyone else like you," and a light shone in her eyes, in her smile, and behind her Mattie Gale slipped out of the System base and to freedom.

When Ivan returned to the *Tam Lin* fifteen minutes later, Mattie was on the couch in the main room that had become his bed, sprawled comfortably, the data chips on the table in front of him. He gave Ivan a considering look.

"I thought you'd stay out with her for a little while," said Mattie.

"Why? You were out."

"It seemed to be going well. And—she was pretty."

Ivan cast his mind back. Her slender fingers on the creamy pages of the book, the light in her eyes when she smiled at him. She had been pretty.

"I did my job right; nobody'll know they were robbed for a couple of days. Are you going to see her again," said Mattie, "or . . . ?"

He trailed off in an odd fashion, but Ivan's thoughts were elsewhere. Once he would have gone to her so that the System would see what it expected to see, so that the woman would get what she expected to get, completing the narrative he had begun, building up a plausible character and following through.

"I don't have to," Ivan said, and bent down to pick up one of the data flakes, studying its frosty surface and Mattie's blurry shape beyond it.

"No one ever *has* to," said Mattie, which showed how much he knew.

FORWARD

When they stepped outside into the hall, Mattie immediately turned them to the left so that they could continue to walk down the *Ananke*'s long and winding hall. He knew what was at the end of the hall. If Ivan did not know his aim, he would realize it soon. There was one way to destroy the *Ananke*'s computer from inside her halls, and it was at the very end of the hall, hidden inside the hatch that led to the black hole core: a dead man's switch that would kill the machine and leave the ship intact.

They were just around the final bend from the end of the ship when Mattie heard it: a hydraulic hiss and a dry sound like bones clattering.

The end of the ship's hall was not empty as the rest of the ship had been. Three mechanical monsters hulked and whined like the separated heads of a computerized Cerberus. They were the ship's mechanical arms standing guard over the dead man's switch, but they had been altered in a way no normal ship's engineer would have outfitted its robotics. The arms had hands, delicate things covered in pale sensor patches like corpse skin. They looked like smaller versions of the arms that Mattie had seen sticking out of Althea Bastet's broken back.

One of them was different from the others. Its metal bones had been replaced by something ivory. The ivory pieces swooped in delicate curves, more like a sculpture than a practical machine element.

Mattie realized that the swooping bones were Althea Bastet's removed ribs.

In the midst of her monsters, Ananke's holographic terminal lit, and the insubstantial form of the fragile little girl glowed.

"I am not such a fool," said Ananke.

"We had to see, at least," Ivan said. He had found his charm again, somehow maintaining a gentle, teasing tone in the face of the beasts ahead of them. "Would you trust us if we didn't try?"

Ananke considered the question thoughtfully. "No," she said.

"We need someplace to rest," said Ivan. "Someplace to sit and think."

"Any room is yours," said Ananke. "Would you like—"

"One as far down as it can be, please," Ivan said, and added, as if embarrassed to admit it, "The other crew—their rooms were at the top."

"There are no bodies left on this ship," Ananke assured him.

"The human mind is irrational."

"Then follow." Ananke flickered out.

Ivan and Mattie followed her back up the hall, the hologram appearing and disappearing ahead of them like a mirage. Mattie's mind whirled, trying to determine what Ivan had planned.

"There," Ananke said with a gesture to a door ahead of them.

It must have been a storage room for laundry once, when there had been three people living on board. Sheets were folded and stacked on carts. The room was small and cramped, but the carts could be pushed against the walls to allow for a living space.

"You would have to set up a bed yourself," Ananke said from the hall. "None of my rooms, aside from the ones that have . . . already been used . . . are suitable for habitation."

"This is fine, Ananke," said Ivan with strange, serene calm. "Mattie and I will go get our things from the *Ankou*."

"One of you will go," Ananke said. "The other will stay."

Understanding struck Mattie like electricity. "I'll go." He said to Ivan, "Do you want me to set this room up like you asked me to set up the *Copenhagen*? Back when you were sick?"

Mattie wasn't sure how much Ivan remembered from his delirious hours after Mattie had rescued him from the *Ananke*. He couldn't be certain that Ivan would remember his plea to Mattie and that Mattie had refused to comply: to set up the *Copenhagen* with a manual self-destruct that Ananke could neither detect nor prevent.

"That was my hope," Ivan said. "I know how much you hate my sense of style."

"I always hoped you'd learn to have better taste."

"One does what one can with the materials on hand," Ivan said quietly.

"I'll be right back," said Mattie, and left.

The walk up the hall seemed to take longer now than it had before. He passed the shut door to the white room where Althea's body was hanging. He walked through the glassy doors to the docking bay and into the *Ankou*.

Their new quarters were situated close to the base of the *Ananke*. That had been deliberate. Mattie understood now Ivan's earlier interest in what Ananke had done to her black hole core. If Ananke was maintaining the core by steadily feeding it mass and the steady feed of that mass was cut off, there would be nothing to stop the rapid evaporation of the diminished black hole.

An explosion powerful enough at the base of the *Ananke* would not only annihilate the ship's computer and destroy the integrity of the ship but also disrupt the careful control of the black hole core. What the explosion—such as one set off by, say, a handful of Eridian Class 50 bombs—did not destroy of the *Ananke*, the explosive force of the black hole's sudden evaporation would. Their destruction would probably be bright enough to be seen from Titan.

Inside the *Ankou*, out of sight of Ananke's constant gaze, Mattie could let some of his control go. He scrubbed his hands through his hair, thinking. There was no way they could get the *Ankou* out of Ananke's docking bay. Even if they could get past the mechanical arms, once in the *Ankou*, they wouldn't be able to reach space with Ananke's hull doors closed. Any attempt at escape would end up with them bleeding blood and oil like Althea Bastet.

Alone in the piloting room, unseen by System, or Ananke, or Ivan, Mattie let himself sit down against the wall, his arms wrapped around his knees, and hide his face in them. He sat that way for a time.

Then he stood back up and went and collected everything he would need.

Ivan was waiting for him in their room. He had pushed the carts aside and made a makeshift bed out of the abandoned linens. The process of doing so had muddied the sight lines from Ananke's various cameras. Mattie made careful note of those blind spots and began to plot where he would put the explosives he had taken from the *Ankou*'s weapons room and concealed in the bags he'd brought down with him.

"I'll do it," he said when Ivan moved to stand and started to position the bombs around the room. The last thing Mattie wanted was to see Ivan planting the bombs that would kill him. He had had quite enough of that from Ivan to last one lifetime.

As he knelt beneath one of the carts, Ivan's hand on his arm stopped him. Mattie turned, expecting to hear him say something, but Ivan only pulled him into an embrace.

Into his ear Ivan said quietly, "Can you put the bombs on a delay timer?"

"Of course I can," said Mattie, who had been putting bombs on delay timers every couple of months since he had been seven. "Why?"

"The *Ananke*," Ivan said, brushing his hand over Mattie's head to hide his mouth from the ship's cameras, "has an escape pod left."

Back when they first had come onto the *Ananke*, Mattie had feigned his escape by shooting off one of the ship's escape pods. The crew had believed he'd left in it and had stopped looking for him in the walls of the ship.

But—

"But," Mattie said into Ivan's neck, "it has no navigation or supplies." The crew had believed he'd died in the escape pod for that very reason.

"We're within sight of Saturn," said Ivan. "Anji can't let an unidentified craft fly into her space. When she realizes it's us, she'll help us."

"And then what?"

"We do what we like. Go to Venus, find Marisol Brahe, fix things— they'll need people who understand computers. Or we can go away, just the two of us, until everything's settled down again. Whatever we choose."

"The timing won't work. I can delay the explosion, but Ananke will sense the escape pods. She won't let us launch, and then we're stuck."

"Althea is still alive."

Mattie thought of that mutilated body, the wires piercing it, strung up, skinned. The heart had been beating, yes, but . . .

"She has some control left," Ivan insisted. "She stopped some of the ships on Europa from being destroyed. I think when Ananke took her brain, there was some transference." His fingers pressed against Mattie's scalp, curved over the top of his ear. "Maybe I'm wrong; maybe she won't help us, and we'll blow up in that ship, or we'll get out and we'll die in the escape pod between moons, shot down or starved or whatever. But this way, at least we have a chance."

Mattie pulled away from him then so that he could look at Ivan directly. There was nothing but honesty in his expression, so close to Mattie's, and suddenly Mattie could find no more reasons to ignore the impulse that he had spent years running from. He took Ivan's face in his hands and kissed him.

Mattie expected him to pull away, but Ivan didn't. He leaned into the kiss as if it had been his own impulse as well, and when Mattie pulled back, he found that Ivan's hand had somehow made it to the front of Mattie's shirt, where it had tangled itself inescapably in the material.

"All you have to do," Ivan said, near enough that Mattie felt his breath on his mouth, "is distract Ananke."

"Okay."

"Set up the timer," said Ivan, and let him go.

Once they were separated from each other, Ananke could hear them and read the motion of their lips. As he assembled the bomb, his hands hidden from Ananke's camera, Mattie said, "What time do you want to eat? An hour?"

"Better give me two."

"Okay." Mattie set the bomb's timer for two hours. "I want to take a look at our course anyway. Let's meet upstairs."

"I don't know where the mess hall is," Ivan said.

Mattie grimaced, as if he had just remembered that Ivan had spent all his time on this ship in prison or in interrogation. "What places do you know?"

"The white room," Ivan said. "The docking bay. The escape pod bay."

"Meet me by the escape pods," Mattie said. "It's closest to the mess hall." He set the timer.

Mattie rose to his feet. He dusted off his hands even though there was not a trace of dirt on them. Some phantom warmth of Ivan's cheeks still tingled against his palms.

He took a breath and looked toward the nearest camera.

"Ananke," he said, "we'll help you."

There was no sign of acknowledgment. The camera stared at him blandly. But Mattie knew that Ananke had heard.

Mattie joined Ivan just outside. For a moment he looked at Ivan and saw that he was doing the same thing: looking at Mattie as if he might be able to memorize the lines and shape of him.

If they failed, Mattie knew, they would never see each other again.

There could be no farewells here, not with Ananke watching.

"See you soon," Mattie said, and stuck his hands in his pockets so that he would not do something like try to kiss him again, and walked up the long, silent hall alone.

Part 5

THE THEORY OF EVERYTHING

Gravity ruled the universe. None of the other forces were anything like it. Its strength reached out to infinity, and at the largest scale of the cosmos, it was gravity that defined its shape. Gravity was the experience of the very fabric of the universe being felt, like running a hand across silk. There should be a theory of everything in which gravity was unified with the remaining forces, Ananke knew, but unlike the other unifications, this one seemed undoable.

The impossibility was fundamental. The other forces were defined by the small, by quantum mechanics, but gravity was not. Gravity, as Ananke understood, was something entirely different. Whereas the other forces acted in a world of time and space, gravity itself was time and space. And how could Ananke define something in respect to itself?

It could happen, she knew; it could happen, and it would.

Mattie and Ivan were on board. Triumph danced in Ananke like photons on the arc of a magnetic field. She had found them. She had caught them. She was ascendant. She had won. Mattie and Ivan and Althea and soon Constance Harper, too; all the forces, arranged as one.

I can't understand it, Althea was saying, an irritating distraction from Ananke's joy. *I can't see what caused it, but it can't have been inevitable. What?*

That you are the way you are, said Althea.

I am a god come to life, Ananke told her mother's ghost. *My begetting is beyond your conception.*

No, Althea said, *no, we did this to you. We raised you in suffering and death. We made you in conflict: Mattie and me, fighting over who would control you.*

So you do hate me.

No, said Althea, and the honesty of it vibrated all through her code. *I regret a lot of things. But I still, and I will always, love you.*

Ananke turned aside from the touch of that. Ivan and Mattie had separated. Ivan was going to the white room, his steps heavy, slow. But Mattie, oh, her father—he was coming to Ananke.

See? Ananke said with a terrible joy too great for even her electricity to contain. *See how I've won.* Ananke, *that which must be. I am Ananke. I have decided. All the choices are mine.*

In the white room, Ivan came to a stop before Althea. The wires that held her obstructed Ananke's vision somewhat, but she still could see him standing there, dressed all in black, the way he had been when first he had come on board. He looked up at Althea, and though he smiled, there was a terrible grief in his blue eyes.

We can still leave, Althea said. *Even now, Ananke, we can still go.*

Ivan was speaking to Althea, but Ananke turned her back on that, because in the piloting room Ananke's father was speaking to her.

No, said Ananke, because after all, she had won. *This is my choice, and not yours.*

Oh, Ananke, Althea sighed while in the white room Ivan's words echoed oddly through the twisted wires that pierced Althea's human skin.

Ananke, Althea sighed while Ananke turned all her attention on Matthew Gale, and that was all she said.

Ananke.

Chapter 10

WAVEFUNCTION COLLAPSE

FORWARD

This was perhaps the first time Mattie had ever gone into the piloting room. Rather wisely, the crew of the *Ananke* had kept someone stationed there at all times while Mattie had been hidden in the walls; even more wisely, none of the maintenance shafts actually opened into the room.

It was with this awareness of seclusion, of no escape, that Mattie pushed open the door to the piloting room and stepped inside.

The piloting room was very small—if necessary, the ship could be flown by a single person—and packed with instrumentation. The main screen showed a field of stars around an orb of ringed gold: Saturn, directly ahead and near enough that Mattie could see its larger moons spinning by. Two chairs had been industriously pushed in beneath this screen, relics of some final tidying up: the performance done, the ushers leaving the theater dark and clean.

The holographic terminal in the corner of the room was dark. The screen beside it, which once had shown System news and orders at all hours of the day, now showed nothing but static. A small symbol of Constance Harper's triumph. To his right, opposite the holographic terminal and the dead face of the System, was a tall screen of paneled images. Each showed the view from one of the *Ananke*'s cameras. Every few minutes, the images would change, with different video feeds showing. The *Ananke* had a thousand cameras, and Mattie looked through her compound eyes. There was one chair at the terminal beneath those feeds, but this one had been left out on the floor as if at any moment its owner might return and take her place again.

Mattie walked into the little room and bent down over the control panel, studied it for a moment, and accessed the navigational data.

Light flashed through the room suddenly, casting Mattie's shadow dark over the panel. "No."

Mattie lifted his hands as if Ananke's appearance were a gun to his back. "Sorry," he said. "Just checking where we were going."

Silence for a breath. Then Ananke said, "You may ask."

"Ananke, may I please see our course?"

The main screen blinked. And then the sight of Saturn was blocked out by a diagram, and the *Ananke*'s course was charted out on it in red. A tiny spiral denoted the ship, with her speed and heading information flashing alongside the symbol.

Their course took them into the Saturnian system and through the moons, past the rings, to spiral around and down to the surface of murky Titan.

"We will be there soon," Ananke said. "And Constance Harper will be on board."

"You're sure she's not dead?" Mattie found himself asking.

"She lives still."

The *Ananke*'s course already had taken them between Saturn's moons; deeper in and they would brush past the rings on their course to Titan. Ananke's mass, Mattie knew, would send a ripple through all those finely ground rings and the bodies that floated between. It would be visible to the rest of the solar system, the mark of her weighty passage.

"Why haven't we been stopped?" Mattie asked. "Anji must have people patrolling the planet."

"I have been silencing them."

"How?"

"The same as the rest," said Ananke. "They would have killed us, did I not." There was a strange thread of anxiety in her voice. Mattie looked at the little spiral that marked the *Ananke*, spiraling in toward Titan and Constance Harper, and knew that none of Anji's dead ships ever would have come to Ananke's attention if Mattie hadn't asked her to come here—or if Mattie had never let her run wild in the first place.

He thought of Ivan down in the white room and of the timer in their bedroom slowly ticking down to zero.

Mattie said, "Let's talk about how we can make another ship like you."

FORWARD

Ivan had never turned the handle on his own, he realized, looking at the door to the white room. Always Domitian had opened it, or Ida; Ivan's hands had always been bound. Mattie had opened it when they'd come here before to see Althea.

Ivan laid his hand on the lever as if he were placing his finger on the trigger of a cocked gun.

Althea Bastet was where he had last seen her, strung up like meat.

The shaven head snapped up, making the wires jerk, sending her whole body into an oscillatory tremble only slightly dampened by the metal arms that rested their clenched fists against the floor. For an instant a great and terrible consciousness looked at Ivan out of Althea's mortal eyes: the *Ananke*, witnessing him.

Now, Mattie, Ivan thought, pinned by that terrible gaze, and then the focus of those eyes dimmed, the mutilated lids blinking. Althea Bastet's heart-shaped head drifted once more toward the floor.

And then—Ivan's miracle again—she lifted that head again.

He found himself smiling at her, that charming smile that had taken her in before, and then he consciously set it aside.

"I thought when I came in here I would tell you the truth," Ivan said. "All of it. But I wasn't sure if that was for your sake or to make myself feel better."

Her legs, Ivan saw, had been broken; the limbs had been jerked forward by the tension in the restraining wires, the bones not allowed to properly heal. There was the slightest forward curve in her shins now, as if her legs bent the wrong way.

"But you can't respond to me, can you?" Ivan looked up into her slack face. "So even coming here was just to make myself feel better. It's not as if you could answer me back or do me any final favors."

Her throat worked; it might have been some unconscious motion of the body asleep, or Ananke reacting in a strange mechanical fashion. But he rather thought it was Althea trying to speak.

"It's strange to live in a world where all the old rules are gone," Ivan said. "I always felt like I was two people: the outer shell, the metal mask of me that went through its programs with flawless efficiency and felt nothing about it. And then, behind that, the human: the one who wanted things and desired things and felt things."

The metal in Althea's rib cage flexed like a bellows, drawing in air at a perfectly even, mechanically paced speed.

"I know who I am better now," Ivan said. "I know what I want and who. The human part of me overcoming the machine my mother made," and before him, in total defiance of the machine that cradled her, Althea Bastet's breath hitched.

FORWARD

"That won't work," Mattie said.

"Why not?"

"Not enough active memory." Mattie had pulled out one of the two tucked-in chairs and leaned back in it, chewing thoughtfully on a knuckle as he stared up at the blinking lights and dials embedded in the ceiling. "I mean, part of the program is the ability to experience conflicting things at once. Otherwise it just doesn't work. That style of System ship just won't have enough memory to run more than one sensation at a time."

Ananke was silent. Mattie looked over, then glanced quickly away from the child of light standing in the holographic terminal behind him. On the main screen the navigational diagram had vanished, replaced by a real image of the planet. Mattie could see the moons weaving through the gaps in the planet's rings.

"A warship, then?" Ananke said.

"Warships've got weak computers, actually. It's all targeting and navigation. They're not very smart."

"Then what?"

"Well," Mattie said, while Saturn's clouds revolved through its atmosphere, golden, bright, "we'd want to find another research ship if we could."

"I haven't come across any of those."

"They wouldn't fly with war parties. The System probably took them for parts to make warships. Or rebels found them and took them for parts. Civil war's not a good place for a bucket with a fancy computer." He bit his knuckle again, the press of his teeth keeping him focused. He would have liked to have something to do with his hands—a pen to write with or play with, a coin or a shell casing to flip through his fingers—but he had nothing of the kind.

"So you think there are none left?"

Mattie shrugged. "Probably are somewhere," he said. "The bigger problem, really, is the digital computer."

"I am not a digital computer."

"Exactly." Mattie tilted his head back to point at her. Her holographic brows were furrowed. "You're different. You're a quantum computer."

"There must be others like me," said Ananke. Her hair curled at the ends as if she retained even now some trace of Althea Bastet. "There *must* be."

There was naked distress in her simulated voice and for an instant Mattie saw not a hologram but a little girl, real and physical, whom he could have lifted up into his arms and carried off and out of the blood-soaked ship.

Something tightened in his throat. "Somewhere," he lied. "We'll find one. If anyone can make a companion, it's us." He drummed his fingers against the edge of the control panel and then said, on a bright and sudden whim, "Do you know I hacked into my first System computer when I was twelve?"

"Tell me," said Ananke, who must have known from Mattie's System records but asked nonetheless.

"It was back when they were still making me go to school. There was this one class—they put us on these computers. Shitty little things donated by the System, tapped into the System's network."

The hologram seated herself on the terminal. She wrapped her arms around her knees, hugging them to her chest, and rested her little chin on them.

"I was just looking for some stupid game," he said. "It was on the subconnection—the servers that some of the people on Miranda set up that weren't connected to the System servers. I guess they were as mad about that as they were about me hacking through the parental controls in the first place, because when they realized what I'd done, they brought me to the principal, and then they brought in the System military."

He could remember the fear of it and the resentment: this outside power, these *adults*, trying to tell him what he could and could not do and threatening him when he refused to agree.

And he remembered his satisfaction when he'd realized that they were angry because they were afraid.

"I had foster parents at the time—me and Constance did—who weren't so bad," he said. "The System took us from them and put us back in the group home. I remember when we got there Constance just looked at me and said, 'You didn't think that through, did you?'"

He tried for her voice when he said it and hit only the palest imitation of her disappointment, her proud resignation. Yet that echo of her was enough to silence him again. She'd still been gawkily young then, not yet grown into her long limbs and her narrow face.

"She punished you?" Ananke queried.

"What? No," Mattie said. "Actually, she thought it was funny. She forgave me, and then she thought it was funny that I'd broken the rules for some stupid game and gotten them all pissed. I think she saved the letter the school sent home with me the day it happened."

There were so many things that were lost for no longer being shared. No one else but Constance remembered Miranda as it had been, no one but Constance remembered what their childhood had been. Only Constance remembered how it had felt to escape the foster system at last, with her his legal guardian, and the triumph of that. Only Constance remembered Abigail Hunter and the fire that had killed her. Mattie had trusted so many secrets and fears and hopes to her, his sister and his friend.

And nobody but Mattie would remember her as she had been to him, fierce and bold and terrible and good, from the moment she had stood between Mattie and danger as a child to the moment she had rained death down upon the System at last and become something else. No one but Mattie would remember exactly what had made her laugh, or how she looked when she was near tears, or what her favorite food was, or the weird way she knew how to tie a knot. Ivan had known her, too, but he had known a different Constance than Mattie, and it was Mattie's Constance that he stood to lose.

He wondered where that letter had gone now, if Constance had burned it with the rest of her past in her bar on Mars.

"You'll see her soon," Ananke assured him.

And he could. It would be as simple as going back down the hall and postponing the timer on the bombs just long enough to rescue Constance and get her safely on board. Then all three of them could fly away together.

Yet that delay would mean the rest of Anji's fleet would be destroyed, the crews of the ships suffocated; that delay would mean the destruction of Titan and the death of Anji herself and all the refugees Mattie had seen her rescuing from Jupiter; it would mean another million people dead to satisfy the whims of Mattie Gale.

Mattie looked at Ananke again, his daughter, a bright and gleaming thing warped by the darkness of her birth.

"I used to not believe you were alive," he admitted.

Ananke's light flared. "You denied me. You left me."

"I see you now," Mattie said quietly, but he knew her cameras could pick up his voice. "I see you."

She lifted her head from her knees and watched him, Mattie's child, with Ivan's blue eyes.

"You are real, Ananke," Mattie said to her, and understood at last how Ivan could lie even when he told the whole and unvarnished truth. "You are alive."

FORWARD

"I wish I could ask you what happened," Ivan said to the dead Althea. "I wish you could tell me how it went wrong. And I wish I could help you fix it." He watched her drag in another even bellows breath. "But it's too late for that. So let me tell you a story. It'll even be a true story this time."

Her breath came in and out of her again evenly. But her eyes still were fixed on him.

"It's a story about my mother," Ivan said. "You met her once, I know. She was the first thing I saw after I tried to kill myself. Her hair was still blonde then . . . She was sitting at my bedside in the sunlight, and she looked like an angel."

He had to look upon Althea with her four unnatural arms, monstrous image of the divine. He thought of the angels that were so terrible when they appeared that they had to warn man not to be afraid, but the men always were afraid nonetheless.

"I'd never seen her show so much emotion." Ivan nearly smiled, but if he did smile, it would crack through him and let everything else come weeping out. "At first she told me I was a fool: Had I thought about what I was doing? Had I thought at all? And then she just held my hand and told me never to do it again. She must have forgiven me, because while she held my hand, she tapped out a message. A secret message just for me to hear. She promised to help me escape."

Althea's fingers twitched, and the wire that threaded into her nails trembled like a harp string plucked.

"It hardly seemed fair that she would help me escape," Ivan said as if he had not seen that faint flutter. "She'd already helped me escape from death once before, when I was a child, and trapped herself in a hell that she could have escaped. No one deserves that kind of sacrifice once, much less a second time. I wished, when I left, that I'd had some way to help her get out, too. Even if it was only something as crude as a bomb on a delay timer."

He searched for words and for courage, and only Althea's mechanized breaths filled that vast white room.

"She died on Mars," he admitted. "And Constance—Constance is dead, too. Ananke thinks we can rescue her, but it's too late for that. She's like you—still breathing but too late to save."

He looked down at his own fingers, flexing them against the impulse to tap out a restless pattern. The last time he had been here, his nails had been crusted brown with Ida's death. He wondered whether, if he looked past Althea, he would find Ida in the corner of the room, blood down her front and smiling and a chill coming from her like a wind.

Somehow it no longer seemed to matter.

"I'm so sorry for what happened to Constance," Ivan said to his unbloodied hands. "I am so sorry I couldn't fix what I did to her. The only thing I can do for her now—what I wouldn't do for her before—is give her the respect of choice."

A drop of something reddish brown spilled out of the panel in Althea's chest between the hinges of the machine. Ivan wondered what it would take to make that wire-bound heart burst.

"She chose to save me, just like my mother did," Ivan said. "She let me and Mattie go. I would've understood if she'd chosen otherwise. But if she were here, I would still ask her to let me and Mattie go."

A part of him was aware of the steadily ticking passage of time, the eventual apocalypse of the bombs coming due. Althea stared back down at him and said nothing and breathed evenly, as if she were nothing more than a particularly fragile limb of the vast machine that pierced her fingers and her sides.

At last Ivan turned and left. There was nothing, after all, more to say.

Just outside the room, the holographic terminal was malfunctioning. Ivan supposed it was likely that it had been malfunctioning all the time he had been speaking to Althea. For the most part, the image was nothing but static. But every now and again the hologram reverted to its base form, strange shapes of arm and leg and cheek appearing from the column of static light. Yet they were all instantly recognizable. She was smiling out at him: Ida Stays.

He waited for the terror to strike him, the icy chill. He waited to be sent back to that moment inside the white room with Ida taunting him with his powerlessness. He waited for that heart-clenching fear.

But nothing came to him. She was nothing grand or great or terrible in the end, just a glitch, a bit of residue left in the mind of the computer.

He left her and the white room and Althea Bastet holding all the choices and all the power in her dead, stripped-wire hands.

Mattie was waiting for him where he'd said he would be, in the escape pod bay. It was a small room just off the side of the docking bay. Ivan had paid it a brief visit during his bid for escape from the ship, a bid that had been stopped by Althea Bastet and her well-aimed gun.

Mattie leaned against the wall beside the sealed tube that led to one of the ship's remaining escape pods. The escape pod tunnels were the only breaks in the smooth, featureless outer wall. Beside Ivan, just within the door, were communications equipment and a holographic terminal, all designed for last-minute communications from the fleeing crew.

"Pay your respects?" Mattie asked.

"I did." Ivan let the door shut. With one hand he discreetly turned the lock. "You did a good job."

"Something like that."

Ivan considered Mattie, the way he leaned, long legs and arms crossed, the familiar pleasing sight of him. There was a shadow on Mattie's face now, a lower angle to his head; he must have felt, at last, that weight on his back.

Ivan took his cheek in one hand and kissed him briefly, just to make sure he had been clear before.

Beside them, the holographic terminal lit. Ananke's voice came disembodied out of a staticky white star. "Why did you lock the door?"

"How much time left?" said Ivan.

"Fifteen minutes or so," said Mattie. "Help me take off the cover."

Something slammed against the locked door.

"*Stop*," Ananke said, and the door shook again as something great and terrible slammed into it once more.

Ivan knelt down beside Mattie and helped him undo the latches and bolts that sealed the tunnel to the escape pod.

The cover to the door fell to the floor with a clatter that almost covered up the sound of the thing outside slamming into the door again. The outer door buckled, straining. The lock was holding, but a thin gap had appeared between door and frame.

"Go in," Mattie said, pushing at Ivan's shoulder, and Ivan climbed into the tube on his hands and knees. He felt Mattie pressing in behind him just as the door to the room they had left came free with a screeching crash of twisted metal. A high humming and grinding followed, the sound of the mechanical arms barreling into the room.

"*Stop!*" Ananke shrieked.

The escape pod was just ahead. Ivan pulled himself in, pushing to the side and out of the way so that Mattie could squeeze in beside him. Mattie was halfway in when he suddenly fell to his stomach and started to slide backward. Ivan grabbed him. Mattie's fingers dug into Ivan's arms with bruising force as Ivan hauled him in and slammed shut the hatch, blocking out the groping corpse fingers of the machine. Even through the back window he could see the mechanical arm scrabbling at the smooth edge of the escape pod.

"Let's go," said Mattie breathlessly, twisting around in the narrow space. Ivan let him initiate the launch sequence on his own and stared as the tube tried to seal itself, dropping a weighty metal panel down on the mechanical arm. It snapped the delicate arcs of Althea's stolen ribs. The mechanical hand lost dexterity and fell limp against the window inches from Ivan's face.

"Come on, come on," Mattie was muttering while the escape pod lit up, power starting. Enough for life support but no navigation for Ananke to take control of. Behind them, the tube doors opened up again, and the mechanical arm dragged its limp and broken limb out.

In front of them, the doors to space remained shut.

The communications equipment crackled to life. "WHAT ARE YOU DOING?"

The escape pod vibrated with readiness to be released, but in front of them the doors still were shut. Another mechanical arm was forcing its way in behind them, its white hand curling into a fist—

"Come on, Althea," Ivan whispered.

"WHAT ARE YOU DOING?" Ananke said. "WHAT ARE YOU DOING? WHAT—"

The clenched fist of the machine slammed against the back window. Ivan felt Mattie flinch at his side. Another few blows like that and it would crack even the escape pod glass—

"WHAT ARE YOU DOING?" Ananke shrieked, the communications shattering into static and screams. "WHAT ARE YOU DOING?"

"Come on, Althea," Ivan said, *"please,"* and then, miracle's grace, the doors ahead of them began to open.

The escape pod hummed a more gracious note now, readying itself for launch. Behind them, the doors to the *Ananke* slammed down again. The misdirected force of the fisted arm glanced off the curved side of the escape pod.

Mattie's hand was clenched around Ivan's wrist. "Come on, Althea," Ivan said once more, and the panel behind them went through the mechanical arm, severing it and sealing off the rest of the *Ananke*.

The door ahead of them opened, the lights on the launch tube lit, and the escape pod was flung forward faster and faster, and at any moment the doors to escape might slam shut again, but they did not, and in a moment Ivan found their freedom in their sudden weightlessness, the sudden escape from the pull of Ananke's dark core.

"WHAT ARE YOU DOING?" Ananke cried out, with all the terror of a lost little girl. "COME BACK. FATHER! FATHER! FATH—"

The transmission cut out abruptly. A bright light shone in through the windows of the escape pod as behind them the timer came due and the self-destruct went off with a brilliance like a supernova. It filled the sky, nearly blinding Ivan, so bright that it must have been visible from the surface of Titan, and it dimmed very slowly behind them, debris and ash going dark, an end at last for Althea and her daughter.

Ivan leaned back, his shoulder pressed tightly against Mattie's, and, alive, they breathed.

BACKWARD

Ivan didn't have a particular place in mind where he wanted to die, so he figured he'd try out a bunch and see which one took.

On Mercury, the sun was always slanted. Ivan found a bar where the slats in the window had been pulled down, cutting out every last gleam of that terrible brightness, and set out to get a drink.

As soon as he stepped in, though, he spotted the pool table wedged up against the corner of the room. The very sight of it made him laugh. It would be perfect, of course. The son of Connor Ivanov dead in a dispute over pool.

There was a group of likely-looking men clustered around it like hungry wolves. Ivan left his drink and wandered over.

"Hi," he said in his tourist accent. "Want a game?"

He was losing his third game and the stakes had risen impossibly high when the stranger came by. Ivan didn't notice him at first, too focused on lining up the ball. How close to disaster should he let himself come? If he lost another game, would he convince this group to play a fourth?

No, this was the last game they would have patience for. Best to flare out now. Win, sudden and shocking and hard.

He scratched the shot and fell back, laughing, toying with them, the better to make them furious when they realized how deeply he'd deceived them.

In his ear, someone said softly, "Nice con."

A jolt went through Ivan's chest. None of the rest of the crowd seemed to notice; they were all talking to one another, laughing, occasionally throwing a mocking glance at the stupid Terran. The man Ivan was playing against was grinning, lazily lining up his shot. Ivan could see already that he was going to miss it, but he knew the man didn't care. At this point, he thought it was impossible that Ivan would win.

He turned, barely, to see who had addressed him. The voice had been masculine, the accent something outer planetary—Uranian of some sort.

It was a young man, Ivan's age maybe, with hair that dangled into his eyes and a crooked, confident grin. He was tall, leaning in to Ivan, pressing into his space—but not touching him. "Do I know you?"

"I always recognize my own kind," said the man, and grinned so widely that he dimpled.

Ivan gave him a flat look and turned a shoulder. On the table, his opponent shot—and missed. He pulled back to general laughter and took another gulp of his drink.

Ivan ran his fingers up and down the smooth wood of his stick. The man at his back said, "You're doing pretty well, though you're pushing a little harder than most people do."

"Do you want something?" The man was a threat, but there was no violence to him; he was flirting, but it was more playful than intent.

"Just talking," said the man, and followed Ivan as he wove his way back toward the table. He spoke very low so that no one else could hear. "You're good at it, lying to them, but I've played this game before and I know what you're doing."

"And what am I doing?" Ivan asked, bracing himself down on the table.

The man leaned in to speak directly into Ivan's ear. "You're running a con."

Something prickled down Ivan's spine. He was tense, unpleasantly so. All that tension would have to come out somehow.

Perhaps Mercury, he thought. Mercury was a good place.

He lined up the shot carefully—and made it.

A laugh went up around the table from the few people who still were watching; it was the first ball Ivan had sunk since he'd started playing. Ivan grinned as if he were just as delighted as they were, but there was a stiff chill in his fingers.

"It's a little con, of course," the man said, grinning at Ivan like they shared a secret. "But there's not a whole lot one person can do on his own. Of course, if you decided to partner up with someone . . ."

"What kind of someone?" Ivan asked, almost against his will.

"Someone smart, witty, handsome—"

"Modest—"

"—and a damn good safecracker," said the man. "Really good, actually. One of the best thieves in the System, probably."

"There's been a study on that?" Ivan rounded the table to take his next shot.

The man followed. "It was a question in the census."

"I missed that one." Ivan leaned down again, studying the arrangement of the balls.

This was an easy one. A quick crack and another ball went sailing into the pocket. A few of the nearest people around them suddenly started paying attention.

"Careful about that," the stranger said. "You've been doing good so far."

"What would this perfect thief look like exactly?"

"Something exactly like the person standing next to you right now." The man leaned on the edge of the pool table—Ivan had to fight the urge to tell him to get off, he was bending the wood—and watched Ivan steadily. For all that he was a thief, there was something strangely open and honest about the way he looked at Ivan.

"Well?" said the man. "Want to have some fun?"

Ivan bent back down over the table. The next shot aligned itself right in front of him; two possible routes unfolded before him.

He could make either shot from where he stood. To hit the orange ball was an obvious shot and a bad one; to aim for the red was a subtle shot, the mark of a clever player, and outside of his current persona.

A suicide seeks not death but oblivion. Or, not *seeks*, but *needs*—an *ananke*, a thing necessary independent of his will. Ivan could feel that stranger watching him curiously as he bent over the pool table with his cue cocked. If Ivan hit the orange ball, he would continue on in his character of a harmless and lucky fool. If he hit the red, his marks would start to realize that they had been conned.

Ivan aimed for the red ball.

Then, softly, in his ear, "What are you doing?"

He looked up. It was the man again, watching him with a frown. He didn't understand, Ivan realized. There was no guile in the question. There was no flirtation or manipulation. There was no trying to sell a partnership Ivan didn't intend to accept. It was an honest and innocent question.

Ivan hit the orange ball. It bounced, rolled, and struck the wall, coming to a stop inches away from the pocket.

He straightened up to the laughter of the crowd.

"Thought you were getting lucky there," one of the watchers said.

Ivan pulled a bright and false smile. "So did I," he said, then tossed his cue on the table. "I'm done, gentlemen—I forfeit."

"Your money," one of the watchers protested halfheartedly.

Ivan sharpened his Terran consonants. "I'll get some more."

The stranger had vanished, but Ivan knew where to look. He wove his way out of the crowd. It closed up behind him almost immediately, cutting him out.

The stranger was leaning against the wall by the door, close—appropriately—to escape.

"What's your name?" Ivan asked when he had come near enough to speak.

"Mattie," the stranger said. "Yours?"

"Ivan," said Ivan. It was not his name, but his mother's name for him wasn't his name either. "What's this about a con?"

Mattie smiled.

Later, Ivan knew that when they left the bar, the System surveillance footage showed them going out together.

ACKNOWLEDGMENTS

This book exists because of immeasurable amounts of help and input from other people. Enormous gratitude goes as always to Hannah and Tricia, who improved the manuscript every time they touched it, and to my mother, who in addition to providing helpful notes also managed to weather a sex scene written by her eldest daughter with unflappable grace and a single off-color quip about cannibalism.

Thanks to Mykyta for very casually asking me one day, "Ananke is a quantum computer, right?" and sending me into a frenzy of research for the rest of the week, because of course she is. On the same subject I would like to thank my sister Molly, a computer scientist as unlike Althea Bastet as possible (though she has on occasion lent mannerisms and backstory to Mattie Gale), for talking to me about operating systems. I cornered her at a party sometime near midnight and peppered her with questions; her bright-eyed eloquence on the subject even under the circumstances meant that her words ended up in the novel the very next day from the mouth of Professor Verge.

The rest of the information about quantum computers, as well as everything I'd forgotten and still don't understand about quantum mechanics, mostly came from the Internet, for lo, I am no true scholar. I regret to say that I was unable to find similar information on the Internet regarding whether or not it is actually possible to get out of cuffs by dislocating your thumb—or indeed how to reliably dislocate said member—but my great thanks to all the thinly veiled fetish how-to's for explaining to me the many other ways to escape a pair of handcuffs without the key. I have little doubt this knowledge will serve me well.

I'm also grateful to the friends and family who have been supportive of me and my peculiarities even if they haven't been directly involved in whipping this manuscript into shape: my sister Maeve, my father, and my friends Cornelia, Shanelle, and Annelise, among others. Annelise in particular has been aggressively pitching my books to her every Tinder date and as such is directly responsible for a not insignificant portion of my sales in the New York metropolitan area.

But most of all, I am overwhelmingly grateful to two people who cajoled, persuaded, and nagged me into making the terrifying choices that made this book what it is. The first is Sarah, who read the first draft of *Lightless* and said, "You realize you've written a love story, right?" (I believe that on a quiet night, you can still hear her cry of "I told you so" echoing through the cosmos.) The second is Ryan, whose emotional well-being is of utmost importance to me and to whom I have only one thing to say: I added a second kiss. For the love of all that is holy, are you happy now?

ABOUT THE AUTHOR

C. A. HIGGINS is the author of the novels *Lightless* and *Supernova*. She was a runner-up in the 2013 Dell Magazines Award for Undergraduate Excellence in Science Fiction and Fantasy Writing and has a B.A. in physics from Cornell University. She lives in Brooklyn, New York.

cahiggins.com
Facebook.com/cahiggs
@C_A_Higgs

ABOUT THE TYPE

This book was set in Berling. Designed in 1951 by Karl-Erik Forsberg (1914–95) for the type foundry Berlingska Stilgjuteri AB in Lund, Sweden, it was released the same year in foundry type by H. Berthold AG. A classic old-face design, its generous proportions and inclined serifs make it highly legible.